MW01275384

The Chouans, and
A Passion in the Desert

Honoré de Balzac

Translated by Katharine Prescott Wormeley
and Ernest Dowson

The Chouans

Translated by Katharine Prescott Wormeley

DEDICATION

To Monsieur Theodore Dablin, Merchant.

To my first friend, my first work.

De Balzac.

I

AN AMBUSCADE

Early in the year VIII., at the beginning of Vendemiaire, or, to conform to our own calendar, towards the close of September, 1799, a hundred or so of peasants and a large number of citizens, who had left Fougeres in the morning on their way to Mayenne, were going up the little mountain of La Pelerine, half-way between Fougeres and Ernee, a small town where travellers along that road are in the habit of resting. This company, divided into groups that were more or less numerous, presented a collection of such fantastic costumes and a mixture of individuals belonging to so many and diverse localities and professions that it will be well to describe their characteristic differences, in order to give to this history the vivid local coloring to which so much value is attached in these days,— though some critics do assert that it injures the representation of sentiments.

Many of the peasants, in fact the greater number, were barefooted, and wore no other garments than a large goatskin, which covered them from the neck to the knees, and trousers of white and very coarse linen, the ill-woven texture of which betrayed the slovenly industrial habits of the region. The straight locks of their long hair mingling with those of the goatskin hid their faces, which were bent on the ground, so completely that the garment might have been thought their own skin, and they themselves mistaken at first sight for a species of the animal which served them as clothing. But through this tangle of hair their eyes were presently seen to shine like dew-drops in a thicket, and their glances, full of human intelligence, caused fear rather than pleasure to those who met them. Their heads were covered with a dirty head-gear of red flannel, not unlike the Phrygian cap which the Republic had lately adopted as an emblem of liberty. Each man carried over his shoulder a heavy stick of knotted oak, at the end of which hung a linen bag with little in it. Some wore, over the red cap, a coarse felt hat, with a broad brim adorned by a sort of woollen chenille of many colors which was fastened round it. Others were clothed entirely in the coarse linen of which the trousers and wallets of all were made, and showed nothing that was distinctive of the new order of civilization. Their long hair fell upon the collar of a round jacket with square pockets,

1

which reached to the hips only, a garment peculiar to the peasantry
of western France. Beneath this jacket, which was worn open, a
waistcoat of the same linen with large buttons was visible. Some of
the company marched in wooden shoes; others, by way of economy,
carried them in their hand. This costume, soiled by long usage,
blackened with sweat and dust, and less original than that of the
other men, had the historic merit of serving as a transition between
the goatskins and the brilliant, almost sumptuous, dress of a few
individuals dispersed here and there among the groups, where they
shone like flowers. In fact, the blue linen trousers of these last, and
their red or yellow waistcoats, adorned with two parallel rows of
brass buttons and not unlike breast-plates, stood out as vividly
among the white linen and shaggy skins of their companions as the
corn-flowers and poppies in a wheat-field. Some of them wore
wooden shoes, which the peasants of Brittany make for themselves;
but the greater number had heavy hobnailed boots, and coats of
coarse cloth cut in the fashion of the old regime, the shape of which
the peasants have religiously retained even to the present day. The
collars of their shirts were held together by buttons in the shape of
hearts or anchors. The wallets of these men seemed to be better than
those of their companions, and several of them added to their
marching outfit a flask, probably full of brandy, slung round their
necks by a bit of twine. A few burgesses were to be seen in the midst
of these semi-savages, as if to show the extremes of civilization in
this region. Wearing round hats, or flapping brims or caps, high-
topped boots, or shoes and gaiters, they exhibited as many and as
remarkable differences in their costume as the peasants themselves.
About a dozen of them wore the republican jacket known by the
name of "la carmagnole." Others, well-to-do mechanics, no doubt,
were clothed from head to foot in one color. Those who had most
pretension to their dress wore swallow-tail coats or surtouts of blue
or green cloth, more or less defaced. These last, evidently characters,
marched in boots of various kinds, swinging heavy canes with the
air and manner of those who take heart under misfortune. A few
heads carefully powdered, and some queues tolerably well braided
showed the sort of care which a beginning of education or prosperity
inspires. A casual spectator observing these men, all surprised to
find themselves in one another's company, would have thought
them the inhabitants of a village driven out by a conflagration. But
the period and the region in which they were gave an altogether
different interest to this body of men. Any one initiated into the
secrets of the civil discords which were then agitating the whole of
France could easily have distinguished the few individuals on whose

fidelity the Republic might count among these groups, almost entirely made up of men who four years earlier were at war with her.

One other and rather noticeable sign left no doubt upon the opinions which divided the detachment. The Republicans alone marched with an air of gaiety. As to the other individuals of the troop, if their clothes showed marked differences, their faces at least and their attitudes wore a uniform expression of ill-fortune. Citizens and peasantry, their faces all bore the imprint of deepest melancholy; their silence had something sullen in it; they all seemed crushed under the yoke of a single thought, terrible no doubt but carefully concealed, for their faces were impenetrable, the slowness of their gait alone betraying their inward communings. From time to time a few of them, noticeable for the rosaries hanging from their necks (dangerous as it was to carry that sign of a religion which was suppressed, rather than abolished) shook their long hair and raised their heads defiantly. They covertly examined the woods, and paths, and masses of rock which flanked the road, after the manner of a dog with his nose to the wind trying to scent his game; and then, hearing nothing but the monotonous tramp of the silent company, they lowered their heads once more with the old expression of despair, like criminals on their way to the galleys to live or die.

The march of this column upon Mayenne, the heterogeneous elements of which it was composed, and the divers sentiments which evidently pervaded it, will explain the presence of another troop which formed the head of the detachment. About a hundred and fifty soldiers, with arms and baggage, marched in the advance, commanded by the *chief of a half-brigade*. We may mention here, for the benefit of those who did not witness the drama of the Revolution, that this title was made to supersede that of colonel, proscribed by patriots as too aristocratic. These soldiers belonged to a demi-brigade of infantry quartered at Mayenne. During these troublous times the inhabitants of the west of France called all the soldiers of the Republic "Blues." This nickname came originally from their blue and red uniforms, the memory of which is still so fresh as to render a description superfluous. A detachment of the Blues was therefore on this occasion escorting a body of recruits, or rather conscripts, all displeased at being taken to Mayenne where military discipline was about to force upon them the uniformity of thought, clothing, and gait which they now lacked entirely.

This column was a contingent slowly and with difficulty raised in the district of Fougeres, from which it was due under the levy ordered by the executive Directory of the Republic on the preceding 10th Messidor. The government had asked for a hundred million of francs and a hundred thousand men as immediate reinforcements for the armies then fighting the Austrians in Italy, the Prussians in Germany, and menaced in Switzerland by the Russians, in whom Suwarow had inspired hopes of the conquest of France. The departments of the West, known under the name of La Vendee, Brittany, and a portion of Lower Normandy, which had been tranquil for the last three years (thanks to the action of General Hoche), after a struggle lasting nearly four, seemed to have seized this new occasion of danger to the nation to break out again. In presence of such aggressions the Republic recovered its pristine energy. It provided in the first place for the defence of the threatened departments by giving the responsibility to the loyal and patriotic portion of the inhabitants. In fact, the government in Paris, having neither troops nor money to send to the interior, evaded the difficulty by a parliamentary gasconade. Not being able to send material aid to the faithful citizens of the insurgent departments, it gave them its "confidence." Possibly the government hoped that this measure, by arming the insurgents against each other, would stifle the insurrection at its birth. This ordinance, the cause of future fatal reprisals, was thus worded: "Independent companies of troops shall be organized in the Western departments." This impolitic step drove the West as a body into so hostile an attitude that the Directory despaired of immediately subduing it. Consequently, it asked the Assemblies to pass certain special measures relating to the independent companies authorized by the ordinance. In response to this request a new law had been promulgated a few days before this history begins, organizing into regular legions the various weak and scattered companies. These legions were to bear the names of the departments, —Sarthe, Orne, Mayenne, Ille-et-Vilaine, Morbihan, Loire-Inferieure, and Maine-et-Loire. "These legions," said the law, "will be specially employed to fight the Chouans, and cannot, under any pretence, be sent to the frontier."

The foregoing irksome details will explain both the weakness of the Directory and the movement of this troop of men under escort of the Blues. It may not be superfluous to add that these finely patriotic Directorial decrees had no realization beyond their insertion among the statutes. No longer restrained, as formerly, by great moral ideas, by patriotism, nor by terror, which enforced their execution, these later decrees of the Republic created millions and drafted soldiers without the slightest benefit accruing to its exchequer or its armies. The mainspring of the Revolution was worn-out by clumsy handling, and the application of the laws took the impress of circumstances instead of controlling them.

The departments of Mayenne and Ille-et-Vilaine were at this time under the command of an old officer who, judging on the spot of the measures that were most opportune to take, was anxious to wring from Brittany every one of her contingents, more especially that of Fougeres, which was known to be a hot-bed of "Chouannerie." He hoped by this means to weaken its strength in these formidable districts. This devoted soldier made use of the illusory provisions of the new law to declare that he would equip and arm at once all recruits, and he announced that he held at their disposal the one month's advanced pay promised by the government to these exceptional levies. Though Brittany had hitherto refused all kinds of military service under the Republic, the levies were made under the new law on the faith of its promises, and with such promptness that even the commander was startled. But he was one of those wary old watch-dogs who are hard to catch napping. He no sooner saw the contingents arriving one after the other than he suspected some secret motive for such prompt action. Possibly he was right in ascribing it to the fact of getting arms. At any rate, no sooner were the Fougeres recruits obtained than, without delaying for laggards, he took immediate steps to fall back towards Alencon, so as to be near a loyal neighborhood,—though the growing disaffection along the route made the success of this measure problematical. This old officer, who, under instruction of his superiors, kept secret the disasters of our armies in Italy and Germany and the disturbing news from La Vendee, was attempting on the morning when this history begins, to make a forced march on Mayenne, where he was resolved to execute the law according to his own good pleasure, and fill the half-empty companies of his own brigade with his Breton conscripts. The word "conscript" which later became so celebrated, had just now for the first time taken the place in the government decrees of the word *requisitionnaire* hitherto applied to all Republican recruits.

Before leaving Fougeres the chief secretly issued to his own men ample supplies of ammunition and sufficient rations of bread for the whole detachment, so as to conceal from the conscripts the length of the march before them. He intended not to stop at Ernee (the last stage before Mayenne), where the men of the contingent might find a way of communicating with the Chouans who were no doubt hanging on his flanks. The dead silence which reigned among the recruits, surprised at the manoeuvring of the old republican, and their lagging march up the mountain excited to the very utmost the distrust and watchfulness of the chief—whose name was Hulot. All the striking points in the foregoing description had been to him matters of the keenest interest; he marched in silence, surrounded by five young officers, each of whom respected the evident preoccupation of their leader. But just as Hulot reached the summit of La Pelerine he turned his head, as if by instinct, to inspect the anxious faces of the recruits, and suddenly broke silence. The slow advance of the Bretons had put a distance of three or four hundred feet between themselves and their escort. Hulot's face contorted after a fashion peculiar to himself.

"What the devil are those dandies up to?" he exclaimed in a sonorous voice. "Creeping instead of marching, I call it."

At his first words the officers who accompanied him turned spasmodically, as if startled out of sleep by a sudden noise. The sergeants and corporals followed their example, and the whole company paused in its march without receiving the wished for "Halt!" Though the officers cast a first look at the detachment, which was creeping like an elongated tortoise up the mountain of La Pelerine, these young men, all dragged, like many others, from important studies to defend their country, and in whom war had not yet smothered the sentiment of art, were so much struck by the scene which lay spread before their eyes that they made no answer to their chief's remark, the real significance of which was unknown to them. Though they had come from Fougeres, where the scene which now presented itself to their eyes is also visible (but with certain differences caused by the change of perspective), they could not resist pausing to admire it again, like those dilettanti who enjoy all music the more when familiar with its construction.

From the summit of La Pelerine the traveller's eye can range over the great valley of Couesnon, at one of the farthest points of which, along the horizon, lay the town of Fougeres. From here the officers could see, to its full extent, the basin of this intervale, as remarkable for the fertility of its soil as for the variety of its aspects. Mountains of gneiss and slate rose on all sides, like an ampitheatre, hiding their ruddy flanks behind forests of oak, and forming on their declivities other and lesser valleys full of dewy freshness. These rocky heights made a vast enclosure, circular in form, in the centre of which a meadow lay softly stretched, like the lawn of an English garden. A number of evergreen hedges, defining irregular pieces of property which were planted with trees, gave to this carpet of verdure a character of its own, and one that is somewhat unusual among the landscapes of France; it held the teeming secrets of many beauties in its various contrasts, the effects of which were fine enough to arrest the eye of the most indifferent spectator.

At this particular moment the scene was brightened by the fleeting glow with which Nature delights at times in heightening the beauty of her imperishable creations. While the detachment was crossing the valley, the rising sun had slowly scattered the fleecy mists which float above the meadows of a September morning. As the soldiers turned to look back, an invisible hand seemed to lift from the landscape the last of these veils—a delicate vapor, like a diaphanous gauze through which the glow of precious jewels excites our curiosity. Not a cloud could be seen on the wide horizon to mark by its silvery whiteness that the vast blue arch was the firmament; it seemed, on the contrary, a dais of silk, held up by the summits of the mountains and placed in the atmosphere, to protect that beautiful assemblage of fields and meadows and groves and brooks.

The group of young officers paused to examine a scene so filled with natural beauties. The eyes of some roved among the copses, which the sterner tints of autumn were already enriching with their russet tones, contrasting the more with the emerald-green of the meadows in which they grew; others took note of a different contrast, made by the ruddy fields, where the buckwheat had been cut and tied in sheaves (like stands of arms around a bivouac), adjoining other fields of rich ploughed land, from which the rye was already harvested. Here and there were dark slate roofs above which puffs of white smoke were rising. The glittering silver threads of the winding brooks caught the eye, here and there, by one of those optic lures which render the soul —one knows not how or why—perplexed and dreamy. The fragrant freshness of the autumn breeze, the stronger odors of the forest, rose like a waft of incense to the admirers of this beautiful region, who noticed with delight its rare wild-flowers, its vigorous vegetation, and its verdure, worthy of England, the very word being common to the two languages. A few cattle gave life to the scene, already so dramatic. The birds sang, filling the valley with a sweet, vague melody that quivered in the air. If a quiet imagination will picture to itself these rich fluctuations of light and shade, the vaporous outline of the mountains, the mysterious perspectives which were seen where the trees gave an opening, or the streamlets ran, or some coquettish little glade fled away in the distance; if memory will color, as it were, this sketch, as fleeting as the moment when it was taken, the persons for whom such pictures are not without charm will have an imperfect image of the magic scene which delighted the still impressionable souls of the young officers.

Thinking that the poor recruits must be leaving, with regret, their own country and their beloved customs, to die, perhaps, in foreign lands, they involuntarily excused a tardiness their feelings comprehended. Then, with the generosity natural to soldiers, they disguised their indulgence under an apparent desire to examine into the military position of the land. But Hulot, whom we shall henceforth call the commandant, to avoid giving him the inharmonious title of "chief of a half-brigade" was one of those soldiers who, in critical moments, cannot be caught by the charms of a landscape, were they even those of a terrestrial paradise. He shook his head with an impatient gesture and contracted the thick, black eyebrows which gave so stern an expression to his face.

"Why the devil don't they come up?" he said, for the second time, in a hoarse voice, roughened by the toils of war.

"You ask why?" replied a voice.

Hearing these words, which seemed to issue from a horn, such as the peasants of the western valleys use to call their flocks, the commandant turned sharply round, as if pricked by a sword, and beheld, close behind him, a personage even more fantastic in appearance than any of those who were now being escorted to Mayenne to serve the Republic. This unknown man, short and thick-set in figure and broad-shouldered, had a head like a bull, to which, in fact, he bore more than one resemblance. His nose seemed shorter than it was, on account of the thick nostrils. His full lips, drawn from the teeth which were white as snow, his large and round black eyes with their shaggy brows, his hanging ears and tawny hair,—seemed to belong far less to our fine Caucasian race than to a breed of herbivorous animals. The total absence of all the usual characteristics of the social man made that bare head still more remarkable. The face, bronzed by the sun (its angular outlines presenting a sort of vague likeness to the granite which forms the soil of the region), was the only visible portion of the body of this singular being. From the neck down he was wrapped in a "sarrau" or smock, a sort of russet linen blouse, coarser in texture than that of the trousers of the less fortunate conscripts. This "sarrau," in which an antiquary would have recognized the "saye," or the "sayon" of the Gauls, ended at his middle, where it was fastened to two leggings of goatskin by slivers, or thongs of wood, roughly cut,—some of them still covered with their peel or bark. These hides of the nanny-goat (to give them the name by which they were known to the peasantry) covered his legs and thighs, and masked all appearance of human shape. Enormous sabots hid his feet. His long and shining hair fell straight, like the goat's hair, on either side of his face, being parted in the centre like the hair of certain statues of the Middle-Ages which are still to be seen in our cathedrals. In place of the knotty stick which the conscripts carried over their shoulders, this man held against his breast as though it were a musket, a heavy whip, the lash of which was closely braided and seemed to be twice as long as that of an ordinary whip. The sudden apparition of this strange being seemed easily explained. At first sight some of the officers took him for a recruit or conscript (the words were used indiscriminately) who had outstripped the column. But the commandant himself was singularly surprised by the man's presence; he showed no alarm, but his face grew thoughtful. After looking the intruder well over, he repeated, mechanically, as if preoccupied with anxious thought: "Yes, why don't they come on? do you know, you?"

"Because," said the gloomy apparition, with an accent which proved his difficulty in speaking French, "there Maine begins" (pointing with his huge, rough hand towards Ernee), "and Bretagne ends."

Then he struck the ground sharply with the handle of his heavy whip close to the commandant's feet. The impression produced on the spectators by the laconic harangue of the stranger was like that of a tom-tom in the midst of tender music. But the word "harangue" is insufficient to reproduce the hatred, the desires of vengeance expressed by the haughty gesture of the hand, the brevity of the speech, and the look of sullen and cool-blooded energy on the countenance of the speaker. The coarseness and roughness of the man, —chopped out, as it seemed by an axe, with his rough bark still left on him,—and the stupid ignorance of his features, made him seem, for the moment, like some half-savage demigod. He stood stock-still in a prophetic attitude, as though he were the Genius of

Brittany rising from a slumber of three years, to renew a war in which victory could only be followed by twofold mourning.

"A pretty fellow this!" thought Hulot; "he looks to me like the emissary of men who mean to argue with their muskets."

Having growled these words between his teeth, the commandant cast his eyes in turn from the man to the valley, from the valley to the detachment, from the detachment to the steep acclivities on the right of the road, the ridges of which were covered with the broom and gorse of Brittany; then he suddenly turned them full on the stranger, whom he subjected to a mute interrogation, which he ended at last by roughly demanding, "Where do you come from?"

His eager, piercing eye strove to detect the secrets of that impenetrable face, which never changed from the vacant, torpid expression in which a peasant when doing nothing wraps himself.

"From the country of the Gars," replied the man, without showing any uneasiness.

"Your name?"

"Marche-a-Terre."

"Why do you call yourself by your Chouan name in defiance of the law?"

Marche-a-Terre, to use the name he gave to himself, looked at the commandant with so genuine an air of stupidity that the soldier believed the man had not understood him.

"Do you belong to the recruits from Fougeres?"

To this inquiry Marche-a-Terre replied by the bucolic "I don't know," the hopeless imbecility of which puts an end to all inquiry. He seated himself by the roadside, drew from his smock a few pieces of thin, black buckwheat-bread,—a national delicacy, the dismal delights of which none but a Breton can understand,—and began to eat with stolid indifference. There seemed such a total absence of all human intelligence about the man that the officers compared him in turn to the cattle browsing in the valley pastures, to the savages of America, or the aboriginal inhabitants of the Cape of Good Hope.

Deceived by his behavior, the commandant himself was about to turn a deaf ear to his own misgivings, when, casting a last prudence glance on the man whom he had taken for the herald of an approaching carnage, he suddenly noticed that the hair, the smock, and the goatskin leggings of the stranger were full of thorns, scraps of leaves, and bits of trees and bushes, as though this Chouan had lately made his way for a long distance through thickets and underbrush. Hulot looked significantly at his adjutant Gerard who stood beside him, pressed his hand firmly, and said in a low voice: "We came for wool, but we shall go back sheared."

The officers looked at each other silently in astonishment.

It is necessary here to make a digression, or the fears of the commandant will not be intelligible to those stay-at-home persons who are in the habit of doubting everything because they have seen nothing, and who might therefore deny the existence of Marche-a-Terre and the peasantry of the West, whose conduct, in the times we are speaking of, was often sublime.

The word "gars" pronounced "ga" is a relic of the Celtic language. It has passed from low Breton into French, and the word in our present speech has more ancient associations than any other. The "gais" was the principal weapon of the Gauls; "gaisde" meant armed; "gais" courage; "gas," force. The word has an analogy with the Latin word "vir" man, the root of "virtus" strength, courage. The present dissertation is excusable as of national interest; besides, it may help to restore the use of such words as: "gars, garcon, garconette, garce, garcette," now discarded from our speech as unseemly; whereas their origin is so warlike that we shall use them from time to time in the course of this history. "She is a famous 'garce'!" was a compliment little understood by Madame de Stael when it was paid to her in a little village of La Vendee, where she spent a few days of her exile.

Brittany is the region in all France where the manners and customs of the Gauls have left their strongest imprint. That portion of the province where, even to our own times, the savage life and superstitious ideas of our rude ancestors still continue—if we may use the word—rampant, is called "the country of the Gars." When a canton (or district) is inhabited by a number of half-savages like the one who has just appeared upon the scene, the inhabitants call them "the Gars of such or such a parish." This classic name is a reward for the fidelity with which they struggle to preserve the traditions of the language and manners of their Gaelic ancestors; their lives show to this day many remarkable and deeply embedded vestiges of the beliefs and superstitious practices of those ancient times. Feudal customs are still maintained. Antiquaries find Druidic monuments still standing. The genius of modern civilization shrinks from forcing its way through those impenetrable primordial forests. An unheard-of ferociousness, a brutal obstinacy, but also a regard for the sanctity of an oath; a complete ignoring of our laws, our customs, our dress, our modern coins, our language, but withal a patriarchal simplicity and virtues that are heroic,—unite in keeping the inhabitants of this region more impoverished as to all intellectual knowledge than the Redskins, but also as proud, as crafty, and as enduring as they. The position which Brittany occupies in the centre of Europe makes it more interesting to observe than Canada. Surrounded by light whose beneficent warmth never reaches it, this region is like a frozen coal left black in the middle of a glowing fire. The efforts made by several noble minds to win this glorious part of France, so rich in neglected treasures, to social life and to prosperity have all, even when sustained by government, come to nought against the inflexibility of a population given over to the habits of immemorial routine. This unfortunate condition is partly accounted for by the nature of the land, broken by ravines, mountain torrents, lakes, and marshes, and bristling with hedges or earth-works which make a sort of citadel of every field; without roads, without canals, and at the mercy of prejudices which scorn our modern agriculture. These will further be shown with all their dangers in our present history.

The picturesque lay of the land and the superstitions of the inhabitants prevent the formation of communities and the benefits arising from the exchange and comparison of ideas. There are no villages. The rickety buildings which the people call homes are sparsely scattered through the wilderness. Each family lives as in a desert. The only meetings among them are on Sundays and feast-days in the parish church. These silent assemblies, under the eye of the rector (the only ruler of these rough minds) last some hours. After listening to the awful words of the priest they return to their noisome hovels for another week; they leave them only to work, they return to them only to sleep. No one ever visits them, unless it is the rector. Consequently, it was the voice of the priesthood which roused Brittany against the Republic, and sent thousands of men, five years before this history begins, to the support of the first Chouannerie. The brothers Cottereau, whose name was given to that first uprising, were bold smugglers, plying their perilous trade between Laval and Fougeres. The insurrections of Brittany had nothing fine or noble about them; and it may be truly said that if La Vendee turned its brigandage into a great war, Brittany turned war into a brigandage. The proscription of princes, the destruction of religion, far from inspiring great sacrifices, were to the Chouans pretexts for mere pillage; and the events of this intestine warfare had all the savage moroseness of their own natures. When the real defenders of the monarchy came to recruit men among these ignorant and violent people they vainly tried to give, for the honor of the white flag, some grandeur to the enterprises which had hitherto rendered the brigands odious; the Chouans remain in history as a memorable example of the danger of uprousing the uncivilized masses of the nation.

The sketch here made of a Breton valley and of the Breton men in the detachment of recruits, more especially that of the "gars" who so suddenly appeared on the summit of Mont Pelerine, gives a brief but faithful picture of the province and its inhabitants. A trained imagination can by the help of these details obtain some idea of the theatre of the war and of the men who were its instruments. The flowering hedges of the beautiful valleys concealed the combatants. Each field was a fortress, every tree an ambush; the hollow trunk of each old willow hid a stratagem. The place for a fight was everywhere. Sharpshooters were lurking at every turn for the Blues, whom laughing young girls, unmindful of their perfidy, attracted within range,—for had they not made pilgrimages with their fathers and their brothers, imploring to be taught wiles, and receiving absolution from their wayside Virgin of rotten wood? Religion, or rather the fetichism of these ignorant creatures, absolved such murders of remorse.

Thus, when the struggle had once begun, every part of the country was dangerous,—in fact, all things were full of peril, sound as well as silence, attraction as well as fear, the family hearth or the open country. Treachery was everywhere, but it was treachery from conviction. The people were savages serving God and the King after the fashion of Red Indians. To make this sketch of the struggle exact and true at all points, the historian must add that the moment Hoche had signed his peace the whole country subsided into smiles and friendliness. Families who were rending each other to pieces over night, were supping together without danger the next day.

The very moment that Commandant Hulot became aware of the secret treachery betrayed by the hairy skins of Marche-a-Terre, he was convinced that this peace, due to the genius of Hoche, the stability of which he had always doubted, was at an end. The civil war, he felt, was about to be renewed,—doubtless more terrible than ever after a cessation of three years. The Revolution, mitigated by the events of the 9th Thermidor, would doubtless return to the old terrors which had made it odious to sound minds. English gold would, as formerly, assist in the national discords. The Republic, abandoned by young Bonaparte who had seemed to be its tutelary genius, was no longer in a condition to resist its enemies from without and from within,—the worst and most cruel of whom were the last to appear. The Civil War, already threatened by various partial uprisings, would assume a new and far more serious aspect if the Chouans were now to attack so strong an escort. Such were the reflections that filled the mind of the commander (though less succinctly formulated) as soon as he perceived, in the condition of Marche-a-Terre's clothing, the signs of an ambush carefully planned.

The silence which followed the prophetic remark of the commandant to Gerard gave Hulot time to recover his self-possession. The old soldier had been shaken. He could not hinder his brow from clouding as he felt himself surrounded by the horrors of a warfare the atrocities of which would have shamed even cannibals. Captain Merle and the adjutant Gerard could not explain to themselves the evident dread on the face of their leader as he looked at Marche-a-Terre eating his bread by the side of the road. But Hulot's face soon cleared; he began to rejoice in the opportunity to fight for the Republic, and he joyously vowed to escape being the dupe of the Chouans, and to fathom the wily and impenetrable being whom they had done him the honor to employ against him.

Before taking any resolution he set himself to study the position in which it was evident the enemy intended to surprise him. Observing that the road where the column had halted was about to pass through a sort of gorge, short to be sure, but flanked with woods from which several paths appeared to issue, he frowned heavily, and said to his two friends, in a low voice of some emotion:—

"We're in a devil of a wasp's-nest."

"What do you fear?" asked Gerard.

14

"Fear? Yes, that's it, *fear*," returned the commandant. "I have always had a fear of being shot like a dog at the edge of a wood, without a chance of crying out 'Who goes there?'"

"Pooh!" said Merle, laughing, "'Who goes there' is all humbug."

"Are we in any real danger?" asked Gerard, as much surprised by Hulot's coolness as he was by his evident alarm.

"Hush!" said the commandant, in a low voice. "We are in the jaws of the wolf; it is as dark as a pocket; and we must get some light. Luckily, we've got the upper end of the slope!"

So saying, he moved, with his two officers, in a way to surround Marche-a-Terre, who rose quickly, pretending to think himself in the way.

"Stay where you are, vagabond!" said Hulot, keeping his eye on the apparently indifferent face of the Breton, and giving him a push which threw him back on the place where he had been sitting.

"Friends," continued Hulot, in a low voice, speaking to the two officers. "It is time I should tell you that it is all up with the army in Paris. The Directory, in consequence of a disturbance in the Assembly, has made another clean sweep of our affairs. Those pentarchs,—puppets, I call them,—those directors have just lost a good blade; Bernadotte has abandoned them."

"Who will take his place?" asked Gerard, eagerly.

"Milet-Mureau, an old blockhead. A pretty time to choose to let fools sail the ship! English rockets from all the headlands, and those cursed Chouan cockchafers in the air! You may rely upon it that some one behind those puppets pulled the wire when they saw we were getting the worst of it."

"How getting the worst of it?"

"Our armies are beaten at all points," replied Hulot, sinking his voice still lower. "The Chouans have intercepted two couriers; I only received my despatches and last orders by a private messenger sent by Bernadotte just as he was leaving the ministry. Luckily, friends have written me confidentially about this crisis. Fouche has discovered that the tyrant Louis XVIII. has been advised by traitors in Paris to send a leader to his followers in La Vendee. It is thought that Barras is betraying the Republic. At any rate, Pitt and the princes have sent a man, a *ci-devant*, vigorous, daring, full of talent, who intends, by uniting the Chouans with the Vendeans, to pluck the cap of liberty from the head of the Republic. The fellow has lately landed in the Morbihan; I was the first to hear of it, and I sent the news to those knaves in Paris. 'The Gars' is the name he goes by. All those beasts," he added, pointing to Marche-a-Terre, "stick on names which would give a stomach-ache to honest patriots if they bore them. The Gars is now in this district. The presence of that fellow" — and again he signed to Marche-a-Terre—"as good as tells me he is on our back. But they can't teach an old monkey to make faces; and you've got to help me to get my birds safe into their cage, and as quick as a flash too. A pretty fool I should be if I allowed that *ci-devant*, who dares to come from London with his British gold, to trap me like a crow!"

On learning these secret circumstances, and being well aware that their leader was never unnecessarily alarmed, the two officers saw the dangers of the position. Gerard was about to ask some questions on the political state of Paris, some details of which Hulot had evidently passed over in silence, but a sign from his commander stopped him, and once more drew the eyes of all three to the Chouan. Marche-a-Terre gave no sign of disturbance at being watched. The curiosity of the two officers, who were new to this species of warfare, was greatly excited by this beginning of an affair which seemed to have an almost romantic interest, and they began to joke about it. But Hulot stopped them at once.

"God's thunder!" he cried. "Don't smoke upon the powder-cask; wasting courage for nothing is like carrying water in a basket. Gerard," he added, in the ear of his adjutant, "get nearer, by degrees, to that fellow, and watch him; at the first suspicious action put your sword through him. As for me, I must take measures to carry on the ball if our unseen adversaries choose to open it."

The Chouan paid no attention to the movements of the young officer, and continued to play with his whip, and fling out the lash of it as though he were fishing in the ditch.

Meantime the commandant was saying to Merle, in a low voice: "Give ten picked men to a sergeant, and post them yourself above us on the summit of this slope, just where the path widens to a ledge; there you ought to see the whole length of the route to Ernee. Choose a position where the road is not flanked by woods, and where the sergeant can overlook the country. Take Clef-des-Coeurs; he is very intelligent. This is no laughing matter; I wouldn't give a farthing for our skins if we don't turn the odds in our favor at once."

While Merle was executing this order with a rapidity of which he fully understood the importance, the commandant waved his right hand to enforce silence on the soldiers, who were standing at ease, and laughing and joking around him. With another gesture he ordered them to take up arms. When quiet was restored he turned his eyes from one end of the road to the other, listened with anxious attention as though he hoped to detect some stifled sound, some echo of weapons, or steps which might give warning of the expected attack. His black eye seemed to pierce the woods to an extraordinary depth. Perceiving no indications of danger, he next consulted, like a savage, the ground at his feet, to discover, if possible, the trail of the invisible enemies whose daring was well known to him. Desperate at seeing and hearing nothing to justify his fears, he turned aside from the road and ascended, not without difficulty, one or two hillocks. The other officers and the soldiers, observing the anxiety of a leader in whom they trusted and whose worth was known to them, knew that his extreme watchfulness meant danger; but not suspecting its imminence, they merely stood still and held their breaths by instinct. Like dogs endeavoring to guess the intentions of a huntsman, whose orders are incomprehensible to them though they faithfully obey him, the soldiers gazed in turn at the valley, at the woods by the roadside, at the stern face of their leader, endeavoring to read their fate. They questioned each other with their eyes, and more than one smile ran from lip to lip.

When Hulot returned to his men with an anxious look, Beau-Pied, a young sergeant who passed for the wit of his company, remarked in a low voice: "Where the deuce have we poked ourselves that an old trooper like Hulot should pull such a gloomy face? He's as solemn as a council of war."

Hulot gave the speaker a stern look, silence being ordered in the ranks. In the hush that ensued, the lagging steps of the conscripts on the creaking sand of the road produced a recurrent sound which added a sort of vague emotion to the general excitement. This indefinable feeling can be understood only by those who have felt their hearts beat in the silence of the night from a painful expectation heightened by some noise, the monotonous recurrence of which seems to distil terror into their minds, drop by drop.

The thought of the commandant, as he returned to his men, was: "Can I be mistaken?" He glanced, with a concentrated anger which flashed like lightning from his eyes, at the stolid, immovable Chouan; a look of savage irony which he fancied he detected in the man's eyes, warned him not to relax in his precautions. Just then Captain Merle, having obeyed Hulot's orders, returned to his side.

"We did well, captain," said the commandant, "to put the few men whose patriotism we can count upon among those conscripts at the rear. Take a dozen more of our own bravest fellows, with sub-lieutenant Lebrun at their head, and make a rear-guard of them; they'll support the patriots who are there already, and help to shove on that flock of birds and close up the distance between us. I'll wait for you."

The captain disappeared. The commander's eye singled out four men on whose intelligence and quickness he knew he might rely, and he beckoned to them, silently, with the well-known friendly gesture of moving the right forefinger rapidly and repeatedly toward the nose. They came to him.

"You served with me under Hoche," he said, "when we brought to reason those brigands who call themselves 'Chasseurs du Roi'; you know how they hid themselves to swoop down on the Blues."

At this commendation of their intelligence the four soldiers nodded with significant grins. Their heroically martial faces wore that look of careless resignation to fate which evidenced the fact that since the struggle had begun between France and Europe, the ideas of the private soldiers had never passed beyond the cartridge-boxes on their backs or the bayonets in front of them. With their lips drawn together like a purse when the strings are tightened, they looked at their commander attentively with inquiring eyes.

"You know," continued Hulot, who possessed the art of speaking picturesquely as soldier to soldiers, "that it won't do for old hares like us to be caught napping by the Chouans,—of whom there are plenty all round us, or my name's not Hulot. You four are to march in advance and beat up both sides of this road. The detachment will hang fire here. Keep your eyes about you; don't get picked off; and bring me news of what you find—quick!"

So saying he waved his hand towards the suspected heights along the road. The four men, by way of thanks raised the backs of their hands to their battered old three-cornered hats, discolored by rain and ragged with age, and bent their bodies double. One of them, named Larose, a corporal well-known to Hulot, remarked as he clicked his musket: "We'll play 'em a tune on the clarinet, commander."

They started, two to right and two to left of the road; and it was not without some excitement that their comrades watched them disappear. The commandant himself feared that he had sent them to their deaths, and an involuntary shudder seized him as he saw the last of them. Officers and soldiers listened to the gradually lessening sound of their footsteps, with feelings all the more acute because they were carefully hidden. There are occasions when the risk of four lives causes more excitement and alarm than all the slain at Jemmapes. The faces of those trained to war have such various and fugitive expressions that a painter who has to describe them is forced to appeal to the recollections of soldiers and to leave civilians to imagine these dramatic figures; for scenes so rich in detail cannot be rendered in writing, except at interminable length.

Just as the bayonets of the four men were finally lost to sight, Captain Merle returned, having executed the commandant's orders with rapidity. Hulot, with two or three sharp commands, put his troop in line of battle and ordered it to return to the summit of La Pelerine where his little advanced-guard were stationed; walking last himself and looking backward to note any changes that might occur in a scene which Nature had made so lovely, and man so terrible. As he reached the spot where he had left the Chouan, Marche-a-Terre, who had seen with apparent indifference the various movements of the commander, but who was now watching with extraordinary intelligence the two soldiers in the woods to the right, suddenly gave the shrill and piercing cry of the *chouette*, or screech-owl. The three famous smugglers already mentioned were in the habit of using the various intonations of this cry to warn each other of danger or of any event that might concern them. From this came the nickname of "Chuin" which means *chouette* or owl in the dialect of that region. This corrupted word came finally to mean the whole body of those who, in the first uprising, imitated the tactics and the signals of the smugglers.

When Hulot heard that suspicious sound he stopped short and examined the man intently; then he feigned to be taken in by his stupid air, wishing to keep him by him as a barometer which might indicate the movements of the enemy. He therefore checked Gerard, whose hand was on his sword to despatch him; but he placed two soldiers beside the man he now felt to be a spy, and ordered them in a loud, clear voice to shoot him at the next sound he made. In spite of his imminent danger Marche-a-Terre showed not the slightest emotion. The commandant, who was studying him, took note of this apparent insensibility, and remarked to Gerard: "That fool is not so clever as he means to be! It is far from easy to read the face of a Chouan, but the fellow betrays himself by his anxiety to show his nerve. Ha! ha! if he had only pretended fear I should have taken him for a stupid brute. He and I might have made a pair! I came very near falling into the trap. Yes, we shall undoubtedly be attacked; but let 'em come; I'm all ready now."

As he said these words in a low voice, rubbing his hands with an air of satisfaction, he looked at the Chouan with a jeering eye. Then he crossed his arms on his breast and stood in the road with his favorite officers beside him awaiting the result of his arrangements. Certain that a fight was at hand, he looked at his men composedly.

"There'll be a row," said Beau-Pied to his comrades in a low voice. "See, the commandant is rubbing his hands."

In critical situations like that in which the detachment and its commander were now placed, life is so clearly at stake that men of nerve make it a point of honor to show coolness and self-possession. These are the moments in which to judge men's souls. The commandant, better informed of the danger than his two officers, took pride in showing his tranquillity. With his eyes moving from Marche-a-Terre to the road and thence to the woods he stood expecting, not without dread, a general volley from the Chouans, whom he believed to be hidden like brigands all around him; but his face remained impassible. Knowing that the eyes of the soldiers were turned upon him, he wrinkled his brown cheeks pitted with the small-pox, screwed his upper lip, and winked his right eye, a grimace always taken for a smile by his men; then he tapped Gerard on the shoulder and said: "Now that things are quiet tell me what you wanted to say just now."

"I wanted to ask what this new crisis means, commandant?" was the reply.

"It is not new," said Hulot. "All Europe is against us, and this time she has got the whip hand. While those Directors are fighting together like horses in a stable without any oats, and letting the government go to bits, the armies are left without supplies or reinforcements. We are getting the worst of it in Italy; we've evacuated Mantua after a series of disasters on the Trebia, and Joubert has just lost a battle at Novi. I only hope Massena may be able to hold the Swiss passes against Suwarow. We're done for on the Rhine. The Directory have sent Moreau. The question is, Can he defend the frontier? I hope he may, but the Coalition will end by invading us, and the only general able to save the nation is, unluckily, down in that devilish Egypt; and how is he ever to get back, with England mistress of the Mediterranean?"

"Bonaparte's absence doesn't trouble me, commandant," said the young adjutant Gerard, whose intelligent mind had been developed by a fine education. "I am certain the Revolution cannot be brought to naught. Ha! we soldiers have a double mission,—not merely to defend French territory, but to preserve the national soul, the generous principles of liberty, independence, and rights of human reason awakened by our Assemblies and gaining strength, as I believe, from day to day. France is like a traveller bearing a light: he protects it with one hand, and defends himself with the other. If your news is true, we have never the last ten years been so surrounded with people trying to blow it out. Principles and nation are in danger of perishing together."

"Alas, yes," said Hulot, sighing. "Those clowns of Directors have managed to quarrel with all the men who could sail the ship. Bernadotte, Carnot, all of them, even Talleyrand, have deserted us. There's not a single good patriot left, except friend Fouche, who holds 'em through the police. There's a man for you! It was he who warned me of a coming insurrection; and here we are, sure enough, caught in a trap."

"If the army doesn't take things in hand and manage the government," said Gerard, "those lawyers in Paris will put us back just where we were before the Revolution. A parcel of ninnies! what do they know about governing?"

"I'm always afraid they'll treat with the Bourbons," said Hulot. "Thunder! if they did *that* a pretty pass we should be in, we soldiers!"

"No, no, commandant, it won't come to that," said Gerard. "The army, as you say, will raise its voice, and—provided it doesn't choose its words from Pichegru's vocabulary—I am persuaded we have not hacked ourselves to pieces for the last ten years merely to manure the flax and let others spin the thread."

"Well," interposed Captain Merle, "what we have to do now is to act as good patriots and prevent the Chouans from communicating with La Vendee; for, if they once come to an understanding and England gets her finger into the pie, I wouldn't answer for the cap of the Republic, one and invisible."

As he spoke the cry of an owl, heard at a distance, interrupted the conversation. Again the commander examined Marche-a-Terre, whose impassible face still gave no sign. The conscripts, their ranks closed up by an officer, now stood like a herd of cattle in the road, about a hundred feet distant from the escort, which was drawn up in line of battle. Behind them stood the rear-guard of soldiers and patriots, picked men, commanded by Lieutenant Lebrun. Hulot cast his eyes over this arrangement of his forces and looked again at the picket of men posted in advance upon the road. Satisfied with what he saw he was about to give the order to march, when the tricolor cockades of the two soldiers he had sent to beat the woods to the left caught his eye; he waited therefore till the two others, who had gone to the right, should reappear.

"Perhaps the ball will open over there," he said to his officers, pointing to the woods from which the two men did not emerge.

While the first two made their report Hulot's attention was distracted momentarily from Marche-a-Terre. The Chouan at once sent his owl's-cry to an apparently vast distance, and before the men who guarded him could raise their muskets and take aim he had struck them a blow with his whip which felled them, and rushed away. A terrible discharge of fire-arms from the woods just above the place where the Chouan had been sitting brought down six or eight soldiers. Marche-a-Terre, at whom several men had fired without touching him, vanished into the woods after climbing the slope with the agility of a wild-cat; as he did so his sabots rolled into the ditch and his feet were seen to be shod with the thick, hobnailed boots always worn by the Chouans.

At the first cries uttered by the Chouans, the conscripts sprang into the woods to the right like a flock of birds taking flight at the approach of a man.

"Fire on those scoundrels!" cried Hulot.

The company fired, but the conscripts knew well how to shelter themselves behind trees, and before the soldiers could reload they were out of sight.

"What's the use of *decreeing* levies in the departments?" said Hulot. "It is only such idiots as the Directory who would expect any good of a draft in this region. The Assembly had much better stop voting more shoes and money and ammunition, and see that we get what belongs to us."

At this moment the two skirmishers sent out on the right were seen returning with evident difficulty. The one that was least wounded supported his comrade, whose blood was moistening the earth. The two poor fellows were half-way down the slope when Marche-a-Terre showed his ugly face, and took so true an aim that both Blues fell together and rolled heavily into the ditch. The Chouan's monstrous head was no sooner seen than thirty muzzles were levelled at him, but, like a figure in a pantomime, he disappeared in a second among the tufts of gorse. These events, which have taken so many words to tell, happened instantaneously, and in another moment the rear-guard of patriots and soldiers had joined the main body of the escort.

"Forward!" cried Hulot.

The company moved quickly to the higher and more open ground on which the picket guard was already stationed. There, the commander formed his troop once more into line of battle; but, as the Chouans made no further hostile demonstrations, he began to think that the deliverance of the conscripts might have been the sole object of the ambuscade.

"Their cries," he said to his two friends, "prove that they are not numerous. We'll advance at a quick step, and possibly we may be able to reach Ernee without getting them on our backs."

These words were overheard by one of the patriot conscripts, who stepped from the ranks, and said respectfully:—

"General, I have already fought the Chouans; may I be allowed a word?"

"A lawyer," whispered Hulot to Merle. "They always want to harangue. Argue away," he said to the young man.

"General, the Chouans have no doubt brought arms for those escaped recruits. Now, if we try to outmarch them, they will catch us in the woods and shoot every one of us before we can get to Ernee. We must argue, as you call it, with cartridges. During the skirmish, which will last more time than you think for, some of us ought to go back and fetch the National Guard and the militia from Fougeres."

"Then you think there are a good many Chouans?"

"Judge for yourself, citizen commander."

He led Hulot to a place where the sand had been stirred as with a rake; then he took him to the opening of a wood-path, where the leaves were scattered and trampled into the earth,—unmistakable signs of the passage of a large body of men.

"Those were the 'gars' from Vitre," said the man, who came himself from Fougeres; "they are on their way to Lower Normandy."

"What is your name?" asked Hulot.

"Gudin, commander."

"Well, then, Gudin, I make you a corporal. You seem to me trustworthy. Select a man to send to Fougeres; but stay yourself with me. In the first place, however, take two or three of your comrades and bring in the muskets and ammunition of the poor fellows those brigands have rolled into the ditch. These Bretons," added Hulot to Gerard, "will make famous infantry if they take to rations."

The Chouans

Gudin's emissary started on a run to Fougeres by a wood-road to the left; the soldiers looked to their arms, and awaited an attack; the commandant passed along their line, smiling to them, and then placed himself with his officers, a little in front of it. Silence fell once more, but it was of short duration. Three hundred or more Chouans, their clothing identical with that of the late recruits, burst from the woods to the right with actual howls and planted themselves, without any semblance of order, on the road directly in front of the feeble detachment of the Blues. The commandant thereupon ranged his soldiers in two equal parts, each with a front of ten men. Between them, he placed the twelve recruits, to whom he hastily gave arms, putting himself at their head. This little centre was protected by the two wings, of twenty-five men each, which manoeuvred on either side of the road under the orders of Merle and Gerard; their object being to catch the Chouans on the flank and prevent them from posting themselves as sharp-shooters among the trees, where they could pick off the Blues without risk to themselves; for in these wars the Republican troops never knew where to look for an enemy.

These arrangements, hastily made, gave confidence to the soldiers, and they advanced in silence upon the Chouans. At the end of a few seconds each side fired, with the loss of several men. At this moment the two wings of the Republicans, to whom the Chouans had nothing to oppose, came upon their flanks, and, with a close, quick volley, sent death and disorder among the enemy. This manoeuvre very nearly equalized the numerical strength of the two parties. But the Chouan nature was so intrepid, their will so firm, that they did not give way; their losses scarcely staggered them; they simply closed up and attempted to surround the dark and well-formed little party of the Blues, which covered so little ground that it looked from a distance like a queen-bee surrounded by the swarm.

The Chouans might have carried the day at this moment if the two wings commanded by Merle and Gerard had not succeeded in getting in two volleys which took them diagonally on their rear. The Blues of the two wings ought to have remained in position and continued to pick off in this way their terrible enemies; but excited by the danger of their little main body, then completely surrounded by the Chouans, they flung themselves headlong into the road with fixed bayonets and made the battle even for a few moments. Both sides fought with a stubbornness intensified by the cruelty and fury of the partisan spirit which made this war exceptional. Each man, observant of danger, was silent. The scene was gloomy and cold as death itself. Nothing was heard through the clash of arms and the grinding of the sand under foot but the moans and exclamations of those who fell, either dead or badly wounded. The twelve loyal recruits in the republican main body protected the commandant (who was guiding his men and giving orders) with such courage that more than once several soldiers called out "Bravo, conscripts!"

Hulot, imperturbable and with an eye to everything, presently remarked among the Chouans a man who, like himself, was evidently surrounded by picked men, and was therefore, no doubt, the leader of the attacking party. He was eager to see this man distinctly, and he made many efforts to distinguish his features, but in vain; they were hidden by the red caps and broad-brimmed hats of those about him. Hulot did, however, see Marche-a-Terre beside this leader, repeating his orders in a hoarse voice, his own carbine, meanwhile, being far from inactive. The commandant grew impatient at being thus baffled. Waving his sword, he urged on the recruits and charged the centre of the Chouans with such fury that he broke through their line and came close to their chief, whose face, however, was still hidden by a broad-brimmed felt hat with a white cockade. But the invisible leader, surprised at so bold an attack, retreated a step or two and raised his hat abruptly, thus enabling Hulot to get a hasty idea of his appearance.

He was young,—Hulot thought him to be about twenty-five; he wore a hunting-jacket of green cloth, and a white belt containing pistols. His heavy shoes were hobnailed like those of the Chouans; leather leggings came to his knees covering the ends of his breeches of very coarse drilling, and completing a costume which showed off a slender and well-poised figure of medium height. Furious that the Blues should thus have approached him, he pulled his hat again over his face and sprang towards them. But he was instantly surrounded by Marche-a-Terre and several Chouans. Hulot thought he perceived between the heads which clustered about this young leader, a broad red ribbon worn across his chest. The eyes of the commandant, caught by this royal decoration (then almost forgotten by republicans), turned quickly to the young man's face, which, however, he soon lost sight of under the necessity of controlling and protecting his own little troop. Though he had barely time to notice a pair of brilliant eyes (the color of which escaped him), fair hair and delicate features bronzed by the sun, he was much struck by the dazzling whiteness of the neck, relieved by a black cravat carelessly knotted. The fiery attitude of the young leader proved him to be a

26

soldier of the stamp of those who bring a certain conventional poesy into battle. His well-gloved hand waved above his head a sword which gleamed in the sunlight. His whole person gave an impression both of elegance and strength. An air of passionate self-devotion, enhanced by the charms of youth and distinguished manners, made this *emigre* a graceful image of the French *noblesse*. He presented a strong contrast to Hulot, who, ten feet distant from him, was quite as vivid an image of the vigorous Republic for which the old soldier was fighting; his stern face, his well-worn blue uniform with its shabby red facings and its blackened epaulettes hanging back of his shoulders, being visible signs of its needs and character.

The graceful attitude and expression of the young man were not lost on the commandant, who exclaimed as he pressed towards him: "Come on, opera-dancer, come on, and let me crush you!"

The royalist leader, provoked by his momentary disadvantage, advanced with an angry movement, but at the same moment the men who were about him rushed forward and flung themselves with fury on the Blues. Suddenly a soft, clear voice was heard above the din of battle saying: "Here died Saint-Lescure! Shall we not avenge him?"

At the magic words the efforts of the Chouans became terrible, and the soldiers of the Republic had great difficulty in maintaining themselves without breaking their little line of battle.

"If he wasn't a young man," thought Hulot, as he retreated step by step, "we shouldn't have been attacked in this way. Who ever heard of the Chouans fighting an open battle? Well, all the better! they won't shoot us off like dogs along the road." Then, raising his voice till it echoed through the woods, he exclaimed, "Come on, my men! Shall we let ourselves be *fooled* by those brigands?"

The word here given is but a feeble equivalent of the one the brave commandant used; but every veteran can substitute the real one, which was far more soldierly in character.

"Gerard! Merle!" added Hulot, "call in your men, form them into a battalion, take the rear, fire upon those dogs, and let's make an end of this!"

The order was difficult to obey, for the young chief, hearing Hulot's voice, cried out: "By Saint Anne of Auray, don't let them get away! Spread out, spread out, my lads!" and each of the two wings of the Blues was followed by Chouans who were fully as obstinate and far superior in numbers. The Republicans were surrounded on all sides by the Goatskins uttering their savage cries, which were more like howls.

"Hold your tongues, gentlemen," cried Beau-Pied; "we can't hear ourselves be killed."

This jest revived the courage of the Blues. Instead of fighting only at one point, the Republicans spread themselves to three different points on the table-land of La Pelerine, and the rattle of musketry woke all the echoes of the valleys, hitherto so peaceful beneath it. Victory might have remained doubtful for many hours, or the fight might have come to an end for want of combatants, for Blues and Chouans were equally brave and obstinate. Each side was growing more and more incensed, when the sound of a drum in the distance told that the body of men must be crossing the valley of Couesnon.

"There's the National Guard of Fougeres!" cried Gudin, in a loud voice; "my man has brought them."

The words reached the ears of the young leader of the Chouans and his ferocious aide-de-camp, and the royalists made a hasty retrograde movement, checked, however, by a brutal shout from Marche-a-Terre. After two or three orders given by the leader in a low voice, and transmitted by Marche-a-Terre in the Breton dialect, the Chouans made good their retreat with a cleverness which disconcerted the Republicans and even the commandant. At the first word of command they formed in line, presenting a good front, behind which the wounded retreated, and the others reloaded their guns. Then, suddenly, with the agility already shown by Marche-a-Terre, the wounded were taken over the brow of the eminence to the right of the road, while half the others followed them slowly to occupy the summit, where nothing could be seen of them by the Blues but their bold heads. There they made a rampart of the trees and pointed the muzzles of their guns on the Republicans, who were rapidly reformed under reiterated orders from Hulot and turned to face the remainder of the Chouans, who were still before them in the road. The latter retreated slowly, disputing the ground and wheeling so as to bring themselves under cover of their comrades' fire. When they reached the broad ditch which bordered the road, they scaled the high bank on the other side, braving the fire of the Republicans, which was sufficiently well-directed to fill the ditch with dead bodies. The Chouans already on the summit answered with a fire that was no less deadly. At that moment the National Guard of Fougeres reached the scene of action at a quick step, and its mere presence put an end to the affair. The Guard and some of the soldiers crossed the road and began to enter the woods, but the commandant called to them in his martial voice, "Do you want to be annihilated over there?"

The victory remained to the Republicans, though not without heavy loss. All the battered old hats were hung on the points of the bayonets and the muskets held aloft, while the soldiers shouted with one voice: "Vive la Republique!" Even the wounded, sitting by the roadside, shared in the general enthusiasm; and Hulot, pressing Gerard's hand, exclaimed:—

"Ha, ha! those are what I call *veterans!*"

Merle was directed to bury the dead in a ravine; while another party of men attended to the removal of the wounded. The carts and horses of the neighborhood were put into requisition, and the suffering men were carefully laid on the clothing of the dead. Before the little column started, the National Guard of Fougeres turned over to Hulot a Chouan, dangerously wounded, whom they had captured at the foot of the slope up which his comrades had escaped, and where he had fallen from weakness.

"Thanks for your help, citizens," said the commandant. "God's thunder! if it hadn't been for you, we should have had a pretty bad quarter of an hour. Take care of yourselves; the war has begun. Adieu, friends." Then, turning to the prisoner, he asked, "What's the name of your general?"

"The Gars."

"Who? Marche-a-Terre?"

"No, the Gars."

"Where does the Gars come from?"

To this question the prisoner, whose face was convulsed with suffering, made no reply; he took out his beads and began to say his prayers.

"The Gars is no doubt that young *ci-devant* with the black cravat, — sent by the tyrant and his allies Pitt and Coburg."

At that words the Chouan raised his head proudly and said: "Sent by God and the king!" He uttered the words with an energy which exhausted his strength. The commandant saw the difficulty of questioning a dying man, whose countenance expressed his gloomy fanaticism, and he turned away his head with a frown. Two soldiers, friends of those whom Marche-a-Terre had so brutally killed with the butt of his whip, stepped back a pace or two, took aim at the Chouan, whose fixed eyes did not blink at the muzzles of their guns, fired at short range, and brought him down. When they approached the dead body to strip it, the dying man found strength to cry out loudly, "Vive le roi!"

"Yes, yes, you canting hypocrite," cried Clef-des-Coeurs; "go and make your report to that Virgin of yours. Didn't he shout in our faces, 'Vive le roi!' when we thought him cooked?"

"Here are his papers, commandant," said Beau-Pied.

"Ho! ho!" cried Clef-des-Coeurs. "Come, all of you, and see this minion of the good God with colors on his stomach!"

Hulot and several soldiers came round the body, now entirely naked, and saw upon its breast a blue tattooing in the form of a swollen heart. It was the sign of initiation into the brotherhood of the Sacred Heart. Above this sign were the words, "Marie Lambrequin," no doubt the man's name.

"Look at that, Clef-des-Coeurs," said Beau-Pied; "it would take you a hundred years to find out what that accoutrement is good for."

"What should I know about the Pope's uniform?" replied Clef-des-Coeurs, scornfully.

"You worthless bog-trotter, you'll never learn anything," retorted Beau-Pied. "Don't you see that they've promised that poor fool that he shall live again, and he has painted his gizzard in order to find himself?"

At this sally—which was not without some foundation—even Hulot joined in the general hilarity. At this moment Merle returned, and the burial of the dead being completed and the wounded placed more or less comfortably in two carts, the rest of the late escort formed into two lines round the improvised ambulances, and descended the slope of the mountain towards Maine, where the beautiful valley of La Pelerine, a rival to that of Couesnon lay before it.

Hulot with his two officers followed the troop slowly, hoping to get safely to Ernee where the wounded could be cared for. The fight we have just described, which was almost forgotten in the midst of the greater events which were soon to occur, was called by the name of the mountain on which it took place. It obtained some notice at the West, where the inhabitants, observant of this second uprising, noticed on this occasion a great change in the manner in which the Chouans now made war. In earlier days they would never have attacked so large a detachment. According to Hulot the young royalist whom he had seen was undoubtedly the Gars, the new general sent to France by the princes, who, following the example of the other royalist chiefs, concealed his real name and title under one of those pseudonyms called "noms de guerre." This circumstance made the commandant quite as uneasy after his melancholy victory as he had been before it while expecting the attack. He turned several times to consider the table-land of La Pelerine which he was leaving behind him, across which he could still hear faintly at intervals the drums of the National Guard descending into the valley of Couesnon at the same time that the Blues were descending into that of La Pelerine.

"Can either of you," he said to his two friends, "guess the motives of that attack of the Chouans? To them, fighting is a matter of business, and I can't see what they expected to gain by this attack. They have lost at least a hundred men, and we"—he added, screwing up his right cheek and winking by way of a smile, "have lost only sixty. God's thunder! I don't understand that sort of speculation. The scoundrels needn't have attacked us; we might just as well have been allowed to pass like letters through the post—No, I don't see what good it has done them to bullet-hole our men," he added, with a sad shake of his head toward the carts. "Perhaps they only intended to say good-day to us."

"But they carried off our recruits, commander," said Merle.

"The recruits could have skipped like frogs into the woods at any time, and we should never have gone after them, especially if those fellows had fired a single volley," returned Hulot. "No, no, there's something behind all this." Again he turned and looked at La Pelerine. "See!" he cried; "see there!"

Though they were now at a long distance from the fatal plateau, they could easily distinguish Marche-a-Terre and several Chouans who were again occupying it.

"Double-quick, march!" cried Hulot to his men, "open your compasses and trot the steeds faster than that! Are your legs frozen?"

These words drove the little troop into a rapid motion.

"There's a mystery, and it's hard to make out," continued Hulot, speaking to his friends. "God grant it isn't explained by muskets at Ernee. I'm very much afraid that we shall find the road to Mayenne cut off by the king's men."

* * * * *

The strategical problem which troubled the commandant was causing quite as much uneasiness to the persons whom he had just seen on the summit of Mont Pelerine. As soon as the drums of the National Guard were out of hearing and Marche-a-Terre had seen the Blues at the foot of the declivity, he gave the owl's cry joyously, and the Chouans reappeared, but their numbers were less. Some were no doubt busy in taking care of the wounded in the little village of La Pelerine, situated on the side of the mountain which looks toward the valley of Couesnon. Two or three chiefs of what were called the "Chasseurs du Roi" clustered about Marche-a-Terre. A few feet apart sat the young noble called The Gars, on a granite rock, absorbed in thoughts excited by the difficulties of his enterprise, which now began to show themselves. Marche-a-Terre screened his forehead with his hand from the rays of the sun, and looked gloomily at the road by which the Blues were crossing the valley of

The Chouans

La Pelerine. His small black eyes could see what was happening on the hill-slopes on the other side of the valley.

"The Blues will intercept the messenger," said the angry voice of one of the leaders who stood near him.

"By Saint Anne of Auray!" exclaimed another. "Why did you make us fight? Was it to save your own skin from the Blues?"

Marche-a-Terre darted a venomous look at his questioner and struck the ground with his heavy carbine.

"Am I your leader?" he asked. Then after a pause he added, pointing to the remains of Hulot's detachment, "If you had all fought as I did, not one of those Blues would have escaped, and the coach could have got here safely."

"They'd never have thought of escorting it or holding it back if we had let them go by without a fight. No, you wanted to save your precious skin and get out of their hands—He has bled us for the sake of his own snout," continued the orator, "and made us lose twenty thousand francs in good coin."

"Snout yourself!" cried Marche-a-Terre, retreating three steps and aiming at his aggressor. "It isn't that you hate the Blues, but you love the gold. Die without confession and be damned, for you haven't taken the sacrament for a year."

This insult so incensed the Chouan that he turned pale and a low growl came from his chest as he aimed in turn at Marche-a-Terre. The young chief sprang between them and struck their weapons from their hands with the barrel of his own carbine; then he demanded an explanation of the dispute, for the conversation had been carried on in the Breton dialect, an idiom with which he was not familiar.

"Monsieur le marquis," said Marche-a-Terre, as he ended his account of the quarrel, "it is all the more unreasonable in them to find fault with me because I have left Pille-Miche behind me; he'll know how to save the coach for us."

"What!" exclaimed the young man, angrily, "are you waiting here, all of you, to pillage that coach?—a parcel of cowards who couldn't

33

win a victory in the first fight to which I led you! But why should you win if that's your object? The defenders of God and the king are thieves, are they? By Saint Anne of Auray! I'd have you know, we are making war against the Republic, and not robbing travellers. Those who are guilty in future of such shameful actions shall not receive absolution, nor any of the favors reserved for the faithful servants of the king."

A murmur came from the group of Chouans, and it was easy to see that the authority of the new chief was about to be disputed. The young man, on whom this effect of his words was by no means lost, was thinking of the best means of maintaining the dignity of his command, when the trot of a horse was heard in the vicinity. All heads turned in the direction from which the sound came. A lady appeared, sitting astride of a little Breton horse, which she put at a gallop as soon as she saw the young leader, so as to reach the group of Chouans as quickly as possible.

"What is the matter?" she said, looking first at the Chouans and then at their chief.

"Could you believe it, madame? they are waiting to rob the diligence from Mayenne to Fougeres when we have just had a skirmish, in order to release the conscripts of Fougeres, which has cost us a great many men without defeating the Blues."

"Well, where's the harm of that?" asked the young lady, to whom the natural shrewdness of a woman explained the whole scene. "You have lost men, but there's no lack of others; the coach is bringing gold, and there's always a lack of that. We bury men, who go to heaven, and we take money, which goes into the pockets of heroes. I don't see the difficulty."

The Chouans approved of her speech by unanimous smiles.

"Do you see nothing in all that to make you blush?" said the young man, in a low voice. "Are you in such need of money that you must pillage on the high-road?"

"I am so eager for it, marquis, that I should put my heart in pawn if it were not already captured," she said, smiling coquettishly. "But where did you get the strange idea that you could manage Chouans without letting them rob a few Blues here and there? Don't you know the saying, 'Thieving as an owl'?—and that's a Chouan. Besides," she said, raising her voice to be heard by the men, "it is just; haven't the Blues seized the property of the Church, and our own?"

Another murmur, very different from the growl with which the Chouans had answered their leader, greeted these words. The young man's face grew darker; he took the young lady aside and said in the annoyed tone of a well-bred man, "Will those gentlemen be at La Vivetiere on the appointed day?"

"Yes," she replied, "all of them, the Claimant, Grand-Jacques, and perhaps Ferdinand."

"Then allow me to return there. I cannot sanction such robbery. Yes, madame, I call it robbery. There may be honor in being robbed, but—"

"Well, well," she said, interrupting him, "then I shall have your share of the booty, and I am much obliged to you for giving it up to me; the extra sum will be extremely useful, for my mother has delayed sending me money, so that I am almost destitute."

"Adieu!" cried the marquis.

He turned away, but the lady ran after him.

"Why won't you stay with me?" she said, giving him the look, half-despotic, half-caressing, with which women who have a right to a man's respect let him know their wishes.

"You are going to pillage that coach?"

"Pillage? what a word!" she said. "Let me explain to you—"

"Explain nothing," he said, taking her hand and kissing it with the superficial gallantry of a courtier. "Listen to me," he added after a short pause: "if I were to stay here while they capture that diligence our people would kill me, for I should certainly—"

"Not kill them," she said quickly, "for they would bind your hands, with all the respect that is due to your rank; then, having levied the necessary contribution for their equipment, subsistence, and munitions from our enemies, they would unbind you and obey you blindly."

"And you wish me to command such men under such circumstances? If my life is necessary to the cause which I defend allow me at any rate to save the honor of my position. If I withdraw now I can ignore this base act. I will return, in order to escort you."

So saying, he rapidly disappeared. The young lady listened to his receding steps with evident displeasure. When the sound on the dried leaves ceased, she stood for a moment as if confounded, then she hastily returned to the Chouans. With a gesture of contempt she said to Marche-a-Terre, who helped her to dismount, "That young man wants to make regular war on the Republic! Ah, well! he'll get over that in a few days. How he treated me!" she thought, presently.

She seated herself on the rock where the marquis had been sitting, and silently awaited the arrival of the coach. It was one of the phenomena of the times, and not the least of them, that this young and noble lady should be flung by violent partisanship into the struggle of monarchies against the spirit of the age, and be driven by the strength of her feelings into actions of which it may almost be said she was not conscious. In this she resembled others of her time who were led away by an enthusiasm which was often productive of noble deeds. Like her, many women played heroic or blameworthy parts in the fierce struggle. The royalist cause had no emissaries so devoted and so active as these women; but none of the heroines on that side paid for mistaken devotion or for actions forbidden to their sex, with a greater expiation than did this lady when, seated on that wayside rock, she was forced to admire the young leader's noble disdain and loyalty to principle. Insensibly she dropped into reverie. Bitter memories made her long for the innocence of her early years, and regret that she had escaped being a victim of the Revolution whose victorious march could no longer be arrested by feeble hands.

The coach, which, as we now see, had much to do with the attack of the Chouans, had started from the little town of Ernee a few moments before the skirmishing began. Nothing pictures a region so well as the state of its social material. From this point of view the coach deserves a mention. The Revolution itself was powerless to destroy it; in fact, it still rolls to this present day. When Turgot bought up the privileges of a company, obtained under Louis XIV., for the exclusive right of transporting travellers from one part of the

36

kingdom to another, and instituted the lines of coaches called the "turgotines," all the old vehicles of the former company flocked into the provinces. One of these shabby coaches was now plying between Mayenne and Fougeres. A few objectors called it the "turgotine," partly to mimic Paris and partly to deride a minister who attempted innovations. This turgotine was a wretched cabriolet on two high wheels, in the depths of which two persons, if rather fat, could with difficulty have stowed themselves. The narrow quarters of this rickety machine not admitting of any crowding, and the box which formed the seat being kept exclusively for the postal service, the travellers who had any baggage were forced to keep it between their legs, already tortured by being squeezed into a sort of little box in shape like a bellows. The original color of coach and running-gear was an insoluble enigma. Two leather curtains, very difficult to adjust in spite of their long service, were supposed to protect the occupants from cold and rain. The driver, perched on a plank seat like those of the worst Parisian "coucous," shared in the conversation by reason of his position between his victims, biped and quadruped. The equipage presented various fantastic resemblances to decrepit old men who have gone through a goodly number of catarrhs and apoplexies and whom death respects; it moaned as it rolled, and squeaked spasmodically. Like a traveller overtaken by sleep, it rocked alternately forward and back, as though it tried to resist the violent action of two little Breton horses which dragged it along a road which was more than rough. This monument of a past era contained three travellers, who, on leaving Ernee, where they had changed horses, continued a conversation begun with the driver before reaching the little town.

"What makes you think the Chouans are hereabouts?" said the coachman. "The Ernee people tell me that Commandant Hulot has not yet started from Fougeres."

"Ho, ho, friend driver!" said the youngest of the travellers, "you risk nothing but your own carcass! If you had a thousand francs about you, as I have, and were known to be a good patriot, you wouldn't take it so easy."

"You are pretty free with your tongue, any way," said the driver, shaking his head.

"Count your lambs, and the wolf will eat them," remarked another of the travellers.

The Chouans

This man, who was dressed in black, seemed to be about forty years old, and was, probably, the rector of some parish in the neighborhood. His chin rested on a double fold of flesh, and his florid complexion indicated a priest. Though short and fat, he displayed some agility when required to get in or out of the vehicle.

"Perhaps you are both Chouans!" cried the man of the thousand francs, whose ample goatskin, covering trousers of good cloth and a clean waistcoat, bespoke a rich farmer. "By the soul of Saint Robespierre! I swear you shall be roughly handled."

He turned his gray eyes from the driver to his fellow-travellers and showed them a pistol in his belt.

"Bretons are not afraid of that," said the rector, disdainfully. "Besides, do we look like men who want your money?"

Every time the word "money" was mentioned the driver was silent, and the rector had wit enough to doubt whether the patriot had any at all, and to suspect that the driver was carrying a good deal.

"Are you well laden, Coupiau?" he asked.

"Oh, no, Monsieur Gudin," replied the coachman. "I'm carrying next to nothing."

The priest watched the faces of the patriot and Coupiau as the latter made this answer, and both were imperturbable.

"So much the better for you," remarked the patriot. "I can now take measures to save my property in case of danger."

Such despotic assumption nettled Coupiau, who answered gruffly: "I am the master of my own carriage, and so long as I drive you—"

"Are you a patriot, or are you a Chouan?" said the other, sharply interrupting him.

"Neither the one nor the other," replied Coupiau. "I'm a postilion, and, what is more, a Breton,—consequently, I fear neither Blues nor nobles."

"Noble thieves!" cried the patriot, ironically.

"They only take back what was stolen from them," said the rector, vehemently.

The two men looked at each other in the whites of their eyes, if we may use a phrase so colloquial. Sitting back in the vehicle was a third traveller who took no part in the discussion, and preserved a deep silence. The driver and the patriot and even Gudin paid no attention to this mute individual; he was, in truth, one of those uncomfortable, unsocial travellers who are found sometimes in a stage-coach, like a patient calf that is being carried, bound, to the nearest market. Such travellers begin by filling their legal space, and end by sleeping, without the smallest respect for their fellow- beings, on a neighbor's shoulder. The patriot, Gudin, and the driver had let him alone, thinking him asleep, after discovering that it was useless to talk to a man whose stolid face betrayed an existence spent in measuring yards of linen, and an intellect employed in selling them at a good percentage above cost. This fat little man, doubled-up in his corner, opened his porcelain-blue eyes every now and then, and looked at each speaker with a sort of terror. He appeared to be afraid of his fellow-travellers and to care very little about the Chouans. When he looked at the driver, however, they seemed to be a pair of free-masons. Just then the first volley of musketry was heard on La Pelerine. Coupiau, frightened, stopped the coach.

"Oh! oh!" said the priest, as if he had some means of judging, "it is a serious engagement; there are many men."

"The trouble for us, Monsieur Gudin," cried Coupiau, "is to know which side will win."

The faces of all became unanimously anxious.

"Let us put up the coach at that inn which I see over there," said the patriot; "we can hide it till we know the result of the fight."

The advice seemed so good that Coupiau followed it. The patriot helped him to conceal the coach behind a wood-pile; the abbe seized the occasion to pull Coupiau aside and say to him, in a low voice: "Has he really any money?"

"Hey, Monsieur Gudin, if it gets into the pockets of your Reverence, they won't be weighed down with it."

When the Blues marched by, after the encounter on La Pelerine, they were in such haste to reach Ernee that they passed the little inn without halting. At the sound of their hasty march, Gudin and the innkeeper, stirred by curiosity, went to the gate of the courtyard to watch them. Suddenly, the fat ecclesiastic rushed to a soldier who was lagging in the rear.

"Gudin!" he cried, "you wrong-headed fellow, have you joined the Blues? My lad, you are surely not in earnest?"

"Yes, uncle," answered the corporal. "I've sworn to defend France."

"Unhappy boy! you'll lose your soul," said the uncle, trying to rouse his nephew to the religious sentiments which are so powerful in the Breton breast.

"Uncle," said the young man, "if the king had placed himself at the head of his armies, I don't say but what—"

"Fool! who is talking to you about the king? Does your republic give abbeys? No, it has upset everything. How do you expect to get on in life? Stay with us; sooner or later we shall triumph and you'll be counsellor to some parliament."

"Parliaments!" said young Gudin, in a mocking tone. "Good-bye, uncle."

"You sha'n't have a penny at my death," cried his uncle, in a rage. "I'll disinherit you."

"Thank you, uncle," said the Republican, as they parted.

The fumes of the cider which the patriot copiously bestowed on Coupiau during the passage of the little troop had somewhat dimmed the driver's perceptions, but he roused himself joyously when the innkeeper, having questioned the soldiers, came back to the inn and announced that the Blues were victorious. He at once brought out the coach and before long it was wending its way across the valley.

When the Blues reached an acclivity on the road from which the plateau of La Pelerine could again be seen in the distance, Hulot turned round to discover if the Chouans were still occupying it, and the sun, glinting on the muzzles of the guns, showed them to him, each like a dazzling spot. Giving a last glance to the valley of La Pelerine before turning into that of Ernee, he thought he saw Coupiau's vehicle on the road he had just traversed.

"Isn't that the Mayenne coach?" he said to his two officers.

They looked at the venerable turgotine, and easily recognized it.

"But," said Hulot, "how did we fail to meet it?"

Merle and Gerard looked at each other in silence.

"Another enigma!" cried the commandant. "But I begin to see the meaning of it all."

At the same moment Marche-a-Terre, who also knew the turgotine, called his comrades' attention to it, and the general shout of joy which they sent up roused the young lady from her reflections. She advanced a little distance and saw the coach, which was beginning the ascent of La Pelerine with fatal rapidity. The luckless vehicle soon reached the plateau. The Chouans, who had meantime hidden themselves, swooped on their prey with hungry celerity. The silent traveller slipped to the floor of the carriage, bundling himself up into the semblance of a bale.

"Well done!" cried Coupiau from his wooden perch, pointing to the man in the goatskin; "you must have scented this patriot who has lots of gold in his pouch—"

The Chouans greeted these words with roars of laughter, crying out: "Pille-Miche! hey, Pille-Miche! Pille-Miche!"

Amid the laughter, to which Pille-Miche responded like an echo, Coupiau came down from his seat quite crestfallen. When the famous Cibot, otherwise called Pille-Miche, helped his neighbor to get out of the coach, a respectful murmur was heard among the Chouans.

"It is the Abbe Gudin!" cried several voices. At this respected name every hat was off, and the men knelt down before the priest as they asked his blessing, which he gave solemnly.

"Pille-Miche here could trick Saint Peter and steal the keys of Paradise," said the rector, slapping that worthy on the shoulder. "If it hadn't been for him, the Blues would have intercepted us."

Then, noticing the lady, the abbe went to speak to her apart. Marche-a-Terre, who had meantime briskly opened the boot of the cabriolet, held up to his comrades, with savage joy, a bag, the shape of which betrayed its contents to be rolls of coin. It did not take long to divide the booty. Each Chouan received his share, so carefully apportioned that the division was made without the slightest dispute. Then Marche-a-Terre went to the lady and the priest, and offered them each about six thousand francs.

"Can I conscientiously accept this money, Monsieur Gudin?" said the lady, feeling a need of justification.

"Why not, madame? In former days the Church approved of the confiscation of the property of Protestants, and there's far more reason for confiscating that of these revolutionists, who deny God, destroy chapels, and persecute religion."

The abbe then joined example to precept by accepting, without the slightest scruple, the novel sort of tithe which Marche-a-Terre offered to him. "Besides," he added, "I can now devote all I possess to the service of God and the king; for my nephew has joined the Blues, and I disinherit him."

Coupiau was bemoaning himself and declaring that he was ruined.

"Join us," said Marche-a-Terre, "and you shall have your share."

"They'll say I let the coach be robbed on purpose if I return without signs of violence."

"Oh, is that all?" exclaimed Marche-a-Terre.

He gave a signal and a shower of bullets riddled the turgotine. At this unexpected volley the old vehicle gave forth such a lamentable cry that the Chouans, superstitious by nature, recoiled in terror; but Marche-a-Terre caught sight of the pallid face of the silent traveller rising from the floor of the coach.

"You've got another fowl in your coop," he said in a low voice to Coupiau.

"Yes," said the driver; "but I make it a condition of my joining you that I be allowed to take that worthy man safe and sound to Fougeres. I'm pledged to it in the name of Saint Anne of Auray."

"Who is he?" asked Pille-Miche.

"That I can't tell you," replied Coupiau.

"Let him alone!" said Marche-a-Terre, shoving Pille-Miche with his elbow; "he has vowed by Saint Anne of Auray, and he must keep his word."

"Very good," said Pille-Miche, addressing Coupiau; "but mind you don't go down the mountain too fast; we shall overtake you,—a good reason why; I want to see the cut of your traveller, and give him his passport."

Just then the gallop of a horse coming rapidly up the slopes of La Pelerine was heard, and the young chief presently reappeared. The lady hastened to conceal the bag of plunder which she held in her hand.

"You can keep that money without any scruple," said the young man, touching the arm which the lady had put behind her. "Here is a letter for you which I have just found among mine which were waiting for me at La Vivetiere; it is from your mother." Then, looking at the Chouans who were disappearing into the woods, and at the turgotine which was now on its way to the valley of Couesnon, he added: "After all my haste I see I am too late. God grant I am deceived in my suspicions!"

"It was my poor mother's money!" cried the lady, after opening her letter, the first lines of which drew forth her exclamation.

A smothered laugh came from the woods, and the young man himself could not help smiling as he saw the lady holding in her hand the bag containing her share in the pillage of her own money. She herself began to laugh.

"Well, well, marquis, God be praised! this time, at least, you can't blame me," she said, smiling.

"Levity in everything! even your remorse!" said the young man.

She colored and looked at the marquis with so genuine a contrition that he was softened. The abbe politely returned to her, with an equivocal manner, the sum he had received; then he followed the young leader who took the by-way through which he had come. Before following them the lady made a sign to Marche-a-Terre, who came to her.

"Advance towards Mortagne," she said to him in a low voice. "I know that the Blues are constantly sending large sums of money in coin to Alencon to pay for their supplies of war. If I allow you and your comrades to keep what you captured to-day it is only on condition that you repay it later. But be careful that the Gars knows nothing of the object of the expedition; he would certainly oppose it; in case of ill-luck, I will pacify him."

"Madame," said the marquis, after she had rejoined him and had mounted his horse *en croupe*, giving her own to the abbe, "my friends in Paris write me to be very careful of what we do; the Republic, they say, is preparing to fight us with spies and treachery."

"It wouldn't be a bad plan," she replied; "they have clever ideas, those fellows. I could take part in that sort of war and find foes."

"I don't doubt it!" cried the marquis. "Pichegru advises me to be cautious and watchful in my friendships and relations of every kind. The Republic does me the honor to think me more dangerous than all the Vendeans put together, and counts on certain of my weaknesses to lay hands upon me."

"Surely you will not distrust me?" she said, striking his heart with the hand by which she held to him.

"Are you a traitor, madame?" he said, bending towards her his forehead, which she kissed.

"In that case," said the abbe, referring to the news, "Fouche's police will be more dangerous for us than their battalions of recruits and counter-Chouans."

44

"Yes, true enough, father," replied the marquis.

"Ah! ah!" cried the lady. "Fouche means to send women against you, does he? I shall be ready for them," she added in a deeper tone of voice and after a slight pause.

* * * * *

At a distance of three or four gunshots from the plateau, now abandoned, a little scene was taking place which was not uncommon in those days on the high-roads. After leaving the little village of La Pelerine, Pille-Miche and Marche-a-Terre again stopped the turgotine at a dip in the road. Coupiau got off his seat after making a faint resistance. The silent traveller, extracted from his hiding place by the two Chouans, found himself on his knees in a furze bush.

"Who are you?" asked Marche-a-Terre in a threatening voice.

The traveller kept silence until Pille-Miche put the question again and enforced it with the butt end of his gun.

"I am Jacques Pinaud," he replied, with a glance at Coupiau; "a poor linen-draper."

Coupiau made a sign in the negative, not considering it an infraction of his promise to Saint Anne. The sign enlightened Pille-Miche, who took aim at the luckless traveller, while Marche-a-Terre laid before him categorically a terrible ultimatum.

"You are too fat to be poor. If you make me ask you your name again, here's my friend Pille-Miche, who will obtain the gratitude and good-will of your heirs in a second. Who are you?" he added, after a pause.

"I am d'Orgemont, of Fougeres."

"Ah! ah!" cried the two Chouans.

"I didn't tell your name, Monsieur d'Orgemont," said Coupiau. "The Holy Virgin is my witness that I did my best to protect you."

"Inasmuch as you are Monsieur d'Orgemont, of Fougeres," said Marche-a-Terre, with an air of ironical respect, "we shall let you go

45

in peace. Only, as you are neither a good Chouan nor a true Blue (thought it was you who bought the property of the Abbey de Juvigny), you will pay us three hundred crowns of six francs each for your ransom. Neutrality is worth that, at least."

"Three hundred crowns of six francs each!" chorussed the luckless banker, Pille-Miche, and Coupiau, in three different tones.

"Alas, my good friend," continued d'Orgemont, "I'm a ruined man. The last forced loan of that devilish Republic for a hundred millions sucked me dry, taxed as I was already."

"How much did your Republic get out of you?"

"A thousand crowns, my dear man," replied the banker, with a piteous air, hoping for a reduction.

"If your Republic gets forced loans out of you for such big sums as that you must see that you would do better with us; our government would cost you less. Three hundred crowns, do you call that dear for your skin?"

"Where am I to get them?"

"Out of your strong-box," said Pille-Miche; "and mind that the money is forthcoming, or we'll singe you still."

"How am I to pay it to you?" asked d'Orgemont.

"Your country-house at Fougeres is not far from Gibarry's farm where my cousin Galope-Chopine, otherwise called Cibot, lives. You can pay the money to him," said Pille-Miche.

"That's not business-like," said d'Orgemont.

"What do we care for that?" said Marche-a-Terre. "But mind you remember that if that money is not paid to Galope-Chopine within two weeks we shall pay you a little visit which will cure your gout. As for you, Coupiau," added Marche-a-Terre, "your name in future is to be Mene-a-Bien."

So saying, the two Chouans departed. The traveller returned to the vehicle, which, thanks to Coupiau's whip, now made rapid progress to Fougeres.

"If you'd only been armed," said Coupiau, "we might have made some defence."

"Idiot!" cried d'Orgemont, pointing to his heavy shoes. "I have ten thousand francs in those soles; do you think I would be such a fool as to fight with that sum about me?"

Mene-a-Bien scratched his ear and looked behind him, but his new comrades were out of sight.

Hulot and his command stopped at Ernee long enough to place the wounded in the hospital of the little town, and then, without further hindrance, they reached Mayenne. There the commandant cleared up his doubts as to the action of the Chouans, for on the following day the news of the pillage of the turgotine was received.

A few days later the government despatched to Mayenne so strong a force of "patriotic conscripts," that Hulot was able to fill the ranks of his brigade. Disquieting rumors began to circulate about the insurrection. A rising had taken place at all the points where, during the late war, the Chouans and Bretons had made their chief centres of insurrection. The little town of Saint-James, between Pontorson and Fougeres was occupied by them, apparently for the purpose of making it for the time being a headquarters of operations and supplies. From there they were able to communicate with Normandy and the Morbihan without risk. Their subaltern leaders roamed the three provinces, roused all the partisans of monarchy, and gave consistence and unity to their plans. These proceedings coincided with what was going on in La Vendee, where the same intrigues, under the influence of four famous leaders (the Abbe Vernal, the Comte de Fontaine, De Chatillon, and Suzannet), were agitating the country. The Chevalier de Valois, the Marquis d'Esgrignon, and the Troisvilles were, it was said, corresponding with these leaders in the department of the Orne. The chief of the great plan of operations which was thus developing slowly but in formidable proportions was really "the Gars,"—a name given by the Chouans to the Marquis de Montauran on his arrival from England. The information sent to Hulot by the War department proved correct in all particulars. The marquis gained after a time sufficient ascendancy over the Chouans to make them understand the true object of the war, and to persuade them that the excesses of which they were guilty brought disgrace upon the cause they had adopted. The daring nature, the nerve, coolness, and capacity of this young nobleman awakened the hopes of all the enemies of the Republic, and suited so thoroughly the grave and even solemn enthusiasm of those regions that even the least zealous partisans of the king did their part in preparing a decisive blow in behalf of the defeated monarchy.

Hulot received no answer to the questions and the frequent reports which he addressed to the government in Paris.

But the news of the almost magical return of General Bonaparte and the events of the 18th Brumaire were soon current in the air. The military commanders of the West understood then the silence of the ministers. Nevertheless, they were only the more impatient to be released from the responsibility that weighed upon them; and they were in every way desirous of knowing what measures the new government was likely to take. When it was known to these soldiers that General Bonaparte was appointed First Consul of the Republic their joy was great; they saw, for the first time, one of their own profession called to the management of the nation. France, which had made an idol of this young hero, quivered with hope. The vigor and energy of the nation revived. Paris, weary of its long gloom, gave itself up to fetes and pleasures of which it had been so long deprived. The first acts of the Consulate did not diminish any hopes, and Liberty felt no alarm. The First Consul issued a proclamation to the inhabitants of the West. The eloquent allocutions addressed to the masses which Bonaparte had, as it were, invented, produced effects in those days of patriotism and miracle that were absolutely startling. His voice echoed through the world like the voice of a prophet, for none of his proclamations had, as yet, been belied by defeat.

INHABITANTS:

An impious war again inflames the West.

The makers of these troubles are traitors sold to the English, or brigands who seek in civil war opportunity and license for misdeeds.

To such men the government owes no forbearance, nor any declaration of its principles.

But there are citizens, dear to France, who have been misled by their wiles. It is so such that truth and light are due.

Unjust laws have been promulgated and executed; arbitrary acts have threatened the safety of citizens and the liberty of consciences; mistaken entries on the list of *emigres* imperil citizens; the great principles of social order have been violated.

The Consuls declare that liberty of worship having been guaranteed by the Constitution, the law of 11 Prairial, year III., which gives the use of edifices built for religious worship to all citizens, shall be executed.

The government will pardon; it will be merciful to repentance; its mercy will be complete and absolute; but it will punish whosoever, after this declaration, shall dare to resist the national sovereignty.

"Well," said Hulot, after the public reading of this Consular manifesto, "Isn't that paternal enough? But you'll see that not a single royalist brigand will be changed by it."

The commandant was right. The proclamation merely served to strengthen each side in their own convictions. A few days later Hulot and his colleagues received reinforcements. The new minister of war notified them that General Brune was appointed to command the troops in the west of France. Hulot, whose experience was known to the government, had provisional control in the departments of the Orne and Mayenne. An unusual activity began to show itself in the government offices. Circulars from the minister of war and the minister of police gave notice that vigorous measures entrusted to the military commanders would be taken to stifle the insurrection at its birth. But the Chouans and the Vendeans had profited by the inaction of the Directory to rouse the whole region and virtually take possession of it. A new Consular proclamation was therefore issued. This time, it was the general speaking to his troops: —

SOLDIERS:

There are none but brigands, *emigres*, and hirelings of England now remaining in the West.

The army is composed of more than fifty thousand brave men. Let me speedily hear from them that the rebel chiefs have ceased to live.

Glory is won by toil alone; if it could be had by living in barracks in a town, all would have it.

Soldiers, whatever be the rank you hold in the army, the gratitude of the nation awaits you. To be worthy of it, you must brave the inclemencies of weather, ice, snow, and the excessive coldness of the nights; you must surprise your enemies at daybreak, and exterminate those wretches, the disgrace of France.

Make a short and sure campaign; be inexorable to those brigands, and maintain strict discipline.

National Guards, join the strength of your arms to that of the line.

If you know among you any men who fraternize with the brigands, arrest them. Let them find no refuge; pursue them; if traitors dare to harbor and defend them, let them perish together.

"What a man!" cried Hulot. "It is just as it was in the army of Italy — he rings in the mass, and he says it himself. Don't you call that talking, hey?"

"Yes, but he speaks by himself and in his own name," said Gerard, who began to feel alarmed at the possible results of the 18th Brumaire.

"And where's the harm, since he's a soldier?" said Merle.

A group of soldiers were clustered at a little distance before the same proclamation posted on a wall. As none of them could read, they gazed at it, some with a careless eye, others with curiosity, while two or three hunted about for a citizen who looked learned enough to read it to them.

"Now you tell us, Clef-des-Coeurs, what that rag of a paper says," cried Beau-Pied, in a saucy tone to his comrade.

"Easy to guess," replied Clef-des-Coeurs.

At these words the other men clustered round the pair, who were always ready to play their parts.

"Look there," continued Clef-des-Coeurs, pointing to a coarse woodcut which headed the proclamation and represented a pair of compasses, —which had lately superseded the level of 1793. "It means that the troops—that's us—are to march firm; don't you see the compasses are open, both legs apart?—that's an emblem."

"Such much for your learning, my lad; it isn't an emblem—it's called a problem. I've served in the artillery," continued Beau-Pied, "and problems were meat and drink to my officers."

"I say it's an emblem."

"It's a problem."

"What will you bet?"

"Anything."

"Your German pipe?"

"Done!"

"By your leave, adjutant, isn't that thing an emblem, and not a problem?" said Clef-des-Coeurs, following Gerard, who was thoughtfully walking away.

"It is both," he replied, gravely.

"The adjutant was making fun of you," said Beau-Pied. "That paper means that our general in Italy is promoted Consul, which is a fine grade, and we are to get shoes and overcoats."

II

ONE OF FOUCHE'S IDEAS

One morning towards the end of Brumaire just as Hulot was exercising his brigade, now by order of his superiors wholly concentrated at Mayenne, a courier arrived from Alencon with despatches, at the reading of which his face betrayed extreme annoyance.

"Forward, then!" he cried in an angry tone, sticking the papers into the crown of his hat. "Two companies will march with me towards Mortagne. The Chouans are there. You will accompany me," he said to Merle and Gerard. "May be I created a nobleman if I can understand one word of that despatch. Perhaps I'm a fool! well, anyhow, forward, march! there's no time to lose."

"Commandant, by your leave," said Merle, kicking the cover of the ministerial despatch with the toe of his boot, "what is there so exasperating in that?"

"God's thunder! nothing at all—except that we are fooled."

When the commandant gave vent to this military oath (an object it must be said of Republican atheistical remonstrance) it gave warning of a storm; the diverse intonations of the words were degrees of a thermometer by which the brigade could judge of the patience of its commander; the old soldier's frankness of nature had made this knowledge so easy that the veriest little drummer-boy knew his Hulot by heart, simply by observing the variations of the grimace with which the commander screwed up his cheek and snapped his eyes and vented his oath. On this occasion the tone of smothered rage with which he uttered the words made his two friends silent and circumspect. Even the pits of the small-pox which dented that veteran face seemed deeper, and the skin itself browner than usual. His broad queue, braided at the edges, had fallen upon one of his epaulettes as he replaced his three-cornered hat, and he flung it back with such fury that the ends became untied. However, as he stood stock-still, his hands clenched, his arms crossed tightly over his breast, his mustache bristling, Gerard ventured to ask him presently: "Are we to start at once?"

"Yes, if the men have ammunition."

"They have."

"Shoulder arms! Left wheel, forward, march!" cried Gerard, at a sign from the commandant.

The drum-corps marched at the head of the two companies designated by Gerard. At the first roll of the drums the commandant, who still stood plunged in thought, seemed to rouse himself, and he left the town accompanied by his two officers, to whom he said not a word. Merle and Gerard looked at each other silently as if to ask, "How long is he going to keep us in suspense?" and, as they marched, they cautiously kept an observing eye on their leader, who continued to vent rambling words between his teeth. Several times these vague phrases sounded like oaths in the ears of his soldiers, but not one of them dared to utter a word; for they all, when occasion demanded, maintained the stern discipline to which the veterans who had served under Bonaparte in Italy were accustomed. The greater part of them had belonged, like Hulot, to the famous battalions which capitulated at Mayenne under a promise not to serve again on the frontier, and the army called them "Les Mayencais." It would be difficult to find leaders and men who more thoroughly understood each other.

At dawn of the day after their departure Hulot and his troop were on the high-road to Alencon, about three miles from that town towards Mortagne, at a part of the road which leads through pastures watered by the Sarthe. A picturesque vista of these meadows lay to the left, while the woodlands on the right which flank the road and join the great forest of Menil-Broust, serve as a foil to the delightful aspect of the river-scenery. The narrow causeway is bordered on each side by ditches the soil of which, being constantly thrown out upon the fields, has formed high banks covered with furze,—the name given throughout the West to this prickly gorse. This shrub, which spreads itself in thorny masses, makes excellent fodder in winter for horses and cattle; but as long as it was not cut the Chouans hid themselves behind its breastwork of dull green. These banks bristling with gorse, signifying to travellers their approach to Brittany, made this part of the road at the period of which we write as dangerous as it was beautiful; it was these dangers which compelled the hasty departure of Hulot and his soldiers, and it was here that he at last let out the secret of his wrath.

He was now on his return, escorting an old mail-coach drawn by post-horses, which the weariness of his soldiers, after their forced march, was compelling to advance at a snail's pace. The company of Blues from the garrison at Mortagne, who had escorted the rickety vehicle to the limits of their district, where Hulot and his men had met them, could be seen in the distance, on their way back to their quarters, like so many black specks. One of Hulot's companies was in the rear, the other in advance of the carriage. The commandant, who was marching with Merle and Gerard between the advance guard and the carriage, suddenly growled out: "Ten thousand thunders! would you believe that the general detached us from Mayenne to escort two petticoats?"

"But, commandant," remarked Gerard, "when we came up just now and took charge I observed that you bowed to them not ungraciously."

"Ha! that's the infamy of it. Those dandies in Paris ordered the greatest attention paid to their damned females. How dare they dishonor good and brave patriots by trailing us after petticoats? As for me, I march straight, and I don't choose to have to do with other people's zigzags. When I saw Danton taking mistresses, and Barras too, I said to them: 'Citizens, when the Republic called you to govern, it was not that you might authorize the vices of the old regime!' You may tell me that women—oh yes! we must have women, that's all right. Good soldiers of course must have women, and good women; but in times of danger, no! Besides, where would be the good of sweeping away the old abuses if patriots bring them back again? Look at the First Consul, there's a man! no women for him; always about his business. I'd bet my left mustache that he doesn't know the fool's errand we've been sent on!"

"But, commandant," said Merle, laughing, "I have seen the tip-end of the nose of the young lady, and I'll declare the whole world needn't be ashamed to feel an itch, as I do, to revolve round that carriage and get up a bit of a conversation."

"Look out, Merle," said Gerard; "the veiled beauties have a man accompanying them who seems wily enough to catch you in a trap."

"Who? that *incroyable* whose little eyes are ferreting from one side of the road to the other, as if he saw Chouans? The fellow seems to have no legs; the moment his horse is hidden by the carriage, he looks like a duck with its head sticking out of a pate. If that booby can hinder me from kissing the pretty linnet—"

"'Duck'! 'linnet'! oh, my poor Merle, you have taken wings indeed! But don't trust the duck. His green eyes are as treacherous as the eyes of a snake, and as sly as those of a woman who forgives her husband. I distrust the Chouans much less than I do those lawyers whose faces are like bottles of lemonade."

"Pooh!" cried Merle, gaily. "I'll risk it—with the commandant's permission. That woman has eyes like stars, and it's worth playing any stakes to see them."

"Caught, poor fellow!" said Gerard to the commandant; "he is beginning to talk nonsense!"

Hulot made a face, shrugged his shoulders, and said: "Before he swallows the soup, I advise him to smell it."

"Bravo, Merle," said Gerard, judging by his friend's lagging step that he meant to let the carriage overtake him. Isn't he a happy fellow? He is the only man I know who can laugh over the death of a comrade without being thought unfeeling."

"He's the true French soldier," said Hulot, in a grave tone.

"Just look at him pulling his epaulets back to his shoulders, to show he is a captain," cried Gerard, laughing,—"as if his rank mattered!"

The coach toward which the officer was pivoting did, in fact, contain two women, one of whom seemed to be the servant of the other.

"Such women always run in couples," said Hulot.

A lean and sharp-looking little man ambled his horse sometimes before, sometimes behind the carriage; but, though he was evidently accompanying these privileged women, no one had yet seen him speak to them. This silence, a proof either of respect or contempt, as the case might be; the quantity of baggage belonging to the lady, whom the commandant sneeringly called "the princess"; everything, even to the clothes of her attendant squire, stirred Hulot's bile. The dress of the unknown man was a good specimen of the fashions of the day then being caricatured as "incroyable,"—unbelievable, unless seen. Imagine a person trussed up in a coat, the front of which was so short that five or six inches of the waistcoat came below it, while the skirts were so long that they hung down behind like the tail of a cod,—the term then used to describe them. An enormous cravat was wound about his neck in so many folds that the little head which protruded from that muslin labyrinth certainly did justify Captain Merle's comparison. The stranger also wore tight-fitting trousers and Suwaroff boots. A huge blue-and-white cameo pinned his shirt; two watch-chains hung from his belt; his hair, worn in ringlets on each side of his face, concealed nearly the whole forehead; and, for a last adornment, the collar of his shirt and that of his coat came so high that his head seemed enveloped like a bunch of flowers in a horn of paper. Add to these queer accessories, which were combined in utter want of harmony, the burlesque contradictions in color of yellow trousers, scarlet waistcoat, cinnamon coat, and a correct idea will be gained of the supreme good taste which all dandies blindly obeyed in the first years of the Consulate. This costume, utterly uncouth, seemed to have been invented as a final test of grace, and to show that there was nothing too ridiculous for fashion to consecrate. The rider seemed to be about thirty years old, but he was really twenty-two; perhaps he owed this appearance of age to debauchery, possibly to the perils of the period. In spite of his preposterous dress, he had a certain elegance of manner which proved him to be a man of some breeding.

When the captain had dropped back close to the carriage, the dandy seemed to fathom his design, and favored it by checking his horse. Merle, who had flung him a sardonic glance, encountered one of those impenetrable faces, trained by the vicissitudes of the Revolution to hide all, even the most insignificant, emotion. The moment the curved end of the old triangular hat and the captain's epaulets were seen by the occupants of the carriage, a voice of angelic sweetness said: "Monsieur l'officier, will you have the kindness to tell us at what part of the road we now are?"

There is some inexpressible charm in the question of an unknown traveller, if a woman,—a world of adventure is in every word; but if the woman asks for assistance or information, proving her weakness or ignorance of certain things, every man is inclined to construct some impossible tale which shall lead to his happiness. The words, "Monsieur l'officier," and the polite tone of the question stirred the captain's heart in a manner hitherto unknown to him. He tried to examine the lady, but was cruelly disappointed, for a jealous veil concealed her features; he could barely see her eyes, which shone through the gauze like onyx gleaming in the sunshine.

"You are now three miles from Alencon, madame," he replied.

"Alencon! already!" and the lady threw herself, or, rather, she gently leaned back in the carriage, and said no more.

"Alencon?" said the other woman, apparently waking up; "then you'll see it again."

She caught sight of the captain and was silent. Merle, disappointed in his hope of seeing the face of the beautiful incognita, began to examine that of her companion. She was a girl about twenty-six years of age, fair, with a pretty figure and the sort of complexion, fresh and white and well-fed, which characterizes the women of Valognes, Bayeux, and the environs of Alencon. Her blue eyes showed no great intelligence, but a certain firmness mingled with tender feeling. She wore a gown of some common woollen stuff. The fashion of her hair, done up closely under a Norman cap, without any pretension, gave a charming simplicity to her face. Her attitude, without, of course, having any of the conventional nobility of society, was not without the natural dignity of a modest young girl, who can look back upon her past life without a single cause for repentance. Merle knew her at a glance for one of those wild flowers which are sometimes taken from their native fields to Parisian hot-houses, where so many blasting rays are concentrated, without ever losing the purity of their color or their rustic simplicity. The naive attitude of the girl and her modest glance showed Merle very plainly that she did not wish a listener. In fact, no sooner had he withdrawn than the two women began a conversation in so low a tone that only a murmur of it reached his ear.

"You came away in such a hurry," said the country-girl, "that you hardly took time to dress. A pretty-looking sight you are now! If we are going beyond Alencon, you must really make your toilet."

"Oh! oh! Francine!" cried the lady.

"What is it?"

"This is the third time you have tried to make me tell you the reasons for this journey and where we are going."

"Have I said one single word which deserves that reproach?"

"Oh, I've noticed your manoeuvring. Simple and truthful as you are, you have learned a little cunning from me. You are beginning to hold questioning in horror; and right enough, too, for of all the known ways of getting at a secret, questions are, to my mind, the silliest."

"Well," said Francine, "since nothing escapes you, you must admit, Marie, that your conduct would excite the curiosity of a saint. Yesterday without a penny, to-day your hands are full of gold; at Mortagne they give you the mail-coach which was pillaged and the driver killed, with government troops to protect you, and you are followed by a man whom I regard as your evil genius."

"Who? Corentin?" said the young lady, accenting the words by two inflections of her voice expressive of contempt, a sentiment which appeared in the gesture with which she waved her hand towards the rider. "Listen, Francine," she said. "Do you remember Patriot, the monkey I taught to imitate Danton?"

"Yes, mademoiselle."

"Well, were you afraid of him?"

"He was chained."

"And Corentin is muzzled, my dear."

"We used to play with Patriot by the hour," said Francine, —"I know that; but he always ended by serving us some bad trick." So saying, Francine threw herself hastily back close to her mistress, whose hands she caught and kissed in a coaxing way; saying in a tone of deep affection: "You know what I mean, Marie, but you will not answer me. How can you, after all that sadness which did so grieve me—oh, indeed it grieved me!—how can you, in twenty-four hours, change about and become so gay? you, who talked of suicide! Why have you changed? I have a right to ask these questions of your soul—it is mine, my claim to it is before that of others, for you will never be better loved than you are by me. Speak, mademoiselle."

"Why, Francine, don't you see all around you the secret of my good spirits? Look at the yellowing tufts of those distant tree-tops; not one is like another. As we look at them from this distance don't they seem like an old bit of tapestry? See the hedges from behind which the Chouans may spring upon us at any moment. When I look at that gorse I fancy I can see the muzzles of their guns. Every time the road is shady under the trees I fancy I shall hear firing, and then my heart beats and a new sensation comes over me. It is neither the shuddering of fear nor an emotion of pleasure; no, it is better than either, it is the stirring of everything within me—it is life! Why shouldn't I be gay when a little excitement is dropped into my monotonous existence?"

"Ah! you are telling me nothing, cruel girl! Holy Virgin!" added Francine, raising her eyes in distress to heaven; "to whom will she confess herself if she denies the truth to me?"

"Francine," said the lady, in a grave tone, "I can't explain to you my present enterprise; it is horrible."

"Why do wrong when you know it to be wrong?"

"How can I help it? I catch myself thinking as if I were fifty, and acting as if I were still fifteen. You have always been my better self, my poor Francine, but in this affair I must stifle conscience. And," she added after a pause, "I cannot. Therefore, how can you expect me to take a confessor as stern as you?" and she patted the girl's hand.

"When did I ever blame your actions?" cried Francine. "Evil is so mixed with good in your nature. Yes, Saint Anne of Auray, to whom I pray to save you, will absolve you for all you do. And, Marie, am I not here beside you, without so much as knowing where you go?" and she kissed her hands with effusion.

"But," replied Marie, "you may yet desert me, if your conscience—"

"Hush, hush, mademoiselle," cried Francine, with a hurt expression. "But surely you will tell me—"

"Nothing!" said the young lady, in a resolute voice. "Only—and I wish you to know it—I hate this enterprise even more than I hate him whose gilded tongue induced me to undertake it. I will be rank and own to you that I would never have yielded to their wishes if I had not foreseen, in this ignoble farce, a mingling of love and danger which tempted me. I cannot bear to leave this empty world without at least attempting to gather the flowers that it owes me,—whether I perish in the attempt or not. But remember, for the honor of my memory, that had I ever been a happy woman, the sight of their great knife, ready to fall upon my neck, would not have driven me to accept a part in this tragedy—for it is a tragedy. But now," she said, with a gesture of disgust, "if it were countermanded, I should instantly fling myself into the Sarthe. It would not be destroying life, for I have never lived."

"Oh, Saint Anne of Auray, forgive her!"

"What are you so afraid of? You know very well that the dull round of domestic life gives no opportunity for my passions. That would be bad in most women, I admit; but my soul is made of a higher sensibility and can bear great tests. I might have been, perhaps, a gentle being like you. Why, why have I risen above or sunk beneath the level of my sex? Ah! the wife of Bonaparte is a happy woman! Yes, I shall die young, for I am gay, as you say,—gay at this pleasure-party, where there is blood to drink, as that poor Danton used to say. There, there, forget what I am saying; it is the woman of fifty who speaks. Thank God! the girl of fifteen is still within me."

The young country-girl shuddered. She alone knew the fiery, impetuous nature of her mistress. She alone was initiated into the mysteries of a soul rich with enthusiasm, into the secret emotions of a being who, up to this time, had seen life pass her like a shadow she could not grasp, eager as she was to do so. After sowing broadcast with full hands and harvesting nothing, this woman was still virgin in soul, but irritated by a multitude of baffled desires. Weary of a struggle without an adversary, she had reached in her despair to the point of preferring good to evil, if it came in the form of enjoyment; evil to good, if it offered her some poetic emotion; misery to mediocrity, as something nobler and higher; the gloomy and mysterious future of present death to a life without hopes or even without sufferings. Never in any heart was so much powder heaped ready for the spark, never were so many riches for love to feed on; no daughter of Eve was ever moulded, with a greater mixture of gold in her clay. Francine, like an angel of earth, watched over this being whose perfections she adored, believing that she obeyed a celestial mandate in striving to bring that spirit back among the choir of seraphim whence it was banished for the sin of pride.

"There is the clock-tower of Alencon," said the horseman, riding up to the carriage.

"I see it," replied the young lady, in a cold tone.

"Ah, well," he said, turning away with all the signs of servile submission, in spite of his disappointment.

"Go faster," said the lady to the postilion. "There is no longer any danger; go at a fast trot, or even a gallop, if you can; we are almost into Alencon."

As the carriage passed the commandant, she called out to him, in a sweet voice: —

"We will meet at the inn, commandant. Come and see me."

"Yes, yes," growled the commandant. "'The inn'! 'Come and see me'! Is that how you speak to an officer in command of the army?" and he shook his fist at the carriage, which was now rolling rapidly along the road.

"Don't be vexed, commandant, she has got your rank as general up her sleeve," said Corentin, laughing, as he endeavored to put his horse into a gallop to overtake the carriage.

"I sha'n't let myself be fooled by any such folks as they," said Hulot to his two friends, in a growling tone. "I'd rather throw my general's coat into that ditch than earn it out of a bed. What are these birds after? Have you any idea, either of you?"

"Yes," said Merle, "I've an idea that that's the handsomest women I ever saw! I think you're reading the riddle all wrong. Perhaps she's the wife of the First Consul."

"Pooh! the First Consul's wife is old, and this woman is young," said Hulot. "Besides, the order I received from the minister gives her name as Mademoiselle de Verneuil. She is a *ci-devant*. Don't I know 'em? They all plied one trade before the Revolution, and any man could make himself a major, or a general in double-quick time; all he had to do was to say 'Dear heart' to them now and then."

While each soldier opened his compasses, as the commandant was wont to say, the miserable vehicle which was then used as the mail-coach drew up before the inn of the Trois Maures, in the middle of the main street of Alencon. The sound of the wheels brought the landlord to the door. No one in Alencon could have expected the arrival of the mail-coach at the Trois Maures, for the murderous attack upon the coach at Mortagne was already known, and so many people followed it along the street that the two women, anxious to escape the curiosity of the crowd, ran quickly into the kitchen, which forms the inevitable antechamber to all Western inns. The landlord was about to follow them, after examining the coach, when the postilion caught him by the arm.

"Attention, citizen Brutus," he said; "there's an escort of the Blues behind us; but it is I who bring you these female citizens; they'll pay like *ci-devant* princesses, therefore—"

"Therefore, we'll drink a glass of wine together presently, my lad," said the landlord.

After glancing about the kitchen, blackened with smoke, and noticing a table bloody from raw meat, Mademoiselle de Verneuil flew into the next room with the celerity of a bird; for she shuddered at the sight and smell of the place, and feared the inquisitive eyes of a dirty *chef*, and a fat little woman who examined her attentively.

"What are we to do, wife?" said the landlord. "Who the devil could have supposed we would have so many on our hands in these days? Before I serve her a decent breakfast that woman will get impatient. Stop, an idea! evidently she is a person of quality. I'll propose to put her with the one we have upstairs. What do you think?"

When the landlord went to look for the new arrival he found only Francine, to whom he spoke in a low voice, taking her to the farther end of the kitchen, so as not to be overheard.

"If the ladies wish," he said, "to be served in private, as I have no doubt they wish to do, I have a very nice breakfast all ready for a lady and her son, and I dare say wouldn't mind sharing it with you; they are persons of condition," he added, mysteriously.

He had hardly said the words before he felt a tap on his back from the handle of a whip. He turned hastily and saw behind him a short, thick-set man, who had noiselessly entered from a side room,—an apparition which seemed to terrify the hostess, the cook, and the scullion. The landlord turned pale when he saw the intruder, who shook back the hair which concealed his forehead and eyes, raised himself on the points of his toes to reach the other's ears, and said to him in a whisper: "You know the cost of an imprudence or a betrayal, and the color of the money we pay it in. We are generous in that coin."

He added a gesture which was like a horrible commentary to his words. Though the rotundity of the landlord prevented Francine from seeing the stranger, who stood behind him, she caught certain words of his threatening speech, and was thunderstruck at hearing the hoarse tones of a Breton voice. She sprang towards the man, but he, seeming to move with the agility of a wild animal, had already darted through a side door which opened on the courtyard. Utterly amazed, she ran to the window. Through its panes, yellowed with smoke, she caught sight of the stranger as he was about to enter the stable. Before doing so, however, he turned a pair of black eyes to the upper story of the inn, and thence to the mail-coach in the yard, as if to call some friend's attention to the vehicle. In spite of his muffling goatskin and thanks to this movement which allowed her to see his face, Francine recognized the Chouan, Marche-a-Terre, with his heavy whip; she saw him, indistinctly, in the obscurity of the stable, fling himself down on a pile of straw, in a position which enabled him to keep an eye on all that happened at the inn. Marche-a-Terre curled himself up in such a way that the cleverest spy, at any distance far or near, might have taken him for one of those huge dogs that drag the hand-carts, lying asleep with his muzzle on his paws.

The behavior of the Chouan proved to Francine that he had not recognized her. Under the hazardous circumstances which she felt her mistress to be in, she scarcely knew whether to regret or to rejoice in this unconsciousness. But the mysterious connection between the landlord's offer (not uncommon among innkeepers, who can thus kill two birds with one stone), and the Chouan's threats, piqued her curiosity. She left the dirty window from which she could see the formless heap which she knew to be Marche-a-Terre, and returned to the landlord, who was still standing in the attitude of a man who feels he has made a blunder, and does not know how to get out of it. The Chouan's gesture had petrified the poor fellow. No one in the West was ignorant of the cruel refinements of torture with which the "Chasseurs du Roi" punished those who were even suspected of indiscretion; the landlord felt their knives already at his throat. The cook looked with a shudder at the iron stove on which they often "warmed" ("chauffaient") the feet of those they suspected. The fat landlady held a knife in one hand and a half-peeled potato in the other, and gazed at her husband with a stupefied air. Even the scullion puzzled himself to know the reason of their speechless terror. Francine's curiosity was naturally excited by this silent scene, the principal actor of which was visible to all, though departed. The girl was gratified at the evident power of the Chouan, and though by nature too simple and humble for the tricks of a lady's maid, she was also far too anxious to penetrate the mystery not to profit by her advantages on this occasion.

"Mademoiselle accepts your proposal," she said to the landlord, who jumped as if suddenly awakened by her words.

"What proposal?" he asked with genuine surprise.

"What proposal?" asked Corentin, entering the kitchen.

"What proposal?" asked Mademoiselle de Verneuil, returning to it.

"What proposal?" asked a fourth individual on the lower step of the staircase, who now sprang lightly into the kitchen.

"Why, the breakfast with your persons of distinction," replied Francine, impatiently.

"Distinction!" said the ringing and ironical voice of the person who had just come down the stairway. "My good fellow, that strikes me as a very poor inn joke; but if it's the company of this young female citizen that you want to give us, we should be fools to refuse it. In my mother's absence, I accept," he added, striking the astonished innkeeper on the shoulder.

The charming heedlessness of youth disguised the haughty insolence of the words, which drew the attention of every one present to the new-comer. The landlord at once assumed the countenance of Pilate washing his hands of the blood of that just man; he slid back two steps to reach his wife's ear, and whispered, "You are witness, if any harm comes of it, that it is not my fault. But, anyhow," he added, in a voice that was lower still, "go and tell Monsieur Marche-a-Terre what has happened."

The traveller, who was a young man of medium height, wore a dark blue coat and high black gaiters coming above the knee and over the breeches, which were also of blue cloth. This simple uniform, without epaulets, was that of the pupils of the Ecole Polytechnique. Beneath this plain attire Mademoiselle de Verneuil could distinguish at a glance the elegant shape and nameless *something* that tells of natural nobility. The face of the young man, which was rather ordinary at first sight, soon attracted the eye by the conformation of certain features which revealed a soul capable of great things. A bronzed skin, curly fair hair, sparkling blue eyes, a delicate nose, motions full of ease, all disclosed a life guided by noble sentiments and trained to the habit of command. But the most characteristic signs of his nature were in the chin, which was dented like that of Bonaparte, and in the lower lip, which joined the upper one with a graceful curve, like that of an acanthus leaf on the capital of a Corinthian column. Nature had given to these two features of his face an irresistible charm.

"This young man has singular distinction if he is really a republican," thought Mademoiselle de Verneuil.

To see all this at a glance, to brighten at the thought of pleasing, to bend her head softly and smile coquettishly and cast a soft look able to revive a heart that was dead to love, to veil her long black eyes with lids whose curving lashes made shadows on her cheeks, to choose the melodious tones of her voice and give a penetrating charm to the formal words, "Monsieur, we are very much obliged to you,"—all this charming by-play took less time than it has taken to describe it. After this, Mademoiselle de Verneuil, addressing the landlord, asked to be shown to a room, saw the staircase, and disappeared with Francine, leaving the stranger to discover whether her reply was intended as an acceptance or a refusal.

"Who is that woman?" asked the Polytechnique student, in an airy manner, of the landlord, who still stood motionless and bewildered.

"That's the female citizen Verneuil," replied Corentin, sharply, looking jealously at the questioner; "a *ci-devant*; what is she to you?"

The stranger, who was humming a revolutionary tune, turned his head haughtily towards Corentin. The two young men looked at each other for a moment like cocks about to fight, and the glance they exchanged gave birth to a hatred which lasted forever. The blue eye of the young soldier was as frank and honest as the green eye of the other man was false and malicious; the manners of the one had native grandeur, those of the other were insinuating; one was eager in his advance, the other deprecating; one commanded respect, the other sought it.

"Is the citizen du Gua Saint-Cyr here?" said a peasant, entering the kitchen at that moment.

"What do you want of him?" said the young man, coming forward.

The peasant made a low bow and gave him a letter, which the young cadet read and threw into the fire; then he nodded his head and the man withdrew.

"No doubt you've come from Paris, citizen?" said Corentin, approaching the stranger with a certain ease of manner, and a pliant, affable air which seemed intolerable to the citizen du Gua.

"Yes," he replied, shortly.

"I suppose you have been graduated into some grade of the artillery?"

"No, citizen, into the navy."

"Ah! then you are going to Brest?" said Corentin, interrogatively.

But the young sailor turned lightly on the heels of his shoes without deigning to reply, and presently disappointed all the expectations which Mademoiselle de Verneuil had based on the charm of his appearance. He applied himself to ordering his breakfast with the eagerness of a boy, questioned the cook and the landlady about their receipts, wondered at provincial customs like a Parisian just out of his shell, made as many objections as any fine lady, and showed the more lack of mind and character because his face and manner had seemed to promise them. Corentin smiled with pity when he saw the face he made on tasting the best cider of Normandy.

"Heu!" he cried; "how can you swallow such stuff as that? It is meat and drink both. I don't wonder the Republic distrusts a province where they knock their harvest from trees with poles, and shoot travellers from the ditches. Pray don't put such medicine as that on the table; give us some good Bordeaux, white and red. And above all, do see if there is a good fire upstairs. These country-people are so backward in civilization!" he added. "Alas!" he sighed, "there is but one Paris in the world; what a pity it is I can't transport it to sea! Heavens! spoil-sauce!" he suddenly cried out to the cook; "what makes you put vinegar in that fricassee when you have lemons? And, madame," he added, "you gave me such coarse sheets I couldn't close my eyes all night." Then he began to twirl a huge cane, executing with a silly sort of care a variety of evolutions, the greater or less precision and agility of which were considered proofs of a young man's standing in the class of the Incroyables, so-called.

"And it is with such dandies as that," said Corentin to the landlord confidentially, watching his face, "that the Republic expects to improve her navy!"

"That man," said the young sailor to the landlady, in a low voice, "is a spy of Fouche's. He has 'police' stamped on his face, and I'll swear that spot he has got on his chin is Paris mud. Well, set a thief to catch—"

Just then a lady to whom the young sailor turned with every sign of outward respect, entered the kitchen of the inn.

"My dear mamma," he said. "I am glad you've come. I have recruited some guests in your absence."

"Guests?" she replied; "what folly!"

"It is Mademoiselle de Verneuil," he said in a low voice.

"She perished on the scaffold after the affair of Savenay; she went to Mans to save her brother the Prince de Loudon," returned his mother, rather brusquely.

"You are mistaken, madame," said Corentin, gently, emphasizing the word "madame"; "there are two demoiselles de Verneuil; all great houses, as you know, have several branches."

The lady, surprised at this freedom, drew back a few steps to examine the speaker; she turned her black eyes upon him, full of the keen sagacity so natural to women, seeking apparently to discover in what interest he stepped forth to explain Mademoiselle de Verneuil's birth. Corentin, on the other hand, who was studying the lady cautiously, denied her in his own mind the joys of motherhood and gave her those of love; he refused the possession of a son of twenty to a woman whose dazzling skin, and arched eyebrows, and lashes still unblemished, were the objects of his admiration, and whose abundant black hair, parted on the forehead into simple bands, bought out the youthfulness of an intelligent head. The slight lines of the brow, far from indicating age, revealed young passions. Though the piercing eyes were somewhat veiled, it was either from the fatigue of travelling or the too frequent expression of excitement. Corentin remarked that she was wrapped in a mantle of English material, and that the shape of her hat, foreign no doubt, did not belong to any of the styles called Greek, which ruled the Parisian fashions of the period. Corentin was one of those beings who are compelled by the bent of their natures to suspect evil rather than good, and he instantly doubted the citizenship of the two travellers. The lady, who, on her side, had made her observations on the person of Corentin with equal rapidity, turned to her son with a significant look which may be faithfully translated into the words: "Who is this queer man? Is he of our stripe?"

To this mute inquiry the youth replied by an attitude and a gesture which said: "Faith! I can't tell; but I distrust him." Then, leaving his mother to fathom the mystery, he turned to the landlady and whispered: "Try to find out who that fellow is; and whether he is really accompanying the young lady; and why."

"So," said Madame du Gua, looking at Corentin, "you are quite sure, citizen, that Mademoiselle de Verneuil is living?"

"She is living in flesh and blood as surely, *madame,* as the citizen du Gua Saint-Cyr."

This answer contained a sarcasm, the hidden meaning of which was known to none but the lady herself, and any one but herself would have been disconcerted by it. Her son looked fixedly at Corentin, who coolly pulled out his watch without appearing to notice the effect of his answer. The lady, uneasy and anxious to discover at once if the speech meant danger or was merely accidental, said to

Corentin in a natural tone and manner; "How little security there is on these roads. We were attacked by Chouans just beyond Mortagne. My son came very near being killed; he received two balls in his hat while protecting me."

"Is it possible, madame? were you in the mail-coach which those brigands robbed in spite of the escort,—the one we have just come by? You must know the vehicle well. They told me at Mortagne that the Chouans numbered a couple of thousands and that every one in the coach was killed, even the travellers. That's how history is written! Alas! madame," he continued, "if they murder travellers so near to Paris you can fancy how unsafe the roads are in Brittany. I shall return to Paris and not risk myself any farther."

"Is Mademoiselle de Verneuil young and handsome?" said the lady to the hostess, struck suddenly with an idea.

Just then the landlord interrupted the conversation, in which there was something of an angry element, by announcing that breakfast was ready. The young sailor offered his hand to his mother with an air of false familiarity that confirmed the suspicions of Corentin, to whom the youth remarked as he went up the stairway: "Citizen, if you are travelling with the female citizen de Verneuil, and she accepts the landlord's proposal, you can come too."

Though the words were said in a careless tone and were not inviting, Corentin followed. The young man squeezed the lady's hand when they were five or six steps above him, and said, in a low voice: "Now you see the dangers to which your imprudent enterprises, which have no glory in them, expose us. If we are discovered, how are we to escape? And what a contemptible role you force me to play!"

All three reached a large room on the upper floor. Any one who has travelled in the West will know that the landlord had, on such an occasion, brought forth his best things to do honor to his guests, and prepared the meal with no ordinary luxury. The table was carefully laid. The warmth of a large fire took the dampness from the room. The linen, glass, and china were not too dingy. Corentin saw at once that the landlord had, as they say familiarly, cut himself into quarters to please the strangers. "Consequently," thought he, "these people are not what they pretend to be. That young man is clever. I took him for a fool, but I begin to believe him as shrewd as myself."

The Chouans

The sailor, his mother, and Corentin awaited Mademoiselle de
Verneuil, whom the landlord went to summon. But the handsome
traveller did not come. The youth expected that she would make
difficulties, and he left the room, humming the popular song,
"Guard the nation's safety," and went to that of Mademoiselle de
Verneuil, prompted by a keen desire to get the better of her scruples
and take her back with him. Perhaps he wanted to solve the doubts
which filled his mind; or else to exercise the power which all men
like to think they wield over a pretty woman.

"May I be hanged if he's a Republican," thought Corentin, as he saw
him go. "He moves his shoulders like a courtier. And if that's his
mother," he added, mentally, looking at Madame du Gua, "I'm the
Pope! They are Chouans; and I'll make sure of their quality."

The door soon opened and the young man entered, holding the hand
of Mademoiselle de Verneuil, whom he led to the table with an air of
self-conceit that was nevertheless courteous. The devil had not
allowed that hour which had elapsed since the lady's arrival to be
wasted. With Francine's assistance, Mademoiselle de Verneuil had
armed herself with a travelling-dress more dangerous, perhaps, than
any ball-room attire. Its simplicity had precisely that attraction
which comes of the skill with which a woman, handsome enough to
wear no ornaments, reduces her dress to the position of a secondary
charm. She wore a green gown, elegantly cut, the jacket of which,
braided and frogged, defined her figure in a manner that was hardly
suitable for a young girl, allowing her supple waist and rounded
bust and graceful motions to be fully seen. She entered the room
smiling, with the natural amenity of women who can show a fine set
of teeth, transparent as porcelain between rosy lips, and dimpling
cheeks as fresh as those of childhood. Having removed the close
hood which had almost concealed her head at her first meeting with
the young sailor, she could now employ at her ease the various little
artifices, apparently so artless, with which a woman shows off the
beauties of her face and the grace of her head, and attracts
admiration for them. A certain harmony between her manners and
her dress made her seem so much younger than she was that
Madame du Gua thought herself beyond the mark in supposing her
over twenty. The coquetry of her apparel, evidently worn to please,
was enough to inspire hope in the young man's breast; but
Mademoiselle de Verneuil bowed to him, as she took her place, with
a slight inclination of her head and without looking at him, putting
him aside with an apparently light-hearted carelessness which

disconcerted him. This coolness might have seemed to an observer neither caution nor coquetry, but indifference, natural or feigned. The candid expression on the young lady's face only made it the more impenetrable. She showed no consciousness of her charms, and was apparently gifted with the pretty manners that win all hearts, and had already duped the natural self-conceit of the young sailor. Thus baffled, the youth returned to his own seat with a sort of vexation.

Mademoiselle de Verneuil took Francine, who accompanied her, by the hand and said, in a caressing voice, turning to Madame de Gua: "Madame, will you have the kindness to allow this young girl, who is more a friend than a servant to me, to sit with us? In these perilous times such devotion as hers can only be repaid by the heart; indeed, that is very nearly all that is left to us."

Madame du Gua replied to the last words, which were said half aside, with a rather unceremonious bow that betrayed her annoyance at the beauty of the new-comer. Then she said, in a low voice, to her son: "'Perilous times,' 'devotion,' 'madame,' 'servant'! that is not Mademoiselle de Verneuil; it is some girl sent here by Fouche."

The guests were about to sit down when Mademoiselle de Verneuil noticed Corentin, who was still employed in a close scrutiny of the mother and son, who were showing some annoyance at his glances.

"Citizen," she said to him, "you are no doubt too well bred to dog my steps. The Republic, when it sent my parents to the scaffold, did not magnanimously provide me with a guardian. Though you have, from extreme and chivalric gallantry accompanied me against my will to this place" (she sighed), "I am quite resolved not to allow your protecting care to become a burden to you. I am safe now, and you can leave me."

She gave him a fixed and contemptuous look. Corentin understood her; he repressed the smile which almost curled the corners of his wily lips as he bowed to her respectfully.

"Citoyenne," he said, "it is always an honor to obey you. Beauty is the only queen a Republican can serve."

Mademoiselle de Verneuil's eyes, as she watched him depart, shone with such natural pleasure, she looked at Francine with a smile of intelligence which betrayed so much real satisfaction, that Madame du Gua, who grew prudent as she grew jealous, felt disposed to relinquish the suspicions which Mademoiselle de Verneuil's great beauty had forced into her mind.

"It may be Mademoiselle de Verneuil, after all," she whispered to her son.

"But that escort?" answered the young man, whose vexation at the young lady's indifference allowed him to be cautious. "Is she a prisoner or an emissary, a friend or an enemy of the government?"

Madame du Gua made a sign as if to say that she would soon clear up the mystery.

However, the departure of Corentin seemed to lessen the young man's distrust, and he began to cast on Mademoiselle de Verneuil certain looks which betrayed an immoderate admiration for women, rather than the respectful warmth of a dawning passion. The young girl grew more and more reserved, and gave all her attentions to Madame du Gua. The youth, angry with himself, tried, in his vexation, to turn the tables and seem indifferent. Mademoiselle de Verneuil appeared not to notice this manoeuvre; she continued to be simple without shyness and reserved without prudery.

This chance meeting of personages who, apparently, were not destined to become intimate, awakened no agreeable sympathy on either side. There was even a sort of vulgar embarrassment, an awkwardness which destroyed all the pleasure which Mademoiselle de Verneuil and the young sailor had begun by expecting. But women have such wonderful conventional tact, they are so intimately allied with each other, or they have such keen desires for emotion, that they always know how to break the ice on such occasions. Suddenly, as if the two beauties had the same thought, they began to tease their solitary knight in a playful way, and were soon vying with each other in the jesting attention which they paid to him; this unanimity of action left them free. At the end of half an hour, the two women, already secret enemies, were apparently the best of friends. The young man then discovered that he felt as angry with Mademoiselle de Verneuil for her friendliness and freedom as he had been with her reserve. In fact, he was so annoyed by it that he regretted, with a sort of dumb anger, having allowed her to breakfast with them.

"Madame," said Mademoiselle de Verneuil, "is your son always as gloomy as he is at this moment?"

"Mademoiselle," he replied, "I ask myself what is the good of a fleeting happiness. The secret of my gloom is the evanescence of my pleasure."

"That is a madrigal," she said, laughing, "which rings of the Court rather than the Polytechnique."

"My son only expressed a very natural thought, mademoiselle," said Madame du Gua, who had her own reasons for placating the stranger.

"Then laugh while you may," said Mademoiselle de Verneuil, smiling at the young man. "How do you look when you have really something to weep for, if what you are pleased to call a happiness makes you so dismal?"

This smile, accompanied by a provoking glance which destroyed the consistency of her reserve, revived the youth's feelings. But inspired by her nature, which often impels a woman to do either too much or too little under such circumstances, Mademoiselle de Verneuil, having covered the young man with that brilliant look full of love's promises, immediately withdrew from his answering expression into a cold and severe modesty,—a conventional performance by which a woman sometimes hides a true emotion. In a moment, a single moment, when each expected to see the eyelids of the other lowered, they had communicated to one another their real thoughts; but they veiled their glances as quickly as they had mingled them in that one flash which convulsed their hearts and enlightened them. Confused at having said so many things in a single glance, they dared no longer look at each other. Mademoiselle de Verneuil withdrew into cold politeness, and seemed to be impatient for the conclusion of the meal.

"Mademoiselle, you must have suffered very much in prison?" said Madame du Gua.

"Alas, madame, I sometimes think that I am still there."

"Is your escort sent to protect you, mademoiselle, or to watch you? Are you still suspected by the Republic?"

Mademoiselle felt instinctively that Madame du Gua had no real interest in her, and the question alarmed her.

"Madame," she replied, "I really do not know myself the exact nature of my relations to the Republic."

"Perhaps it fears you?" said the young man, rather satirically.

"We must respect her secrets," interposed Madame du Gua.

"Oh, madame, the secrets of a young girl who knows nothing of life but its misfortunes are not interesting."

"But," answered Madame du Gua, wishing to continue a conversation which might reveal to her all that she wanted to know, "the First Consul seems to have excellent intentions. They say that he is going to remove the disabilities of the *emigres*."

"That is true, madame," she replied, with rather too much eagerness, "and if so, why do we rouse Brittany and La Vendee? Why bring civil war into France?"

This eager cry, in which she seemed to share her own reproach, made the young sailor quiver. He looked earnestly at her, but was unable to detect either hatred or love upon her face. Her beautiful skin, the delicacy of which was shown by the color beneath it, was impenetrable. A sudden and invincible curiosity attracted him to this strange creature, to whom he was already drawn by violent desires.

"Madame," said Mademoiselle de Verneuil, after a pause, "may I ask if you are going to Mayenne?"

"Yes, mademoiselle," replied the young man with a questioning look.

"Then, madame," she continued, "as your son serves the Republic" (she said the words with an apparently indifferent air, but she gave her companions one of those furtive glances the art of which belongs to women and diplomatists), "you must fear the Chouans, and an escort is not to be despised. We are now almost travelling companions, and I hope you will come with me to Mayenne."

Mother and son hesitated, and seemed to consult each other's faces.

"I am not sure, mademoiselle," said the young man, "that it is prudent in me to tell you that interests of the highest importance require our presence to-night in the neighborhood of Fougeres, and we have not yet been able to find a means of conveyance; but women are so naturally generous that I am ashamed not to confide in you. Nevertheless," he added, "before putting ourselves in your hands, I ought to know whether we shall get out of them safe and sound. In short, mademoiselle, are you the sovereign or the slave of your Republican escort? Pardon my frankness, but your position does not seem to me exactly natural—"

"We live in times, monsieur, when nothing takes place naturally. You can accept my proposal without anxiety. Above all," she added, emphasizing her words, "you need fear no treachery in an offer made by a woman who has no part in political hatreds."

"A journey thus made is not without danger," he said, with a look which gave significance to that commonplace remark.

"What is it you fear?" she answered, smiling sarcastically. "I see no peril for any one."

"Is this the woman who a moment ago shared my desires in her eyes?" thought the young man. "What a tone in her voice! she is laying a trap for me."

At that instant a shrill cry of an owl which appeared to have perched on the chimney top vibrated in the air like a warning.

"What does that mean?" said Mademoiselle de Verneuil. "Our journey together will not begin under favorable auspices. Do owls in these woods screech by daylight?" she added, with a surprised gesture.

"Sometimes," said the young man, coolly. "Mademoiselle," he continued, "we may bring you ill-luck; you are thinking of that, I am sure. We had better not travel together."

These words were said with a calmness and reserve which puzzled Mademoiselle de Verneuil.

"Monsieur," she replied, with truly aristocratic insolence, "I am far from wishing to compel you. Pray let us keep the little liberty the Republic leaves us. If Madame were alone, I should insist—"

The heavy step of a soldier was heard in the passage, and the Commandant Hulot presently appeared in the doorway with a frowning brow.

"Come here, colonel," said Mademoiselle de Verneuil, smiling and pointing to a chair beside her. "Let us talk over the affairs of State. But what is the matter with you? Are there Chouans here?"

The commandant stood speechless on catching sight of the young man, at whom he looked with peculiar attention.

"Mamma, will you take some more hare? Mademoiselle, you are not eating," said the sailor to Francine, seeming busy with the guests.

But Hulot's astonishment and Mademoiselle de Verneuil's close observation had something too dangerously serious about them to be ignored.

"What is it, citizen?" said the young man, abruptly; "do you know me?"

"Perhaps I do," replied the Republican.

"You are right; I remember you at the School."

"I never went to any school," said the soldier, roughly. "What school do you mean?"

"The Polytechnique."

"Ha, ha, those barracks where they expect to make soldiers in dormitories," said the veteran, whose aversion for officers trained in that nursery was insurmountable. "To what arm do you belong?"

"I am in the navy."

The Chouans

"Ha!" cried Hulot, smiling vindictively, "how many of your fellow-students are in the navy? Don't you know," he added in a serious tone, "that none but the artillery and the engineers graduate from there?"

The young man was not disconcerted.

"An exception was made in my favor, on account of the name I bear," he answered. "We are all naval men in our family."

"What is the name of your family, citizen?" asked Hulot.

"Du Gua Saint-Cyr."

"Then you were not killed at Mortagne?"

"He came very near being killed," said Madame du Gua, quickly; "my son received two balls in—"

"Where are your papers?" asked Hulot, not listening to the mother.

"Do you propose to read them?" said the young man, cavalierly; his blue eye, keen with suspicion, studied alternately the gloomy face of the commandant and that of Mademoiselle de Verneuil.

"A stripling like you to pretend to fool me! Come, produce your papers, or—"

"La! la! citizen, I'm not such a babe as I look to be. Why should I answer you? Who are you?"

"The commander of this department," answered Hulot.

"Oh, then, of course, the matter is serious; I am taken with arms in my hand," and he held a glass full of Bordeaux to the soldier.

"I am not thirsty," said Hulot. "Come, your papers."

At that instant the rattle of arms and the tread of men was heard in the street. Hulot walked to the window and gave a satisfied look which made Mademoiselle de Verneuil tremble. That sign of interest on her part seemed to fire the young man, whose face had grown cold and haughty. After feeling in the pockets of his coat he drew forth an elegant portfolio and presented certain papers to the commandant, which the latter read slowly, comparing the description given in the passport with the face and figure of the young man before him. During this prolonged examination the owl's cry rose again; but this time there was no difficulty whatever in recognizing a human voice. The commandant at once returned the papers to the young man, with a scoffing look.

"That's all very fine," he said; "but I don't like the music. You will come with me to headquarters."

"Why do you take him there?" asked Mademoiselle de Verneuil, in a tone of some excitement.

"My good lady," replied the commandant, with his usual grimace, "that's none of your business."

Irritated by the tone and words of the old soldier, but still more at the sort of humiliation offered to her in presence of a man who was under the influence of her charms, Mademoiselle de Verneuil rose, abandoning the simple and modest manner she had hitherto adopted; her cheeks glowed and her eyes shone as she said in a quiet tone but with a trembling voice: "Tell me, has this young man met all the requirements of the law?"

"Yes—apparently," said Hulot ironically.

"Then, I desire that you will leave him, *apparently*, alone," she said. "Are you afraid he will escape you? You are to escort him with me to Mayenne; he will be in the coach with his mother. Make no objection; it is my will—Well, what?" she added, noticing Hulot's grimace; "do you suspect him still?"

"Rather."

"What do you want to do with him?"

"Oh, nothing; balance his head with a little lead perhaps. He's a giddy-pate!" said the commandant, ironically.

"Are you joking, colonel?" cried Mademoiselle de Verneuil.

"Come!" said the commandant, nodding to the young man, "make haste, let us be off."

At this impertinence Mademoiselle de Verneuil became calm and smiling.

"Do not go," she said to the young man, protecting him with a gesture that was full of dignity.

"Oh, what a beautiful head!" said the youth to his mother, who frowned heavily.

Annoyance, and many other sentiments, aroused and struggled with, did certainly bring fresh beauties to the young woman's face. Francine, Madame du Gua, and her son had all risen from their seats. Mademoiselle de Verneuil hastily advanced and stood between them and the commandant, who smiled amusedly; then she rapidly unfastened the frogged fastenings of her jacket. Acting with that blindness which often seizes women when their self-love is threatened and they are anxious to show their power, as a child is impatient to play with a toy that has just been given to it, she took from her bosom a paper and presented it to Hulot.

"Read that," she said, with a sarcastic laugh.

Then she turned to the young man and gave him, in the excitement of her triumph, a look in which mischief was mingled with an expression of love. Their brows cleared, joy flushed each agitated face, and a thousand contradictory thoughts rose in their hearts. Madame du Gua noted in that one look far more of love than of pity in Mademoiselle de Verneuil's intervention; and she was right. The handsome creature blushed beneath the other woman's gaze, understanding its meaning, and dropped her eyelids; then, as if aware of some threatening accusation, she raised her head proudly and defied all eyes. The commandant, petrified, returned the paper, countersigned by ministers, which enjoined all authorities to obey the orders of this mysterious lady. Having done so, he drew his sword, laid it across his knees, broke the blade, and flung away the pieces.

"Mademoiselle, you probably know what you are about; but a Republican has his own ideas, and his own dignity. I cannot serve where women command. The First Consul will receive my resignation to-morrow; others, who are not of my stripe, may obey you. I do not understand my orders and therefore I stop short,—all the more because I am supposed to understand them."

There was silence for a moment, but it was soon broken by the young lady, who went up to the commandant and held out her hand, saying, "Colonel, though your beard is somewhat long, you may kiss my hand; you are, indeed, a man!"

"I flatter myself I am, mademoiselle," he replied, depositing a kiss upon the hand of this singular young woman rather awkwardly. "As for you, friend," he said, threatening the young man with his finger, "you have had a narrow escape this time."

"Commandant," said the youth, "it is time all this nonsense should cease; I am ready to go with you, if you like, to headquarters."

"And bring your invisible owl, Marche-a-Terre?"

"Who is Marche-a-Terre?" asked the young man, showing all the signs of genuine surprise.

"Didn't he hoot just now?"

"What did that hooting have to do with me, I should like to know? I supposed it was your soldiers letting you know of their arrival."

"Nonsense, you did not think that."

"Yes, I did. But do drink that glass of Bordeaux; the wine is good."

Surprised at the natural behaviour of the youth and also by the frivolity of his manners and the youthfulness of his face, made even more juvenile by the careful curling of his fair hair, the commandant hesitated in the midst of his suspicions. He noticed that Madame du Gua was intently watching the glances that her son gave to Mademoiselle de Verneuil, and he asked her abruptly: "How old are you, *citoyenne*?"

"Ah, Monsieur l'officier," she said, "the rules of the Republic are very severe; must I tell you that I am thirty-eight?"

"May I be shot if I believe it! Marche-a-Terre is here; it was he who gave that cry; you are Chouans in disguise. God's thunder! I'll search the inn and make sure of it!"

Just then a hoot, somewhat like those that preceded it, came from the courtyard; the commandant rushed out, and missed seeing the pallor that covered Madame du Gua's face as he spoke. Hulot saw at once that the sound came from a postilion harnessing his horses to the coach, and he cast aside his suspicions, all the more because it seemed absurd to suppose that the Chouans would risk themselves in Alencon. He returned to the house confounded.

"I forgive him now, but later he shall pay dear for the anxiety he has given us," said the mother to the son, in a low voice, as Hulot re-entered the room.

The brave old officer showed on his worried face the struggle that went on in his mind betwixt a stern sense of duty and the natural kindness of his heart. He kept his gruff air, partly, perhaps, because he fancied he had deceived himself, but he took the glass of Bordeaux, and said: "Excuse me, comrade, but your Polytechnique does send such young officers—"

"The Chouans have younger ones," said the youth, laughing.

"For whom did you take my son?" asked Madame du Gua.

"For the Gars, the leader sent to the Chouans and the Vendeans by the British cabinet; his real name is Marquis de Montauran."

The commandant watched the faces of the suspected pair, who looked at each other with a puzzled expression that seemed to say: "Do you know that name?" "No, do you?" "What is he talking about?" "He's dreaming."

The sudden change in the manner of Marie de Verneuil, and her torpor as she heard the name of the royalist general was observed by no one but Francine, the only person to whom the least shade on that young face was visible. Completely routed, the commandant picked up the bits of his broken sword, looked at Mademoiselle de Verneuil, whose ardent beauty was beginning to find its way to his heart, and said: "As for you, mademoiselle, I take nothing back, and to-morrow these fragments of my sword will reach Bonaparte, unless—"

"Pooh! what do I care for Bonaparte, or your republic, or the king, or the Gars?" she cried, scarcely repressing an explosion of ill-bred temper.

A mysterious emotion, the passion of which gave to her face a dazzling color, showed that the whole world was nothing to the girl the moment that one individual was all in all to her. But she suddenly subdued herself into forced calmness, observing, like a trained actor, that the spectators were watching her. The commandant rose hastily and went out. Anxious and agitated, Mademoiselle de Verneuil followed him, stopped him in the corridor, and said, in an almost solemn tone: "Have you any good reason to suspect that young man of being the Gars?"

"God's thunder! mademoiselle, that fellow who rode here with you came back to warn me that the travellers in the mail-coach had all been murdered by the Chouans; I knew that, but what I didn't know was the name of the murdered persons,—it was Gua de Saint-Cyr!"

"Oh! if Corentin is at the bottom of all this, nothing surprises me," she cried, with a gesture of disgust.

The commandant went his way without daring to look at Mademoiselle de Verneuil, whose dangerous beauty began to affect him.

"If I had stayed two minutes longer I should have committed the folly of taking back my sword and escorting her," he was saying to himself as he went down the stairs.

As Madame du Gua watched the young man, whose eyes were fixed on the door through which Mademoiselle de Verneuil had passed, she said to him in a low voice: "You are incorrigible. You will perish through a woman. A doll can make you forget everything. Why did you allow her to breakfast with us? Who is a Demoiselle de Verneuil escorted by the Blues, who accepts a breakfast from strangers and disarms an officer with a piece of paper hidden in the bosom of her gown like a love-letter? She is one of those contemptible creatures by whose aid Fouche expects to lay hold of you, and the paper she showed the commandant ordered the Blues to assist her against you."

"Eh! madame," he replied in a sharp tone which went to the lady's heart and turned her pale; "her generous action disproves your supposition. Pray remember that the welfare of the king is the sole bond between us. You, who have had Charette at your feet must find the world without him empty; are you not living to avenge him?"

The lady stood still and pensive, like one who sees from the shore the wreck of all her treasures, and only the more eagerly longs for the vanished property.

Mademoiselle de Verneuil re-entered the room; the young man exchanged a smile with her and gave her a glance full of gentle meaning. However uncertain the future might seem, however ephemeral their union, the promises of their sudden love were only the more endearing to them. Rapid as the glance was, it did not escape the sagacious eye of Madame du Gua, who instantly understood it; her brow clouded, and she was unable to wholly conceal her jealous anger. Francine was observing her; she saw the eyes glitter, the cheeks flush; she thought she perceived a diabolical spirit in the face, stirred by some sudden and terrible revulsion. But lightning is not more rapid, nor death more prompt than this brief exhibition of inward emotion. Madame du Gua recovered her lively manner with such immediate self-possession that Francine fancied herself mistaken. Nevertheless, having once perceived in this woman a violence of feeling that was fully equal to that of Mademoiselle de Verneuil, she trembled as she foresaw the clash with which such natures might come together, and the girl shuddered when she saw Mademoiselle de Verneuil go up to the young man with a passionate look and, taking him by the hand, draw him close beside her and into the light, with a coquettish glance that was full of witchery.

"Now," she said, trying to read his eyes, "own to me that you are not the citizen du Gua Saint-Cyr."

"Yes, I am, mademoiselle."

"But he and his mother were killed yesterday."

"I am very sorry for that," he replied, laughing. "However that may be, I am none the less under a great obligation to you, for which I shall always feel the deepest gratitude and only wish I could prove it to you."

"I thought I was saving an *emigre*, but I love you better as a Republican."

The words escaped her lips as it were impulsively; she became confused; even her eyes blushed, and her face bore no other expression than one of exquisite simplicity of feeling; she softly released the young man's hand, not from shame at having pressed it, but because of a thought too weighty, it seemed, for her heart to bear, leaving him drunk with hope. Suddenly she appeared to regret this freedom, permissible as it might be under the passing circumstances of a journey. She recovered her conventional manner, bowed to the lady and her son, and taking Francine with her, left the room. When they reached their own chamber Francine wrung her hands and tossed her arms, as she looked at her mistress, saying: "Ah, Marie, what a crowd of things in a moment of time! who but you would have such adventures?"

Mademoiselle de Verneuil sprang forward and clasped Francine round the neck.

"Ah! this is life indeed—I am in heaven!"

"Or hell," retorted Francine.

"Yes, hell if you like!" cried Mademoiselle de Verneuil. "Here, give me your hand; feel my heart, how it beats. There's fever in my veins; the whole world is now a mere nothing to me! How many times have I not seen that man in my dreams! Oh! how beautiful his head is—how his eyes sparkle!"

"Will he love you?" said the simple peasant-woman, in a quivering voice, her face full of sad foreboding.

"How can you ask me that!" cried Mademoiselle de Verneuil. "But, Francine, tell me," she added throwing herself into a pose that was half serious, half comic, "will it be very hard to love me?"

"No, but will he love you always?" replied Francine, smiling.

They looked at each other for a moment speechless,—Francine at revealing so much knowledge of life, and Marie at the perception, which now came to her for the first time, of a future of happiness in her passion. She seemed to herself hanging over a gulf of which she had wanted to know the depth, and listening to the fall of the stone she had flung, at first heedlessly, into it.

"Well, it is my own affair," she said, with the gesture of a gambler. "I should never pity a betrayed woman; she has no one but herself to blame if she is abandoned. I shall know how to keep, either living or dead, the man whose heart has once been mine. But," she added, with some surprise and after a moment's silence, "where did you get your knowledge of love, Francine?"

"Mademoiselle," said the peasant-woman, hastily, "hush, I hear steps in the passage."

"Ah! not *his* steps!" said Marie, listening. "But you are evading an answer; well, well, I'll wait for it, or guess it."

Francine was right, however. Three taps on the door interrupted the conversation. Captain Merle appeared, after receiving Mademoiselle de Verneuil's permission to enter.

With a military salute to the lady, whose beauty dazzled him, the soldier ventured on giving her a glance, but he found nothing better to say than: "Mademoiselle, I am at your orders."

"Then you are to be my protector, in place of the commander, who retires; is that so?"

"No, my superior is the adjutant-major Gerard, who has sent me here."

"Your commandant must be very much afraid of me," she said.

"Beg pardon, mademoiselle, Hulot is afraid of nothing. But women, you see, are not in his line; it ruffled him to have a general in a mob-cap."

"And yet," continued Mademoiselle de Verneuil, "it was his duty to obey his superiors. I like subordination, and I warn you that I shall allow no one to disobey me."

"That would be difficult," replied Merle, gallantly.

"Let us consult," said Mademoiselle de Verneuil. "You can get fresh troops here and accompany me to Mayenne, which I must reach this evening. Shall we find other soldiers there, so that I might go on at once, without stopping at Mayenne? The Chouans are quite ignorant of our little expedition. If we travel at night, we can avoid meeting any number of them, and so escape an attack. Do you think this feasible?"

"Yes, mademoiselle."

"What sort of road is it between Mayenne and Fougeres?"

"Rough; all up and down, a regular squirrel-wheel."

"Well, let us start at once. As we have nothing to fear near Alencon, you can go before me; we'll join you soon."

"One would think she had seen ten years' service," thought Merle, as he departed. "Hulot is mistaken; that young girl is not earning her living out of a feather-bed. Ten thousand carriages! if I want to be adjutant-major I mustn't be such a fool as to mistake Saint-Michael for the devil."

During Mademoiselle de Verneuil's conference with the captain, Francine had slipped out for the purpose of examining, through a window of the corridor, the spot in the courtyard which had excited her curiosity on arriving at the inn. She watched the stable and the heaps of straw with the absorption of one who was saying her prayers to the Virgin, and she presently saw Madame du Gua approaching Marche-a-Terre with the precaution of a cat that dislikes to wet its feet. When the Chouan caught sight of the lady, he rose and stood before her in an attitude of deep respect. This singular circumstance aroused Francine's curiosity; she slipped into the courtyard and along the walls, avoiding Madame du Gua's notice, and trying to hide herself behind the stable door. She walked on tiptoe, scarcely daring to breathe, and succeeded in posting herself close to Marche-a-Terre, without exciting his attention.

"If, after all this information," the lady was saying to the Chouan, "it proves not to be her real name, you are to fire upon her without pity, as you would on a mad dog."

"Agreed!" said Marche-a-Terre.

The lady left him. The Chouan replaced his red woollen cap upon his head, remained standing, and was scratching his ear as if puzzled when Francine suddenly appeared before him, apparently by magic.

"Saint Anne of Auray!" he exclaimed. Then he dropped his whip, clasped his hands, and stood as if in ecstasy. A faint color illuminated his coarse face, and his eyes shone like diamonds dropped on a muck-heap. "Is it really the brave girl from Cottin?" he muttered, in a voice so smothered that he alone heard it. "You *are* fine," he said, after a pause, using the curious word, "godaine," a superlative in the dialect of those regions used by lovers to express the combination of fine clothes and beauty.

"I daren't touch you," added Marche-a-Terre, putting out his big hand nevertheless, as if to weigh the gold chain which hung round her neck and below her waist.

"You had better not, Pierre," replied Francine, inspired by the instinct which makes a woman despotic when not oppressed. She drew back haughtily, after enjoying the Chouan's surprise; but she compensated for the harshness of her words by the softness of her glance, saying, as she once more approached him: "Pierre, that lady was talking to you about my young mistress, wasn't she?"

Marche-a-Terre was silent; his face struggled, like the dawn, between clouds and light. He looked in turn at Francine, at the whip he had dropped, and at the chain, which seemed to have as powerful an attraction for him as the Breton girl herself. Then, as if to put a stop to his own uneasiness, he picked up his whip and still kept silence.

"Well, it is easy to see that that lady told you to kill my mistress," resumed Francine, who knew the faithful discretion of the peasant, and wished to relieve his scruples.

Marche-a-Terre lowered his head significantly. To the Cottin girl that was answer enough.

"Very good, Pierre," she said; "if any evil happens to her, if a hair of her head is injured, you and I will have seen each other for the last time; for I shall be in heaven, and you will go to hell."

The possessed of devils whom the Church in former days used to exorcise with great pomp were not more shaken and agitated than

Marche-a-Terre at this prophecy, uttered with a conviction that gave it certainty. His glance, which at first had a character of savage tenderness, counteracted by a fanaticism as powerful in his soul as love, suddenly became surly, as he felt the imperious manner of the girl he had long since chosen. Francine interpreted his silence in her own way.

"Won't you do anything for my sake?" she said in a tone of reproach.

At these words the Chouan cast a glance at his mistress from eyes that were black as a crow's wing.

"Are you free?" he asked in a growl that Francine alone could have understood.

"Should I be here if I were not?" she replied indignantly. "But you, what are you doing here? Still playing bandit, still roaming the country like a mad dog wanting to bite. Oh! Pierre, if you were wise, you would come with me. This beautiful young lady, who, I ought to tell you, was nursed when a baby in our home, has taken care of me. I have two hundred francs a year from a good investment. And Mademoiselle has bought me my uncle Thomas's big house for fifteen hundred francs, and I have saved two thousand beside."

But her smiles and the announcement of her wealth fell dead before the dogged immovability of the Chouan.

"The priests have told us to go to war," he replied. "Every Blue we shoot earns one indulgence."

"But suppose the Blues shoot you?"

He answered by letting his arms drop at his sides, as if regretting the poverty of the offering he should thus make to God and the king.

"What will become of me?" exclaimed the young girl, sorrowfully.

Marche-a-Terre looked at her stupidly; his eyes seemed to enlarge; tears rolled down his hairy cheeks upon the goatskin which covered him, and a low moan came from his breast.

"Saint Anne of Auray!—Pierre, is this all you have to say to me after a parting of seven years? You have changed indeed."

"I love you the same as ever," said the Chouan, in a gruff voice.

"No," she whispered, "the king is first."

"If you look at me like that I shall go," he said.

"Well, then, adieu," she replied, sadly.

"Adieu," he repeated.

He seized her hand, wrung it, kissed it, made the sign of the cross, and rushed into the stable, like a dog who fears that his bone will be taken from him.

"Pille-Miche," he said to his comrade. "Where's your tobacco-box?"

"Ho! *sacre bleu*! what a fine chain!" cried Pille-Miche, fumbling in a pocket constructed in his goatskin.

Then he held out to Marche-a-Terre the little horn in which Bretons put the finely powdered tobacco which they prepare themselves during the long winter nights. The Chouan raised his thumb and made a hollow in the palm of his hand, after the manner in which an "Invalide" takes his tobacco; then he shook the horn, the small end of which Pille-Miche had unscrewed. A fine powder fell slowly from the little hole pierced in the point of this Breton utensil. Marche-a-Terre went through the same process seven or eight times silently, as if the powder had power to change the current of his thoughts. Suddenly he flung the horn to Pille-Miche with a gesture of despair, and caught up a gun which was hidden in the straw.

"Seven or eight shakes at once! I suppose you think that costs nothing!" said the stingy Pille-Miche.

"Forward!" cried Marche-a-Terre in a hoarse voice. "There's work before us."

Thirty or more Chouans who were sleeping in the straw under the mangers, raised their heads, saw Marche-a-Terre on his feet, and disappeared instantly through a door which led to the garden, from which it was easy to reach the fields.

When Francine left the stable she found the mail-coach ready to start. Mademoiselle de Verneuil and her new fellow-travellers were already in it. The girl shuddered as she saw her young mistress sitting side by side with the woman who had just ordered her death. The young man had taken his seat facing Marie, and as soon as Francine was in hers the heavy vehicle started at a good pace.

The sun had swept away the gray autumnal mists, and its rays were brightening the gloomy landscape with a look of youth and holiday. Many lovers fancy that such chance accidents of the sky are premonitions. Francine was surprised at the strange silence which fell upon the travellers. Mademoiselle de Verneuil had recovered her cold manner, and sat with her eyes lowered, her head slightly inclined, and her hands hidden under a sort of mantle in which she had wrapped herself. If she raised her eyes it was only to look at the passing scenery. Certain of being admired, she rejected admiration; but her apparent indifference was evidently more coquettish than natural. Purity, which gives such harmony to the diverse expressions by which a simple soul reveals itself, could lend no charm to a being whose every instinct predestined her to the storms of passion. Yielding himself up to the pleasures of this dawning intrigue, the young man did not try to explain the contradictions which were obvious between the coquetry and the enthusiasm of this singular young girl. Her assumed indifference allowed him to examine at his ease a face which was now as beautiful in its calmness as it had been when agitated. Like the rest of us, he was not disposed to question the sources of his enjoyment.

It is difficult for a pretty woman to avoid the glances of her companions in a carriage when their eyes fasten upon her as a visible distraction to the monotony of a journey. Happy, therefore, in being able to satisfy the hunger of his dawning passion, without offence or avoidance on the part of its object, the young man studied the pure and brilliant lines of the girl's head and face. To him they were a picture. Sometimes the light brought out the transparent rose of the nostrils and the double curve which united the nose with the upper lip; at other times a pale glint of sunshine illuminated the tints of the skin, pearly beneath the eyes and round the mouth, rosy on the cheeks, and ivory-white about the temples and throat. He admired the contrasts of light and shade caused by the masses of black hair surrounding her face and giving it an ephemeral grace,—for all is fleeting in a woman; her beauty of to-day is often not that of yesterday, fortunately for herself, perhaps! The young man, who was still at an age when youth delights in the nothings which are the all of love, watched eagerly for each movement of the eyelids, and the seductive rise and fall of her bosom as she breathed. Sometimes he fancied, suiting the tenor of his thoughts, that he could see a meaning in the expression of the eyes and the imperceptible inflection of the lips. Every gesture betrayed to him the soul, every motion a new aspect of the young girl. If a thought stirred those mobile features, if a sudden blush suffused the cheeks, or a smile brought life into the face, he found a fresh delight in trying to discover the secrets of this mysterious creature. Everything about her was a snare to the soul and a snare to the senses. Even the silence that fell between them, far from raising an obstacle to the understanding of their hearts, became the common ground for mutual thoughts. But after a while the many looks in which their eyes encountered each other warned Marie de Verneuil that the silence was compromising her, and she turned to Madame du Gua with one of those commonplace remarks which open the way to conversation; but even in so doing she included the young man.

"Madame," she said, "how could you put your son into the navy? have you not doomed yourself to perpetual anxiety?"

"Mademoiselle, the fate of women, of mothers, I should say, is to tremble for the safety of their dear ones."

"Your son is very like you."

"Do you think so, mademoiselle?"

The smile with which the young man listened to these remarks increased the vexation of his pretended mother. Her hatred grew with every passionate glance he turned on Marie. Silence or conversation, all increased the dreadful wrath which she carefully concealed beneath a cordial manner.

"Mademoiselle," said the young man, "you are quite mistaken. Naval men are not more exposed to danger than soldiers. Women ought not to dislike the navy; we sailors have a merit beyond that of the military, —we are faithful to our mistresses."

"Oh, from necessity," replied Mademoiselle de Verneuil, laughing.

"But even so, it is fidelity," said Madame du Gua, in a deep voice.

The conversation grew lively, touching upon subjects that were interesting to none but the three travellers, for under such circumstances intelligent persons given new meanings to commonplace talk; but every word, insignificant as it might seem, was a mutual interrogation, hiding the desires, hopes, and passions which agitated them. Marie's cleverness and quick perception (for she was fully on her guard) showed Madame du Gua that calumny and treachery could alone avail to triumph over a rival as formidable through her intellect as by her beauty. The mail-coach presently overtook the escort, and then advanced more slowly. The young man, seeing a long hill before them, proposed to the young lady that they should walk. The friendly politeness of his offer decided her, and her consent flattered him.

"Is Madame of our opinion?" she said, turning to Madame du Gua. "Will she walk, too?"

"Coquette!" said the lady to herself, as she left the coach.

Marie and the young man walked together, but a little apart. The sailor, full of ardent desires, was determined to break the reserve that checked him, of which, however, he was not the dupe. He fancied that he could succeed by dallying with the young lady in that tone of courteous amiability and wit, sometimes frivolous, sometimes serious, which characterized the men of the exiled aristocracy. But the smiling Parisian beauty parried him so mischievously, and rejected his frivolities with such disdain, evidently preferring the stronger ideas and enthusiasms which he betrayed from time to time in spite of himself, that he presently began to understand the true way of pleasing her. The conversation then changed. He realized the hopes her expressive face had given him; yet, as he did so, new difficulties arose, and he was still forced to suspend his judgment on a girl who seemed to take delight in thwarting him, a siren with whom he grew more and more in love. After yielding to the seduction of her beauty, he was still more attracted to her mysterious soul, with a curiosity which Marie perceived and took pleasure in exciting. Their intercourse assumed, insensibly, a character of intimacy far removed from the tone of indifference which Mademoiselle de Verneuil endeavored in vain to give to it.

Though Madame du Gua had followed the lovers, the latter had unconsciously walked so much more rapidly than she that a distance of several hundred feet soon separated them. The charming pair trod the fine sand beneath their feet, listening with childlike delight to the union of their footsteps, happy in being wrapped by the same ray of a sunshine that seemed spring-like, in breathing with the same breath autumnal perfumes laden with vegetable odors which seemed a nourishment brought by the breezes to their dawning love. Though to them it may have been a mere circumstance of their fortuitous meeting, yet the sky, the landscape, the season of the year, did communicate to their emotions a tinge of melancholy gravity which gave them an element of passion. They praised the weather and talked of its beauty; then of their strange encounter, of the coming rupture of an intercourse so delightful; of the ease with which, in travelling, friendships, lost as soon as made, are formed. After this last remark, the young man profited by what seemed to be a tacit permission to make a few tender confidences, and to risk an avowal of love like a man who was not unaccustomed to such situations.

"Have you noticed, mademoiselle," he said, "how little the feelings of the heart follow the old conventional rules in the days of terror in which we live? Everything about us bears the stamp of suddenness. We love in a day, or we hate on the strength of a single glance. We are bound to each other for life in a moment, or we part with the celerity of death itself. All things are hurried, like the convulsions of the nation. In the midst of such dangers as ours the ties that bind should be stronger than under the ordinary course of life. In Paris during the Terror, every one came to know the full meaning of a clasp of the hand as men do on a battle-field."

"People felt the necessity of living fast and ardently," she answered, "for they had little time to live." Then, with a glance at her companion which seemed to tell him that the end of their short intercourse was approaching, she added, maliciously: "You are very well informed as to the affairs of life, for a young man who has just left the Ecole Polytechnique!"

"What are you thinking of me?" he said after a moment's silence. "Tell me frankly, without disguise."

"You wish to acquire the right to speak to me of myself," she said laughing.

"You do not answer me," he went on after a slight pause. "Take care, silence is sometimes significant."

"Do you think I cannot guess all that you would like to say to me? Good heavens! you have already said enough."

"Oh, if we understand each other," he replied, smiling, "I have obtained more than I dared hope for."

She smiled in return so graciously that she seemed to accept the courteous struggle into which all men like to draw a woman. They persuaded themselves, half in jest, half in earnest, that they never could be more to each other than they were at that moment. The young man fancied, therefore, he might give reins to a passion that could have no future; the young woman felt she might smile upon it. Marie suddenly struck her foot against a stone and stumbled.

"Take my arm," said her companion.

"It seems I must," she replied; "you would be too proud if I refused; you would fancy I feared you."

"Ah, mademoiselle," he said, pressing her arm against his heart that she might feel the beating of it, "you flatter my pride by granting such a favor."

"Well, the readiness with which I do so will cure your illusions."

"Do you wish to save me from the danger of the emotions you cause?"

"Stop, stop!" she cried; "do not try to entangle me in such boudoir riddles. I don't like to find the wit of fools in a man of your character. See! here we are beneath the glorious sky, in the open country; before us, above us, all is grand. You wish to tell me that I am beautiful, do you not? Well, your eyes have already told me so; besides, I know it; I am not a woman whom mere compliments can please. But perhaps you would like," this with satirical emphasis, "to talk about your *sentiments*? Do you think me so simple as to believe that sudden sympathies are powerful enough to influence a whole life through the recollections of one morning?"

"Not the recollections of a morning," he said, "but those of a beautiful woman who has shown herself generous."

"You forget," she retorted, laughing, "half my attractions,—a mysterious woman, with everything odd about her, name, rank, situation, freedom of thought and manners."

"You are not mysterious to me!" he exclaimed. "I have fathomed you; there is nothing that could be added to your perfections except a little more faith in the love you inspire."

"Ah, my poor child of eighteen, what can you know of love?" she said smiling. "Well, well, so be it!" she added, "it is a fair subject of conversation, like the weather when one pays a visit. You shall find that I have neither false modesty nor petty fears. I can hear the word love without blushing; it has been so often said to me without one echo of the heart that I think it quite unmeaning. I have met with it everywhere, in books, at the theatre, in society,—yes, everywhere, and never have I found in it even a semblance of its magnificent ideal."

"Did you seek that ideal?"

"Yes."

The word was said with such perfect ease and freedom that the young man made a gesture of surprise and looked at Marie fixedly, as if he had suddenly changed his opinion on her character and real position.

"Mademoiselle," he said with ill-concealed devotion, "are you maid or wife, angel or devil?"

"All," she replied, laughing. "Isn't there something diabolic and also angelic in a young girl who has never loved, does not love, and perhaps will never love?"

"Do you think yourself happy thus?" he asked with a free and easy tone and manner, as though already he felt less respect for her.

"Oh, happy, no," she replied. "When I think that I am alone, hampered by social conventions that make me deceitful, I envy the privileges of a man. But when I also reflect on the means which nature has bestowed on us women to catch and entangle you men in the invisible meshes of a power which you cannot resist, then the part assigned to me in the world is not displeasing to me. And then again, suddenly, it does seem very petty, and I feel that I should despise a man who allowed himself to be duped by such vulgar seductions. No sooner do I perceive our power and like it, than I know it to be horrible and I abhor it. Sometimes I feel within me that longing towards devotion which makes my sex so nobly beautiful; and then I feel a desire, which consumes me, for dominion and power. Perhaps it is the natural struggle of the good and the evil principle in which all creatures live here below. Angel or devil! you have expressed it. Ah! to-day is not the first time that I have recognized my double nature. But we women understand better than you men can do our own shortcomings. We have an instinct which shows us a perfection in all things to which, nevertheless, we fail to attain. But," she added, sighing as she glanced at the sky; "that which enhances us in your eyes is—"

"Is what?" he said.

"—that we are all struggling, more or less," she answered, "against a thwarted destiny."

"Mademoiselle, why should we part to-night?"

"Ah!" she replied, smiling at the passionate look which he gave her, "let us get into the carriage; the open air does not agree with us."

Marie turned abruptly; the young man followed her, and pressed her arm with little respect, but in a manner that expressed his imperious admiration. She hastened her steps. Seeing that she wished to escape an importune declaration, he became the more ardent; being determined to win a first favor from this woman, he risked all and said, looking at her meaningly:—

"Shall I tell you a secret?"

"Yes, quickly, if it concerns you."

"I am not in the service of the Republic. Where are you going? I shall follow you."

At the words Marie trembled violently. She withdrew her arm and covered her face with both hands to hide either the flush or the pallor of her cheeks; then she suddenly uncovered her face and said in a voice of deep emotion:—

"Then you began as you would have ended, by deceiving me?"

"Yes," he said.

At this answer she turned again from the carriage, which was now overtaking them, and began to almost run along the road.

"I thought," he said, following her, "that the open air did not agree with you?"

"Oh! it has changed," she replied in a grave tone, continuing to walk on, a prey to agitating thoughts.

"You do not answer me," said the young man, his heart full of the soft expectation of coming pleasure.

"Oh!" she said, in a strained voice, "the tragedy begins."

"What tragedy?" he asked.

She stopped short, looked at the young student from head to foot with a mingled expression of fear and curiosity; then she concealed her feelings that were agitating her under the mask of an impenetrable calmness, showing that for a girl of her age she had great experience of life.

"Who are you?" she said,—"but I know already; when I first saw you I suspected it. You are the royalist leader whom they call the Gars. The ex-bishop of Autun was right in saying we should always believe in presentiments which give warning of evil."

"What interest have you in knowing the Gars?"

"What interest has he in concealing himself from me who have already saved his life?" She began to laugh, but the merriment was forced. "I have wisely prevented you from saying that you love me. Let me tell you, monsieur, that I abhor you. I am republican, you are royalist; I would deliver you up if you were not under my protection, and if I had not already saved your life, and if—" she stopped. These violent extremes of feeling and the inward struggle which she no longer attempted to conceal alarmed the young man, who tried, but in vain, to observe her calmly. "Let us part here at once,—I insist upon it; farewell!" she said. She turned hastily back, made a few steps, and then returned to him. "No, no," she continued, "I have too great an interest in knowing who you are. Hide nothing from me; tell me the truth. Who are you? for you are no more a pupil of the Ecole Polytechnique than you are eighteen years old."

"I am a sailor, ready to leave the ocean and follow you wherever your imagination may lead you. If I have been so lucky as to rouse your curiosity in any particular I shall be very careful not to lessen it. Why mingle the serious affairs of real life with the life of the heart in which we are beginning to understand each other?"

"Our souls might have understood each other," she said in a grave voice. "But I have no right to exact your confidence. You will never know the extent of your obligations to me; I shall not explain them."

They walked a few steps in silence.

"My life does interest you," said the young man.

"Monsieur, I implore you, tell me your name or else be silent. You are a child," she added, with an impatient movement of her shoulders, "and I feel a pity for you."

The obstinacy with which she insisted on knowing his name made the pretended sailor hesitate between prudence and love. The vexation of a desired woman is powerfully attractive; her anger, like her submission, is imperious; many are the fibres she touches in a man's heart, penetrating and subjugating it. Was this scene only another aspect of Mademoiselle de Verneuil's coquetry? In spite of his sudden passion the unnamed lover had the strength to distrust a woman thus bent on forcing from him a secret of life and death.

"Why has my rash indiscretion, which sought to give a future to our present meeting, destroyed the happiness of it?" he said, taking her hand, which she left in his unconsciously.

Mademoiselle de Verneuil, who seemed to be in real distress, was silent.

"How have I displeased you?" he said. "What can I do to soothe you?"

"Tell me your name."

He made no reply, and they walked some distance in silence. Suddenly Mademoiselle de Verneuil stopped short, like one who has come to some serious determination.

"Monsieur le Marquis de Montauran," she said, with dignity, but without being able to conceal entirely the nervous trembling of her features, "I desire to do you a great service, whatever it may cost me. We part here. The coach and its escort are necessary for your protection, and you must continue your journey in it. Fear nothing from the Republicans; they are men of honor, and I shall give the adjutant certain orders which he will faithfully execute. As for me, I shall return on foot to Alencon with my maid, and take a few of the soldiers with me. Listen to what I say, for your life depends on it. If, before you reach a place of safety, you meet that odious man you saw in my company at the inn, escape at once, for he will instantly betray you. As for me,—" she paused, "as for me, I fling myself back into the miseries of life. Farewell, monsieur, may you be happy; farewell."

She made a sign to Captain Merle, who was just then reaching the brow of the hill behind her. The marquis was taken unawares by her sudden action.

"Stop!" he cried, in a tone of despair that was well acted.

This singular caprice of a girl for whom he would at that instant have thrown away his life so surprised him that he invented, on the spur of the moment, a fatal fiction by which to hide his name and satisfy the curiosity of his companion.

"You have almost guessed the truth," he said. "I am an *emigre*, condemned to death, and my name is Vicomte de Bauvan. Love of my country has brought me back to France to join my brother. I hope to be taken off the list of *emigres* through the influence of Madame de Beauharnais, now the wife of the First Consul; but if I fail in this, I mean to die on the soil of my native land, fighting beside my friend Montauran. I am now on my way secretly, by means of a passport he has sent me, to learn if any of my property in Brittany is still unconfiscated."

While the young man spoke Mademoiselle de Verneuil examined him with a penetrating eye. She tried at first to doubt his words, but being by nature confiding and trustful, she slowly regained an expression of serenity, and said eagerly, "Monsieur, are you telling me the exact truth?"

"Yes, the exact truth," replied the young man, who seemed to have no conscience in his dealings with women.

Mademoiselle de Verneuil gave a deep sigh, like a person who returns to life.

"Ah!" she exclaimed, "I am very happy."

"Then you hate that poor Montauran?"

"No," she said; "but I could not make you understand my meaning. I was not willing that *you* should meet the dangers from which I will try to protect him,—since he is your friend."

"Who told you that Montauran was in danger?"

"Ah, monsieur, even if I had not come from Paris, where his enterprise is the one thing talked of, the commandant at Alencon said enough to show his danger."

"Then let me ask you how you expect to save him from it."

"Suppose I do not choose to answer," she replied, with the haughty air that women often assume to hide an emotion. "What right have you to know my secrets?"

"The right of a man who loves you."

"Already?" she said. "No, you do not love me. I am only an object of passing gallantry to you,—that is all. I am clear-sighted; did I not penetrate your disguise at once? A woman who knows anything of good society could not be misled, in these days, by a pupil of the Polytechnique who uses choice language, and conceals as little as you do the manners of a *grand seigneur* under the mask of a Republican. There is a trifle of powder left in your hair, and a fragrance of nobility clings to you which a woman of the world cannot fail to detect. Therefore, fearing that the man whom you saw accompanying me, who has all the shrewdness of a woman, might make the same discovery, I sent him away. Monsieur, let me tell you that a true Republican officer just from the Polytechnique would not have made love to me as you have done, and would not have taken me for a pretty adventuress. Allow me, Monsieur de Bauvan, to preach you a little sermon from a woman's point of view. Are you too juvenile to know that of all the creatures of my sex the most difficult to subdue is that same adventuress,—she whose price is ticketed and who is weary of pleasure. That sort of woman requires, they tell me, constant seduction; she yields only to her own caprices; any attempt to please her argues, I should suppose, great conceit on the part of a man. But let us put aside that class of women, among whom you have been good enough to rank me; you ought to understand that a young woman, handsome, brilliant, and of noble birth (for, I suppose, you will grant me those advantages), does not sell herself, and can only be won by the man who loves her in one way. You understand me? If she loves him and is willing to commit a folly, she must be justified by great and heroic reasons. Forgive me this logic, rare in my sex; but for the sake of your happiness,—and my own," she added, dropping her head, —"I will not allow either of us to deceive the other, nor will I permit you to think that Mademoiselle de Verneuil, angel or devil, maid or wife, is capable of being seduced by commonplace gallantry."

"Mademoiselle," said the marquis, whose surprise, though he concealed it, was extreme, and who at once became a man of the great world, "I entreat you to believe that I take you to be a very noble person, full of the highest sentiments, or—a charming girl, as you please."

"I don't ask all that," she said, laughing. "Allow me to keep my incognito. My mask is better than yours, and it pleases me to wear it, —if only to discover whether those who talk to me of love are sincere. Therefore, beware of me! Monsieur," she cried, catching his arm vehemently, "listen to me; if you were able to prove that your love is true, nothing, no human power, could part us. Yes, I would fain unite myself to the noble destiny of some great man, and marry a vast ambition, glorious hopes! Noble hearts are never faithless, for constancy is in their fibre; I should be forever loved, forever happy, —I would make my body a stepping-stone by which to raise the man who loved me; I would sacrifice all things to him, bear all things from him, and love him forever,—even if he ceased to love me. I have never before dared to confess to another heart the secrets of mine, nor the passionate enthusiasms which exhaust me; but I tell you something of them now because, as soon as I have seen you in safety, we shall part forever."

"Part? never!" he cried, electrified by the tones of that vigorous soul which seemed to be fighting against some overwhelming thought.

"Are you free?" she said, with a haughty glance which subdued him.

"Free! yes, except for the sentence of death which hangs over me."

She added presently, in a voice full of bitter feeling: "If all this were not a dream, a glorious life might indeed be ours. But I have been talking folly; let us beware of committing any. When I think of all you would have to be before you could rate me at my proper value I doubt everything—"

"I doubt nothing if you will only grant me—"

"Hush!" she cried, hearing a note of true passion in his voice, "the open air is decidedly disagreeing with us; let us return to the coach."

That vehicle soon came up; they took their places and drove on several miles in total silence. Both had matter for reflection, but henceforth their eyes no longer feared to meet. Each now seemed to have an equal interest in observing the other, and in mutually hiding important secrets; but for all that they were drawn together by one and the same impulse, which now, as a result of this interview, assumed the dimensions of a passion. They recognized in each other qualities which promised to heighten all the pleasures to be derived from either their contest or their union. Perhaps both of them, living a life of adventure, had reached the singular moral condition in which, either from weariness or in defiance of fate, the mind rejects serious reflection and flings itself on chance in pursuing an enterprise precisely because the issues of chance are unknown, and the interest of expecting them vivid. The moral nature, like the physical nature, has its abysses into which strong souls love to plunge, risking their future as gamblers risk their fortune. Mademoiselle de Verneuil and the young marquis had obtained a revelation of each other's minds as a consequence of this interview, and their intercourse thus took rapid strides, for the sympathy of their souls succeeded to that of their senses. Besides, the more they felt fatally drawn to each other, the more eager they were to study the secret action of their minds. The so-called Vicomte de Bauvan, surprised at the seriousness of the strange girl's ideas, asked himself how she could possibly combine such acquired knowledge of life with so much youth and freshness. He thought he discovered an extreme desire to appear chaste in the modesty and reserve of her attitudes. He suspected her of playing a part; he questioned the nature of his own pleasure; and ended by choosing to consider her a clever actress. He was right; Mademoiselle de Verneuil, like other women of the world, grew the more reserved the more she felt the warmth of her own feelings, assuming with perfect naturalness the appearance of prudery, beneath which such women veil their desires. They all wish to offer themselves as virgins on love's altar; and if they are not so, the deception they seek to practise is at least a homage which they pay to their lovers. These thoughts passed rapidly through the mind of the young man and gratified him. In fact, for both, this mutual examination was an advance in their intercourse, and the lover soon came to that phase of passion in which a man finds in the defects of his mistress a reason for loving her the more.

Mademoiselle de Verneuil was thoughtful. Perhaps her imagination led her over a greater extent of the future than that of the young *emigre*, who was merely following one of the many impulses of his life as a man; whereas Marie was considering a lifetime, thinking to make it beautiful, and to fill it with happiness and with grand and noble sentiments. Happy in such thoughts, more in love with her ideal than with the actual reality, with the future rather than with the present, she desired now to return upon her steps so as to better establish her power. In this she acted instinctively, as all women act. Having agreed with her soul that she would give herself wholly up, she wished—if we may so express it—to dispute every fragment of the gift; she longed to take back from the past all her words and looks and acts and make them more in harmony with the dignity of a woman beloved. Her eyes at times expressed a sort of terror as she

thought of the interview just over, in which she had shown herself aggressive. But as she watched the face before her, instinct with power, and felt that a being so strong must also be generous, she glowed at the thought that her part in life would be nobler than that of most women, inasmuch as her lover was a man of character, a man condemned to death, who had come to risk his life in making war against the Republic. The thought of occupying such a soul to the exclusion of all rivals gave a new aspect to many matters. Between the moment, only five hours earlier, when she composed her face and toned her voice to allure the young man, and the present moment, when she was able to convulse him with a look, there was all the difference to her between a dead world and a living one.

In the condition of soul in which Mademoiselle de Verneuil now existed external life seemed to her a species of phantasmagoria. The carriage passed through villages and valleys and mounted hills which left no impressions on her mind. They reached Mayenne; the soldiers of the escort were changed; Merle spoke to her; she replied; they crossed the whole town and were again in the open country; but the faces, houses, streets, landscape, men, swept past her like the figments of a dream. Night came, and Marie was travelling beneath a diamond sky, wrapped in soft light, and yet she was not aware that darkness had succeeded day; that Mayenne was passed; that Fougeres was near; she knew not even where she was going. That she should part in a few hours from the man she had chosen, and who, she believed, had chosen her, was not for her a possibility. Love is the only passion which looks to neither past nor future. Occasionally her thoughts escaped in broken words, in phrases devoid of meaning, though to her lover's ears they sounded like promises of love. To the two witnesses of this birth of passion she seemed to be rushing onward with fearful rapidity. Francine knew Marie as well as Madame du Gua knew the marquis, and their experience of the past made them await in silence some terrible finale. It was, indeed, not long before the end came to the drama which Mademoiselle de Verneuil had called, without perhaps imagining the truth of her words, a tragedy.

When the travellers were about three miles beyond Mayenne they heard a horseman riding after them with great rapidity. When he reached the carriage he leaned towards it to look at Mademoiselle de Verneuil, who recognized Corentin. That offensive personage made her a sign of intelligence, the familiarity of which was deeply

mortifying; then he turned away, after chilling her to the bone with a look full of some base meaning. The young *emigre* seemed painfully affected by this circumstance, which did not escape the notice of his pretended mother; but Marie softly touched him, seeming by her eyes to take refuge in his heart as thought it were her only haven. His brow cleared at this proof of the full extent of his mistress's attachment, coming to him as it were by accident. An inexplicable fear seemed to have overcome her coyness, and her love was visible for a moment without a veil. Unfortunately for both of them, Madame du Gua saw it all; like a miser who gives a feast, she seemed to count the morsels and begrudge the wine.

Absorbed in their happiness the lovers arrived, without any consciousness of the distance they had traversed, at that part of the road which passed through the valley of Ernee. There Francine noticed and showed to her companions a number of strange forms which seemed to move like shadows among the trees and gorse that surrounded the fields. When the carriage came within range of these shadows a volley of musketry, the balls of which whistled above their heads, warned the travellers that the shadows were realities. The escort had fallen into a trap.

Captain Merle now keenly regretted having adopted Mademoiselle de Verneuil's idea that a rapid journey by night would be a safe one,—an error which had led him to reduce his escort from Mayenne to sixty men. He at once, under Gerard's orders, divided his little troop into two columns, one on each side of the road, which the two officers marched at a quick step among the gorse hedges, eager to meet the assailants, though ignorant of their number. The Blues beat the thick bushes right and left with rash intrepidity, and replied to the Chouans with a steady fire.

Mademoiselle de Verneuil's first impulse was to jump from the carriage and run back along the road until she was out of sight of the battle; but ashamed of her fears, and moved by the feeling which impels us all to act nobly under the eyes of those we love, she presently stood still, endeavoring to watch the combat coolly.

The marquis followed her, took her hand, and placed it on his breast.

"I was afraid," she said, smiling, "but now—"

Just then her terrified maid cried out: "Marie, take care!"

But as she said the words, Francine, who was springing from the carriage, felt herself grasped by a strong hand. The sudden weight of that enormous hand made her shriek violently; she turned, and was instantly silenced on recognizing Marche-a-Terre.

"Twice I owe to chance," said the marquis to Mademoiselle de Verneuil, "the revelation of the sweetest secrets of the heart. Thanks to Francine I now know you bear the gracious name of Marie,—Marie, the name I have invoked in my distresses,—Marie, a name I shall henceforth speak in joy, and never without sacrifice, mingling religion and love. There can be no wrong where prayer and love go together."

They clasped hands, looked silently into each other's eyes, and the excess of their emotion took away from them the power to express it.

"There's no danger for *the rest of you*," Marche-a-Terre was saying roughly to Francine, giving to his hoarse and guttural voice a reproachful tone, and emphasizing his last words in a way to stupefy the innocent peasant-girl. For the first time in her life she saw ferocity in that face. The moonlight seemed to heighten the effect of it. The savage Breton, holding his cap in one hand and his heavy carbine in the other, dumpy and thickset as a gnome, and bathed in that white light the shadows of which give such fantastic aspects to forms, seemed to belong more to a world of goblins than to reality. This apparition and its tone of reproach came upon Francine with the suddenness of a phantom. He turned rapidly to Madame du Gua, with whom he exchanged a few eager words, which Francine, who had somewhat forgotten the dialect of Lower Brittany, did not understand. The lady seemed to be giving him a series of orders. The short conference ended by an imperious gesture of the lady's hand pointing out to the Chouan the lovers standing a little distance apart. Before obeying, Marche-a-Terre glanced at Francine whom he seemed to pity; he wished to speak to her, and the girl was aware that his silence was compulsory. The rough and sunburnt skin of his forehead wrinkled, and his eyebrows were drawn violently together. Did he think of disobeying a renewed order to kill Mademoiselle de Verneuil? The contortion of his face made him all the more hideous to Madame du Gua, but to Francine the flash of his eye seemed almost gentle, for it taught her to feel intuitively that the violence of his savage nature would yield to her will as a woman, and that she reigned, next to God, in that rough heart.

The lovers were interrupted in their tender interview by Madame du Gua, who ran up to Marie with a cry, and pulled her away as though some danger threatened her. Her real object however, was to enable a member of the royalist committee of Alencon, whom she saw approaching them, to speak privately to the Gars.

"Beware of the girl you met at the hotel in Alencon; she will betray you," said the Chevalier de Valois, in the young man's ear; and immediately he and his little Breton horse disappeared among the bushes from which he had issued.

The firing was heavy at that moment, but the combatants did not come to close quarters.

"Adjutant," said Clef-des-Coeurs, "isn't it a sham attack, to capture our travellers and get a ransom."

"The devil is in it, but I believe you are right," replied Gerard, darting back towards the highroad.

Just then the Chouan fire slackened, for, in truth, the whole object of the skirmish was to give the chevalier an opportunity to utter his warning to the Gars. Merle, who saw the enemy disappearing across the hedges, thought best not to follow them nor to enter upon a fight that was uselessly dangerous. Gerard ordered the escort to take its former position on the road, and the convoy was again in motion without the loss of a single man. The captain offered his hand to Mademoiselle de Verneuil to replace her in the coach, for the young nobleman stood motionless, as if thunderstruck. Marie, amazed at his attitude, got into the carriage alone without accepting the politeness of the Republican; she turned her head towards her lover, saw him still motionless, and was stupefied at the sudden change which had evidently come over him. The young man slowly returned, his whole manner betraying deep disgust.

"Was I not right?" said Madame du Gua in his ear, as she led him to the coach. "We have fallen into the hands of a creature who is trafficking for your head; but since she is such a fool as to have fallen in love with you, for heaven's sake don't behave like a boy; pretend to love her at least till we reach La Vivetiere; once there —But," she thought to herself, seeing the young man take his place with a dazed air, as if bewildered, "can it be that he already loves her?"

The coach rolled on over the sandy road. To Mademoiselle de Verneuil's eyes all seemed changed. Death was gliding beside her love. Perhaps it was only fancy, but, to a woman who loves, fancy is as vivid as reality. Francine, who had clearly understood from Marche-a-Terre's glance that Mademoiselle de Verneuil's fate, over which she had commanded him to watch, was in other hands than his, looked pale and haggard, and could scarcely restrain her tears when her mistress spoke to her. To her eyes Madame du Gua's female malignancy was scarcely concealed by her treacherous smiles, and the sudden changes which her obsequious attentions to Mademoiselle de Verneuil made in her manners, voice, and expression was of a nature to frighten a watchful observer. Mademoiselle de Verneuil herself shuddered instinctively, asking herself, "Why should I fear? She is his mother." Then she trembled in every limb as the thought crossed her mind, "Is she really his mother?" An abyss suddenly opened before her, and she cast a look upon the mother and son, which finally enlightened her. "That woman loves him!" she thought. "But why has she begun these attentions after showing me such coolness? Am I lost? or—is she afraid of me?"

As for the young man, he was flushed and pale by turns; but he kept a quiet attitude and lowered his eyes to conceal the emotions which agitated him. The graceful curve of his lips was lost in their close compression, and his skin turned yellow under the struggle of his stormy thoughts. Mademoiselle de Verneuil was unable to decide whether any love for her remained in his evident anger. The road, flanked by woods at this particular point, became darker and more gloomy, and the obscurity prevented the eyes of the silent travellers from questioning each other. The sighing of the wind, the rustling of the trees, the measured step of the escort, gave that almost solemn character to the scene which quickens the pulses. Mademoiselle de Verneuil could not long try in vain to discover the reason of this change. The recollection of Corentin came to her like a flash, and reminded her suddenly of her real destiny. For the first time since the morning she reflected seriously on her position. Until then she had yielded herself up to the delight of loving, without a thought of the past or of the future. Unable to bear the agony of her mind, she sought, with the patience of love, to obtain a look from the young man's eyes, and when she did so her paleness and the quiver in her face had so penetrating an influence over him that he wavered; but the softening was momentary.

"Are you ill, mademoiselle?" he said, but his voice had no gentleness; the very question, the look, the gesture, all served to convince her that the events of this day belonged to a mirage of the soul which was fast disappearing like mists before the wind.

"Am I ill?" she replied, with a forced laugh. "I was going to ask you the same question."

"I supposed you understood each other," remarked Madame du Gua with specious kindliness.

Neither the young man nor Mademoiselle de Verneuil replied. The girl, doubly insulted, was angered at feeling her powerful beauty powerless. She knew she could discover the cause of the present situation the moment she chose to do so; but, for the first time, perhaps, a woman recoiled before a secret. Human life is sadly fertile in situations where, as a result of either too much meditation or of some catastrophe, our thoughts seem to hold to nothing; they have no substance, no point of departure, and the present has no hooks by which to hold to the past or fasten on the future. This was Mademoiselle de Verneuil's condition at the present moment. Leaning back in the carriage, she sat there like an uprooted shrub. Silent and suffering, she looked at no one, wrapped herself in her grief, and buried herself so completely in the unseen world, the refuge of the miserable, that she saw nothing around her. Crows crossed the road in the air above them cawing, but although, like all strong hearts, hers had a superstitious corner, she paid no attention to the omen. The party travelled on in silence. "Already parted?" Mademoiselle de Verneuil was saying to herself. "Yet no one about us has uttered one word. Could it be Corentin? It is not his interest to speak. Who can have come to this spot and accused me? Just loved, and already abandoned! I sow attraction, and I reap contempt. Is it my perpetual fate to see happiness and ever lose it?" Pangs hitherto unknown to her wrung her heart, for she now loved truly and for the first time. Yet she had not so wholly delivered herself to her lover that she could not take refuge from her pain in the natural pride and dignity of a young and beautiful woman. The secret of her love—a secret often kept by women under torture itself—had not escaped her lips. Presently she rose from her reclining attitude, ashamed that she had shown her passion by her silent sufferings; she shook her head with a light-hearted action, and showed a face, or rather a mask, that was gay and smiling, then she raised her voice to disguise the quiver of it.

"Where are we?" she said to Captain Merle, who kept himself at a certain distance from the carriage.

"About six miles from Fougeres, mademoiselle."

"We shall soon be there, shall we not?" she went on, to encourage a conversation in which she might show some preference for the young captain.

"A Breton mile," said Merle much delighted, "has the disadvantage of never ending; when you are at the top of one hill you see a valley and another hill. When you reach the summit of the slope we are now ascending you will see the plateau of Mont Pelerine in the distance. Let us hope the Chouans won't take their revenge there. Now, in going up hill and going down hill one doesn't make much headway. From La Pelerine you will still see—"

The young *emigre* made a movement at the name which Marie alone noticed.

"What is La Pelerine?" she asked hastily, interrupting the captain's description of Breton topography.

"It is the summit of a mountain," said Merle, "which gives its name to the Maine valley through which we shall presently pass. It separates this valley from that of Couesnon, at the end of which is the town of Fougeres, the chief town in Brittany. We had a fight there last Vendemiaire with the Gars and his brigands. We were escorting Breton conscripts, who meant to kill us sooner than leave their own land; but Hulot is a rough Christian, and he gave them—"

"Did you see the Gars?" she asked. "What sort of man is he?"

Her keen, malicious eyes never left the so-called vicomte's face.

"Well, mademoiselle," replied Merle, nettled at being always interrupted, "he is so like citizen du Gua, that if your friend did not wear the uniform of the Ecole Polytechnique I could swear it was he."

Mademoiselle de Verneuil looked fixedly at the cold, impassible young man who had scorned her, but she saw nothing in him that betrayed the slightest feeling of alarm. She warned him by a bitter smile that she had now discovered the secret so treacherously kept; then in a jesting voice, her nostrils dilating with pleasure, and her head so turned that she could watch the young man and yet see Merle, she said to the Republican: "That new leader gives a great deal of anxiety to the First Consul. He is very daring, they say; but he has the weakness of rushing headlong into adventures, especially with women."

"We are counting on that to get even with him," said the captain. "If we catch him for only an hour we shall put a bullet in his head. He'll do the same to us if he meets us, so *par pari*—"

"Oh!" said the *emigre*, "we have nothing to fear. Your soldiers cannot go as far as La Pelerine, they are tired, and, if you consent, we can all rest a short distance from here. My mother stops at La Vivetiere, the road to which turns off a few rods farther on. These ladies might like to stop there too; they must be tired with their long drive from Alencon without resting; and as mademoiselle," he added, with forced politeness, "has had the generosity to give safety as well as pleasure to our journey, perhaps she will deign to accept a supper from my mother; and I think, captain," he added, addressing Merle, "the times are not so bad but what we can find a barrel of cider for your men. The Gars can't have taken all, at least my mother thinks not—"

"Your mother?" said Mademoiselle de Verneuil, interrupting him in a tone of irony, and making no reply to his invitation.

"Does my age seem more improbable to you this evening, mademoiselle?" said Madame du Gua. "Unfortunately I was married very young, and my son was born when I was fifteen."

"Are you not mistaken, madame?—when you were thirty, perhaps."

Madame du Gua turned livid as she swallowed the sarcasm. She would have liked to revenge herself on the spot, but was forced to smile, for she was determined at any cost, even that of insult, to discover the nature of the feelings that actuated the young girl; she therefore pretended not to have understood her.

"The Chouans have never had a more cruel leader than the Gars, if we are to believe the stories about him," she said, addressing herself vaguely to both Francine and her mistress.

"Oh, as for cruel, I don't believe that," said Mademoiselle de Verneuil; "he knows how to lie, but he seems rather credulous himself. The leader of a party ought not to be the plaything of others."

"Do you know him?" asked the *emigre*, quietly.

"No," she replied, with a disdainful glance, "but I thought I did."

"Oh, mademoiselle, he's a *malin*, yes a *malin*," said Captain Merle, shaking his head and giving with an expressive gesture the peculiar meaning to the word which it had in those days but has since lost. "Those old families do sometimes send out vigorous shoots. He has just returned from a country where, they say, the *ci-devants* didn't find life too easy, and men ripen like medlars in the straw. If that fellow is really clever he can lead us a pretty dance. He has already formed companies of light infantry who oppose our troops and neutralize the efforts of the government. If we burn a royalist village he burns two of ours. He can hold an immense tract of country and force us to spread out our men at the very moment when we want them on one spot. Oh, he knows what he is about."

"He is cutting his country's throat," said Gerard in a loud voice, interrupting the captain.

"Then," said the *emigre*, "if his death would deliver the nation, why don't you catch him and shoot him?"

As he spoke he tried to look into the depths of Mademoiselle de Verneuil's soul, and one of those voiceless scenes the dramatic vividness and fleeting sagacity of which cannot be reproduced in language passed between them in a flash. Danger is always interesting. The worst criminal threatened with death excites pity. Though Mademoiselle de Verneuil was now certain that the lover who had cast her off was this very leader of the Chouans, she was not ready to verify her suspicions by giving him up; she had quite another curiosity to satisfy. She preferred to doubt or to believe as her passion led her, and she now began deliberately to play with peril. Her eyes, full of scornful meaning, bade the young chief notice the soldiers of the escort; by thus presenting to his mind triumphantly an image of his danger she made him feel that his life depended on a word from her, and her lips seemed to quiver on the verge of pronouncing it. Like an American Indian, she watched every muscle of the face of her enemy, tied, as it were, to the stake, while she brandished her tomahawk gracefully, enjoying a revenge that was still innocent, and torturing like a mistress who still loves.

"If I had a son like yours, madame," she said to Madame du Gua, who was visibly frightened, "I should wear mourning from the day when I had yielded him to danger; I should know no peace of mind."

No answer was made to this speech. She turned her head repeatedly to the escort and then suddenly to Madame du Gua, without detecting the slightest secret signal between the lady and the Gars which might have confirmed her suspicions on the nature of their intimacy, which she longed to doubt. The young chief calmly smiled, and bore without flinching the scrutiny she forced him to undergo; his attitude and the expression of his face were those of a man indifferent to danger; he even seemed to say at times: "This is your chance to avenge your wounded vanity—take it! I have no desire to lessen my contempt for you."

Mademoiselle de Verneuil began to study the young man from the vantage-ground of her position with coolness and dignity; at the bottom of her heart she admired his courage and tranquillity. Happy in discovering that the man she loved bore an ancient title (the distinctions of which please every woman), she also found pleasure in meeting him in their present situation, where, as champion of a cause ennobled by misfortune, he was fighting with all the faculties of a strong soul against a Republic that was constantly victorious. She rejoiced to see him brought face to face with danger, and still displaying the courage and bravery so powerful on a woman's heart; again and again she put him to the test, obeying perhaps the instinct which induces a woman to play with her victim as a cat plays with a mouse.

"By virtue of what law do you put the Chouans to death?" she said to Merle.

"That of the 14th of last Fructidor, which outlaws the insurgent departments and proclaims martial law," replied the Republican.

"May I ask why I have the honor to attract your eyes?" she said presently to the young chief, who was attentively watching her.

"Because of a feeling which a man of honor cannot express to any woman, no matter who she is," replied the Marquis de Montauran, in a low voice, bending down to her. "We live in times," he said aloud, "when women do the work of the executioner and wield the axe with even better effect."

She looked at de Montauran fixedly; then, delighted to be attacked by the man whose life she held in her hands, she said in a low voice, smiling softly: "Your head is a very poor one; the executioner does not want it; I shall keep it myself."

The marquis looked at the inexplicable girl, whose love had overcome all, even insult, and who now avenged herself by forgiving that which women are said never to forgive. His eyes grew less stern, less cold; a look of sadness came upon his face. His love was stronger than he suspected. Mademoiselle de Verneuil, satisfied with these faint signs of a desired reconciliation, glanced at him tenderly, with a smile that was like a kiss; then she leaned back once more in the carriage, determined not to risk the future of this happy drama, believing she had assured it with her smile. She was so beautiful! She knew so well how to conquer all obstacles to love! She was so accustomed to take all risks and push on at all hazards! She loved the unexpected, and the tumults of life—why should she fear?

Before long the carriage, under the young chief's directions, left the highway and took a road cut between banks planted with apple-trees, more like a ditch than a roadway, which led to La Vivetiere. The carriage now advanced rapidly, leaving the escort to follow slowly towards the manor-house, the gray roofs of which appeared and disappeared among the trees. Some of the men lingered on the way to knock the stiff clay of the road-bed from their shoes.

"This is devilishly like the road to Paradise," remarked Beau-Pied.

Thanks to the impatience of the postilion, Mademoiselle de Verneuil soon saw the chateau of La Vivetiere. This house, standing at the end of a sort of promontory, was protected and surrounded by two deep lakelets, and could be reached only by a narrow causeway. That part of the little peninsula on which the house and gardens were placed was still further protected by a moat filled with water from the two lakes which it connected. The house really stood on an island that was well-nigh impregnable,—an invaluable retreat for a chieftain, who could be surprised there only by treachery.

Mademoiselle de Verneuil put her head out of the carriage as she heard the rusty hinges of the great gates open to give entrance to an arched portal which had been much injured during the late war. The gloomy colors of the scene which met her eyes almost extinguished the thoughts of love and coquetry in which she had been indulging. The carriage entered a large courtyard that was nearly square, bordered on each side by the steep banks of the lakelets. Those sterile shores, washed by water, which was covered with large green patches, had no other ornament than aquatic trees devoid of foliage, the twisted trunks and hoary heads of which, rising from the reeds and rushes, gave them a certain grotesque likeness to gigantic marmosets. These ugly growths seemed to waken and talk to each other when the frogs deserted them with much croaking, and the water-fowl, startled by the sound of the wheels, flew low upon the surface of the pools. The courtyard, full of rank and seeded grasses, reeds, and shrubs, either dwarf or parasite, excluded all impression of order or of splendor. The house appeared to have been long abandoned. The roof seemed to bend beneath the weight of the various vegetations which grew upon it. The walls, though built of the smooth, slaty stone which abounds in that region, showed many rifts and chinks where ivy had fastened its rootlets. Two main buildings, joined at the angle by a tall tower which faced the lake, formed the whole of the chateau, the doors and swinging, rotten shutters, rusty balustrades, and broken windows of which seemed ready to fall at the first tempest. The north wind whistled through these ruins, to which the moon, with her indefinite light, gave the character and outline of a great spectre. But the colors of those gray-blue granites, mingling with the black and tawny schists, must have been seen in order to understand how vividly a spectral image was suggested by the empty and gloomy carcass of the building. Its disjointed stones and paneless windows, the battered tower and broken roofs gave it the aspect of a skeleton; the birds of prey which flew from it, shrieking, added another feature to this vague resemblance. A few tall pine-trees standing behind the house waved their dark foliage above the roof, and several yews cut into formal shapes at the angles of the building, festooned it gloomily like the ornaments on a hearse. The style of the doors, the coarseness of the decorations, the want of harmony in the architecture, were all characteristic of the feudal manors of which Brittany was proud; perhaps justly proud, for they maintained upon that Gaelic ground a species of monumental history of the nebulous period which preceded the establishment of the French monarchy.

Mademoiselle de Verneuil, to whose imagination the word "chateau" brought none but its conventional ideas, was affected by the funereal aspect of the scene. She sprang from the carriage and stood apart gazing at in terror, and debating within herself what action she ought to take. Francine heard Madame du Gua give a sigh of relief as she felt herself in safety beyond reach of the Blues; an exclamation escaped her when the gates were closed, and she saw the carriage and its occupants within the walls of this natural fortress.

The Marquis de Montauran turned hastily to Mademoiselle de Verneuil, divining the thoughts that crowded in her mind.

"This chateau," he said, rather sadly, "was ruined by the war, just as my plans for our happiness have been ruined by you."

"How ruined?" she asked in surprise.

"Are you indeed 'beautiful, brilliant, and of noble birth'?" he asked ironically, repeating the words she had herself used in their former conversation.

"Who has told you to the contrary?"

"Friends, in whom I put faith; who care for my safety and are on the watch against treachery."

"Treachery!" she exclaimed, in a sarcastic tone. "Have you forgotten Hulot and Alencon already? You have no memory,—a dangerous defect in the leader of a party. But if friends," she added, with increased sarcasm, "are so all-powerful in your heart, keep your friends. Nothing is comparable to the joys of friendship. Adieu; neither I nor the soldiers of the Republic will stop here."

She turned towards the gateway with a look of wounded pride and scorn, and her motions as she did so displayed a dignity and also a despair which changed in an instant the thoughts of the young man; he felt that the cost of relinquishing his desires was too great, and he gave himself up deliberately to imprudence and credulity. He loved; and the lovers had no desire now to quarrel with each other.

"Say but one word and I will believe you," he said, in a supplicating voice.

"One word?" she answered, closing her lips tightly, "not a single word; not even a gesture."

"At least, be angry with me," he entreated, trying to take the hand she withheld from him,—"that is, if you dare to be angry with the leader of the rebels, who is now as sad and distrustful as he was lately happy and confiding."

Marie gave him a look that was far from angry, and he added: "You have my secret, but I have not yours."

The alabaster brow appeared to darken at these words; she cast a look of annoyance on the young chieftain, and answered, hastily: "Tell you my secret? Never!"

In love every word, every glance has the eloquence of the moment; but on this occasion Mademoiselle de Verneuil's exclamation revealed nothing, and, clever as Montauran might be, its secret was impenetrable to him, though the tones of her voice betrayed some extraordinary and unusual emotion which piqued his curiosity.

"You have a singular way of dispelling suspicion," he said.

"Do you still suspect me?" she replied, looking him in the eye, as if to say, "What rights have you over me?"

"Mademoiselle," said the young man, in a voice that was submissive and yet firm, "the authority you exercise over Republican troops, this escort—"

"Ah, that reminds me! My escort and I," she asked, in a slightly satirical tone, "your protectors, in short,—will they be safe here?"

"Yes, on the word of a gentleman. Whoever you be, you and your party have nothing to fear in my house."

The promise was made with so loyal and generous an air and manner that Mademoiselle de Verneuil felt absolutely secure as to the safety of the Republican soldiers. She was about to speak when Madame du Gua's approach silenced her. That lady had either overheard or guessed part of their conversation, and was filled with anxiety at no longer perceiving any signs of animosity between them. As soon as the marquis caught sight of her, he offered his hand to Mademoiselle de Verneuil and led her hastily towards the house, as if to escape an undesired companion.

"I am in their way," thought Madame du Gua, remaining where she was. She watched the lovers walking slowly towards the portico, where they stopped, as if satisfied to have placed some distance between themselves and her. "Yes, yes, I am in their way," she repeated, speaking to herself; "but before long that creature will not be in mine; the lake, God willing, shall have her. I'll help him keep his word as a gentleman; once under the water, she has nothing to fear, — what can be safer than that?"

She was looking fixedly at the still mirror of the little lake to the right when suddenly she heard a rustling among the rushes and saw in the moonlight the face of Marche-a-Terre rising behind the gnarled trunk of an old willow. None but those who knew the Chouan well could have distinguished him from the tangle of branches of which he seemed a part. Madame du Gua looked about her with some distrust; she saw the postilion leading his horses to a stable in the wing of the chateau which was opposite to the bank where Marche-a-Terre was hiding; Francine, with her back to her, was going towards the two lovers, who at that moment had forgotten the whole earth. Madame du Gua, with a finger on her lip to demand silence, walked towards the Chouan, who guessed rather than heard her question, "How many of you are here?"

"Eighty-seven."

"They are sixty-five; I counted them."

"Good," said the savage, with sullen satisfaction.

Attentive to all Francine's movements, the Chouan disappeared behind the willow, as he saw her turn to look for the enemy over whom she was keeping an instinctive watch.

Six or eight persons, attracted by the noise of the carriage-wheels, came out on the portico, shouting: "It is the Gars! it is he; here he is!" On this several other men ran out, and their coming interrupted the lovers. The Marquis de Montauran went hastily up to them, making an imperative gesture for silence, and pointing to the farther end of the causeway, where the Republican escort was just appearing. At the sight of the well-known blue uniforms with red facings, and the glittering bayonets, the amazed conspirators called out hastily, "You have surely not betrayed us?"

"If I had, I should not warn you," said the marquis, smiling bitterly. "Those Blues," he added, after a pause, "are the escort of this young lady, whose generosity has delivered us, almost miraculously, from a danger we were in at Alencon. I will tell you about it later. Mademoiselle and her escort are here in safety, on my word as a gentleman, and we must all receive them as friends."

Madame du Gua and Francine were now on the portico; the marquis offered his hand to Mademoiselle de Verneuil, the group of gentlemen parted in two lines to allow them to pass, endeavoring, as they did so, to catch sight of the young lady's features; for Madame du Gua, who was following behind, excited their curiosity by secret signs.

Mademoiselle de Verneuil saw, with surprise, that a large table was set in the first hall, for about twenty guests. The dining-room opened into a vast salon, where the whole party were presently assembled. These rooms were in keeping with the dilapidated appearance of the outside of the house. The walnut panels, polished by age, but rough and coarse in design and badly executed, were loose in their places and ready to fall. Their dingy color added to the gloom of these apartments, which were barren of curtains and mirrors; a few venerable bits of furniture in the last stages of decay alone remained, and harmonized with the general destruction. Marie noticed maps and plans stretched out upon long tables, and in the corners of the room a quantity of weapons and stacked carbines. These things bore witness, though she did not know it, to an important conference between the leaders of the Vendeans and those of the Chouans.

The marquis led Mademoiselle de Verneuil to a large and worm-eaten armchair placed beside the fireplace; Francine followed and stood behind her mistress, leaning on the back of that ancient bit of furniture.

"You will allow me for a moment to play the part of master of the house," he said, leaving the two women and mingling with the groups of his other guests.

Francine saw the gentlemen hasten, after a few words from Montauran, to hide their weapons, maps, and whatever else might arouse the suspicions of the Republican officers. Some took off their broad leather belts containing pistols and hunting-knives. The marquis requested them to show the utmost prudence, and went himself to see to the reception of the troublesome guests whom fate had bestowed upon him.

Mademoiselle de Verneuil, who had raised her feet to the fire and was now warming them, did not turn her head as Montauran left the room, thus disappointing those present, who were anxious to see her. Francine alone saw the change produced upon the company by the departure of the young chief. The gentlemen gathered hastily round Madame du Gua, and during a conversation carried on in an undertone between them, they all turned several times to look curiously at the stranger.

"You know Montauran," Madame du Gua said to them; "he has fallen in love with that worthless girl, and, as you can easily understand, he thinks all my warnings selfish. Our friends in Paris, Messieurs de Valois and d'Esgrignon, have warned him of a trap set for him by throwing some such creature at his head; but in spite of this he allows himself to be fooled by the first woman he meets,—a girl who, if my information is correct, has stolen a great name only to disgrace it."

The speaker, in whom our readers have already recognized the lady who instigated the attack on the "turgotine," may be allowed to keep the name which she used to escape the dangers that threatened her in Alencon. The publication of her real name would only mortify a noble family already deeply afflicted at the misconduct of this woman; whose history, by the bye, has already been given on another scene.

The curiosity manifested by the company of men soon became impertinent and almost hostile. A few harsh words reached Francine's ear, and after a word said to her mistress the girl retreated into the embrasure of a window. Marie rose, turned towards the insolent group, and gave them a look full of dignity and even disdain. Her beauty, the elegance of her manners, and her pride changed the behavior of her enemies, and won her the flattering murmur which escaped their lips. Two or three men, whose outward appearance seemed to denote the habits of polite society and the gallantry acquired in courts, came towards her; but her propriety of demeanor forced them to respect her, and none dared speak to her;

so that, instead of being herself arraigned by the company, it was she who appeared to judge of them. These chiefs of a war undertaken for God and the king bore very little resemblance to the portraits her fancy had drawn of them. The struggle, really great in itself, shrank to mean proportions as she observed these provincial noblemen, all, with one or two vigorous exceptions, devoid of significance and virility. Having made to herself a poem of such heroes, Marie suddenly awakened to the truth. Their faces expressed to her eyes more a love of scheming than a love of glory; self-interest had evidently put arms into their hands. Still, it must be said that these men did become heroic when brought into action. The loss of her illusions made Mademoiselle de Verneuil unjust, and prevented her from recognizing the real devotion which rendered several of these men remarkable. It is true that most of those now present were commonplace. A few original and marked faces appeared among them, but even these were belittled by the artificiality and the etiquette of aristocracy. If Marie generously granted intellect and perception to the latter, she also discerned in them a total absence of the simplicity, the grandeur, to which she had been accustomed among the triumphant men of the Republic. This nocturnal assemblage in the old ruined castle made her smile; the scene seemed symbolic of the monarchy. But the thought came to her with delight that the marquis at least played a noble part among these men, whose only remaining merit in her eyes was devotion to a lost cause. She pictured her lover's face upon the background of this company, rejoicing to see it stand forth among those paltry and puny figures who were but the instruments of his great designs.

The footsteps of the marquis were heard in the adjoining room. Instantly the company separated into little groups and the whisperings ceased. Like schoolboys who have plotted mischief in the master's absence, they hurriedly became silent and orderly. Montauran entered. Marie had the happiness of admiring him among his fellows, of whom he was the youngest, the handsomest, and the chief. Like a king in his court, he went from group to group, distributing looks and nods and words of encouragement or warning, with pressure of the hands and smiles; doing his duty as leader of a party with a grace and self-possession hardly to be expected in the young man whom Marie had so lately accused of heedlessness.

The presence of the marquis put an end to the open curiosity bestowed on Mademoiselle de Verneuil, but Madame du Gua's scandalous suggestions bore fruit. The Baron du Guenic, familiarly called "l'Intime," who by rank and name had the best right among those present to treat Montauran familiarly, took the young leader by the arm and led him apart.

"My dear marquis," he said; "we are much disturbed at seeing you on the point of committing an amazing folly."

"What do you mean by that?"

"Do you know where that girl comes from, who she is, and what her schemes about you are?"

"Don't trouble yourself, my dear Intime; between you and me my fancy for her will be over to-morrow."

"Yes; but suppose that creature betrays you to-night?"

"I'll answer that when you tell me why she has not done it already," said Montauran, assuming with a laugh an air of conceit. "My dear fellow, look at that charming girl, watch her manners, and dare to tell me she is not a woman of distinction. If she gave you a few favorable looks wouldn't you feel at the bottom of your soul a respect for her? A certain lady has prejudiced you. I will tell you this: if she were the lost creature our friends are trying to make her out, I would, after what she and I have said to each other, kill her myself."

"Do you suppose," said Madame du Gua, joining them, "that Fouche is fool enough to send you a common prostitute out of the streets? He has provided seductions according to your deserts. You may choose to be blind, but your friends are keeping their eyes open to protect you."

"Madame," replied the Gars, his eyes flashing with anger, "be warned; take no steps against that lady, nor against her escort; if you do, nothing shall save you from my vengeance. I choose that Mademoiselle de Verneuil is to be treated with the utmost respect, and as a lady belonging to my family. We are, I believe, related to the de Verneuils."

The opposition the marquis was made to feel produced the usual effect of such obstacles on all young men. Though he had, apparently, treated Mademoiselle de Verneuil rather lightly, and left it to be supposed that his passion for her was a mere caprice, he now, from a feeling of pride, made immense strides in his relation to her. By openly protecting her, his honor became concerned in compelling respect to her person; and he went from group to group assuring his friends, in the tone of a man whom it was dangerous to contradict, that the lady was really Mademoiselle de Verneuil. The doubts and gossip ceased at once. As soon as Montauran felt that harmony was restored and anxiety allayed, he returned to his mistress eagerly, saying in a low voice: —

"Those mischievous people have robbed me of an hour's happiness."

"I am glad you have come back to me," she said, smiling. "I warn you that I am inquisitive; therefore you must not get tired of my questions. Tell me, in the first place, who is that worthy in a green cloth jacket?"

"That is the famous Major Brigaut, a man from the Marais, a comrade of the late Mercier, called La Vendee."

"And that fat priest with the red face to whom he is talking at this moment about me?" she went on.

"Do you want to know what they are saying?"

"Do I want to know it? What a useless question!"

"But I could not tell it without offending you."

"If you allow me to be insulted in your house without avenging me, marquis, adieu!" she said. "I will not stay another moment. I have some qualms already about deceiving these poor Republicans, loyal and confiding as they are!"

She made a few hasty steps; the marquis followed her.

"Dear Marie, listen to me. On my honor, I have silenced their evil speaking, without knowing whether it was false or true. But, placed as I am, if friends whom we have in all the ministries in Paris warn me to beware of every woman I meet, and assure me that Fouche has employed against me a Judith of the streets, it is not unnatural that my best friends here should think you too beautiful to be an honest woman."

As he spoke the marquis plunged a glance into Mademoiselle de Verneuil's eyes. She colored, and was unable to restrain her tears.

"I deserve these insults," she said. "I wish you really thought me that despicable creature and still loved me; then, indeed, I could no longer doubt you. I believed in you when you were deceiving me, and you will not believe me now when I am true. Let us make an end of this, monsieur," she said, frowning, but turning pale as death, —"adieu!"

She rushed towards the dining-room with a movement of despair.

"Marie, my life is yours," said the young marquis in her ear.

She stopped short and looked at him.

"No, no," she said, "I will be generous. Farewell. In coming with you here I did not think of my past nor of your future—I was beside myself."

"You cannot mean that you will leave me now when I offer you my life?"

"You offer it in a moment of passion—of desire."

"I offer it without regret, and forever," he replied.

She returned to the room they had left. Hiding his emotions the marquis continued the conversation.

"That fat priest whose name you asked is the Abbe Gudin, a Jesuit, obstinate enough—perhaps I ought to say devoted enough,—to remain in France in spite of the decree of 1793, which banished his order. He is the firebrand of the war in these regions and a propagandist of the religious association called the Sacre-Coeur. Trained to use religion as an instrument, he persuades his followers that if they are killed they will be brought to life again, and he knows how to rouse their fanaticism by shrewd sermons. You see, it is necessary to work upon every man's selfish interests to attain a great end. That is the secret of all political success."

"And that vigorous, muscular old man, with the repulsive face, who is he? I mean the one in the ragged gown of a barrister."

"Barrister! he aspires to be considered a brigadier-general. Did you never hear of de Longuy?"

"Is that he!" exclaimed Mademoiselle de Verneuil, horrified. "You employ such men as that?"

"Hush! he'll hear you. Do you see that other man in malignant conversation with Madame du Gua?"

"The one in black who looks like a judge?"

"That is one of our go-betweens, La Billardiere, son of a councillor to the Breton Parliament, whose real name is something like Flamet; he is in close correspondence with the princes."

"And his neighbor? the one who is just putting up his white clay pipe, and uses all the fingers of his right hand to snap the box, like a countryman."

"By Jove, you are right; he was game-keeper to the deceased husband of that lady, and now commands one of the companies I send against the Republican militia. He and Marche-a-Terre are the two most conscientious vassals the king has here."

"But she—who is she?"

"Charette's last mistress," replied the marquis. "She wields great influence over all these people."

"Is she faithful to his memory?"

For all answer the marquis gave a dubious smile.

"Do you think well of her?"

"You are very inquisitive."

"She is my enemy because she can no longer be my rival," said Mademoiselle de Verneuil, laughing. "I forgive her her past errors if she forgives mine. Who is that officer with the long moustache?"

"Permit me not to name him; he wants to get rid of the First Consul by assassination. Whether he succeeds or not you will hear of him. He is certain to become famous."

"And you have come here to command such men as these!" she exclaimed in horror. "Are *they* they king's defenders? Where are the gentlemen and the great lords?"

"Where?" said the marquis, coolly, "they are in all the courts of Europe. Who else should win over kings and cabinets and armies to serve the Bourbon cause and hurl them at that Republic which threatens monarchies and social order with death and destruction?"

"Ah!" she said, with generous emotion, "be to me henceforth the source from which I draw the ideas I must still acquire about your cause—I consent. But let me still remember that you are the only noble who does his duty in fighting France with Frenchmen, without the help of foreigners. I am a woman; I feel that if my child struck me in anger I could forgive him; but if he saw me beaten by a stranger, and consented to it, I should regard him as a monster."

"You shall remain a Republican," said the marquis, in the ardor produced by the generous words which confirmed his hopes.

"Republican! no, I am that no longer. I could not now respect you if you submitted to the First Consul," she replied. "But neither do I like to see you at the head of men who are pillaging a corner of France, instead of making war against the whole Republic. For whom are you fighting? What do you expect of a king restored to his throne by your efforts? A woman did that great thing once, and the liberated king allowed her to be burned. Such men are the anointed of the Lord, and there is danger in meddling with sacred things. Let God take care of his own, and place, displace, and replace them on their purple seats. But if you have counted the cost, and seen the poor return that will come to you, you are tenfold greater in my eyes than I thought you—"

"Ah! you are bewitching. Don't attempt to indoctrinate my followers, or I shall be left without a man."

"If you would let me convert you, only you," she said, "we might live happily a thousand leagues away from all this."

"These men whom you seem to despise," said the marquis, in a graver tone, "will know how to die when the struggle comes, and all their misdeeds will be forgotten. Besides, if my efforts are crowned with some success, the laurel leaves of victory will hide all."

"I see no one but you who is risking anything."

"You are mistaken; I am not the only one," he replied, with true modesty. "See, over there, the new leaders from La Vendee. The first, whom you must have heard of as 'Le Grand Jacques,' is the Comte de Fontain; the other is La Billardiere, whom I mentioned to you just now."

"Have you forgotten Quiberon, where La Billardiere played so equivocal a part?" she said, struck by a sudden recollection.

"La Billardiere took a great deal upon himself. Serving princes is far from lying on a bed of roses."

"Ah! you make me shudder!" cried Marie. "Marquis," she continued, in a tone which seemed to indicate some mysterious personal reticence, "a single instant suffices to destroy illusions and to betray secrets on which the life and happiness of many may depend—" she stopped, as though she feared she had said too much; then she added, in another tone, "I wish I could be sure that those Republican soldiers were in safety."

"I will be prudent," he said, smiling to disguise his emotion; "but say no more about your soldiers; have I not answered for their safety on my word as a gentleman?"

"And after all," she said, "what right have I to dictate to you? Be my master henceforth. Did I not tell you it would drive me to despair to rule a slave?"

"Monsieur le marquis," said Major Brigaut, respectfully, interrupting the conversation, "how long are the Blues to remain here?"

"They will leave as soon as they are rested," said Marie.

The marquis looked about the room and noticed the agitation of those present. He left Mademoiselle de Verneuil, and his place beside her was taken at once by Madame du Gua, whose smiling and treacherous face was in no way disconcerted by the young chief's bitter smile. Just then Francine, standing by the window, gave a stifled cry. Marie, noticing with amazement that the girl left the room, looked at Madame du Gua, and her surprise increased as she saw the pallor on the face of her enemy. Anxious to discover the meaning of Francine's abrupt departure, she went to the window, where Madame du Gua followed her, no doubt to guard against any suspicions which might arise in her mind. They returned together to the chimney, after each had cast a look upon the shore and the lake,—Marie without seeing anything that could have caused Francine's flight, Madame du Gua seeing that which satisfied her she was being obeyed.

The lake, at the edge of which Marche-a-Terre had shown his head, where Madame du Gua had seen him, joined the moat in misty curves, sometimes broad as ponds, in other places narrow as the artificial streamlets of a park. The steep bank, washed by its waters, lay a few rods from the window. Francine, watching on the surface of the water the black lines thrown by the willows, noticed, carelessly at first, the uniform trend of their branches, caused by a light breeze then prevailing. Suddenly she thought she saw against the glassy surface a figure moving with the spontaneous and irregular motion of life. The form, vague as it was, seemed to her that of a man. At first she attributed what she saw to the play of the moonlight upon the foliage, but presently a second head appeared, then several others in the distance. The shrubs upon the bank were bent and then violently straightened, and Francine saw the long hedge undulating like one of those great Indian serpents of fabulous size and shape. Here and there, among the gorse and taller brambles, points of light could be seen to come and go. The girl's attention redoubled, and she thought she recognized the foremost of the dusky figures; indistinct as its outlines were, the beating of her heart convinced her it was no other than her lover, Marche-a-Terre. Eager to know if this mysterious approach meant treachery, she ran to the courtyard. When she reached the middle of its grass plot she looked alternately at the two wings of the building and along the steep shores, without discovering, on the inhabited side of the house, any sign of this silent approach. She listened attentively and heard a slight rustling, like that which might be made by the footfalls of some wild animal in the silence of the forest. She quivered, but did not tremble. Though young and innocent, her anxious curiosity suggested a ruse. She saw the coach and slipped into it, putting out her head to listen, with the caution of a hare giving ear to the sound of the distant hunters. She saw Pille-Miche come out of the stable, accompanied by two peasants, all three carrying bales of straw; these they spread on the ground in a way to form a long bed of litter before the inhabited wing of the house, parallel with the bank, bordered by dwarf trees.

"You're spreading straw as if you thought they'd sleep here! Enough, Pille-Miche, enough!" said a low, gruff voice, which Francine recognized.

"And won't they sleep here?" returned Pille-Miche with a laugh. "I'm afraid the Gars will be angry!" he added, too low for Francine to hear.

"Well, let him," said Marche-a-Terre, in the same tone, "we shall have killed the Blues anyway. Here's that coach, which you and I had better put up."

Pille-Miche pulled the carriage by the pole and Marche-a-Terre pushed it by one of the wheels with such force that Francine was in the barn and about to be locked up before she had time to reflect on her situation. Pille-Miche went out to fetch the barrel of cider, which the marquis had ordered for the escort; and Marche-a-Terre was passing along the side of the coach, to leave the barn and close the door, when he was stopped by a hand which caught and held the long hair of his goatskin. He recognized a pair of eyes the gentleness of which exercised a power of magnetism over him, and he stood stock-still for a moment under their spell. Francine sprang from the carriage, and said, in the nervous tone of an excited woman: "Pierre, what news did you give to that lady and her son on the road? What is going on here? Why are you hiding? I must know all."

These words brought a look on the Chouan's face which Francine had never seen there before. The Breton led his innocent mistress to the door; there he turned her towards the blanching light of the moon, and answered, as he looked in her face with terrifying eyes: "Yes, by my damnation, Francine, I will tell you, but not until you have sworn on these beads (and he pulled an old chaplet from beneath his goatskin) —on this relic, which *you know well*," he continued, "to answer me truly one question."

Francine colored as she saw the chaplet, which was no doubt a token of their love. "It was on that," he added, much agitated, "that you swore—"

He did not finish the sentence. The young girl placed her hand on the lips of her savage lover and silenced him.

"Need I swear?" she said.

He took his mistress gently by the hand, looked at her for a moment and said: "Is the lady you are with really Mademoiselle de Verneuil?"

Francine stood with hanging arms, her eyelids lowered, her head bowed, pale and speechless.

"She is a strumpet!" cried Marche-a-Terre, in a terrifying voice.

At the word the pretty hand once more covered his lips, but this time he sprang back violently. The girl no longer saw a lover; he had turned to a wild beast in all the fury of its nature. His eyebrows were drawn together, his lips drew apart, and he showed his teeth like a dog which defends its master.

"I left you pure, and I find you muck. Ha! why did I ever leave you! You are here to betray us; to deliver up the Gars!"

These sentences sounded more like roars than words. Though Francine was frightened, she raised her angelic eyes at this last accusation and answered calmly, as she looked into his savage face: "I will pledge my eternal safety that that is false. That's an idea of the lady you are serving."

He lowered his head; then she took his hand and nestling to him with a pretty movement said: "Pierre, what is all this to you and me? I don't know what you understand about it, but I can't make it out. Recollect one thing: that noble and beautiful young lady has been my benefactress; she is also yours—we live together like two sisters. No harm must ever come to her where we are, you and I—in our lifetime at least. Swear it! I trust no one here but you."

"I don't command here," said the Chouan, in a surly tone.

His face darkened. She caught his long ears and twisted them gently as if playing with a cat.

"At least," she said, seeing that he looked less stern, "promise me to use all the power you have to protect our benefactress."

He shook his head as if he doubted of success, and the motion made her tremble. At this critical moment the escort was entering the courtyard. The tread of the soldiers and the rattle of their weapons awoke the echoes and seemed to put an end to Marche-a-Terre's indecision.

"Perhaps I can save her," he said, "if you make her stay in the house. And mind," he added, "whatever happens, you must stay with her and keep silence; if not, no safety."

"I promise it," she replied in terror.

"Very good; then go in—go in at once, and hide your fears from every one, even your mistress."

"Yes."

She pressed his hand; he stood for a moment watching her with an almost paternal air as she ran with the lightness of a bird up the portico; then he slipped behind the bushes, like an actor darting behind the scenes as the curtain rises on a tragedy.

"Do you know, Merle," said Gerard as they reached the chateau, "that this place looks to me like a mousetrap?"

"So I think," said the captain, anxiously.

The two officers hastened to post sentinels to guard the gate and the causeway; then they examined with great distrust the precipitous banks of the lakes and the surroundings of the chateau.

"Pooh!" said Merle, "we must do one of two things: either trust ourselves in this barrack with perfect confidence, or else not enter it at all."

"Come, let's go in," replied Gerard.

The soldiers, released at the word of command, hastened to stack their muskets in conical sheaves, and to form a sort of line before the litter of straw, in the middle of which was the promised barrel of cider. They then divided into groups, to whom two peasants began to distribute butter and rye-bread. The marquis appeared in the portico to welcome the officers and take them to the salon. As Gerard went up the steps he looked at both ends of the portico, where some venerable larches spread their black branches; and he called up Clef-des-Coeurs and Beau-Pied.

"You will each reconnoitre the gardens and search the bushes, and post a sentry before your line."

"May we light our fire before starting, adjutant?" asked Clef-des-Coeurs.

Gerard nodded.

"There! you see, Clef-des-Coeurs," said Beau-Pied, "the adjutant's wrong to run himself into this wasp's-nest. If Hulot was in command we shouldn't be cornered here—in a saucepan!"

"What a stupid you are!" replied Clef-des-Coeurs, "haven't you guessed, you knave of tricks, that this is the home of the beauty our jovial Merle has been whistling round? He'll marry her to a certainty—that's as clear as a well-rubbed bayonet. A woman like that will do honor to the brigade."

"True for you," replied Beau-Pied, "and you may add that she gives pretty good cider—but I can't drink it in peace till I know what's behind those devilish hedges. I always remember poor Larose and Vieux-Chapeau rolling down the ditch at La Pelerine. I shall recollect Larose's queue to the end of my days; it went hammering down like the knocker of a front door."

"Beau-Pied, my friend; you have too much imagination for a soldier; you ought to be making songs at the national Institute."

"If I've too much imagination," retorted Beau-Pied, "you haven't any; it will take you some time to get your degree as consul."

A general laugh put an end to the discussion, for Clef-des-Coeurs found no suitable reply in his pouch with which to floor his adversary.

"Come and make our rounds; I'll go to the right," said Beau-Pied.

"Very good, I'll take the left," replied his comrade. "But stop one minute, I must have a glass of cider; my throat is glued together like the oiled-silk of Hulot's best hat."

The left bank of the gardens, which Clef-des-Coeurs thus delayed searching at once, was, unhappily, the dangerous slope where Francine had seen the moving line of men. All things go by chance in war.

As Gerard entered the salon and bowed to the company he cast a penetrating eye on the men who were present. Suspicions came forcibly to his mind, and he went at once to Mademoiselle de Verneuil and said in a low voice: "I think you had better leave this place immediately. We are not safe here."

"What can you fear while I am with you?" she answered, laughing. "You are safer here than you would be at Mayenne."

A woman answers for her lover in good faith. The two officers were reassured. The party now moved into the dining-room after some discussion about a guest, apparently of some importance, who had not appeared. Mademoiselle de Verneuil was able, thanks to the silence which always reigns at the beginning of a meal, to give some attention to the character of the assemblage, which was curious enough under existing circumstances. One thing struck her with surprise. The Republican officers seemed superior to the rest of the assembly by reason of their dignified appearance. Their long hair tied behind in a queue drew lines beside their foreheads which gave, in those days, an expression of great candor and nobleness to young heads. Their threadbare blue uniforms with the shabby red facings, even their epaulets flung back behind their shoulders (a sign throughout the army, even among the leaders, of a lack of overcoats), —all these things brought the two Republican officers into strong relief against the men who surrounded them.

"Oh, they are the Nation, and that means liberty!" thought Marie; then, with a glance at the royalists, she added, "on the other side is a man, a king, and privileges." She could not refrain from admiring Merle, so thoroughly did that gay soldier respond to the ideas she had formed of the French trooper who hums a tune when the balls are whistling, and jests when a comrade falls. Gerard was more imposing. Grave and self-possessed, he seemed to have one of those truly Republican spirits which, in the days of which we write, crowded the French armies, and gave them, by means of these noble individual devotions, an energy which they had never before possessed. "That is one of my men with great ideals," thought Mademoiselle de Verneuil. "Relying on the present, which they rule, they destroy the past for the benefit of the future."

The thought saddened her because she could not apply it to her lover; towards whom she now turned, to discard by a different admiration, these beliefs in the Republic she was already beginning to dislike. Looking at the marquis, surrounded by men who were bold enough, fanatical enough, and sufficiently long-headed as to the future to give battle to a victorious Republic in the hope of restoring a dead monarchy, a proscribed religion, fugitive princes, and lost privileges, "He," thought she, "has no less an aim than the others; clinging to those fragments, he wants to make a future from the past." Her mind, thus grasped by conflicting images, hesitated between the new and the old wrecks. Her conscience told her that the one was fighting for a man, the other for a country; but she had now reached, through her feelings, the point to which reason will also bring us, namely: to a recognition that the king *is* the Nation.

The steps of a man echoed in the adjoining room, and the marquis rose from the table to greet him. He proved to be the expected guest, and seeing the assembled company he was about to speak, when the Gars made him a hasty sign, which he concealed from the Republicans, to take his place and say nothing. The more the two officers analyzed the faces about them, the more their suspicions increased. The clerical dress of the Abbe Gudin and the singularity of the Chouan garments were so many warnings to them; they redoubled their watchfulness, and soon discovered many discrepancies between the manners of the guests and the topics of their conversation. The republicanism of some was quite as exaggerated as the aristocratic bearing of others was unmistakable. Certain glances which they detected between the marquis and his guests, certain words of double meaning imprudently uttered, but above all the fringe of beard which was round the necks of several of the men and was very ill-concealed by their cravats, brought the officers at last to a full conviction of the truth, which flashed upon their minds at the same instant. They gave each other one look, for Madame du Gua had cleverly separated them and they could only impart their thoughts by their eyes. Such a situation demanded the utmost caution. They did not know whether they and their men were masters of the situation, or whether they had been drawn into a trap, or whether Mademoiselle de Verneuil was the dupe or the accomplice of this inexplicable state of things. But an unforeseen event precipitated a crisis before they had fully recognized the gravity of their situation.

The new guest was one of those solid men who are square at the base and square at the shoulders, with ruddy skins; men who lean backward when they walk, seeming to displace much atmosphere about them, and who appear to think that more than one glance of the eye is needful to take them in. Notwithstanding his rank, he had taken life as a joke from which he was to get as much amusement as possible; and yet, although he knelt at his own shrine only, he was kind, polite, and witty, after the fashion of those noblemen who, having finished their training at court, return to live on their estates, and never suspect that they have, at the end of twenty years, grown rusty. Men of this type fail in tact with imperturbable coolness, talk folly wittily, distrust good with extreme shrewdness, and take incredible pains to fall into traps.

When, by a play of his knife and fork which proclaimed him a good feeder, he had made up for lost time, he began to look round on the company. His astonishment was great when he observed the two Republican officers, and he questioned Madame du Gua with a look, while she, for all answer, showed him Mademoiselle de Verneuil in the same way. When he saw the siren whose demeanor had silenced the suspicions Madame du Gua had excited among the guests, the face of the stout stranger broke into one of those insolent, ironical smiles which contain a whole history of scandal. He leaned to his next neighbor and whispered a few words, which went from ear to ear and lip to lip, passing Marie and the two officers, until they reached the heart of one whom they struck to death. The leaders of the Vendeans and the Chouans assembled round that table looked at the Marquis de Montauran with cruel curiosity. The eyes of Madame du Gua, flashing with joy, turned from the marquis to Mademoiselle de Verneuil, who was speechless with surprise. The Republican officers, uneasy in mind, questioned each other's thoughts as they awaited the result of this extraordinary scene. In a moment the forks remained inactive in every hand, silence reigned, and every eye was turned to the Gars. A frightful anger showed upon his face, which turned waxen in tone. He leaned towards the guest from whom the rocket had started and said, in a voice that seemed muffled in crape, "Death of my soul! count, is that true?"

"On my honor," said the count, bowing gravely.

The marquis lowered his eyes for a moment, then he raised them and looked fixedly at Marie, who, watchful of his struggle, knew that look to be her death-warrant.

"I would give my life," he said in a low voice, "for revenge on the spot."

Madame du Gua understood the words from the mere movement of the young man's lips, and she smiled upon him as we smile at a friend whose regrets are about to cease. The scorn felt for Mademoiselle de Verneuil and shown on every face, brought to its height the growing indignation of the two Republicans, who now rose hastily:—

"Do you want anything, citizens?" asked Madame du Gua.

"Our swords, *citoyenne*," said Gerard, sarcastically.

"You do not need them at table," said the marquis, coldly.

"No, but we are going to play at a game you know very well," replied Gerard. "This is La Pelerine over again."

The whole party seemed dumfounded. Just then a volley, fired with terrible regularity, echoed through the courtyard. The two officers sprang to the portico; there they beheld a hundred or so of Chouans aiming at the few soldiers who were not shot down at the first discharge; these they fired upon as upon so many hares. The Bretons swarmed from the bank, where Marche-a-Terre had posted them at the peril of their lives; for after the last volley, and mingling with the cries of the dying, several Chouans were heard to fall into the lake, where they were lost like stones in a gulf. Pille-Miche took aim at Gerard; Marche-a-Terre held Merle at his mercy.

"Captain," said the marquis to Merle, repeating to the Republican his own words, "you see that men are like medlars, they ripen on the straw." He pointed with a wave of his hand to the entire escort of the Blues lying on the bloody litter where the Chouans were despatching those who still breathed, and rifling the dead bodies with incredible rapidity. "I was right when I told you that your soldiers will not get as far as La Pelerine. I think, moreover, that your head will fill with lead before mine. What say you?"

Montauran felt a horrible necessity to vent his rage. His bitter sarcasm, the ferocity, even the treachery of this military execution, done without his orders, but which he now accepted, satisfied in some degree the craving of his heart. In his fury he would fain have annihilated France. The dead Blues, the living officers, all innocent of the crime for which he demanded vengeance, were to him the cards by which a gambler cheats his despair.

"I would rather perish than conquer as you are conquering," said Gerard. Then, seeing the naked and bloody corpses of his men, he cried out, "Murdered basely, in cold blood!"

"That was how you murdered Louis XVI., monsieur," said the marquis.

"Monsieur," replied Gerard, haughtily, "there are mysteries in a king's trial which you could never comprehend."

"Do you dare to accuse the king?" exclaimed the marquis.

"Do you dare to fight your country?" retorted Gerard.

"Folly!" said the marquis.

"Parricide!" exclaimed the Republican.

"Well, well," cried Merle, gaily, "a pretty time to quarrel at the moment of your death."

"True," said Gerard, coldly, turning to the marquis. "Monsieur, if it is your intention to put us to death, at least have the goodness to shoot us at once."

"Ah! that's like you, Gerard," said Merle, "always in a hurry to finish things. But if one has to travel far and can't breakfast on the morrow, at least we might sup."

Gerard sprang forward without a word towards the wall. Pille-Miche covered him, glancing as he did so at the motionless marquis, whose silence he took for an order, and the adjutant-major fell like a tree. Marche-a-Terre ran to share the fresh booty with Pille-Miche; like two hungry crows they disputed and clamored over the still warm body.

"If you really wish to finish your supper, captain, you can come with me," said the marquis to Merle.

The captain followed him mechanically, saying in a low voice: "It is that devil of a strumpet that caused all this. What will Hulot say?"

"Strumpet!" cried the marquis in a strangled voice, "then she is one?"

The captain seemed to have given Montauran a death-blow, for he re-entered the house with a staggering step, pale, haggard, and undone.

Another scene had meanwhile taken place in the dining-room, which assumed, in the marquis's absence, such a threatening character that Marie, alone without her protector, might well fancy she read her death-warrant in the eyes of her rival. At the noise of the volley the guests all sprang to their feet, but Madame du Gua remained seated.

"It is nothing," she said; "our men are despatching the Blues." Then, seeing the marquis outside on the portico, she rose. "Mademoiselle whom you here see," she continued, with the calmness of concentrated fury, "came here to betray the Gars! She meant to deliver him up to the Republic."

"I could have done so twenty times to-day and yet I saved his life," said Mademoiselle de Verneuil.

Madame du Gua sprang upon her rival like lightning; in her blind excitement she tore apart the fastenings of the young girl's spencer, the stuff, the embroidery, the corset, the chemise, and plunged her savage hand into the bosom where, as she well knew, a letter lay hidden. In doing this her jealousy so bruised and tore the palpitating throat of her rival, taken by surprise at the sudden attack, that she left the bloody marks of her nails, feeling a sort of pleasure in making her submit to so degrading a prostitution. In the feeble struggle which Marie made against the furious woman, her hair became unfastened and fell in undulating curls about her shoulders; her face glowed with outraged modesty, and tears made their burning way along her cheeks, heightening the brilliancy of her eyes, as she quivered with shame before the looks of the assembled men. The hardest judge would have believed in her innocence when he saw her sorrow.

Hatred is so uncalculating that Madame du Gua did not perceive she had overshot her mark, and that no one listened to her as she cried triumphantly: "You shall now see, gentlemen, whether I have slandered that horrible creature."

"Not so horrible," said the bass voice of the guest who had thrown the first stone. "But for my part, I like such horrors."

"Here," continued the cruel woman, "is an order signed by Laplace, and counter-signed by Dubois, minister of war." At these names several heads were turned to her. "Listen to the wording of it," she went on.

"'The military citizen commanders of all grades, the district administrators, the *procureur-syndics*, et cetera, of the insurgent departments, and particularly those of the localities in which the ci-devant Marquis de Montauran, leader of the brigands and otherwise known as the Gars, may be found, are hereby commanded to give aid and assistance to the *citoyenne* Marie Verneuil and to obey the orders which she may give them at her discretion.'

"A worthless hussy takes a noble name to soil it with such treachery," added Madame du Gua.

A movement of astonishment ran through the assembly.

"The fight is not even if the Republic employs such pretty women against us," said the Baron du Guenic gaily.

"Especially women who have nothing to lose," said Madame du Gua.

"Nothing?" cried the Chevalier du Vissard. "Mademoiselle has a property which probably brings her in a pretty good sum."

"The Republic must like a joke, to send strumpets for ambassadors," said the Abbe Gudin.

"Unfortunately, Mademoiselle seeks the joys that kill," said Madame du Gua, with a horrible expression of pleasure at the end she foresaw.

"Then why are you still living?" said her victim, rising to her feet, after repairing the disorder of her clothes.

This bitter sarcasm excited a sort of respect for so brave a victim, and silenced the assembly. Madame du Gua saw a satirical smile on the lips of the men, which infuriated her, and paying no attention to the marquis and Merle who were entering the room, she called to the Chouan who followed them. "Pille-Miche!" she said, pointing to Mademoiselle de Verneuil, "take her; she is my share of the booty, and I turn her over to you—do what you like with her."

At these words the whole assembly shuddered, for the hideous heads of Pille-Miche and Marche-a-Terre appeared behind the marquis, and the punishment was seen in all its horror.

Francine was standing with clasped hands as though paralyzed. Mademoiselle de Verneuil, who recovered her presence of mind before the danger that threatened her, cast a look of contempt at the assembled men, snatched the letter from Madame du Gua's hand, threw up her head with a flashing eye, and darted towards the door where Merle's sword was still leaning. There she came upon the marquis, cold and motionless as a statue. Nothing pleaded for her on his fixed, firm features. Wounded to the heart, life seemed odious to her. The man who had pledged her so much love must have heard the odious jests that were cast upon her, and stood there silently a witness of the infamy she had been made to endure. She might, perhaps, have forgiven him his contempt, but she could not forgive his having seen her in so humiliating a position, and she flung him a look that was full of hatred, feeling in her heart the birth of an unutterable desire for vengeance. With death beside her, the sense of impotence almost strangled her. A whirlwind of passion and madness rose in her head; the blood which boiled in her veins made everything about her seem like a conflagration. Instead of killing herself, she seized the sword and thrust it though the marquis. But the weapon slipped between his arm and side; he caught her by the wrist and dragged her from the room, aided by Pille-Miche, who had flung himself upon the furious creature when she attacked his master. Francine shrieked aloud. "Pierre! Pierre! Pierre!" she cried in heart-rending tones, as she followed her mistress.

The marquis closed the door on the astonished company. When he reached the portico he was still holding the woman's wrist, which he clasped convulsively, while Pille-Miche had almost crushed the bones of her arm with his iron fingers, but Marie felt only the burning hand of the young leader.

"You hurt me," she said.

For all answer he looked at her a moment.

"Have you some base revenge to take—like that woman?" she said. Then, seeing the dead bodies on the heap of straw, she cried out, shuddering: "The faith of a gentleman! ha! ha! ha!" With a frightful laugh she added: "Ha! the glorious day!"

"Yes," he said, "a day without a morrow."

He let go her hand and took a long, last look at the beautiful creature he could scarcely even then renounce. Neither of these proud natures yielded. The marquis may have looked for a tear, but the eyes of the girl were dry and scornful. Then he turned quickly, and left the victim to Pille-Miche.

"God will hear me, marquis," she called. "I will ask Him to give you a glorious day without a morrow."

Pille-Miche, not a little embarrassed with so rich a prize, dragged her away with some gentleness and a mixture of respect and scorn. The marquis, with a sigh, re-entered the dining-room, his face like that of a dead man whose eyes have not been closed.

Merle's presence was inexplicable to the silent spectators of this tragedy; they looked at him in astonishment and their eyes questioned each other. Merle saw their amazement, and, true to his native character, he said, with a smile: "Gentlemen, you will scarcely refuse a glass of wine to a man who is about to make his last journey."

It was just as the company had calmed down under the influence of these words, said with a true French carelessness which pleased the Vendeans, that Montauran returned, his face pale, his eyes fixed.

"Now you shall see," said Merle, "how death can make men lively."

"Ah!" said the marquis, with a gesture as if suddenly awaking, "here you are, my dear councillor of war," and he passed him a bottle of *vin de Grave.*

"Oh, thanks, citizen marquis," replied Merle. "Now I can divert myself."

At this sally Madame du Gua turned to the other guests with a smile, saying, "Let us spare him the dessert."

"That is a very cruel vengeance, madame," he said. "You forget my murdered friend who is waiting for me; I never miss an appointment."

"Captain," said the marquis, throwing him his glove, "you are free; that's your passport. The Chasseurs du Roi know that they must not kill all the game."

"So much the better for me!" replied Merle, "but you are making a mistake; we shall come to close quarters before long, and I'll not let you off. Though your head can never pay for Gerard's, I want it and I shall have it. Adieu. I could drink with my own assassins, but I cannot stay with those of my friend"; and he disappeared, leaving the guests astonished at his coolness.

"Well, gentlemen, what do you think of the lawyers and surgeons and bailiffs who manage the Republic," said the Gars, coldly.

"God's-death! marquis," replied the Comte de Bauvan; "they have shocking manners; that fellow presumed to be impertinent, it seems to me."

The captain's hasty retreat had a motive. The despised, humiliated woman, who was even then, perhaps, being put to death, had so won upon him during the scene of her degradation that he said to himself, as he left the room, "If she is a prostitute, she is not an ordinary one, and I'll marry her." He felt so sure of being able to rescue her from the savages that his first thought, when his own life was given to him, was to save hers. Unhappily, when he reached the portico, he found the courtyard deserted. He looked about him, listened to the silence, and could hear nothing but the distant shouts and laughter of the Chouans, who were drinking in the gardens and dividing their booty. He turned the corner to the fatal wing before which his men had been shot, and from there he could distinguish, by the feeble light of a few stray lanterns, the different groups of the Chasseurs du Roi. Neither Pille-Miche, nor Marche-a-Terre, nor the girl were visible; but he felt himself gently pulled by the flap of his uniform, and, turning round, saw Francine on her knees.

"Where is she?" he asked.

"I don't know; Pierre drove me back and told me not to stir from here."

"Which way did they go?"

"That way," she replied, pointing to the causeway.

The captain and Francine then noticed in that direction a line of strong shadows thrown by the moonlight on the lake, and among them that of a female figure.

"It is she!" cried Francine.

Mademoiselle de Verneuil seemed to be standing, as if resigned, in the midst of other figures, whose gestures denoted a debate.

"There are several," said the captain. "Well, no matter, let us go to them."

"You will get yourself killed uselessly," said Francine.

"I have been killed once before to-day," he said gaily.

They both walked towards the gloomy gateway which led to the causeway; there Francine suddenly stopped short.

"No," she said, gently, "I'll go no farther; Pierre told me not to meddle; I believe in him; if we go on we shall spoil all. Do as you please, officer, but leave me. If Pierre saw us together he would kill you."

Just then Pille-Miche appeared in the gateway and called to the postilion who was left in the stable. At the same moment he saw the captain and covered him with his musket, shouting out, "By Saint Anne of Auray! the rector was right enough in telling us the Blues had signed a compact with the devil. I'll bring you to life, I will!"

"Stop! my life is sacred," cried Merle, seeing his danger. "There's the glove of your Gars," and he held it out.

"Ghosts' lives are not sacred," replied the Chouan, "and I sha'n't give you yours. Ave Maria!"

He fired, and the ball passed through his victim's head. The captain fell. When Francine reached him she heard him mutter the words, "I'd rather die with them than return without them."

The Chouan sprang upon the body to strip it, saying, "There's one good thing about ghosts, they come to life in their clothes." Then, recognizing the Gars' glove, that sacred safeguard, in the captain's hand, he stopped short, terrified. "I wish I wasn't in the skin of my mother's son!" he exclaimed, as he turned and disappeared with the rapidity of a bird.

To understand this scene, so fatal to poor Merle, we must follow Mademoiselle de Verneuil after the marquis, in his fury and despair, had abandoned her to Pille-Miche. Francine had caught Marche-a-Terre by the arm and reminded him, with sobs, of the promise he had made her. Pille-Miche was already dragging away his victim like a heavy bundle. Marie, her head and hair hanging back, turned her eyes to the lake; but held as she was in a grasp of iron she was forced to follow the Chouan, who turned now and then to hasten her steps, and each time that he did so a jovial thought brought a hideous smile upon his face.

"Isn't she a morsel!" he cried, with a coarse laugh.

Hearing the words, Francine recovered speech.

"Pierre?"

"Well, what?"

"He'll kill her."

"Not at once."

"Then she'll kill herself, she will never submit; and if she dies I shall die too."

"Then you love her too much, and she shall die," said Marche-a-Terre.

"Pierre! if we are rich and happy we owe it all to her; but, whether or no, you promised me to save her."

"Well, I'll try; but you must stay here, and don't move."

Francine at once let go his arm, and waited in horrible suspense in the courtyard where Merle found her. Meantime Marche-a-Terre joined his comrade at the moment when the latter, after dragging his victim to the barn, was compelling her to get into the coach. Pille-Miche called to him to help in pulling out the vehicle.

"What are you going to do with all that?" asked Marche-a-Terre.

"The Grande Garce gave me the woman, and all that belongs to her is mine."

"The coach will put a sou or two in your pocket; but as for the woman, she'll scratch your eyes out like a cat."

Pille-Miche burst into a roar of laughter.

"Then I'll tie her up and take her home," he answered.

"Very good; suppose we harness the horses," said Marche-a-Terre.

A few moments later Marche-a-Terre, who had left his comrade mounting guard over his prey, led the coach from the stable to the causeway, where Pille-Miche got into it beside Mademoiselle de

Verneuil, not perceiving that she was on the point of making a spring into the lake.

"I say, Pille-Miche!" cried Marche-a-Terre.

"What!"

"I'll buy all your booty."

"Are you joking?" asked the other, catching his prisoner by the petticoat, as a butcher catches a calf that is trying to escape him.

"Let me see her, and I'll set a price."

The unfortunate creature was made to leave the coach and stand between the two Chouans, who each held a hand and looked at her as the Elders must have looked at Susannah.

"Will you take thirty francs in good coin?" said Marche-a-Terre, with a groan.

"Really?"

"Done?" said Marche-a-Terre, holding out his hand.

"Yes, done; I can get plenty of Breton girls for that, and choice morsels, too. But the coach; whose is that?" asked Pille-Miche, beginning to reflect upon his bargain.

"Mine!" cried Marche-a-Terre, in a terrible tone of voice, which showed the sort of superiority his ferocious character gave him over his companions.

"But suppose there's money in the coach?"

"Didn't you say, 'Done'?"

"Yes, I said, 'Done.'"

"Very good; then go and fetch the postilion who is gagged in the stable over there."

"But if there's money in the—"

"Is there any?" asked Marche-a-Terre, roughly, shaking Marie by the arm.

"Yes, about a hundred crowns."

The two Chouans looked at each other.

"Well, well, friend," said Pille-Miche, "we won't quarrel for a female Blue; let's pitch her into the lake with a stone around her neck, and divide the money."

"I'll give you that money as my share in d'Orgemont's ransom," said Marche-a-Terre, smothering a groan, caused by such sacrifice.

Pille-Miche uttered a sort of hoarse cry as he started to find the postilion, and his glee brought death to Merle, whom he met on his way.

Hearing the shot, Marche-a-Terre rushed in the direction where he had left Francine, and found her praying on her knees, with clasped hands, beside the poor captain, whose murder had deeply horrified her.

"Run to your mistress," said the Chouan; "she is saved."

He ran himself to fetch the postilion, returning with all speed, and, as he repassed Merle's body, he noticed the Gars' glove, which was still convulsively clasped in the dead hand.

"Oho!" he cried. "Pille-Miche has blundered horribly—he won't live to spend his crowns."

He snatched up the glove and said to Mademoiselle de Verneuil, who was already in the coach with Francine: "Here, take this glove. If any of our men attack you on the road, call out 'Ho, the Gars!' show the glove, and no harm can happen to you. Francine," he said, turning towards her and seizing her violently, "you and I are quits with that woman; come with me and let the devil have her."

"You can't ask me to abandon her just at this moment!" cried Francine, in distress.

Marche-a-Terre scratched his ear and forehead, then he raised his head, and his mistress saw the ferocious expression of his eyes. "You are right," he said; "I leave you with her one week; if at the end of that time you don't come with me—" he did not finish the sentence, but he slapped the muzzle of his gun with the flat of his hand. After making the gesture of taking aim at her, he disappeared, without waiting for her reply.

No sooner was he gone than a voice, which seemed to issue from the lake, called, in a muffled tone: "Madame, madame!"

The postilion and the two women shuddered, for several corpses were floating near them. A Blue, hidden behind a tree, cautiously appeared.

"Let me get up behind the coach, or I'm a dead man. That damned cider which Clef-des-Coeurs would stop to drink cost more than a pint of blood. If he had done as I did, and made his round, our poor comrades there wouldn't be floating dead in the pond."

* * * * *

While these events were taking place outside the chateau, the leaders sent by the Vendeans and those of the Chouans were holding a council of war, with their glasses in their hands, under the presidency of the Marquis de Montauran. Frequent libations of Bordeaux animated the discussion, which, however, became more serious and important at the end of the meal. After the general plan of military operations had been decided on, the Royalists drank to the health of the Bourbons. It was at that moment that the shot which killed Merle was heard, like an echo of the disastrous war which these gay and noble conspirators were about to make against the Republic. Madame du Gua quivered with pleasure at the thought that she was freed from her rival; the guests looked at each other in silence; the marquis rose from the table and went out.

"He loved her!" said Madame du Gua, sarcastically. "Follow him, Monsieur de Fontaine, and keep him company; he will be as irritating as a fly if we let him sulk."

She went to a window which looked on the courtyard to endeavor to see Marie's body. There, by the last gleams of the sinking moon, she caught sight of the coach being rapidly driven down the avenue of apple-trees. Mademoiselle de Verneuil's veil was fluttering in the wind. Madame du Gua, furious at the sight, left the room hurriedly. The marquis, standing on the portico absorbed in gloomy thought, was watching about a hundred and fifty Chouans, who, having divided their booty in the gardens, were now returning to finish the cider and the rye-bread provided for the Blues. These soldiers of a new species, on whom the monarchy was resting its hopes, dispersed into groups. Some drank the cider; others, on the bank before the portico, amused themselves by flinging into the lake the dead bodies of the Blues, to which they fastened stones. This sight, joined to the other aspects of the strange scene,—the fantastic dress, the savage expressions of the barbarous and uncouth *gars*,—was so new and so amazing to Monsieur de Fontaine, accustomed to the nobler and better-regulated appearance of the Vendean troops, that he seized the occasion to say to the Marquis de Montauran, "What do you expect to do with such brutes?"

"Not very much, my dear count," replied the Gars.

"Will they ever be fit to manoeuvre before the enemy?"

"Never."

"Can they understand or execute an order?"

"No."

"Then what good will they be to you?"

"They will help me to plunge my sword into the entrails of the Republic," replied the marquis in a thundering voice. "They will give me Fougeres in three days, and all Brittany in ten! Monsieur," he added in a gentler voice, "start at once for La Vendee; if d'Auticamp, Suzannet, and the Abbe Bernier will act as rapidly as I do, if they'll not negotiate with the First Consul, as I am afraid they will" (here he wrung the hand of the Vendean chief) "we shall be within reach of Paris in a fortnight."

"But the Republic is sending sixty thousand men and General Brune against us."

"Sixty thousand men! indeed!" cried the marquis, with a scoffing laugh. "And how will Bonaparte carry on the Italian campaign? As for General Brune, he is not coming. The First Consul has sent him against the English in Holland, and General Hedouville, *the friend of our friend Barras*, takes his place here. Do you understand?"

As Monsieur de Fontaine heard these words he gave Montauran a look of keen intelligence which seemed to say that the marquis had not himself understood the real meaning of the words addressed to him. The two leaders then comprehended each other perfectly, and the Gars replied with an undefinable smile to the thoughts expressed in both their eyes: "Monsieur de Fontaine, do you know my arms? our motto is 'Persevere unto death.'"

The Comte de Fontaine took Montauran's hand and pressed it, saying: "I was left for dead at Quatre-Chemins, therefore you need never doubt me. But believe in my experience—times have changed."

"Yes," said La Billardiere, who now joined them. "You are young, marquis. Listen to me; your property has not yet been sold—"

"Ah!" cried Montauran, "can you conceive of devotion without sacrifice?"

"Do you really know the king?"

"I do."

"Then I admire your loyalty."

"The king," replied the young chieftain, "is the priest; I am fighting not for the man, but for the faith."

They parted,—the Vendean leader convinced of the necessity of yielding to circumstances and keeping his beliefs in the depths of his heart; La Billardiere to return to his negotiations in England; and Montauran to fight savagely and compel the Vendeans, by the victories he expected to win, to co-operate in his enterprise.

* * * * *

The events of the day had excited such violent emotions in Mademoiselle de Verneuil's whole being that she lay back almost fainting in the carriage, after giving the order to drive to Fougeres.

Francine was as silent as her mistress. The postilion, dreading some new disaster, made all the haste he could to reach the high-road, and was soon on the summit of La Pelerine. Through the thick white mists of morning Marie de Verneuil crossed the broad and beautiful valley of Couesnon (where this history began) scarcely able to distinguish the slaty rock on which the town of Fougeres stands from the slopes of La Pelerine. They were still eight miles from it. Shivering with cold herself, Mademoiselle de Verneuil recollected the poor soldier behind the carriage, and insisted, against his remonstrances, in taking him into the carriage beside Francine. The sight of Fougeres drew her for a time out of her reflections. The sentinels stationed at the Porte Saint-Leonard refused to allow ingress to the strangers, and she was therefore obliged to exhibit the ministerial order. This at once gave her safety in entering the town, but the postilion could find no other place for her to stop at than the Poste inn.

"Madame," said the Blue whose life she had saved. "If you ever want a sabre to deal some special blow, my life is yours. I am good for that. My name is Jean Falcon, otherwise called Beau-Pied, sergeant of the first company of Hulot's veterans, seventy-second half-brigade, nicknamed 'Les Mayencais.' Excuse my vanity; I can only offer you the soul of a sergeant, but that's at your service."

He turned on his heel and walked off whistling.

"The lower one goes in social life," said Marie, bitterly, "the more we find generous feelings without display. A marquis returns death for life, and a poor sergeant—but enough of that."

When the weary woman was at last in a warm bed, her faithful Francine waited in vain for the affectionate good-night to which she was accustomed; but her mistress, seeing her still standing and evidently uneasy, made her a sign of distress.

"This is called a day, Francine," she said; "but I have aged ten years in it."

The next morning, as soon as she had risen, Corentin came to see her and she admitted him.

"Francine," she exclaimed, "my degradation is great indeed, for the thought of that man is not disagreeable to me."

Still, when she saw him, she felt once more, for the hundredth time, the instinctive repulsion which two years' intercourse had increased rather than lessened.

"Well," he said, smiling, "I felt certain you were succeeding. Was I mistaken? did you get hold of the wrong man?"

"Corentin," she replied, with a dull look of pain, "never mention that affair to me unless I speak of it myself."

He walked up and down the room casting oblique glances at her, endeavoring to guess the secret thoughts of the singular woman whose mere glance had the power of discomfiting at times the cleverest men.

"I foresaw this check," he replied, after a moment's silence. "If you would be willing to establish your headquarters in this town, I have already found a suitable place for you. We are in the very centre of Chouannerie. Will you stay here?"

She answered with an affirmative sign, which enabled Corentin to make conjectures, partly correct, as to the events of the preceding evening.

"I can hire a house for you, a bit of national property still unsold. They are behind the age in these parts. No one has dared buy the old barrack because it belonged to an *emigre* who was thought to be harsh. It is close to the church of Saint Leonard; and on my word of honor the view from it is delightful. Something can really be made of the old place; will you try it?"

"Yes, at once," she cried.

"I want a few hours to have it cleaned and put in order for you, so that you may like it."

"What matter?" she said. "I could live in a cloister or a prison without caring. However, see that everything is in order before night, so that I may sleep there in perfect solitude. Go, leave me; your presence is intolerable. I wish to be alone with Francine; she is better for me than my own company, perhaps. Adieu; go—go, I say."

These words, said volubly with a mingling of coquetry, despotism, and passion, showed she had entirely recovered her self-possession. Sleep had no doubt classified the impressions of the preceding day, and reflection had determined her on vengeance. If a few reluctant signs appeared on her face they only proved the ease with which certain women can bury the better feelings of their souls, and the cruel dissimulation which enables them to smile sweetly while planning the destruction of a victim. She sat alone after Corentin had left her, thinking how she could get the marquis still living into her toils. For the first time in her life this woman had lived according to her inmost desires; but of that life nothing remained but one craving, —that of vengeance,—vengeance complete and infinite. It was her one thought, her sole desire. Francine's words and attentions were unnoticed. Marie seemed to be sleeping with her eyes open; and the long day passed without an action or even a gesture that bore testimony to her thoughts. She lay on a couch which she had made of chairs and pillows. It was late in the evening when a few words escaped her, as if involuntarily.

"My child," she said to Francine, "I understood yesterday what it was to live for love; to-day I know what it means to die for vengeance. Yes, I will give my life to seek him wherever he may be, to meet him, seduce him, make him mine! If I do not have that man, who dared to despise me, at my feet humble and submissive, if I do not make him my lackey and my slave, I shall indeed be base; I shall not be a woman; I shall not be myself."

The house which Corentin now hired for Mademoiselle de Verneuil offered many gratifications to the innate love of luxury and elegance that was part of this girl. The capricious creature took possession of it with regal composure, as of a thing which already belonged to her; she appropriated the furniture and arranged it with intuitive sympathy, as though she had known it all her life. This is a vulgar detail, but one that is not unimportant in sketching the character of so exceptional a person. She seemed to have been already familiarized in a dream with the house in which she now lived on her hatred as she might have lived on her love.

"At least," she said to herself, "I did not rouse insulting pity in him; I do not owe him my life. Oh, my first, my last, my only love! what an end to it!" She sprang upon Francine, who was terrified. "Do you love a man? Oh, yes, yes, I remember; you do. I am glad I have a woman here who can understand me. Ah, my poor Francette, man is a miserable being. Ha! he said he loved me, and his love could not bear the slightest test! But I,—if all men had accused him I would have defended him; if the universe rejected him my soul should have been his refuge. In the old days life was filled with human beings coming and going for whom I did not care; it was sad and dull, but not horrible; but now, now, what is life without him? He will live on, and I not near him! I shall not see him, speak to him, feel him, hold him, press him,—ha! I would rather strangle him myself in his sleep!"

Francine, horrified, looked at her in silence.

"Kill the man you love?" she said, in a soft voice.

"Yes, yes, if he ceases to love me."

But after those ruthless words she hid her face in her hands, and sat down silently.

The next day a man presented himself without being announced. His face was stern. It was Hulot, followed by Corentin. Mademoiselle de Verneuil looked at the commandant and trembled.

"You have come," she said, "to ask me to account for your friends. They are dead."

"I know it," he replied, "and not in the service of the Republic."

"For me, and by me," she said. "You preach the nation to me. Can the nation bring to life those who die for her? Can she even avenge them? But I—I will avenge them!" she cried. The awful images of the catastrophe filled her imagination suddenly, and the graceful creature who held modesty to be the first of women's wiles forgot herself in a moment of madness, and marched towards the amazed commandant brusquely.

"In exchange for a few murdered soldiers," she said, "I will bring to the block a head that is worth a million heads of other men. It is not a woman's business to wage war; but you, old as you are, shall learn good stratagems from me. I'll deliver a whole family to your bayonets —him, his ancestors, his past, his future. I will be as false and treacherous to him as I was good and true. Yes, commandant, I will bring that little noble to my arms, and he shall leave them to go to death. I have no other rival. The wretch himself pronounced his doom, —*a day without a morrow.* Your Republic and I shall be avenged. The Republic!" she cried in a voice the strange intonations of which horrified Hulot. "Is he to die for bearing arms against the nation? Shall I suffer France to rob me of my vengeance? Ah! what a little thing is life! death can expiate but one crime. He has but one head to fall, but I will make him know in one night that he loses more than life. Commandant, you who will kill him," and she sighed, "see that nothing betrays my betrayal; he must die convinced of my fidelity. I ask that of you. Let him know only me—me, and my caresses!"

She stopped; but through the crimson of her cheeks Hulot and Corentin saw that rage and delirium had not entirely smothered all sense of shame. Marie shuddered violently as she said the words; she seemed to listen to them as though she doubted whether she herself had said them, and she made the involuntary movement of a woman whose veil is falling from her.

"But you had him in your power," said Corentin.

"Very likely."

"Why did you stop me when I had him?" asked Hulot.

"I did not know what he would prove to be," she cried. Then, suddenly, the excited woman, who was walking up and down with hurried steps and casting savage glances at the spectators of the storm, calmed down. "I do not know myself," she said, in a man's tone. "Why talk? I must go and find him."

"Go and find him?" said Hulot. "My dear woman, take care; we are not yet masters of this part of the country; if you venture outside of the town you will be taken or killed before you've gone a hundred yards."

"There's never any danger for those who seek vengeance," she said, driving from her presence with a disdainful gesture the two men whom she was ashamed to face.

"What a woman!" cried Hulot as he walked away with Corentin. "A queer idea of those police fellows in Paris to send her here; but she'll never deliver him up to us," he added, shaking his head.

"Oh yes, she will," replied Corentin.

"Don't you see she loves him?" said Hulot.

"That's just why she will. Besides," looking at the amazed commandant, "I am here to see that she doesn't commit any folly. In my opinion, comrade, there is no love in the world worth the three hundred thousand francs she'll make out of this."

When the police diplomatist left the soldier the latter stood looking after him, and as the sound of the man's steps died away he gave a sigh, muttering to himself, "It may be a good thing after all to be such a dullard as I am. God's thunder! if I meet the Gars I'll fight him hand to hand, or my name's not Hulot; for if that fox brings him before me in any of their new-fangled councils of war, my honor will be as soiled as the shirt of a young trooper who is under fire for the first time."

The massacre at La Vivetiere, and the desire to avenge his friends had led Hulot to accept a reinstatement in his late command; in fact, the new minister, Berthier, had refused to accept his resignation under existing circumstances. To the official despatch was added a private letter, in which, without explaining the mission of Mademoiselle de Verneuil, the minister informed him that the affair was entirely outside of the war, and not to interfere with any military operations. The duty of the commanders, he said, was limited to giving assistance to that honorable *citoyenne*, if occasion arose. Learning from his scouts that the movements of the Chouans all tended towards a concentration of their forces in the neighborhood of Fougeres, Hulot secretly and with forced marches brought two battalions of his brigade into the town. The nation's danger, his hatred of aristocracy, whose partisans threatened to convulse so large a section of country, his desire to avenge his murdered friends, revived in the old veteran the fire of his youth.

* * * * *

"So this is the life I craved," exclaimed Mademoiselle de Verneuil, when she was left alone with Francine. "No matter how fast the hours go, they are to me like centuries of thought."

Suddenly she took Francine's hand, and her voice, soft as that of the first red-throat singing after a storm, slowly gave sound to the following words:—

"Try as I will to forget them, I see those two delicious lips, that chin just raised, those eyes of fire; I hear the 'Hue!' of the postilion; I dream, I dream,—why then such hatred on awakening!"

She drew a long sigh, rose, and then for the first time looked out upon the country delivered over to civil war by the cruel leader whom she was plotting to destroy. Attracted by the scene she wandered out to breathe at her ease beneath the sky; and though her steps conducted her at a venture, she was surely led to the Promenade of the town by one of those occult impulses of the soul which lead us to follow hope irrationally. Thoughts conceived under the dominion of that spell are often realized; but we then attribute their pre-vision to a power we call presentiment,—an inexplicable power, but a real one,—which our passions find accommodating, like a flatterer who, among his many lies, does sometimes tell the truth.

III

A DAY WITHOUT A MORROW

The preceding events of this history having been greatly influenced by the formation of the regions in which they happened, it is desirable to give a minute description of them, without which the closing scenes might be difficult of comprehension.

The town of Fougeres is partly built upon a slate rock, which seems to have slipped from the mountains that hem in the broad valley of Couesnon to the west and take various names according to their localities. The town is separated from the mountains by a gorge, through which flows a small river called the Nancon. To the east, the view is the same as from the summit of La Pelerine; to the west, the town looks down into the tortuous valley of the Nancon; but there is a spot from which a section of the great valley and the picturesque windings of the gorge can be seen at the same time. This place, chosen by the inhabitants of the town for their Promenade, and to which the steps of Mademoiselle de Verneuil were now turned, was destined to be the theatre on which the drama begun at La Vivetiere was to end. Therefore, however picturesque the other parts of Fougeres may be, attention must be particularly given to the scenery which meets the eye from this terrace.

To give an idea of the rock on which Fougeres stands, as seen on this side, we may compare it to one of those immense towers circled by Saracen architects with balconies on each story, which were reached by spiral stairways. To add to this effect, the rock is capped by a Gothic church, the small spires, clock-tower, and buttresses of which make its shape almost precisely that of a sugar-loaf. Before the portal of this church, which is dedicated to Saint-Leonard, is a small, irregular square, where the soil is held up by a buttressed wall, which forms a balustrade and communicates by a flight of steps with the Promenade. This public walk, like a second cornice, extends round the rock a few rods below the square of Saint-Leonard; it is a broad piece of ground planted with trees, and it joins the fortifications of the town. About ten rods below the walls and rocks which support this Promenade (due to a happy combination of indestructible slate and patient industry) another circular road exists, called the "Queen's Staircase"; this is cut in the rock itself and leads to a bridge built across the Nancon by Anne of Brittany. Below this road, which forms a third cornice, gardens descend, terrace after terrace, to the river, like shelves covered with flowers.

Parallel with the Promenade, on the other side of the Nancon and across its narrow valley, high rock-formations, called the heights of Saint-Sulpice, follow the stream and descend in gentle slopes to the great valley, where they turn abruptly to the north. Towards the south, where the town itself really ends and the faubourg Saint-Leonard begins, the Fougeres rock makes a bend, becomes less steep, and turns into the great valley, following the course of the river, which it hems in between itself and the heights of Saint-Sulpice, forming a sort of pass through which the water escapes in two streamlets to the Couesnon, into which they fall. This pretty group of rocky hills is called the "Nid-aux-Crocs"; the little vale they surround is the "Val de Gibarry," the rich pastures of which supply the butter known to epicures as that of the "Pree-Valaye."

At the point where the Promenade joins the fortifications is a tower called the "Tour de Papegaut." Close to this square erection, against the side of which the house now occupied by Mademoiselle de Verneuil rested, is a wall, partly built by hands and partly formed of the native rock where it offered a smooth surface. Here stands a gateway leading to the faubourg of Saint-Sulpice and bearing the same name. Above, on a breastwork of granite which commands the three valleys, rise the battlements and feudal towers of the ancient castle of Fougeres, — one of those enormous erections built by the Dukes of Brittany, with lofty walls fifteen feet thick, protected on the east by a pond from which flows the Nancon, the waters of which fill its moats, and on the west by the inaccessible granite rock on which it stands.

Seen from the Promenade, this magnificent relic of the Middle Ages, wrapped in its ivy mantle, adorned with its square or rounded towers, in either of which a whole regiment could be quartered, — the castle, the town, and the rock, protected by walls with sheer surfaces, or by the glacis of the fortifications, form a huge horseshoe, lined with precipices, on which the Bretons have, in course of ages, cut various narrow footways. Here and there the rocks push out like architectural adornments. Streamlets issue from the fissures, where the roots of stunted trees are nourished. Farther on, a few rocky slopes, less perpendicular than the rest, afford a scanty pasture for the goats. On all sides heather, growing from every crevice, flings its rosy garlands over the dark, uneven surface of the ground. At the bottom of this vast funnel the little river winds through meadows that are always cool and green, lying softly like a carpet.

Beneath the castle and among the granite boulders is a church dedicated to Saint-Sulpice, whose name is given to the suburb which lies across the Nancon. This suburb, flung as it were to the bottom of a precipice, and its church, the spire of which does not rise to the height of the rocks which threaten to crush it, are picturesquely watered by several affluents of the Nancon, shaded by trees and brightened by gardens. The whole region of Fougeres, its suburbs, its churches, and the hills of Saint-Sulpice are surrounded by the heights of Rille, which form part of a general range of mountains enclosing the broad valley of Couesnon.

Such are the chief features of this landscape, the principal characteristic of which is a rugged wildness softened by smiling accidents, by a happy blending of the finest works of men's hands with the capricious lay of a land full of unexpected contrasts, by a something, hardly to be explained, which surprises, astonishes, and puzzles. In no other part of France can the traveller meet with such grandiose contrasts as those offered by the great basin of the Couesnon, and the valleys hidden among the rocks of Fougeres and the heights of Rille. Their beauty is of that unspeakable kind in which chance triumphs and all the harmonies of Nature do their part. The clear, limpid, flowing waters, the mountains clothed with the vigorous vegetation of those regions, the sombre rocks, the graceful buildings, the fortifications raised by nature, and the granite towers built by man; combined with all the artifices of light and shade, with the contrasts of the varieties of foliage, with the groups of houses where an active population swarms, with the lonely barren places where the granite will not suffer even the lichen to fasten on its surface, in short, with all the ideas we ask a landscape to possess: grace and awfulness, poesy with its renascent magic, sublime pictures, delightful ruralities,—all these are here; it is Brittany in bloom.

The tower called the Papegaut, against which the house now occupied by Mademoiselle de Verneuil rested, has its base at the very bottom of the precipice, and rises to the esplanade which forms the cornice or terrace before the church of Saint-Leonard. From Marie's house, which was open on three sides, could be seen the horseshoe (which begins at the tower itself), the winding valley of the Nancon, and the square of Saint-Leonard. It is one of a group of wooden buildings standing parallel with the western side of the church, with which they form an alley-way, the farther end of which opens on a steep street skirting the church and leading to the gate of Saint-Leonard, along which Mademoiselle de Verneuil now made her way.

Marie naturally avoided entering the square of the church which was then above her, and turned towards the Promenade. The magnificence of the scene which met her eyes silenced for a moment the tumult of her passions. She admired the vast trend of the valley, which her eyes took in, from the summit of La Pelerine to the plateau where the main road to Vitry passes; then her eyes rested on the Nid-aux-Crocs and the winding gorges of the Val de Gibarry, the crests of which were bathed in the misty glow of the setting sun. She was almost frightened by the depth of the valley of the Nancon, the tallest poplars of which scarcely reached to the level of the gardens below the Queen's Staircase. At this time of day the smoke from the houses in the suburbs and in the valleys made a vapor in the air, through which the various objects had a bluish tinge; the brilliant colors of the day were beginning to fade; the firmament took a pearly tone; the moon was casting its veil of light into the ravine; all things tended to plunge the soul into reverie and bring back the memory of those beloved.

In a moment the scene before her was powerless to hold Marie's thoughts. In vain did the setting sun cast its gold-dust and its crimson sheets to the depths of the river and along the meadows and over the graceful buildings strewn among the rocks; she stood immovable, gazing at the heights of the Mont Saint-Sulpice. The frantic hope which had led her to the Promenade was miraculously realized. Among the gorse and bracken which grew upon those heights she was certain that she recognized, in spite of the goatskins which they wore, a number of the guests at La Vivetiere, and among them the Gars, whose every moment became vivid to her eyes in the softened light of the sinking sun. A few steps back of the ground of men she distinguished her enemy, Madame du Gua. For a moment Marie fancied that she dreamed, but her rival's hatred soon proved to her that the dream was a living one. The attention she was giving to the least little gesture of the marquis prevented her from observing the care with which Madame du Gua aimed a musket at her. But a shot which woke the echoes of the mountains, and a ball that whistled past her warned Mademoiselle de Verneuil of her rival's determination. "She sends me her card," thought Marie, smiling. Instantly a "Qui vive?" echoing from sentry to sentry, from the castle to the Porte Saint-Leonard, proved to the Chouans the alertness of the Blues, inasmuch as the least accessible of their ramparts was so well guarded.

"It is she—and he," muttered Marie to herself.

To seek the marquis, follow his steps and overtake him, was a thought that flashed like lightning through her mind. "I have no weapon!" she cried. She remembered that on leaving Paris she had flung into a trunk an elegant dagger formerly belonging to a sultana, which she had jestingly brought with her to the theatre of war, as some persons take note-books in which to jot down their travelling ideas; she was less attracted by the prospect of shedding blood than by the pleasure of wearing a pretty weapon studded with precious stones, and playing with a blade that was stainless. Three days earlier she had deeply regretted having put this dagger in a trunk, when to escape her enemies at La Vivetiere she had thought for a moment of killing herself. She now returned to the house, found the weapon, put it in her belt, wrapped a large shawl round her shoulders and a black lace scarf about her hair, and covered her head with one of those broad-brimmed hats distinctive of Chouans which belonged to a servant of the house. Then, with the presence of mind which excited passions often give, she took the glove which Marche-a-Terre had given her as a safeguard, and saying, in reply to Francine's terrible looks, "I would seek him in hell," she returned to the Promenade.

The Gars was still at the same place, but alone. By the direction of his telescope he seemed to be examining with the careful attention of a commander the various paths across the Nancon, the Queen's Staircase, and the road leading through the Porte Saint-Sulpice and round the church of that name, where it meets the high-road under range of the guns at the castle. Mademoiselle de Verneuil took one of the little paths made by goats and their keepers leading down from the Promenade, reached the Staircase, then the bottom of the ravine, crossed the Nancon and the suburb, and divining like a bird in the desert her right course among the dangerous precipices of the Mont Saint-Sulpice, she followed a slippery track defined upon the granite, and in spite of the prickly gorse and reeds and loose stones which hindered her, she climbed the steep ascent with an energy greater perhaps than that of a man,—the energy momentarily possessed by a woman under the influence of passion.

Night overtook her as she endeavored by the failing moonlight to make out the path the marquis must have taken; an obstinate quest without reward, for the dead silence about her was sufficient proof of the withdrawal of the Chouans and their leader. This effort of passion collapsed with the hope that inspired it. Finding herself alone, after nightfall, in a hostile country, she began to reflect; and Hulot's advice, together with the recollection of Madame du Gua's attempt, made her tremble with fear. The stillness of the night, so deep in mountain regions, enabled her to hear the fall of every leaf even at a distance, and these slight sounds vibrated on the air as though to give a measure of the silence or the solitude. The wind was blowing across the heights and sweeping away the clouds with violence, producing an alternation of shadows and light, the effect of which increased her fears, and gave fantastic and terrifying semblances to the most harmless objects. She turned her eyes to the houses of Fougeres, where the domestic lights were burning like so many earthly stars, and she presently saw distinctly the tower of Papegaut. She was but a very short distance from her own house, but within that space was the ravine. She remembered the declivities by which she had come, and wondered if there were not more risk in attempting to return to Fougeres than in following out the purpose which had brought her. She reflected that the marquis's glove would surely protect her from the Chouans, and that Madame du Gua was the only enemy to be really feared. With this idea in her mind, Marie clasped her dagger, and tried to find the way to a country house the roofs of which she had noticed as she climbed Saint-Sulpice; but she walked slowly, for she suddenly became aware of the majestic solemnity which oppresses a solitary being in the night time in the midst of wild scenery, where lofty mountains nod their heads like assembled giants. The rustle of her gown, caught by the brambles, made her tremble more than once, and more than once she hastened her steps only to slacken them again as she thought her last hour had come. Before long matters assumed an aspect which the boldest men could not have faced without alarm, and which threw Mademoiselle de Verneuil into the sort of terror that so affects the very springs of life that all things become excessive, weakness as well as strength. The feeblest beings will then do deeds of amazing power; the strongest go mad with fear.

Marie heard at a short distance a number of strange sounds, distinct yet vague, indicative of confusion and tumult, fatiguing to the ear which tried to distinguish them. They came from the ground, which seemed to tremble beneath the feet of a multitude of marching men. A momentary clearness in the sky enabled her to perceive at a little distance long files of hideous figures waving like ears of corn and gliding like phantoms; but she scarcely saw them, for darkness fell again, like a black curtain, and hid the fearful scene which seemed to her full of yellow, dazzling eyes. She turned hastily and ran to the top of a bank to escape meeting three of these horrible figures who were coming towards her.

"Did you see it?" said one.

"I felt a cold wind as it rushed past me," replied a hoarse voice.

"I smelt a damp and graveyard smell," said the third.

"Was it white?" asked the first.

"Why should only *he* come back out of all those we left dead at La Pelerine?" said the second.

"Why indeed?" replied the third. "Why do the Sacre-Coeur men have the preference? Well, at any rate, I'd rather die without confession than wander about as he does, without eating or drinking, and no blood in his body or flesh on his bones."

"Ah!"

This exclamation, or rather this fearful cry, issued from the group as the three Chouans pointed to the slender form and pallid face of Mademoiselle de Verneuil, who fled away with terrified rapidity without a sound.

"Here he is!" "There he is!" "Where?" "There!" "He's gone!" "No!" "Yes!" "Can you see him?" These cries reverberated like the monotonous murmur of waves upon a shore.

Mademoiselle de Verneuil walked bravely in the direction of the house she had seen, and soon came in sight of a number of persons, who all fled away at her approach with every sign of panic fear. She felt impelled to advance by a mysterious power which coerced her;

the lightness of her body, which seemed to herself inexplicable, was another source of terror. These forms which rose in masses at her approach, as if from the ground on which she trod, uttered moans which were scarcely human. At last she reached, not without difficulty, a trampled garden, the hedges and fences of which were broken down. Stopped by a sentry, she showed the glove. The moon lighted her face, and the muzzle of the gun already pointed at her was dropped by the Chouan, who uttered a hoarse cry, which echoed through the place. She now saw large buildings, where a few lighted windows showed the rooms that were occupied, and presently reached the walls without further hindrance. Through the window into which she looked, she saw Madame du Gua and the leaders who were convoked at La Vivetiere. Bewildered at the sight, also by the conviction of her danger, she turned hastily to a little opening protected by iron bars, and saw in a long vaulted hall the marquis, alone and gloomy, within six feet of her. The reflection of the fire, before which he was sitting in a clumsy chair, lighted his face with a vacillating ruddy glow that gave the character of a vision to the scene. Motionless and trembling, the girl stood clinging to the bars, to catch his words if he spoke. Seeing him so depressed, disheartened, and pale, she believed herself to be the cause of his sadness. Her anger changed to pity, her pity to tenderness, and she suddenly knew that it was not revenge alone which had brought her there.

The marquis rose, turned his head, and stood amazed when he saw, as if in a cloud, Mademoiselle de Verneuil's face; then he shook his head with a gesture of impatience and contempt, exclaiming: "Must I forever see the face of that devil, even when awake?"

This utter contempt for her forced a half-maddened laugh from the unhappy girl which made the young leader quiver. He sprang to the window, but Mademoiselle de Verneuil was gone. She heard the steps of a man behind her, which she supposed to be those of the marquis, and, to escape him, she knew no obstacles; she would have scaled walls and flown through air; she would have found and followed a path to hell sooner than have seen again, in flaming letters on the forehead of that man, "I despise you,"—words which an inward voice sounded in her soul with the noise of a trumpet.

After walking a short distance without knowing where she went, she stopped, conscious of a damp exhalation. Alarmed by the sound of voices, she went down some steps which led into a cellar. As she reached the last of them, she stopped to listen and discover the direction her pursuers might take. Above the sounds from the outside, which were somewhat loud, she could hear within the lugubrious moans of a human being, which added to her terror. Rays of light coming down the steps made her fear that this retreat was only too well known to her enemies, and, to escape them, she summoned fresh energy. Some moments later, after recovering her composure of mind, it was difficult for her to conceive by what means she had been able to climb a little wall, in a recess of which she was now hidden. She took no notice at first of the cramped position in which she was, but before long the pain of it became intolerable, for she was bending double under the arched opening of a vault, like the crouching Venus which ignorant persons attempt to squeeze into too narrow a niche. The wall, which was rather thick and built of granite, formed a low partition between the stairway and the cellar whence the groans were issuing. Presently she saw an individual, clothed in a goatskin, enter the cave beneath her, and move about, without making any sign of eager search. Impatient to discover if she had any chance of safety, Mademoiselle de Verneuil waited with anxiety till the light brought by the new-comer lighted the whole cave, where she could partly distinguish a formless but living mass which was trying to reach a part of the wall, with violent and repeated jerks, something like those of a carp lying out of water on a shore.

A small pine torch threw its blue and hazy light into the cave. In spite of the gloomy poetic effects which Mademoiselle de Verneuil's imagination cast about this vaulted chamber, which was echoing to the sounds of a pitiful prayer, she was obliged to admit that the place was nothing more than an underground kitchen, evidently long abandoned. When the formless mass was distinguishable it proved to be a short and very fat man, whose limbs were carefully bound before he had been left lying on the damp stone floor of the kitchen by those who had seized him. When he saw the new-comer approach him with a torch in one hand and a fagot of sticks in the other, the captive gave a dreadful groan, which so wrought upon the sensibilities of Mademoiselle de Verneuil that she forgot her own terror and despair and the cramped position of her limbs, which were growing numb. But she made a great effort and remained still. The Chouan flung the sticks into the fireplace, after trying the strength of an old crane which was fastened to a long iron bar; then he set fire to the wood with his torch. Marie saw with terror that the man was the same Pille-Miche to whom her rival had delivered her, and whose figure, illuminated by the flame, was like that of the little boxwood men so grotesquely carved in Germany. The moans of his prisoner produced a broad grin upon features that were ribbed with wrinkles and tanned by the sun.

"You see," he said to his victim, "that we Christians keep our promises, which you don't. That fire is going to thaw out your legs and tongue and hands. Hey! hey! I don't see a dripping-pan to put under your feet; they are so fat the grease may put out the fire. Your house must be badly furnished if it can't give its master all he wants to warm him."

The victim uttered a sharp cry, as if he hoped someone would hear him through the ceiling and come to his assistance.

"Ho! sing away, Monsieur d'Orgemont; they are all asleep upstairs, and Marche-a-Terre is just behind me; he'll shut the cellar door."

While speaking Pille-Miche was sounding with the butt-end of his musket the mantel-piece of the chimney, the tiles of the floor, the walls and the ovens, to discover, if possible, where the miser hid his gold. This search was made with such adroitness that d'Orgemont kept silence, as if he feared to have been betrayed by some frightened servant; for, though he trusted his secrets to no one, his habits gave plenty of ground for logical deductions. Pille-Miche turned several times sharply to look at his victim, as children do when they try to guess, by the conscious expression of the comrade who has hidden an article, whether they are nearer to or farther away from it. D'Orgemont pretended to be alarmed when the Chouan tapped the ovens, which sounded hollow, and seemed to wish to play upon his eager credulity. Just then three other Chouans rushed down the steps and entered the kitchen. Seeing Marche-a-Terre among them Pille-Miche discontinued his search, after casting upon d'Orgemont a look that conveyed the wrath of his balked covetousness.

"Marie Lambrequin has come to life!" cried Marche-a-Terre, proclaiming by his manner that all other interests were of no account beside this great piece of news.

"I'm not surprised," said Pille-Miche, "he took the sacrament so often; the good God belonged to him."

"Ha! ha!" observed Mene-a-Bien, "that didn't stand him in anything at his death. He hadn't received absolution before the affair at La Pelerine. He had cheapened Goguelu's daughter, and was living in mortal sin. The Abbe Gudin said he'd have to roam round two months as a ghost before he could come to life. We saw him pass us,—he was pale, he was cold, he was thin, he smelt of the cemetery."

"And his Reverence says that if a ghost gets hold of a living man he can force him to be his companion," said the fourth Chouan.

The grotesque appearance of this last speaker drew Marche-a-Terre from the pious reflections he had been making on the accomplishment of this miracle of coming to life which, according to the Abbe Gudin would happen to every true defender of religion and the king.

"You see, Galope-Chopine," he said to the fourth man gravely, "what comes of omitting even the smallest duty commanded by our holy religion. It is a warning to us, given by Saint Anne of Auray, to be rigorous with ourselves for the slightest sin. Your cousin Pille-Miche has asked the Gars to give you the surveillance of Fougeres, and the Gars consents, and you'll be well paid—but you know with what flour we bake a traitor's bread."

"Yes, Monsieur Marche-a-Terre."

"And you know why I tell you that. Some say you like cider and gambling, but you can't play heads or tails now, remember; you must belong to us only, or—"

"By your leave, Monsieur Marche-a-Terre, cider and stakes are two good things which don't hinder a man's salvation."

"If my cousin commits any folly," said Pille-Miche, "it will be out of ignorance."

"In any way he commits it, if harm comes," said Marche-a-Terre, in a voice which made the arched roof tremble, "my gun won't miss him. You will answer for him to me," he added, turning to Pille-Miche; "for if he does wrong I shall take it out on the thing that fills your goatskin."

"But, Monsieur Marche-a-Terre, with all due respect," said Galope-Chopine, "haven't you sometimes taken a counterfeit Chouan for a real one."

"My friend," said Marche-a-Terre in a curt tone, "don't let that happen in your case, or I'll cut you in two like a turnip. As to the emissaries of the Gars, they all carry his glove, but since that affair at La Vivetiere the Grande Garce has added a green ribbon to it."

Pille Miche nudged his comrade by the elbow and showed him d'Orgemont, who was pretending to be asleep; but Pille-Miche and Marche-a-Terre both knew by experience that no one ever slept by the corner of their fire, and though the last words said to Galope-Chopine were almost whispered, they must have been heard by the victim, and the four Chouans looked at him fixedly, thinking perhaps that fear had deprived him of his senses.

Suddenly, at a slight sign from Marche-a-Terre, Pille-Miche pulled off d'Orgemont's shoes and stockings, Mene-a-Bien and Galope-Chopine seized him round the body and carried him to the fire. Then Marche-a-Terre took one of the thongs that tied the fagots and fastened the miser's feet to the crane. These actions and the horrible celerity with which they were done brought cries from the victim, which became heart-rending when Pille-Miche gathered the burning sticks under his legs.

"My friends, my good friends," screamed d'Orgemont, "you hurt me, you kill me! I'm a Christian like you."

"You lie in your throat!" replied Marche-a-Terre. "Your brother denied God; and as for you, you bought the abbey of Juvigny. The Abbe Gudin says we can roast apostates when we find them."

"But, my brothers in God, I don't refuse to pay."

"We gave you two weeks, and it is now two months, and Galope-Chopine here hasn't received the money."

"Haven't you received any of it, Galope-Chopine?" asked the miser, in despair.

"None of it, Monsieur d'Orgemont," replied Galope-Chopine, frightened.

The Chouans

The cries, which had sunk into groans, continuous as the rattle in a
dying throat, now began again with dreadful violence. Accustomed
to such scenes, the four Chouans looked at d'Orgemont, who was
twisting and howling, so coolly that they seemed like travellers
watching before an inn fire till the roast meat was done enough to
eat.

"I'm dying, I'm dying!" cried the victim, "and you won't get my
money."

In spite of these agonizing cries, Pille-Miche saw that the fire did not
yet scorch the skin; he drew the sticks cleverly together so as to make
a slight flame. On this d'Orgemont called out in a quavering voice:
"My friends, unbind me! How much do you want? A hundred
crowns —a thousand crowns—ten thousand crowns—a hundred
thousand crowns—I offer you two hundred thousand crowns!"

The voice became so lamentable that Mademoiselle de Verneuil
forgot her own danger and uttered an exclamation.

"Who spoke?" asked Marche-a-Terre.

The Chouans looked about them with terrified eyes. These men, so
brave in fight, were unable to face a ghost. Pille-Miche alone
continued to listen to the promises which the flames were now
extracting from his victim.

"Five hundred thousand crowns—yes, I'll give them," cried the
victim.

"Well, where are they?" answered Pille-Miche, tranquilly.

"Under the first apple-tree—Holy Virgin! at the bottom of the garden
to the left—you are brigands—thieves! Ah! I'm dying—there's ten
thousand francs—"

"Francs! we don't want francs," said Marche-a-Terre; "those
Republican coins have pagan figures which oughtn't to pass."

"They are not francs, they are good louis d'or. But oh! undo me,
unbind me! I've told you where my life is—my money."

171

The four Chouans looked at each other as if thinking which of their number they could trust sufficiently to disinter the money.

The cannibal cruelty of the scene so horrified Mademoiselle de Verneuil that she could bear it no longer. Though doubtful whether the role of ghost, which her pale face and the Chouan superstitions evidently assigned to her, would carry her safely through the danger, she called out, courageously, "Do you not fear God's anger? Unbind him, brutes!"

The Chouans raised their heads and saw in the air above them two eyes which shone like stars, and they fled, terrified. Mademoiselle de Verneuil sprang into the kitchen, ran to d'Orgemont, and pulled him so violently from the crane that the thong broke. Then with the blade of her dagger she cut the cords which bound him. When the miser was free and on his feet, the first expression of his face was a painful but sardonic grin.

"Apple-tree! yes, go to the apple-tree, you brigands," he said. "Ho, ho! this is the second time I've fooled them. They won't get a third chance at me."

So saying, he caught Mademoiselle de Verneuil's hand, drew her under the mantel-shelf to the back of the hearth in a way to avoid disturbing the fire, which covered only a small part of it; then he touched a spring; the iron back was lifted, and when their enemies returned to the kitchen the heavy door of the hiding-place had already fallen noiselessly. Mademoiselle de Verneuil then understood the carp-like movements she had seen the miser making.

"The ghost has taken the Blue with him," cried the voice of Marche-a-Terre.

The fright of the Chouans must have been great, for the words were followed by a stillness so profound that d'Orgemont and his companion could hear them muttering to themselves: "Ave, sancta Anna Auriaca gratia plena, Dominus tecum," etc.

"They are praying, the fools!" cried d'Orgemont.

"Hush! are you not afraid they will discover us?" said Mademoiselle de Verneuil, checking her companion.

The old man's laugh dissipated her fears.

"That iron back is set in a wall of granite two feet thick," he said. "We can hear them, but they can't hear us."

Then he took the hand of his preserver and placed it near a crevice through which a current of fresh air was blowing. She then perceived that the opening was made in the shaft of the chimney.

"Ai! ai!" cried d'Orgemont. "The devil! how my legs smart!"

The Chouans, having finished their prayer, departed, and the old miser again caught the hand of his companion and helped her to climb some narrow winding steps cut in the granite wall. When they had mounted some twenty of these steps the gleam of a lamp dimly lighted their heads. The miser stopped, turned to his companion, examined her face as if it were a bank note he was doubtful about cashing, and heaved a heavy sigh.

"By bringing you here," he said, after a moment's silence, "I have paid you in full for the service you did me; I don't see why I should give you—"

"Monsieur, I ask nothing of you," she said.

These words, and also, perhaps, the disdainful expression on the beautiful face, reassured the old man, for he answered, not without a sigh, "Ah! if you take it that way, I have gone too far not to continue on."

He politely assisted Marie to climb a few more steps rather strangely constructed, and half willingly, half reluctantly, ushered her into a small closet about four feet square, lighted by a lamp hanging from the ceiling. It was easy to see that the miser had made preparations to spend more than one day in this retreat if the events of the civil war compelled him to hide himself.

"Don't brush against that wall, you might whiten yourself," said d'Orgemont suddenly, as he hurriedly put his hand between the girl's shawl and the stones which seemed to have been lately whitewashed. The old man's action produced quite another effect from that he intended. Marie looked about her and saw in one corner a sort of projection, the shape of which forced from her a cry of terror, for she fancied it was that of a human being standing erect and mortared into the wall. D'Orgemont made a violent sign to her to hold her tongue, and his little eyes of a porcelain blue showed as much fear as those of his companion.

"Fool! do you think I murdered him? It is the body of my brother," and the old man gave a lugubrious sigh. "He was the first sworn-in priest; and this was the only asylum where he was safe against the fury of the Chouans and the other priests. He was my elder brother, and he alone had the patience to each me the decimal calculus. Oh! he was a good priest! He was economical and laid by money. It is four years since he died; I don't know what was the matter with him; perhaps it was that priests are so in the habit of kneeling down to pray that he couldn't get accustomed to standing upright here as I do. I walled him up there; *they'd* have dug him up elsewhere. Some day perhaps I can put him in holy ground, as he used to call it,— poor man, he only took the oath out of fear."

A tear rolled from the hard eyes of the little old man, whose rusty wig suddenly seemed less hideous to the girl, and she turned her eyes respectfully away from his distress. But, in spite of these tender reminiscences, d'Orgemont kept on saying, "Don't go near the wall, you might—"

His eyes never ceased to watch hers, hoping thus to prevent her from examining too closely the walls of the closet, where the close air was scarcely enough to inflate the lungs. Marie succeeded, however, in getting a sufficiently good look in spite of her Argus, and she came to the conclusion that the strange protuberances in the walls were neither more nor less than sacks of coin which the miser had placed there and plastered up.

Old d'Orgemont was now in a state of almost grotesque bewilderment. The pain in his legs, the terror he felt at seeing a human being in the midst of his hoards, could be read in every wrinkle of his face, and yet at the same time his eyes expressed, with unaccustomed fire, a lively emotion excited in him by the presence of his liberator, whose white and rosy cheek invited kisses, and whose velvety black eye sent waves of blood to his heart, so hot that he was much in doubt whether they were signs of life or of death.

"Are you married?" he asked, in a trembling voice.

"No," she said, smiling.

"I have a little something," he continued, heaving a sigh, "though I am not so rich as people think for. A young girl like you must love diamonds, trinkets, carriages, money. I've got all that to give—after my death. Hey! if you will—"

The old man's eyes were so shrewd and betrayed such calculation in this ephemeral love that Mademoiselle de Verneuil, as she shook her head in sign of refusal, felt that his desire to marry her was solely to bury his secret in another himself.

"Money!" she said, with a look of scorn which made him satisfied and angry both; "money is nothing to me. You would be three times as rich as you are, if you had all the gold that I have refused—" she stopped suddenly.

"Don't go near that wall, or—"

"But I hear a voice," she said; "it echoes through that wall,—a voice that is more to me than all your riches."

Before the miser could stop her Marie had laid her hand on a small colored engraving of Louis XV. on horseback; to her amazement it turned, and she saw, in a room beneath her, the Marquis de Montauran, who was loading a musket. The opening, hidden by a little panel on which the picture was gummed, seemed to form some opening in the ceiling of the adjoining chamber, which, no doubt, was the bedroom of the royalist general. D'Orgemont closed the opening with much precaution, and looked at the girl sternly.

"Don't say a word if you love your life. You haven't thrown your grappling-iron on a worthless building. Do you know that the Marquis de Montauran is worth more than one hundred thousand francs a year from lands which have not yet been confiscated? And I read in the Primidi de l'Ille-et-Vilaine a decree of the Consuls putting an end to confiscation. Ha! ha! you'll think the Gars a prettier fellow than ever, won't you? Your eyes are shining like two new louis d'or."

Mademoiselle de Verneuil's face was, indeed, keenly excited when she heard that well-known voice so near her. Since she had been standing there, erect, in the midst as it were of a silver mine, the spring of her mind, held down by these strange events, recovered itself. She seemed to have formed some sinister resolution and to perceive a means of carrying it out.

"There is no return from such contempt," she was saying to herself; "and if he cannot love me, I will kill him—no other woman shall have him."

"No, abbe, no!" cried the young chief, in a loud voice which was heard through the panel, "it must be so."

"Monsieur le marquis," replied the Abbe Gudin, haughtily; "you will scandalize all Brittany if you give that ball at Saint James. It is preaching, not dancing, which will rouse our villagers. Take guns, not fiddles."

"Abbe, you have sense enough to know that it is not in a general assembly of our partisans that I can learn to know these people, or judge of what I may be able to undertake with them. A supper is better for examining faces than all the spying in the world, of which, by the bye, I have a horror; they can be made to talk with glasses in their hand."

Marie quivered, as she listened, and conceived the idea of going to the ball and there avenging herself.

"Do you take me for an idiot with your sermon against dancing?" continued Montauran. "Wouldn't you yourself dance a reed if it would restore your order under its new name of Fathers of the Faith? Don't you know that Bretons come away from the mass and go to dancing? Are you aware that Messieurs Hyde de Neuville and d'Andigne had a conference, five days ago, with the First Consul, on the question of restoring his Majesty Louis XVIII.? Ah, monsieur, the princes are deceived as to the true state of France. The devotions which uphold them are solely those of rank. Abbe, if I have set my feet in blood, at least I will not go into it to my middle without full knowledge of what I do. I am devoted to the king, but not to four hot-heads, not to a man crippled with debt like Rifoel, not to 'chauffeurs,' not to—"

"Say frankly, monsieur, not to abbes who force contributions on the highway to carry on the war," retorted the Abbe Gudin.

"Why should I not say it?" replied the marquis, sharply; "and I'll say, further, that the great and heroic days of La Vendee are over."

"Monsieur le marquis, we can perform miracles without you."

"Yes, like that of Marie Lambrequin, whom I hear you have brought to life," said the marquis, smiling. "Come, come, let us have no rancor, abbe. I know that you run all risks and would shoot a Blue as readily as you say an *oremus*. God willing, I hope to make you assist with a mitre on your head at the king's coronation."

This last remark must have had some magic power, for the click of a musket was heard as the abbe exclaimed, "I have fifty cartridges in my pocket, monsieur le marquis, and my life is the king's."

"He's a debtor of mine," whispered the usurer to Marie. "I don't mean the five or six hundred crowns he has borrowed, but a debt of blood which I hope to make him pay. He can never suffer as much evil as I wish him, the damned Jesuit! He swore the death of my brother, and raised the country against him. Why? Because the poor man was afraid of the new laws." Then, after applying his ear to another part of his hiding-place, he added, "They are all decamping, those brigands. I suppose they are going to do some other miracle elsewhere. I only hope they won't bid me good-bye as they did the last time, by setting fire to my house."

After the lapse of about half an hour, during which time the usurer and Mademoiselle de Verneuil looked at each other as if they were studying a picture, the coarse, gruff voice of Galope-Chopine was heard saying, in a muffled tone: "There's no longer any danger, Monsieur d'Orgemont. But this time, you must allow that I have earned my thirty crowns."

"My dear," said the miser to Marie, "swear to shut your eyes."

Mademoiselle de Verneuil placed one hand over her eyelids; but for greater security d'Orgemont blew out the lamp, took his liberator by the hand, and helped her to make seven or eight steps along a difficult passage. At the end of some minutes he gently removed her hand, and she found herself in the very room the Marquis de Montauran had just quitted, and which was, in fact, the miser's own bedroom.

"My dear girl," said the old man, "you can safely go now. Don't look about you that way. I dare say you have no money with you. Here are ten crowns; they are a little shaved, but they'll pass. When you leave the garden you will see a path that leads straight to the town, or, as they say now, the district. But the Chouans will be at Fougeres, and it is to be presumed that you can't get back there at once. You may want some safe place to hide in. Remember what I say to you, but don't make use of it unless in some great emergency. You will see on the road which leads to Nid-aux-Crocs through the Val de Gibarry, a farmhouse belonging to Cibot—otherwise called Galope-Chopine. Go in, and say to his wife: 'Good-day, Becaniere,' and Barbette will hide you. If Galope-Chopine discovers you he will either take you for the ghost, if it is dark, or ten crowns will master him if it is light. Adieu, our account is squared. But if you choose," he added, waving his hand about him, "all this is yours."

Mademoiselle de Verneuil gave the strange old man a look of thanks, and succeeded in extracting a sigh from him, expressing a variety of emotions.

"You will of course return me my ten crowns; and please remark that I ask no interest. You can pay them to my credit with Maitre Patrat, the notary at Fougeres, who would draw our marriage contract if you consented to be mine. Adieu."

"Adieu," she said, smiling and waving her hand.

"If you ever want money," he called after her, "I'll lend it to you at five per cent; yes, only five—did I say five?—why, she's gone! That girl looks to me like a good one; nevertheless, I'll change the secret opening of my chimney."

Then he took a twelve-pound loaf and a ham, and returned to his hiding-place.

* * * * *

As Mademoiselle de Verneuil walked through the country she seemed to breathe a new life. The freshness of the night revived her after the fiery experience of the last few hours. She tried to follow the path explained to her by d'Orgemont, but the darkness became so dense after the moon had gone down that she was forced to walk hap-hazard, blindly. Presently the fear of falling down some precipice seized her and saved her life, for she stopped suddenly, fancying the ground would disappear before her if she made another step. A cool breeze lifting her hair, the murmur of the river, and her instinct all combined to warn her that she was probably on the verge of the Saint-Sulpice rocks. She slipped her arm around a tree and waited for dawn with keen anxiety, for she heard a noise of arms and horses and human voices; she was grateful to the darkness which saved her from the Chouans, who were evidently, as the miser had said, surrounding Fougeres.

Like fires lit at night as signals of liberty, a few gleams, faintly crimsoned, began to show upon the summits, while the bases of the mountains still retained the bluish tints which contrasted with the rosy clouds that were floating in the valley. Soon a ruby disk rose slowly on the horizon and the skies greeted it; the varied landscape, the bell-tower of Saint-Leonard, the rocks, the meadows buried in shadow, all insensibly reappeared, and the trees on the summits were defined against the skies in the rising glow. The sun freed itself with a graceful spring from the ribbons of flame and ochre and sapphire. Its vivid light took level lines from hill to hill and flowed into the vales. The dusk dispersed, day mastered Nature. A sharp breeze crisped the air, the birds sang, life wakened everywhere. But the girl had hardly time to cast her eyes over the whole of this wondrous landscape before, by a phenomenon not infrequent in these cool regions, the mists spread themselves in sheets, filled the valleys, and rose to the tops of the mountains, burying the great valley beneath a mantle of snow. Mademoiselle de Verneuil fancied for a moment she saw a *mer de glace*, like those of the Alps. Then the vaporous atmosphere rolled like the waves of ocean, lifted impenetrable billows which softly swayed, undulated, and were violently whirled, catching from the sun's rays a vivid rosy tint, and showing here and there in their depths the transparencies of a lake of molten silver. Suddenly the north wind swept this phantasmagoric scene and scattered the mists which laid a dew full of oxygen on the meadows.

Mademoiselle de Verneuil was now able to distinguish a dark mass of men on the rocks of Fougeres. Seven or eight hundred Chouans were running like ants through the suburb of Saint-Sulpice. The sleeping town would certainly have been overpowered in spite of its fortifications and its old gray towers, if Hulot had not been alert. A battery, concealed on a height at the farther end of the basin formed by the ramparts, replied to the first fire of the Chouans by taking them diagonally on the road to the castle. The balls swept the road. Then a company of Blues made a sortie from the Saint-Sulpice gate, profited by the surprise of the royalists to form in line upon the high-road, and poured a murderous fire upon them. The Chouans made no attempt to resist, seeing that the ramparts of the castle were covered with soldiers, and that the guns of the fortress sufficiently protected the Republican advance.

Meantime, however, other Chouans, masters of the little valley of the Nancon, had swarmed up the rocks and reached the Promenade, which was soon covered with goatskins, giving it to Marie's eyes the appearance of a thatched roof, brown with age. At the same moment loud reports were heard from the part of the town which overlooks the valley of Couesnon. Evidently, Fougeres was attacked on all sides and completely surrounded. Flames rising on the western side of the rock showed that the Chouans were setting fire to the suburbs; but these soon ceased, and a column of black smoke which succeeded them showed that the fire was extinguished. Brown and white clouds again hid the scene from Mademoiselle de Verneuil, but they were clouds of smoke from the fire and powder, which the wind dispersed. The Republican commander, as soon as he saw his first orders admirably executed, changed the direction of his battery so as to sweep, successively, the valley of the Nancon, the Queen's Staircase, and the base of the rock of Fougeres. Two guns posted at the gate of Saint-Leonard scattered the ant-hill of Chouans who had seized that position, and the national guard of the town, rushing in haste to the square before the Church, succeeded in dislodging the enemy. The fight lasted only half an hour, and cost the Blues a hundred men. The Chouans, beaten on all sides, retreated under orders from the Gars, whose bold attempt failed (although he did not know this) in consequence of the massacre at La Vivetiere, which had brought Hulot secretly and in all haste to Fougeres. The artillery had arrived only that evening, and the news had not reached Montauran; otherwise, he would certainly have abandoned an enterprise which, if it failed, could only have bad results. As soon as he heard the guns the marquis knew it would be madness to continue, out of mere pride, a surprise which had missed fire. Therefore, not to lose men uselessly, he sent at once to all points of the attack, ordering an immediate retreat. The commandant, seeing his adversary on the rocks of Saint-Sulpice surrounded by a council of men, endeavored to pour a volley upon him; but the spot was cleverly selected, and the young leader was out of danger in a moment. Hulot now changed parts with his opponent and became the aggressor. At the first sign of the Gars' intention, the company stationed under the walls of the castle were ordered to cut off the Chouans' retreat by seizing the upper outlet of the valley of the Nancon.

Notwithstanding her desire for revenge, Mademoiselle de Verneuil's sympathies were with the men commanded by her lover, and she turned hastily to see if the other end of the valley were clear for them; but the Blues, conquerors no doubt on the opposite side of Fougeres, were returning from the valley of Couesnon and taking possession of the Nid-aux-Crocs and that portion of the Saint-Sulpice rocks which overhang the lower end of the valley of the Nancon. The Chouans, thus hemmed in to the narrow fields of the gorge, seemed in danger of perishing to the last man, so cleverly and sagaciously were the commandant's measures taken. But Hulot's cannon were powerless at these two points; and here, the town of Fougeres being quite safe, began one of those desperate struggles which denoted the character of Chouan warfare.

Mademoiselle de Verneuil now comprehended the presence of the masses of men she had seen as she left the town, the meeting of the leaders at d'Orgemont's house, and all the other events of the night, wondering how she herself had escaped so many dangers. The attack, prompted by desperation, interested her so keenly that she stood motionless, watching the living pictures as they presented themselves to her sight. Presently the struggle at the foot of the mountain had a deeper interest for her. Seeing the Blues almost masters of the Chouans, the marquis and his friends rushed into the valley of the Nancon to support their men. The rocks were now covered with straggling groups of furious combatants deciding the question of life or death on a ground and with weapons that were more favorable to the Goatskins. Slowly this moving arena widened. The Chouans, recovering themselves, gained the rocks, thanks to the shrubs and bushes which grew here and there among them. For a moment Mademoiselle de Verneuil felt alarmed as she saw, rather late, her enemies swarming over the summit and defending the dangerous paths by which alone she could descend. Every issue on the mountain was occupied by one or other of the two parties; afraid of encountering them she left the tree behind which she had been sheltering, and began to run in the direction of the farm which d'Orgemont had mentioned to her. After running some time on the slope of Saint-Sulpice which overlooks the valley of Couesnon she saw a cow-shed in the distance, and thought it must belong to the house of Galope-Chopine, who had doubtless left his wife at home and alone during the fight. Mademoiselle de Verneuil hoped to be able to pass a few hours in this retreat until it was possible for her to return to Fougeres without danger. According to all appearance Hulot was to triumph. The Chouans were retreating so rapidly that she heard firing all about her, and the fear of being shot made her hasten to the cottage, the chimney of which was her landmark. The path she was following ended at a sort of shed covered with a furze-roof, supported by four stout trees with the bark still on them. A mud wall formed the back of this shed, under which were a cider-mill, a flail to thresh buckwheat, and several agricultural implements. She stopped before one of the posts, unwilling to cross the dirty bog which formed a sort of courtyard to the house which, in her Parisian ignorance, she had taken for a stable.

The cabin, protected from the north wind by an eminence towering above the roof, which rested against it, was not without a poetry of its own; for the tender shoots of elms, heather, and various rock-flowers wreathed it with garlands. A rustic staircase, constructed between the shed and the house, enabled the inhabitants to go to the top of the rock and breathe a purer air. On the left, the eminence sloped abruptly down, giving to view a series of fields, the first of which belonged no doubt to this farm. These fields were like bowers, separated by banks which were planted with trees. The road which led to them was barred by the trunk of an old, half-rotten tree,—a Breton method of enclosure the name of which may furnish, further on, a digression which will complete the characterization of this region. Between the stairway cut in the schist rock and the path closed by this old tree, in front of the marsh and beneath the overhanging rock, several granite blocks roughly hewn, and piled one upon the other, formed the four corners of the cottage and held up the planks, cobblestones, and pitch amalgam of which the walls were made. The fact that one half of the roof was covered with furze instead of thatch, and the other with shingles or bits of board cut into the form of slates, showed that the building was in two parts; one half, with a broken hurdle for a door, served as a stable, the other half was the dwelling of the owner. Though this hut owed to the neighborhood of the town a few improvements which were wholly absent from such buildings that were five or six miles further off, it showed plainly enough the instability of domestic life and habits to which the wars and customs of feudality had reduced the serf; even to this day many of the peasants of those parts call a seignorial chateau, "The Dwelling."

While examining the place, with an astonishment we can readily conceive, Mademoiselle de Verneuil noticed here and there in the filth of the courtyard a few bits of granite so placed as to form stepping-stones to the house. Hearing the sound of musketry that was evidently coming nearer, she jumped from stone to stone, as if crossing a rivulet, to ask shelter. The house was closed by a door opening in two parts; the lower one of wood, heavy and massive, the upper one a shutter which served as a window. In many of the smaller towns of France the shops have the same type of door though far more decorated, the lower half possessing a call-bell. The door in question opened with a wooden latch worthy of the golden age, and the upper part was never closed except at night, for it was the only opening through which daylight could enter the room. There was, to be sure, a clumsy window, but the glass was thick like the bottom of a bottle, and the lead which held the panes in place took so much room that the opening seemed intended to intercept the light rather than admit it. As soon as Mademoiselle de Verneuil had turned the creaking hinges of the lower door she smelt an intolerable ammoniacal odor, and saw that the beasts in the stable had kicked through the inner partition which separated the stable from the dwelling. The interior of the farmhouse, for such it was, did not belie its exterior.

Mademoiselle de Verneuil was asking herself how it was possible for human beings to live in such habitual filth, when a ragged boy about eight or nine years old suddenly presented his fresh and rosy face, with a pair of fat cheeks, lively eyes, ivory teeth, and a mass of fair hair, which fell in curls upon his half-naked shoulders. His limbs were vigorous, and his attitude had the charm of that amazement and naive curiosity which widens a child's eyes. The little fellow was a picture of beauty.

"Where is your mother?" said Marie, in a gentle voice, stooping to kiss him between the eyes.

After receiving her kiss the child slipped away like an eel, and disappeared behind a muck-heap which was piled at the top of a mound between the path and the house; for, like many Breton farmers who have a system of agriculture that is all their own, Galope-Chopine put his manure in an elevated spot, so that by the time it was wanted for use the rains had deprived it of all its virtue. Alone for a few minutes, Marie had time to make an inventory. The room in which she waited for Barbette was the whole house. The most obvious and sumptuous object was a vast fireplace with a *mantle*-shelf of blue granite. The etymology of that word was shown by a strip of green serge, edged with a pale-green ribbon, cut in scallops, which covered and overhung the whole shelf, on which stood a colored plaster cast of the Holy Virgin. On the pedestal of the statuette were two lines of a religious poem very popular in Brittany:—

> "I am the mother of God,
> Protectress of the sod."

Behind the Virgin a hideous image, daubed with red and blue under pretence of painting, represented Saint-Labre. A green serge bed of the shape called "tomb," a clumsy cradle, a spinning-wheel, common chairs, and a carved chest on which lay utensils, were about the whole of Galope-Chopine's domestic possessions. In front of the window stood a chestnut table flanked by two benches of the same wood, to which the sombre light coming through the thick panes gave the tone of mahogany. An immense cask of cider, under the bung of which Mademoiselle de Verneuil noticed a pool of yellow mud, which had decomposed the flooring, although it was made of scraps of granite conglomerated in clay, proved that the master of the house had a right to his Chouan name, and that the pints galloped down either his own throat or that of his friends. Two enormous jugs full of cider stood on the table. Marie's attention, caught at first by the innumerable spider's-webs which hung from the roof, was fixing itself on these pitchers when the noise of fighting, growing more and more distinct, impelled her to find a hiding-place, without waiting for the woman of the house, who, however, appeared at that moment.

"Good-morning, Becaniere," said Marie, restraining a smile at the appearance of a person who bore some resemblance to the heads which architects attach to window-casings.

"Ha! you come from d'Orgemont?" answered Barbette, in a tone that was far from cordial.

"Yes, where can you hide me? for the Chouans are close by—"

"There," replied Barbette, as much amazed at the beauty as by the strange apparel of a being she could hardly believe to be of her own sex,—"there, in the priest's hiding-place."

She took her to the head of the bed, and was putting her behind it, when they were both startled by the noise of a man springing into the courtyard. Barbette had scarcely time to drop the curtain of the bed and fold it about the girl before she was face to face with a fugitive Chouan.

"Where can I hide, old woman? I am the Comte de Bauvan," said the new-comer.

Mademoiselle de Verneuil quivered as she recognized the voice of the belated guest, whose words, still a secret to her, brought about the catastrophe of La Vivetiere.

"Alas! monseigneur, don't you see, I have no place? What I'd better do is to keep outside and watch that no one gets in. If the Blues come, I'll let you know. If I stay here, and they find me with you, they'll burn my house down."

Barbette left the hut, feeling herself incapable of settling the interests of two enemies who, in virtue of the double role her husband was playing, had an equal right to her hiding-place.

"I've only two shots left," said the count, in despair. "It will be very unlucky if those fellows turn back now and take a fancy to look under this bed."

He placed his gun gently against the headboard behind which Marie was standing among the folds of the green serge, and stooped to see if there was room for him under the bed. He would infallibly have seen her feet, but she, rendered desperate by her danger, seized his gun, jumped quickly into the room, and threatened him. The count broke into a peal of laughter when he caught sight of her, for, in order to hide herself, Marie had taken off her broad-brimmed Chouan hat, and her hair was escaping, in heavy curls, from the lace scarf which she had worn on leaving home.

"Don't laugh, monsieur le comte; you are my prisoner. If you make the least movement, you shall know what an offended woman is capable of doing."

As the count and Marie stood looking at each other with differing emotions, confused voices were heard without among the rocks, calling out, "Save the Gars! spread out, spread out, save the Gars!"

Barbette's voice, calling to her boy, was heard above the tumult with very different sensations by the two enemies, to whom Barbette was really speaking instead of to her son.

"Don't you see the Blues?" she cried sharply. "Come here, you little scamp, or I shall be after you. Do you want to be shot? Come, hide, quick!"

While these things took place rapidly a Blue jumped into the marshy courtyard.

"Beau-Pied!" exclaimed Mademoiselle de Verneuil.

Beau-Pied, hearing her voice, rushed into the cottage, and aimed at the count.

"Aristocrat!" he cried, "don't stir, or I'll demolish you in a wink, like the Bastille."

"Monsieur Beau-Pied," said Mademoiselle de Verneuil, in a persuasive voice, "you will be answerable to me for this prisoner. Do as you like with him now, but you must return him to me safe and sound at Fougeres."

"Enough, madame!"

"Is the road to Fougeres clear?"

"Yes, it's safe enough—unless the Chouans come to life."

Mademoiselle de Verneuil picked up the count's gun gaily, and smiled satirically as she said to her prisoner, "Adieu, monsieur le comte, au revoir!"

Then she darted down the path, having replaced the broad hat upon her head.

"I have learned too late," said the count, "not to joke about the virtue of a woman who has none."

"Aristocrat!" cried Beau-Pied, sternly, "if you don't want me to send you to your *ci-devant* paradise, you will not say a word against that beautiful lady."

Mademoiselle de Verneuil returned to Fougeres by the paths which connect the rocks of Saint-Sulpice with the Nid-aux-Crocs. When she reached the latter height and had threaded the winding way cut in its rough granite, she stopped to admire the pretty valley of the Nancon, lately so turbulent and now so tranquil. Seen from that point, the vale was like a street of verdure. Mademoiselle de Verneuil re-entered the town by the Porte Saint-Leonard. The inhabitants, still uneasy about the fighting, which, judging by the distant firing, was still going on, were waiting the return of the National Guard, to judge of their losses. Seeing the girl in her strange costume, her hair dishevelled, a gun in her hand, her shawl and gown whitened against the walls, soiled with mud and wet with dew, the curiosity of the people was keenly excited,—all the more because the power, beauty, and singularity of this young Parisian had been the subject of much discussion.

Francine, full of dreadful fears, had waited for her mistress throughout the night, and when she saw her she began to speak; but Marie, with a kindly gesture, silenced her.

"I am not dead, my child," she said. "Ah!" she added, after a pause, "I wanted emotions when I left Paris, and I have had them!"

Francine asked if she should get her some food, observing that she must be in great need of it.

"No, no; a bath, a bath!" cried Mademoiselle de Verneuil. "I must dress at once."

Francine was not a little surprised when her mistress required her to unpack the most elegant of the dresses she had brought with her. Having bathed and breakfasted, Marie made her toilet with all the minute care which a woman gives to that important act when she expects to meet the eyes of her lover in a ball-room. Francine could not explain to herself the mocking gaiety of her mistress. It was not the joy of love,—a woman never mistakes that; it was rather an expression of concentrated maliciousness, which to Francine's mind boded evil. Marie herself drew the curtains of the window from which the glorious panorama could be seen, then she moved the sofa to the chimney corner, turning it so that the light would fall becomingly on her face; then she told Francine to fetch flowers, that the room might have a festive air; and when they came she herself directed their arrangement in a picturesque manner. Giving a last

The Chouans

glance of satisfaction at these various preparations she sent Francine
to the commandant with a request that he would bring her prisoner
to her; then she lay down luxuriously on a sofa, partly to rest, and
partly to throw herself into an attitude of graceful weakness, the
power of which is irresistible in certain women. A soft languor, the
seductive pose of her feet just seen below the drapery of her gown,
the plastic ease of her body, the curving of the throat,—all, even the
droop of her slender fingers as they hung from the pillow like the
buds of a bunch of jasmine, combined with her eyes to produce
seduction. She burned certain perfumes to fill the air with those
subtle emanations which affect men's fibres powerfully, and often
prepare the way for conquests which women seek to make without
seeming to desire them. Presently the heavy step of the old soldier
resounded in the adjoining room.

"Well, commandant, where is my captive?" she said.

"I have just ordered a picket of twelve men to shoot him, being taken
with arms in his hand."

"Why have you disposed of my prisoner?" she asked. "Listen to me,
commandant; surely, if I can trust your face, the death of a man *after*
a fight is no particular satisfaction to you. Well, then, give my
Chouan a reprieve, for which I will be responsible, and let me see
him. I assure you that aristocrat has become essential to me, and he
can be made to further the success of our plans. Besides, to shoot a
mere amateur in Chouannerie would be as absurd as to fire on a
balloon when a pinprick would disinflate it. For heaven's sake leave
cruelty to the aristocracy. Republicans ought to be generous.
Wouldn't you and yours have forgiven the victims of Quiberon?
Come, send your twelve men to patrol the town, and dine with me
and bring the prisoner. There is only an hour of daylight left, and
don't you see," she added smiling, "that if you are too late, my toilet
will have lost its effect?"

"But, mademoiselle," said the commandant, amazed.

"Well, what? But I know what you mean. Don't be anxious; the
count shall not escape. Sooner or later that big butterfly will burn
himself in your fire."

The commandant shrugged his shoulders slightly, with the air of a
man who is forced to obey, whether he will or no, the commands of a

pretty woman; and he returned in about half an hour, followed by the Comte de Bauvan.

Mademoiselle de Verneuil feigned surprise and seemed confused that the count should see her in such a negligent attitude; then, after reading in his eyes that her first effect was produced, she rose and busied herself about her guests with well-bred courtesy. There was nothing studied or forced in her motions, smiles, behavior, or voice, nothing that betrayed premeditation or purpose. All was harmonious; no part was over-acted; an observer could not have supposed that she affected the manners of a society in which she had not lived. When the Royalist and the Republic were seated she looked sternly at the count. He, on his part, knew women sufficiently well to feel certain that the offence he had committed against this woman was equivalent to a sentence of death. But in spite of this conviction, and without seeming either gay or gloomy, he had the air of a man who did not take such serious results into consideration; in fact, he really thought it ridiculous to fear death in presence of a pretty woman. Marie's stern manner roused ideas in his mind.

"Who knows," thought he, "whether a count's coronet wouldn't please her as well as that of her lost marquis? Montauran is as lean as a nail, while I—" and he looked himself over with an air of satisfaction. "At any rate I should save my head."

These diplomatic revelations were wasted. The passion the count proposed to feign for Mademoiselle de Verneuil became a violent caprice, which the dangerous creature did her best to heighten.

"Monsieur le comte," she said, "you are my prisoner, and I have the right to dispose of you. Your execution cannot take place without my consent, and I have too much curiosity to let them shoot you at present."

"And suppose I am obstinate enough to keep silence?" he replied gaily.

"With an honest woman, perhaps, but with a woman of the town, no, no, monsieur le comte, impossible!" These words, full of bitter sarcasm, were hissed, as Sully says, in speaking of the Duchesse de Beaufort, from so sharp a beak that the count, amazed, merely looked at his antagonist. "But," she continued, with a scornful glance, "not to contradict you, if I am a creature of that kind I will act like one. Here is your gun," and she offered him his weapon with a mocking air.

"On the honor of a gentleman, mademoiselle—"

"Ah!" she said, interrupting him, "I have had enough of the honor of gentlemen. It was on the faith of that that I went to La Vivetiere. Your leader had sworn to me that I and my escort should be safe there."

"What an infamy!" cried Hulot, contracting his brows.

"The fault lies with monsieur le comte," said Marie, addressing Hulot. "I have no doubt the Gars meant to keep his word, but this gentleman told some calumny about me which confirmed those that Charette's mistress had already invented—"

"Mademoiselle," said the count, much troubled, "with my head under the axe I would swear that I said nothing but the truth."

"In saying what?"

"That you were the—"

"Say the word, mistress of—"

"The Marquis de Lenoncourt, the present duke, a friend of mine," replied the count.

"Now I can let you go to execution," she said, without seeming at all agitated by the outspoken reply of the count, who was amazed at the real or pretended indifference with which she heard his statement. "However," she added, laughing, "you have not wronged me more than that friend of whom you suppose me to have been the—Fie! monsieur le comte; surely you used to visit my father, the Duc de Verneuil? Yes? well then—"

Evidently considering Hulot one too many for the confidence she was about to make, Mademoiselle de Verneuil motioned the count to her side, and said a few words in her ear. Monsieur de Bauvan gave a low ejaculation of surprise and looked with bewilderment at Marie, who completed the effect of her words by leaning against the chimney in the artless and innocent attitude of a child.

"Mademoiselle," cried the count, "I entreat your forgiveness, unworthy as I am of it."

"I have nothing to forgive," she replied. "You have no more ground for repentance than you had for the insolent supposition you proclaimed at La Vivetiere. But this is a matter beyond your comprehension. Only, remember this, monsieur le comte, the daughter of the Duc de Verneuil has too generous a spirit not to take a lively interest in your fate."

"Even after I have insulted you?" said the count, with a sort of regret.

"Some are placed so high that insult cannot touch them. Monsieur le comte,—I am one of them."

As she said the words, the girl assumed an air of pride and nobility which impressed the prisoner and made the whole of this strange intrigue much less clear to Hulot than the old soldier had thought it. He twirled his moustache and looked uneasily at Mademoiselle de Verneuil, who made him a sign, as if to say she was still carrying out her plan.

"Now," continued Marie, after a pause, "let us discuss these matters. Francine, my dear, bring lights."

She adroitly led the conversation to the times which had now, within a few short years, become the "ancien regime." She brought back that period to the count's mind by the liveliness of her remarks and sketches, and gave him so many opportunities to display his wit, by cleverly throwing repartees in his way, that he ended by thinking he had never been so charming; and that idea having rejuvenated him, he endeavored to inspire this seductive young woman with his own good opinion of himself. The malicious creature practised, in return, every art of her coquetry upon him, all the more adroitly because it was mere play to her. Sometimes she let him think he was making rapid progress, and then, as if surprised at the sentiment she was feeling, she showed a sudden coolness which charmed him, and served to increase imperceptibly his impromptu passion. She was like a fisherman who lifts his line from time to time to see if the fish is biting. The poor count allowed himself to be deceived by the innocent air with which she accepted two or three neatly turned compliments. Emigration, Brittany, the Republic, and the Chouans were far indeed from his thoughts. Hulot sat erect and silent as the god Thermes. His want of education made him quite incapable of taking part in a conversation of this kind; he supposed that the talking pair were very witty, but his efforts at comprehension were limited to discovering whether they were plotting against the Republic in covert language.

"Montauran," the count was saying, "has birth and breeding, he is a charming fellow, but he doesn't understand gallantry. He is too young to have seen Versailles. His education is deficient. Instead of diplomatically defaming, he strikes a blow. He may be able to love violently, but he will never have that fine flower of breeding in his gallantry which distinguished Lauzun, Adhemar, Coigny, and so many others! He hasn't the winning art of saying those pretty nothings to women which, after all, they like better than bursts of passion, which soon weary them. Yes, though he has undoubtedly had many love-affairs, he has neither the grace nor the ease that should belong to them."

"I have noticed that myself," said Marie.

"Ah!" thought the count, "there's an inflection in her voice, and a look in her eye which shows me plainly I shall soon be *on terms* with her; and faith! to get her, I'll believe all she wants me to."

He offered her his hand, for dinner was now announced. Mademoiselle de Verneuil did the honors with a politeness and tact which could only have been acquired by the life and training of a court.

"Leave us," she whispered to Hulot as they left the table. "You will only frighten him; whereas, if I am alone with him I shall soon find out all I want to know; he has reached the point where a man tells me everything he thinks, and sees through my eyes only."

"But afterwards?" said Hulot, evidently intending to claim the prisoner.

"Afterwards, he is to be free—free as air," she replied.

"But he was taken with arms in his hand."

"No," she said, making one of those sophistical jokes with which women parry unanswerable arguments, "I had disarmed him. Count," she said, turning back to him as Hulot departed, "I have just obtained your liberty, but—nothing for nothing," she added, laughing, with her head on one side as if to interrogate him.

"Ask all, even my name and my honor," he cried, intoxicated. "I lay them at your feet."

He advanced to seize her hand, trying to make her take his passion for gratitude; but Mademoiselle de Verneuil was not a woman to be thus misled. So, smiling in a way to give some hope to this new lover, she drew back a few steps and said: "You might make me regret my confidence."

"The imagination of a young girl is more rapid than that of a woman," he answered, laughing.

"A young girl has more to lose than a woman."

"True; those who carry a treasure ought to be distrustful."

"Let us quit such conventional language," she said, "and talk seriously. You are to give a ball at Saint-James. I hear that your headquarters, arsenals, and base of supplies are there. When is the ball to be?"

"To-morrow evening."

"You will not be surprised if a slandered woman desires, with a woman's obstinacy, to obtain a public reparation for the insults offered to her, in presence of those who witnessed them. I shall go to your ball. I ask you to give me your protection from the moment I enter the room until I leave it. I ask nothing more than a promise," she added, as he laid his hand on his heart. "I abhor oaths; they are too like precautions. Tell me only that you engage to protect my person from all dangers, criminal or shameful. Promise to repair the wrong you did me, by openly acknowledging that I am the daughter of the Duc de Verneuil; but say nothing of the trials I have borne in being illegitimate,—this will pay your debt to me. Ha! two hours' attendance on a woman in a ball-room is not so dear a ransom for your life, is it? You are not worth a ducat more." Her smile took the insult from her words.

"What do you ask for the gun?" said the count, laughing.

"Oh! more than I do for you."

"What is it?"

"Secrecy. Believe me, my dear count, a woman is never fathomed except by a woman. I am certain that if you say one word of this, I shall be murdered on my way to that ball. Yesterday I had warning enough. Yes, that woman is quick to act. Ah! I implore you," she said, "contrive that no harm shall come to me at the ball."

"You will be there under my protection," said the count, proudly. "But," he added, with a doubtful air, "are you coming for the sake of Montauran?"

"You wish to know more than I know myself," she answered, laughing. "Now go," she added, after a pause. "I will take you to the gate of the town myself, for this seems to me a cannibal warfare."

"Then you do feel some interest in me?" exclaimed the count. "Ah! mademoiselle, permit me to hope that you will not be insensible to my friendship—for that sentiment must content me, must it not?" he added with a conceited air.

"Ah! diviner!" she said, putting on the gay expression a woman assumes when she makes an avowal which compromises neither her dignity nor her secret sentiments.

Then, having slipped on a pelisse, she accompanied him as far as the Nid-aux-Crocs. When they reached the end of the path she said, "Monsieur, be absolutely silent on all this; even to the marquis"; and she laid her finger on both lips.

The count, emboldened by so much kindness, took her hand; she let him do so as though it were a great favor, and he kissed it tenderly.

"Oh! mademoiselle," he cried, on knowing himself beyond all danger, "rely on me for life, for death. Though I owe you a gratitude equal to that I owe my mother, it will be very difficult to restrain my feelings to mere respect."

He sprang into the narrow pathway. After watching him till he reached the rocks of Saint-Sulpice, Marie nodded her head in sign of satisfaction, saying to herself in a low voice: "That fat fellow has given me more than his life for his life! I can make him my creator at a very little cost! Creature or creator, that's all the difference there is between one man and another—"

She did not finish her thought, but with a look of despair she turned and re-entered the Porte Saint-Leonard, where Hulot and Corentin were awaiting her.

"Two more days," she cried, "and then—" She stopped, observing that they were not alone—"he shall fall under your guns," she whispered to Hulot.

The commandant recoiled a step and looked with a jeering contempt, impossible to render, at the woman whose features and expression gave no sign whatever of relenting. There is one thing remarkable about women: they never reason about their blameworthy actions,— feeling carries them off their feet; even in their dissimulation there is an element of sincerity; and in women alone crime may exist without baseness, for it often happens that they do not know how it came about that they committed it.

"I am going to Saint-James, to a ball the Chouans give to-morrow night, and—"

"But," said Corentin, interrupting her, "that is fifteen miles distant; had I not better accompany you?"

"You think a great deal too much of something I never think of at all," she replied, "and that is yourself."

Marie's contempt for Corentin was extremely pleasing to Hulot, who made his well-known grimace as she turned away in the direction of her own house. Corentin followed her with his eyes, letting his face express a consciousness of the fatal power he knew he could exercise over the charming creature, by working upon the passions which sooner or later, he believed, would give her to him.

As soon as Mademoiselle de Verneuil reached home she began to deliberate on her ball-dress. Francine, accustomed to obey without understanding her mistress's motives, opened the trunks, and suggested a Greek costume. The Republican fashions of those days were all Greek in style. Marie chose one which could be put in a box that was easy to carry.

"Francine, my dear, I am going on an excursion into the country; do you want to go with me, or will you stay behind?"

"Stay behind!" exclaimed Francine; "then who would dress you?"

"Where have you put that glove I gave you this morning?"

"Here it is."

"Sew this green ribbon into it, and, above all, take plenty of money." Then noticing that Francine was taking out a number of the new Republican coins, she cried out, "Not those; they would get us murdered. Send Jeremie to Corentin—no, stay, the wretch would follow me—send to the commandant; ask him from me for some six-franc crowns."

With the feminine sagacity which takes in the smallest detail, she thought of everything. While Francine was completing the arrangements for this extraordinary trip, Marie practised the art of imitating an owl, and so far succeeded in rivalling Marche-a-Terre that the illusion was a good one. At midnight she left Fougeres by the gate of Saint-Leonard, took the little path to Nid-aux-Crocs, and started, followed by Francine, to cross the Val de Gibarry with a firm step, under the impulse of that strong will which gives to the body and its bearing such an expression of force. To leave a ball-room with sufficient care to avoid a cold is an important affair to the health of a woman; but let her have a passion in her heart, and her body becomes adamant. Such an enterprise as Marie had now undertaken would have floated in a bold man's mind for a long time; but Mademoiselle de Verneuil had no sooner thought of it than its dangers became to her attractions.

"You are starting without asking God to bless you," said Francine, turning to look at the tower of Saint-Leonard.

The pious Breton stopped, clasped her hands, and said an "Ave" to Saint Anne of Auray, imploring her to bless their expedition; during which time her mistress waited pensively, looking first at the artless attitude of her maid who was praying fervently, and then at the effects of the vaporous moonlight as it glided among the traceries of the church building, giving to the granite all the delicacy of filagree. The pair soon reached the hut of Galope-Chopine. Light as their steps were they roused one of those huge watch-dogs on whose fidelity the Bretons rely, putting no fastening to their doors but a simple latch. The dog ran to the strangers, and his bark became so threatening that they were forced to retreat a few steps and call for help. But no one came. Mademoiselle de Verneuil then gave the owl's cry, and instantly the rusty hinges of the door made a creaking sound, and Galope-Chopine, who had risen hastily, put out his head.

"I wish to go to Saint-James," said Marie, showing the Gars' glove. "Monsieur le Comte de Bauvan told me that you would take me there and protect me on the way. Therefore be good enough to get us two riding donkeys, and make yourself ready to go with us. Time is precious, for if we do not get to Saint-James before to-morrow night I can neither see the ball nor the Gars."

Galope-Chopine, completely bewildered, took the glove and turned it over and over, after lighting a pitch candle about a finger thick and the color of gingerbread. This article of consumption, imported into Brittany from the North, was only one more proof to the eyes in this strange country of a utter ignorance of all commercial principles, even the commonest. After seeing the green ribbon, staring at Mademoiselle de Verneuil, scratching his ear, and drinking a beaker of cider (having first offered a glass to the beautiful lady), Galope-Chopine left her seated before the table and went to fetch the required donkeys.

The violet gleam cast by the pitch candle was not powerful enough to counteract the fitful moonlight, which touched the dark floor and furniture of the smoke-blackened cottage with luminous points. The little boy had lifted his pretty head inquisitively, and above it two cows were poking their rosy muzzles and brilliant eyes through the holes in the stable wall. The big dog, whose countenance was by no means the least intelligent of the family, seemed to be examining the strangers with as much curiosity as the little boy. A painter would have stopped to admire the night effects of this scene, but Marie, not wishing to enter into conversation with Barbette, who sat up in bed and began to show signs of amazement at recognizing her, left the hovel to escape its fetid air and the questions of its mistress. She ran quickly up the stone staircase behind the cottage, admiring the vast details of the landscape, the aspect of which underwent as many changes as spectators made steps either upward to the summits or downward to the valleys. The moonlight was now enveloping like a luminous mist the valley of Couesnon. Certainly a woman whose heart was burdened with a despised love would be sensitive to the melancholy which that soft brilliancy inspires in the soul, by the weird appearance it gives to objects and the colors with which it tints the streams.

The silence was presently broken by the braying of a donkey. Marie went quickly back to the hut, and the party started. Galope-Chopine, armed with a double-barrelled gun, wore a long goatskin, which gave him something the look of Robinson Crusoe. His blotched face, seamed with wrinkles, was scarcely visible under the broad-brimmed hat which the Breton peasants still retain as a tradition of the olden time; proud to have won, after their servitude, the right to wear the former ornament of seignorial heads. This nocturnal caravan, protected by a guide whose clothing, attitudes, and person had something patriarchal about them, bore no little resemblance to the Flight into Egypt as we see it represented by the sombre brush of Rembrandt. Galope-Chopine carefully avoided the main-road and guided the two women through the labyrinth of by-ways which intersect Brittany.

Mademoiselle de Verneuil then understood the Chouan warfare. In threading these complicated paths, she could better appreciate the condition of a country which when she saw it from an elevation had seemed to her so charming, but into which it was necessary to penetrate before the dangers and inextricable difficulties of it could be understood. Round each field, and from time immemorial, the peasants have piled mud walls, about six feet high, and prismatic in shape; on the top of which grow chestnuts, oaks and beeches. The walls thus planted are called hedges (Norman hedges) and the long branches of the trees sweeping over the pathways arch them. Sunken between these walls (made of a clay soil) the paths are like the covered ways of a fortification, and where the granite rock, which in these regions comes to the surface of the ground, does not make a sort of rugged natural pavement, they become so impracticable that the smallest vehicles can only be drawn over them by two pairs of oxen or Breton horses, which are small but usually vigorous. These by-ways are so swampy that foot-passengers have gradually by long usage made other paths beside them on the hedge-banks which are called "rotes"; and these begin and end with each division into fields. In order to cross from one field to another it is necessary to climb the clay banks by means of steps which are often very slippery after a rain.

Travellers have many other obstacles to encounter in these intricate paths. Thus surrounded, each field is closed by what is called in the West an *echalier*. That is a trunk or stout branch of a tree, one end of which, being pierced, is fitted to an upright post which serves as a pivot on which it turns. One end of the *echalier* projects far enough beyond the pivot to hold a weight, and this singular rustic gate, the post of which rests in a hole made in the bank, is so easy to work that a child can handle it. Sometimes the peasants economize the stone which forms the weight by lengthening the trunk or branch beyond the pivot. This method of enclosure varies with the genius of each proprietor. Sometimes it consists of a single trunk or branch, both ends of which are embedded in the bank. In other places it looks like a gate, and is made of several slim branches placed at regular distances like the steps of a ladder lying horizontally. The form turns, like the *echalier*, on a pivot. These "hedges" and *echaliers* give the region the appearance of a huge chess-board, each field forming a square, perfectly isolated from the rest, closed like a fortress and protected by ramparts. The gate, which is very easy to defend, is a dangerous spot for assailants. The Breton peasant thinks he improves his fallow land by encouraging the growth of gorse, a shrub so well treated in these regions that it soon attains the height of a man. This delusion, worthy of a population which puts its manure on the highest spot in the courtyard, has covered the soil to a proportion of one fourth with masses of gorse, in the midst of which a thousand men might ambush. Also there is scarcely a field without a number of old apple-trees, the fruit being used for cider, which kill the vegetation wherever their branches cover the ground. Now, if the reader will reflect on the small extent of open ground within these hedges and large trees whose hungry roots impoverish the soil, he will have an idea of the cultivation and general character of the region through which Mademoiselle de Verneuil was now passing.

It is difficult to say whether the object of these enclosures is to avoid all disputes of possession, or whether the custom is a lazy one of keeping the cattle from straying, without the trouble of watching them; at any rate such formidable barriers are permanent obstacles, which make these regions impenetrable and ordinary warfare impossible. There lies the whole secret of the Chouan war. Mademoiselle de Verneuil saw plainly the necessity the Republic was under to strangle the disaffection by means of police and by negotiation, rather than by a useless employment of military force. What could be done, in fact, with a people wise enough to despise the possession of towns, and hold to that of an open country already furnished with indestructible fortifications? Surely, nothing except negotiate; especially as the whole active strength of these deluded peasants lay in a single able and enterprising leader. She admired the genius of the minister who, sitting in his study, had been able to grasp the true way of procuring peace. She thought she understood the considerations which act on the minds of men powerful enough to take a bird's-eye view of an empire; men whose actions, criminal in the eyes of the masses, are the outcome of a vast and intelligent thought. There is in these terrible souls some mysterious blending of the force of fate and that of destiny, some prescience which suddenly elevates them above their fellows; the masses seek them for a time in their own ranks, then they raise their eyes and see these lordly souls above them.

Such reflections as these seemed to Mademoiselle de Verneuil to justify and even to ennoble her thoughts of vengeance; this travail of her soul and its expectations gave her vigor enough to bear the unusual fatigues of this strange journey. At the end of each property Galope-Chopine made the women dismount from their donkeys and climb the obstructions; then, mounting again, they made their way through the boggy paths which already felt the approach of winter. The combination of tall trees, sunken paths, and enclosed places, kept the soil in a state of humidity which wrapped the travellers in a mantle of ice. However, after much wearisome fatigue, they managed to reach the woods of Marignay by sunrise. The journey then became less difficult, and led by a broad footway through the forest. The arch formed by the branches, and the great size of the trees protected the travellers from the weather, and the many difficulties of the first half of their way did not recur.

They had hardly gone a couple of miles through the woods before they heard a confused noise of distant voices and the tinkling of a bell, the silvery tones of which did not have the monotonous sound given by the movements of cattle. Galope-Chopine listened with great attention, as he walked along, to this melody; presently a puff of wind brought several chanted words to his ear, which seemed to affect him powerfully, for he suddenly turned the wearied donkeys into a by-path, which led away from Saint-James, paying no attention to the remonstrances of Mademoiselle de Verneuil, whose fears were increased by the darkness of the forest path along which their guide now led them. To right and left were enormous blocks of granite, laid one upon the other, of whimsical shape. Across them huge roots had glided, like monstrous serpents, seeking from afar the juicy nourishment enjoyed by a few beeches. The two sides of the road resembled the subterranean grottos that are famous for stalactites. Immense festoons of stone, where the darkling verdure of ivy and holly allied itself to the green-gray patches of the moss and lichen, hid the precipices and the openings into several caves. When the three travellers had gone a few steps through a very narrow path a most surprising spectacle suddenly unfolded itself to Mademoiselle de Verneuil's eyes, and made her understand the obstinacy of her Chouan guide.

A semi-circular basin of granite blocks formed an ampitheatre, on the rough tiers of which rose tall black pines and yellowing chestnuts, one above the other, like a vast circus, where the wintry sun shed its pale colors rather than poured its light, and autumn had spread her tawny carpet of fallen leaves. About the middle of this hall, which seemed to have had the deluge for its architect, stood three enormous Druid stones,—a vast altar, on which was raised an old church-banner. About a hundred men, kneeling with bared heads, were praying fervently in this natural enclosure, where a priest, assisted by two other ecclesiastics, was saying mass. The poverty of the sacerdotal vestments, the feeble voice of the priest, which echoed like a murmur through the open space, the praying men filled with conviction and united by one and the same sentiment, the bare cross, the wild and barren temple, the dawning day, gave the primitive character of the earlier times of Christianity to the scene. Mademoiselle de Verneuil was struck with admiration. This mass said in the depths of the woods, this worship driven back by persecution to its sources, the poesy of ancient times revived in the midst of this weird and romantic nature, these armed and unarmed Chouans, cruel and praying, men yet children, all these things resembled nothing that she had ever seen or yet imagined. She remembered admiring in her childhood the pomps of the Roman church so pleasing to the senses; but she knew nothing of God *alone*, his cross on the altar, his altar the earth. In place of the carved foliage of a Gothic cathedral, the autumnal trees upheld the sky; instead of a thousand colors thrown through stained glass windows, the sun could barely slide its ruddy rays and dull reflections on altar, priest, and people. The men present were a fact, a reality, and not a system,—it was a prayer, not a religion. But human passions, the momentary repression of which gave harmony to the picture, soon reappeared on this mysterious scene and gave it powerful vitality.

As Mademoiselle de Verneuil reached the spot the reading of the gospel was just over. She recognized in the officiating priest, not without fear, the Abbe Gudin, and she hastily slipped behind a granite block, drawing Francine after her. She was, however, unable to move Galope-Chopine from the place he had chosen, and from which he intended to share in the benefits of the ceremony; but she noticed the nature of the ground around her, and hoped to be able to evade the danger by getting away, when the service was over, before the priests. Through a large fissure of the rock that hid her, she saw the Abbe Gudin mounting a block of granite which served him as a pulpit, where he began his sermon with the words, —

"In nomine Patris et Filii, et Spiritus Sancti."

All present made the sign of the cross.

"My dear friends," continued the abbe, "let us pray in the first place for the souls of the dead, —Jean Cochegrue, Nicalos Laferte, Joseph Brouet, Francois Parquoi, Sulpice Coupiau, all of this parish, and dead of wounds received in the fight on Mont Pelerine and at the siege of Fougeres. *De profundis,"* etc.

The psalm was recited, according to custom, by the congregation and the priests, taking verses alternately with a fervor which augured well for the success of the sermon. When it was over the abbe continued, in a voice which became gradually louder and louder, for the former Jesuit was not unaware that vehemence of delivery was in itself a powerful argument with which to persuade his semi-savage hearers.

"These defenders of our God, Christians, have set you an example of duty," he said. "Are you not ashamed of what will be said of you in paradise? If it were not for these blessed ones, who have just been received with open arms by all the saints, our Lord might have thought that your parish is inhabited by Mahometans! —Do you know, men, what is said of you in Brittany and in the king's presence? What! you don't know? Then I shall tell you. They say: 'Behold, the Blues have cast down altars, and killed priests, and murdered the king and queen; they mean to make the parish folk of Brittany Blues like themselves, and send them to fight in foreign lands, away from their churches, where they run the risk of dying without confession and going eternally to hell; and yet the gars of Marignay, whose churches they have burned, stand still with folded arms! Oh! oh! this Republic of damned souls has sold the property of God and that of the nobles at auction; it has shared the proceeds with the Blues; it has decreed, in order to gorge itself with money as it does with blood, that a crown shall be only worth three francs instead of six; and yet the gars of Marignay haven't seized their weapons and driven the Blues from Brittany! Ha! paradise will be closed to them! they can never save their souls!' That's what they say of you in the king's presence! It is your own salvation, Christians, which is at stake. Your souls are to be saved by fighting for religion and the king. Saint Anne of Auray herself appeared to me yesterday at half-past two o'clock; and she said to me these very words which I now repeat to you: 'Are you a priest of Marignay?' 'Yes, madame, ready to serve you.' 'I am Saint Anne of Auray, aunt of God, after the manner of Brittany. I have come to bid you warn the people of Marignay that they must not hope for salvation if they do not take arms. You are to refuse them absolution for their sins unless they serve God. Bless their guns, and those who gain absolution will never miss the Blues, because their guns are sanctified.' She disappeared, leaving an odor of incense behind her. I marked the spot. It is under the oak of the Patte d'Oie; just where that beautiful wooden Virgin was placed by the rector of Saint-James; to whom the crippled mother of Pierre Leroi (otherwise called Marche-a-Terre) came to pray, and was cured of all her pains, because of her son's good deeds. You see her there in the midst of you, and you know that she walks without assistance. It was a miracle—a miracle intended, like the resurrection of Marie Lambrequin to prove to you that God will never forsake the Breton cause so long as the people fight for his servants and for the king. Therefore, my dear brothers, if you wish to save your souls and show yourselves defenders of God and the king, you will obey all the orders of the man whom God has sent to us, and whom we call THE GARS. Then indeed, you will no longer be Mahometans; you will rank with all the gars of Brittany under the flag of God. You can take from the pockets of the Blues the money they have stolen from you; for, if the fields have to go uncultivated while you are making war, God and the king will deliver to you the spoils of your enemies. Shall it be said, Christians, that the gars of Marignay are behind the gars of the Morbihan, the gars of Saint-Georges, of Vitre, or Antrain, who are all faithful to God and the king? Will you let them get all the spoils? Will you stand like heretics, with your arms folded, when other Bretons are saving their souls and saving their king? 'Forsake all, and follow me,' says the Gospel. Have we not forsaken our tithes, we priests? And you, I say to you, forsake all for this holy war! You shall be like the Maccabees. All will be forgiven you. You will find the priests and curates in your midst, and you will conquer! Pay attention to these words, Christians," he said, as he ended; "for this day only have we the power to bless your guns. Those who do not take advantage of the Saint's favor will not find her merciful; she will not forgive them or listen to them as she did in the last war."

This appeal, enforced by the power of a loud voice and by many gestures, the vehemence of which bathed the orator in perspiration, produced, apparently, very little effect. The peasants stood motionless, their eyes on the speaker, like statues; but Mademoiselle de Verneuil presently noticed that this universal attitude was the result of a spell cast by the abbe on the crowd. He had, like great actors, held his audience as one man by addressing their passions and self-interests. He had absolved excesses before committal, and broken the only bonds which held these boorish men to the practice of religious and social precepts. He had prostituted his sacred office to political interests; but it must be said that, in these times of revolution, every man made a weapon of whatever he possessed for the benefit of his party, and the pacific cross of Jesus became as much an instrument of war as the peasant's plough-share.

Seeing no one with whom to advise, Mademoiselle de Verneuil turned to look for Francine, and was not a little astonished to see that she shared in the rapt enthusiasm, and was devoutly saying her chaplet over some beads which Galope-Chopine had probably given her during the sermon.

"Francine," she said, in a low voice, "are you afraid of being a Mahometan?"

"Oh! mademoiselle," replied the girl, "just see Pierre's mother; she is walking!"

Francine's whole attitude showed such deep conviction that Marie understood at once the secret of the homily, the influence of the clergy over the rural masses, and the tremendous effect of the scene which was now beginning.

The peasants advanced one by one and knelt down, presenting their guns to the preacher, who laid them upon the altar. Galope-Chopine offered his old duck-shooter. The three priests sang the hymn "Veni, Creator," while the celebrant wrapped the instruments of death in bluish clouds of incense, waving the smoke into shapes that appeared to interlace one another. When the breeze had dispersed the vapor the guns were returned in due order. Each man received his own on his knees from the hands of the priests, who recited a Latin prayer as they returned them. After the men had regained their places, the profound enthusiasm of the congregation, mute till then, broke forth and resounded in a formidable manner.

"*Domine salvum fac regem!*" was the prayer which the preacher intoned in an echoing voice, and was then sung vehemently by the people. The cry had something savage and warlike in it. The two notes of the word *regem*, readily interpreted by the peasants, were taken with such energy that Mademoiselle de Verneuil's thoughts reverted almost tenderly to the exiled Bourbon family. These recollections awakened those of her past life. Her memory revived the fetes of a court now dispersed, in which she had once a share. The face of the marquis entered her reverie. With the natural mobility of a woman's mind she forgot the scene before her and reverted to her plans of vengeance, which might cost her her life or come to nought under the influence of a look. Seeing a branch of holly the trivial thought crossed her mind that in this decisive moment, when she wished to appear in all her beauty at the ball, she had no decoration for her hair; and she gathered a tuft of the prickly leaves and shining berries with the idea of wearing them.

"Ho! ho! my gun may miss fire on a duck, but on a Blue, never!" cried Galope-Chopine, nodding his head in sign of satisfaction.

Marie examined her guide's face attentively, and found it of the type of those she had just seen. The old Chouan had evidently no more ideas than a child. A naive joy wrinkled his cheeks and forehead as he looked at his gun; but a pious conviction cast upon that expression of his joy a tinge of fanaticism, which brought into his face for an instant the signs of the vices of civilization.

Presently they reached a village, or rather a collection of huts like that of Galope-Chopine, where the rest of the congregation arrived before Mademoiselle de Verneuil had finished the milk and bread and butter which formed the meal. This irregular company was led by the abbe, who held in his hand a rough cross draped with a flag, followed by a gars, who was proudly carrying the parish banner. Mademoiselle de Verneuil was compelled to mingle with this detachment, which was on its way, like herself, to Saint-James, and would naturally protect her from all danger as soon as Galope-Chopine informed them that the Gars glove was in her possession, provided always that the abbe did not see her.

Towards sunset the three travellers arrived safely at Saint-James, a little town which owes its name to the English, by whom it was built in the fourteenth century, during their occupation of Brittany. Before entering it Mademoiselle de Verneuil was witness of a strange scene of this strange war, to which, however, she gave little attention; she feared to be recognized by some of her enemies, and this dread hastened her steps. Five or six thousand peasants were camping in a field. Their clothing was not in any degree warlike; in fact, this tumultuous assembly resembled that of a great fair. Some attention was needed to even observe that these Bretons were armed, for their goatskins were so made as to hide their guns, and the weapons that were chiefly visible were the scythes with which some of the men had armed themselves while awaiting the distribution of muskets. Some were eating and drinking, others were fighting and quarrelling in loud tones, but the greater part were sleeping on the ground. An officer in a red uniform attracted Mademoiselle de Verneuil's attention, and she supposed him to belong to the English service. At a little distance two other officers seemed to be trying to teach a few Chouans, more intelligent than the rest, to handle two cannon, which apparently formed the whole artillery of the royalist army. Shouts hailed the coming of the gars of Marignay, who were recognized by their banner. Under cover of the tumult which the new-comers and the priests excited in the camp, Mademoiselle de Verneuil was able to make her way past it and into the town without danger. She stopped at a plain-looking inn not far from the building where the ball was to be given. The town was so full of strangers that she could only obtain one miserable room. When she was safely in it Galope-Chopine brought Francine the box which contained the ball dress, and having done so he stood stock-still in an attitude of indescribable irresolution. At any other time Mademoiselle de Verneuil would have been much amused to see what a Breton peasant can be like when he leaves his native parish; but now she broke the charm by opening her purse and producing four crowns of six francs each, which she gave him.

"Take it," she said, "and if you wish to oblige me, you will go straight back to Fougeres without entering the camp or drinking any cider."

The Chouan, amazed at her liberality, looked first at the crowns (which he had taken) and then at Mademoiselle de Verneuil; but she made him a sign with her hand and he disappeared.

"How could you send him away, mademoiselle?" said Francine. "Don't you see how the place is surrounded? we shall never get away! and who will protect you here?"

"You have a protector of your own," said Marie maliciously, giving in an undertone Marche-a-Terre's owl cry which she was constantly practising.

Francine colored, and smiled rather sadly at her mistress's gaiety.

"But who is yours?" she said.

Mademoiselle de Verneuil plucked out her dagger, and showed it to the frightened girl, who dropped on a chair and clasped her hands.

"What have you come here for, Marie?" she cried in a supplicating voice which asked no answer.

Mademoiselle de Verneuil was busily twisting the branches of holly which she had gathered.

"I don't know whether this holly will be becoming," she said; "a brilliant skin like mine may possibly bear a dark wreath of this kind. What do you think, Francine?"

Several remarks of the same kind as she dressed for the ball showed the absolute self-possession and coolness of this strange woman. Whoever had listened to her then would have found it hard to believe in the gravity of a situation in which she was risking her life. An Indian muslin gown, rather short and clinging like damp linen, revealed the delicate outlines of her shape; over this she wore a red drapery, numerous folds of which, gradually lengthening as they fell by her side, took the graceful curves of a Greek peplum. This voluptuous garment of the pagan priestesses lessened the indecency of the rest of the attire which the fashions of the time suffered women to wear. To soften its immodesty still further, Marie threw a gauze scarf over her shoulders, left bare and far too low by the red drapery. She wound the long braids of her hair into the flat irregular cone above the nape of the neck which gives such grace to certain antique statues by an artistic elongation of the head, while a few stray locks escaping from her forehead fell in shining curls beside her cheeks. With a form and head thus dressed, she presented a perfect likeness of the noble masterpieces of Greek sculpture. She smiled as she looked with approval at the arrangement of her hair, which brought out the beauties of her face, while the scarlet berries of the holly wreath which she laid upon it repeated charmingly the color of the peplum. As she twisted and turned a few leaves, to give capricious diversity to their arrangement, she examined her whole costume in a mirror to judge of its general effect.

"I am horrible to-night," she said, as though she were surrounded by flatterers. "I look like a statue of Liberty."

She placed the dagger carefully in her bosom leaving the rubies in the hilt exposed, their ruddy reflections attracting the eye to the hidden beauties of her shape. Francine could not bring herself to leave her mistress. When Marie was ready she made various pretexts to follow her. She must help her to take off her mantle, and the overshoes which the mud and muck in the streets compelled her to wear (though the roads had been sanded for this occasion); also the gauze veil which Mademoiselle de Verneuil had thrown over her head to conceal her features from the Chouans who were collecting in the streets to watch the company. The crowd was in fact so great that they were forced to make their way through two hedges of Chouans. Francine no longer strove to detain her mistress, and after giving a few last touches to a costume the greatest charm of which was its exquisite freshness, she stationed herself in the courtyard that she might not abandon this beloved mistress to her fate without being able to fly to her succor; for the poor girl foresaw only evil in these events.

A strange scene was taking place in Montauran's chamber as Marie was on her way to the ball. The young marquis, who had just finished dressing, was putting on the broad red ribbon which distinguished him as first in rank of the assembly, when the Abbe Gudin entered the room with an anxious air.

"Monsieur le marquis, come quickly," he said. "You alone can quell a tumult which has broken out, I don't know why, among the leaders. They talk of abandoning the king's cause. I think that devil of a Rifoel is at the bottom of it. Such quarrels are always caused by some mere nonsense. Madame du Gua reproached him, so I hear, for coming to the ball ill-dressed."

"That woman must be crazy," cried the marquis, "to try to—"

"Rifoel retorted," continued the abbe, interrupting his chief, "that if you had given him the money promised him in the king's name—"

"Enough, enough; I understand it all now. This scene has all been arranged, and you are put forward as ambassador—"

"I, monsieur le marquis!" said the abbe, again interrupting him. "I am supporting you vigorously, and you will, I hope, do me the justice to believe that the restoration of our altars in France and that of the king upon the throne of his fathers are far more powerful incentives to my humble labors than the bishopric of Rennes which you—"

The abbe dared say no more, for the marquis smiled bitterly at his last words. However, the young chief instantly repressed all expression of feeling, his brow grew stern, and he followed the Abbe Gudin into a hall where the worst of the clamor was echoing.

"I recognize no authority here," Rifoel was saying, casting angry looks at all about him and laying his hand on the hilt of his sabre.

"Do you recognize that of common-sense?" asked the marquis, coldly.

The young Chevalier de Vissard, better known under his patronymic of Rifoel, was silent before the general of the Catholic armies.

"What is all this about, gentlemen?" asked the marquis, examining the faces round him.

"This, monsieur le marquis," said a famous smuggler, with the awkwardness of a man of the people who long remains under the yoke of respect to a great lord, though he admits no barriers after he has once jumped them, and regards the aristocrat as an equal only, "*this*," he said, "and you have come in the nick of time to hear it. I am no speaker of gilded phrases, and I shall say things plainly. I commanded five hundred men during the late war. Since we have taken up arms again I have raised a thousand heads as hard as mine for the service of the king. It is now seven years that I have risked my life in the good cause; I don't blame you, but I say that the laborer is worthy of his hire. Now, to begin with, I demand that I be called Monsieur de Cottereau. I also demand that the rank of colonel shall be granted me, or I send in my adhesion to the First Consul! Let me tell you, monsieur le marquis, my men and I have a devilishly importunate creditor who must be satisfied—he's here!" he added, striking his stomach.

"Have the musicians come?" said the marquis, in a contemptuous tone, turning to Madame du Gua.

But the smuggler had dealt boldly with an important topic, and the calculating, ambitious minds of those present had been too long in suspense as to what they might hope for from the king to allow the scorn of their new leader to put an end to the scene. Rifoel hastily blocked the way before Montauran, and seized his hand to oblige him to remain.

"Take care, monsieur le marquis," he said; "you are treating far too lightly men who have a right to the gratitude of him whom you are here to represent. We know that his Majesty has sent you with full powers to judge of our services, and we say that they ought to be recognized and rewarded, for we risk our heads upon the scaffold daily. I know, so far as I am concerned, that the rank of brigadier-general—"

"You mean colonel."

"No, monsieur le marquis; Charette made me a colonel. The rank I mention cannot be denied me. I am not arguing for myself, I speak for my brave brothers-in-arms, whose services ought to be recorded. Your signature and your promise will suffice them for the present; though," he added, in a low voice, "I must say they are satisfied with very little. But," he continued, raising his voice, "when the sun rises on the chateau of Versailles to glorify the return of the monarchy after the faithful have conquered France, *in France*, for the king, will they obtain favors for their families, pensions for widows, and the restitution of their confiscated property? I doubt it. But, monsieur le marquis, we must have certified proof of our services when that time comes. I will never distrust the king, but I do distrust those cormorants of ministers and courtiers, who tingle his ears with talk about the public welfare, the honor of France, the interests of the crown, and other crochets. They will sneer at a loyal Vendean or a brave Chouan, because he is old and the sword he drew for the good cause dangles on his withered legs, palsied with exposure. Can you say that we are wrong in feeling thus?"

"You talk well, Monsieur du Vissard, but you are over hasty," replied the marquis.

"Listen, marquis," said the Comte de Bauvan, in a whisper. "Rifoel has really, on my word, told the truth. You are sure, yourself, to have the ear of the king, while the rest of us only see him at a distance and from time to time. I will own to you that if you do not give me your word as a gentleman that I shall, in due course of time, obtain the place of Master of Woods and Waters in France, the devil take me if I will risk my neck any longer. To conquer Normandy for the king is not an easy matter, and I demand the Order for it. But," he added, coloring, "there's time enough to think of that. God forbid that I should imitate these poor mercenaries and harass you. Speak to the king for me, and that's enough."

Each of the chiefs found means to let the marquis know, in a more or less ingenious manner, the exaggerated price they set upon their services. One modestly demanded the governorship of Brittany; another a barony; this one a promotion; that one a command; and all wanted pensions.

"Well, baron," said the marquis to Monsieur du Guenic, "don't you want anything?"

"These gentlemen have left me nothing but the crown of France, marquis, but I might manage to put up with that—"

"Gentlemen!" cried the Abbe Gudin, in a loud voice, "remember that if you are too eager you will spoil everything in the day of victory. The king will then be compelled to make concessions to the revolutionists."

"To those Jacobins!" shouted the smuggler. "Ha! if the king would let me have my way, I'd answer for my thousand men; we'd soon wring their necks and be rid of them."

"Monsieur *de* Cottereau," said the marquis, "I see some of our invited guests arriving. We must all do our best by attention and courtesy to make them share our sacred enterprise; you will agree, I am sure, that this is not the moment to bring forward your demands, however just they may be."

So saying, the marquis went to the door, as if to meet certain of the country nobles who were entering the room, but the bold smuggler barred his way in a respectful manner.

"No, no, monsieur le marquis, excuse me," he said; "the Jacobins taught me too well in 1793 that it is not he who sows and reaps who eats the bread. Sign this bit of paper for me, and to-morrow I'll bring you fifteen hundred gars. If not, I'll treat with the First Consul."

Looking haughtily about him, the marquis saw plainly that the boldness of the old partisan and his resolute air were not displeasing to any of the spectators of this debate. One man alone, sitting by himself in a corner of the room, appeared to take no part in the scene, and to be chiefly occupied in filling his pipe. The contemptuous air with which he glanced at the speakers, his modest demeanor, and a look of sympathy which the marquis encountered in his eyes, made the young leader observe the man, whom he then recognized as Major Brigaut, and he went suddenly up to him.

"And you, what do you want?" he said.

"Oh, monsieur le marquis, if the king comes back that's all I want."

"But for yourself?"

"For myself? are you joking?"

The marquis pressed the horny hand of the Breton, and said to Madame du Gua, who was near them: "Madame, I may perish in this enterprise before I have time to make a faithful report to the king on the Catholic armies of Brittany. I charge you, in case you live to see the Restoration, not to forget this honorable man nor the Baron du Guenic. There is more devotion in them than in all those other men put together."

He pointed to the chiefs, who were waiting with some impatience till the marquis should reply to their demands. They were all holding papers in their hands, on which, no doubt, their services were recorded over the signatures of the various generals of the former war; and all were murmuring. The Abbe Gudin, the Comte de Bauvan, and the Baron du Guenic were consulting how best to help the marquis in rejecting these extravagant demands, for they felt the position of the young leader to be extremely delicate.

Suddenly the marquis ran his blue eyes, gleaming with satire, over the whole assembly, and said in a clear voice: "Gentlemen, I do not know whether the powers which the king has graciously assigned to me are such that I am able to satisfy your demands. He doubtless did not foresee such zeal, such devotion, on your part. You shall judge yourselves of the duties put upon me,—duties which I shall know how to accomplish."

So saying, he left the room and returned immediately holding in his hand an open letter bearing the royal seal and signature.

"These are the letters-patent in virtue of which you are to obey me," he said. "They authorize me to govern the provinces of Brittany, Normandy, Maine, and Anjou, in the king's name, and to recognize the services of such officers as may distinguish themselves in his armies."

A movement of satisfaction ran through the assembly. The Chouans approached the marquis and made a respectful circle round him. All eyes fastened on the king's signature. The young chief, who was standing near the chimney, suddenly threw the letters into the fire, and they were burned in a second.

"I do not choose to command any," cried the young man, "but those who see a king in the king, and not a prey to prey upon. You are free, gentlemen, to leave me."

Madame du Gua, the Abbe Gudin, Major Brigaut, the Chevalier du Vissard, the Baron du Guenic, and the Comte de Bauvan raised the cry of "Vive le roi!" For a moment the other leaders hesitated; then, carried away by the noble action of the marquis, they begged him to forget what had passed, assuring him that, letters-patent or not, he must always be their leader.

"Come and dance," cried the Comte de Bauvan, "and happen what will! After all," he added, gaily, "it is better, my friends, to pray to God than the saints. Let us fight first, and see what comes of it."

"Ha! that's good advice," said Brigaut. "I have never yet known a day's pay drawn in the morning."

The assembly dispersed about the rooms, where the guests were now arriving. The marquis tried in vain to shake off the gloom which darkened his face. The chiefs perceived the unfavorable impression made upon a young man whose devotion was still surrounded by all the beautiful illusions of youth, and they were ashamed of their action.

However, a joyous gaiety soon enlivened the opening of the ball, at which were present the most important personages of the royalist party, who, unable to judge rightly, in the depths of a rebellious province, of the actual events of the Revolution, mistook their hopes for realities. The bold operations already begun by Montauran, his name, his fortune, his capacity, raised their courage and caused that political intoxication, the most dangerous of all excitements, which does not cool till torrents of blood have been uselessly shed. In the minds of all present the Revolution was nothing more than a passing trouble to the kingdom of France, where, to their belated eyes, nothing was changed. The country belonged as it ever did to the house of Bourbon. The royalists were the lords of the soil as completely as they were four years earlier, when Hoche obtained less a peace than an armistice. The nobles made light of the revolutionists; for them Bonaparte was another, but more fortunate, Marceau. So gaiety reigned. The women had come to dance. A few only of the chiefs, who had fought the Blues, knew the gravity of the situation; but they were well aware that if they talked of the First Consul and his power to their benighted companions, they could not make themselves understood. These men stood apart and looked at the women with indifference. Madame du Gua, who seemed to do the honors of the ball, endeavored to quiet the impatience of the dancers by dispensing flatteries to each in turn. The musicians were tuning their instruments and the dancing was about to begin, when Madame du Gua noticed the gloom on de Montauran's face and went hurriedly up to him.

"I hope it is not that vulgar scene you have just had with those clodhoppers which depresses you?" she said.

She got no answer; the marquis, absorbed in thought, was listening in fancy to the prophetic reasons which Marie had given him in the midst of the same chiefs at La Vivetiere, urging him to abandon the struggle of kings against peoples. But the young man's soul was too proud, too lofty, too full perhaps of conviction, to abandon an enterprise he had once begun, and he decided at this moment, to continue it boldly in the face of all obstacles. He raised his head haughtily, and for the first time noticed that Madame du Gua was speaking to him.

"Your mind is no doubt at Fougeres," she remarked bitterly, seeing how useless her efforts to attract his attention had been. "Ah, monsieur, I would give my life to put *her* within your power, and see you happy with her."

"Then why have you done all you could to kill her?"

"Because I wish her dead or in your arms. Yes, I may have loved the Marquis de Montauran when I thought him a hero, but now I feel only a pitying friendship for him; I see him shorn of all his glory by a fickle love for a worthless woman."

"As for love," said the marquis, in a sarcastic tone, "you judge me wrong. If I loved that girl, madame, I might desire her less; if it were not for you, perhaps I should not think of her at all."

"Here she is!" exclaimed Madame du Gua, abruptly.

The haste with which the marquis looked round went to the heart of the woman; but the clear light of the wax candles enabled her to see every change on the face of the man she loved so violently, and when he turned back his face, smiling at her woman's trick, she fancied there was still some hope of recovering him.

"What are you laughing at?" asked the Comte de Bauvan.

"At a soap-bubble which has burst," interposed Madame du Gua, gaily. "The marquis, if we are now to believe him, is astonished that his heart ever beat the faster for that girl who presumes to call herself Mademoiselle de Verneuil. You know who I mean."

"That girl!" echoed the count. "Madame, the author of a wrong is bound to repair it. I give you my word of honor that she is really the daughter of the Duc de Verneuil."

"Monsieur le comte," said the marquis, in a changed voice, "which of your statements am I to believe,—that of La Vivetiere, or that now made?"

The loud voice of a servant at the door announced Mademoiselle de Verneuil. The count sprang forward instantly, offered his hand to the beautiful woman with every mark of profound respect, and led her through the inquisitive crowd to the marquis and Madame du Gua. "Believe the one now made," he replied to the astonished young leader.

Madame du Gua turned pale at the unwelcome sight of the girl, who stood for a moment, glancing proudly over the assembled company, among whom she sought to find the guests at La Vivetiere. She awaited the forced salutation of her rival, and, without even looking at the marquis, she allowed the count to lead her to the place of honor beside Madame du Gua, whose bow she returned with an air that was slightly protecting. But the latter, with a woman's instinct, took no offense; on the contrary, she immediately assumed a smiling, friendly manner. The extraordinary dress and beauty of Mademoiselle de Verneuil caused a murmur throughout the ballroom. When the marquis and Madame du Gua looked towards the late guests at La Vivetiere they saw them in an attitude of respectful admiration which was not assumed; each seemed desirous of recovering favor with the misjudged young woman. The enemies were in presence of each other.

"This is really magic, mademoiselle," said Madame du Gua; "there is no one like you for surprises. Have you come all alone?"

"All alone," replied Mademoiselle de Verneuil. "So you have only one to kill to-night, madame."

"Be merciful," said Madame du Gua. "I cannot express to you the pleasure I have in seeing you again. I have truly been overwhelmed by the remembrance of the wrongs I have done you, and am most anxious for an occasion to repair them."

"As for those wrongs, madame, I readily pardon those you did to me, but my heart bleeds for the Blues whom you murdered. However, I excuse all, in return for the service you have done me."

Madame du Gua lost countenance as she felt her hand pressed by her beautiful rival with insulting courtesy. The marquis had hitherto stood motionless, but he now seized the arm of the count.

"You have shamefully misled me," he said; "you have compromised my honor. I am not a Geronte of comedy, and I shall have your life or you will have mine."

"Marquis," said the count, haughtily, "I am ready to give you all the explanations you desire."

They passed into the next room. The witnesses of this scene, even those least initiated into the secret, began to understand its nature, so that when the musicians gave the signal for the dancing to begin no one moved.

"Mademoiselle, what service have I rendered you that deserves a return?" said Madame du Gua, biting her lips in a sort of rage.

"Did you not enlighten me as to the true character of the Marquis de Montauran, madame? With what utter indifference that man allowed me to go to my death! I give him up to you willingly!"

"Then why are you here?" asked Madame du Gua, eagerly.

"To recover the respect and consideration you took from me at La Vivetiere, madame. As for all the rest, make yourself easy. Even if the marquis returned to me, you know very well that a return is never love."

Madame du Gua took Mademoiselle de Verneuil's hand with that affectionate touch and motion which women practise to each other, especially in the presence of men.

"Well, my poor dear child," she said, "I am glad to find you so reasonable. If the service I did you was rather harsh," she added, pressing the hand she held, and feeling a desire to rend it as her fingers felt its softness and delicacy, "it shall at least be thorough.

Listen to me, I know the character of the Gars; he meant to deceive you; he neither can nor will marry any woman except—"

"Ah!"

"Yes, mademoiselle, he has accepted his dangerous mission to win the hand of Mademoiselle d'Uxelles, a marriage to which his Majesty has promised his countenance."

"Ah! ah!"

Mademoiselle de Verneuil added not a word to that scornful ejaculation. The young and handsome Chevalier du Vissard, eager to be forgiven for the joke which had led to the insults at La Vivetiere, now came up to her and respectfully invited her to dance. She placed her hand in his, and they took their places in a quadrille opposite to Madame du Gua. The gowns of the royalist women, which recalled the fashions of the exiled court, and their creped and powdered hair seemed absurd as soon as they were contrasted with the attire which republican fashions authorized Mademoiselle de Verneuil to wear. This attire, which was elegant, rich, and yet severe, was loudly condemned but inwardly envied by all the women present. The men could not restrain their admiration for the beauty of her natural hair and the adjustment of a dress the charm of which was in the proportions of the form which it revealed.

At that moment the marquis and the count re-entered the ballroom behind Mademoiselle de Verneuil, who did not turn her head. If a mirror had not been there to inform her of Montauran's presence, she would have known it from Madame du Gua's face, which scarcely concealed, under an apparently indifferent air, the impatience with which she awaited the conflict which must, sooner or later, take place between the lovers. Though the marquis talked with the count and other persons, he heard the remarks of all the dancers who from time to time in the mazes of the quadrille took the place of Mademoiselle de Verneuil and her partner.

"Positively, madame, she came alone," said one.

"She must be a bold woman," replied the lady.

"If I were dressed like that I should feel myself naked," said another woman.

"Oh, the gown is not decent, certainly," replied her partner; "but it is so becoming, and she is so handsome."

"I am ashamed to look at such perfect dancing, for her sake; isn't it exactly that of an opera girl?" said the envious woman.

"Do you suppose that she has come here to intrigue for the First Consul?" said another.

"A joke if she has," replied the partner.

"Well, she can't offer innocence as a dowry," said the lady, laughing.

The Gars turned abruptly to see the lady who uttered this sarcasm, and Madame du Gua looked at him as if to say, "You see what people think of her."

"Madame," said the count, laughing, "so far, it is only women who have taken her innocence away from her."

The marquis privately forgave the count. When he ventured to look at his mistress, whose beauty was, like that of most women, brought into relief by the light of the wax candles, she turned her back upon him as she resumed her place, and went on talking to her partner in a way to let the marquis hear the sweetest and most caressing tones of her voice.

"The First Consul sends dangerous ambassadors," her partner was saying.

"Monsieur," she replied, "you all said that at La Vivetiere."

"You have the memory of a king," replied he, disconcerted at his own awkwardness.

"To forgive injuries one must needs remember them," she said quickly, relieving his embarrassment with a smile.

"Are we all included in that amnesty?" said the marquis, approaching her.

But she darted away in the dance, with the gaiety of a child, leaving him without an answer. He watched her coldly and sadly; she saw it, and bent her head with one of those coquettish motions which the graceful lines of her throat enabled her to make, omitting no movement or attitude which could prove to him the perfection of her figure. She attracted him like hope, and eluded him like a memory. To see her thus was to desire to possess her at any cost. She knew that, and the sense it gave her of her own beauty shed upon her whole person an inexpressible charm. The marquis felt the storm of love, of rage, of madness, rising in his heart; he wrung the count's hand violently, and left the room.

"Is he gone?" said Mademoiselle de Verneuil, returning to her place.

The count gave her a glance and passed into the next room, from which he presently returned accompanied by the Gars.

"He is mine!" she thought, observing his face in the mirror.

She received the young leader with a displeased air and said nothing, but she smiled as she turned away from him; he was so superior to all about him that she was proud of being able to rule him; and obeying an instinct which sways all women more or less, she resolved to let him know the value of a few gracious words by making him pay dear for them. As soon as the quadrille was over, all the gentlemen who had been at La Vivetiere surrounded Mademoiselle de Verneuil, wishing by their flattering attentions to obtain her pardon for the mistake they had made; but he whom she longed to see at her feet did not approach the circle over which she now reigned a queen.

"He thinks I still love him," she thought, "and does not wish to be confounded with mere flatterers."

She refused to dance again. Then, as if the ball were given for her, she walked about on the arm of the Comte de Bauvan, to whom she was pleased to show some familiarity. The affair at La Vivetiere was by this time known to all present, thanks to Madame du Gua, and the lovers were the object of general attention. The marquis dared not again address his mistress; a sense of the wrong he had done her and the violence of his returning passion made her seem to him actually terrible. On her side Marie watched his apparently calm face while she seemed to be observing the ball.

"It is fearfully hot here," she said to the count. "Take me to the other side where I can breathe; I am stifling here."

And she motioned towards a small room where a few card-players were assembled. The marquis followed her. He ventured to hope she had left the crowd to receive him, and this supposed favor roused his passion to extreme violence; for his love had only increased through the resistance he had made to it during the last few days. Mademoiselle de Verneuil still tormented him; her eyes, so soft and velvety for the count, were hard and stern when, as if by accident, they met his. Montauran at last made a painful effort and said, in a muffled voice, "Will you never forgive me?"

"Love forgives nothing, or it forgives all," she said, coldly. "But," she added, noticing his joyful look, "it must be love."

She took the count's arm once more and moved forward into a small boudoir which adjoined the cardroom. The marquis followed her.

"Will you not hear me?" he said.

"One would really think, monsieur," she replied, "that I had come here to meet you, and not to vindicate my own self-respect. If you do not cease this odious pursuit I shall leave the ballroom."

"Ah!" he cried, recollecting one of the crazy actions of the last Duc de Lorraine, "let me speak to you so long as I can hold this live coal in my hand."

He stooped to the hearth and picking up a brand held it tightly. Mademoiselle de Verneuil flushed, took her arm from that of the count, and looked at the marquis in amazement. The count softly withdrew, leaving them alone together. So crazy an action shook Marie's heart, for there is nothing so persuasive in love as courageous folly.

"You only prove to me," she said, trying to make him throw away the brand, "that you are willing to make me suffer cruelly. You are extreme in everything. On the word of a fool and the slander of a woman you suspected that one who had just saved your life was capable of betraying you."

"Yes," he said, smiling, "I have been very cruel to you; but nevertheless, forget it; I shall never forget it. Hear me. I have been shamefully deceived; but so many circumstances on that fatal day told against you—"

"And those circumstances were stronger than your love?"

He hesitated; she made a motion of contempt, and rose.

"Oh, Marie. I shall never cease to believe in you now."

"Then throw that fire away. You are mad. Open your hand; I insist upon it."

He took delight in still resisting the soft efforts of her fingers, but she succeeded in opening the hand she would fain have kissed.

"What good did that do you?" she said, as she tore her handkerchief and laid it on the burn, which the marquis covered with his glove.

Madame du Gua had stolen softly into the cardroom, watching the lovers with furtive eyes, but escaping theirs adroitly; it was, however, impossible for her to understand their conversation from their actions.

"If all that they said of me was true you must admit that I am avenged at this moment," said Marie, with a look of malignity which startled the marquis.

"What feeling brought you here?" he asked.

"Do you suppose, my dear friend, that you can despise a woman like me with impunity? I came here for your sake and for my own," she continued, after a pause, laying her hand on the hilt of rubies in her bosom and showing him the blade of her dagger.

"What does all that mean?" thought Madame du Gua.

"But," she continued, "you still love me; at any rate, you desire me, and the folly you have just committed," she added, taking his hand, "proves it to me. I will again be that I desired to be; and I return to Fougeres happy. Love absolves everything. You love me; I have regained the respect of the man who represents to me the whole world, and I can die."

"Then you still love me?" said the marquis.

"Have I said so?" she replied with a scornful look, delighting in the torture she was making him endure. "I have run many risks to come here. I have saved Monsieur de Bauvan's life, and he, more grateful than others, offers me in return his fortune and his name. You have never even thought of doing that."

The marquis, bewildered by these words, stifled the worst anger he had ever felt, supposing that the count had played him false. He made no answer.

"Ah! you reflect," she said, bitterly.

"Mademoiselle," replied the young man, "your doubts justify mine."

"Let us leave this room," said Mademoiselle de Verneuil, catching sight of a corner of Madame du Gua's gown, and rising. But the wish to reduce her rival to despair was too strong, and she made no further motion to go.

"Do you mean to drive me to hell?" cried the marquis, seizing her hand and pressing it violently.

"Did you not drive me to hell five days ago? are you not leaving me at this very moment uncertain whether your love is sincere or not?"

"But how do I know whether your revenge may not lead you to obtain my life to tarnish it, instead of killing me?"

"Ah! you do not love me! you think of yourself and not of me!" she said angrily, shedding a few tears.

The coquettish creature well knew the power of her eyes when moistened by tears.

"Well, then," he cried, beside himself, "take my life, but dry those tears."

"Oh, my love! my love!" she exclaimed in a stifled voice: "those are the words, the accents, the looks I have longed for, to allow me to prefer your happiness to mine. But," she added, "I ask one more proof of your love, which you say is so great. I wish to stay here only so long as may be needed to show the company that you are mine. I will not even drink a glass of water in the house of a woman who has twice tried to kill me, who is now, perhaps, plotting mischief against us," and she showed the marquis the floating corner of Madame du Gua's drapery. Then she dried her eyes and put her lips to the ear of the young man, who quivered as he felt the caress of her warm breath. "See that everything is prepared for my departure," she said; "you shall take me yourself to Fougeres and there only will I tell you if I love you. For the second time I trust you. Will you trust me a second time?"

"Ah, Marie, you have brought me to a point where I know not what I do. I am intoxicated by your words, your looks, by you—by you, and I am ready to obey you."

"Well, then, make me for an instant very happy. Let me enjoy the only triumph I desire. I want to breathe freely, to drink of the life I have dreamed, to feed my illusions before they are gone forever. Come —come into the ballroom and dance with me."

They re-entered the room together, and though Mademoiselle de Verneuil was as completely satisfied in heart and vanity as any woman ever could be, the unfathomable gentleness of her eyes, the demure smile on her lips, the rapidity of the motions of a gay dance, kept the secret of her thoughts as the sea swallows those of the criminal who casts a weighted body into its depths. But a murmur of admiration ran through the company as, circling in each other's arms, voluptuously interlaced, with heavy heads, and dimmed sight, they waltzed with a sort of frenzy, dreaming of the pleasures they hoped to find in a future union.

A few moments later Mademoiselle de Verneuil and the marquis were in the latter's travelling-carriage drawn by four horses. Surprised to see these enemies hand in hand, and evidently understanding each other, Francine kept silence, not daring to ask her mistress whether her conduct was that of treachery or love. Thanks to the darkness, the marquis did not observe Mademoiselle de Verneuil's agitation as they neared Fougeres. The first flush of dawn showed the towers of Saint-Leonard in the distance. At that moment Marie was saying to herself: "I am going to my death."

As they ascended the first hill the lovers had the same thought; they left the carriage and mounted the rise on foot, in memory of their first meeting. When Marie took the young man's arm she thanked him by a smile for respecting her silence; then, as they reached the summit of the plateau and looked at Fougeres, she threw off her reverie.

"Don't come any farther," she said; "my authority cannot save you from the Blues to-day."

Montauran showed some surprise. She smiled sadly and pointed to a block of granite, as if to tell him to sit down, while she herself stood before him in a melancholy attitude. The rending emotions of her soul no longer permitted her to play a part. At that moment she would have knelt on red-hot coals without feeling them any more than the marquis had felt the fire-brand he had taken in his hand to prove the strength of his passion. It was not until she had contemplated her lover with a look of the deepest anguish that she said to him, at last:—

"All that you have suspected of me is true."

The marquis started.

"Ah! I pray you," she said, clasping her hands, "listen to me without interruption. I am indeed the daughter of the Duc de Verneuil,—but his natural daughter. My mother, a Demoiselle de Casteran, who became a nun to escape the reproaches of her family, expiated her fault by fifteen years of sorrow, and died at Seez, where she was abbess. On her death-bed she implored, for the first time and only for me, the help of the man who had betrayed her, for she knew she was leaving me without friends, without fortune, without a future. The duke accepted the charge, and took me from the roof of Francine's mother, who had hitherto taken care of me; perhaps he liked me because I was beautiful; possibly I reminded him of his youth. He was one of those great lords of the old regime, who took pride in showing how they could get their crimes forgiven by committing them with grace. I will say no more, he was my father. But let me explain to you how my life in Paris injured my soul. The society of the Duc de Verneuil, to which he introduced me, was bitten by that scoffing philosophy about which all France was then enthusiastic because it was wittily professed. The brilliant conversations which charmed my ear were marked by subtlety of perception and by witty contempt for all that was true and spiritual. Men laughed at sentiments, and pictured them all the better because they did not feel them; their satirical epigrams were as fascinating as the light-hearted humor with which they could put a whole adventure into a word; and yet they had sometimes too much wit, and wearied women by making love an art, and not a matter of feeling. I could not resist the tide. And yet my soul was too ardent— forgive this pride—not to feel that their minds had withered their hearts; and the life I led resulted in a perpetual struggle between my natural feelings and beliefs and the vicious habits of mind which I there contracted. Several superior men took pleasure in developing in me that liberty of thought and contempt for public opinion which do tear from a woman her modesty of soul, robbed of which she loses her charm. Alas! my subsequent misfortunes have failed to lessen the faults I learned through opulence. My father," she continued, with a sigh, "the Duc de Verneuil, died, after duly recognizing me as his daughter and making provisions for me by his will, which considerably reduced the fortune of my brother, his legitimate son. I found myself one day without a home and without a protector. My brother contested the will which made me rich. Three years of my late life had developed my vanity. By satisfying all my fancies my father had created in my nature a need of luxury, and given me habits of self-indulgence of which my own mind, young and artless as it then was, could not perceive either the danger or the tyranny. A friend of my father, the Marechal Duc de Lenoncourt, then seventy years old, offered to become my guardian, and I found myself, soon after the termination of the odious suit, in a brilliant home, where I enjoyed all the advantages of which my brother's cruelty had deprived me. Every evening the old marechal came to sit with me and comfort me with kind and consoling words. His white hair and the many proofs he gave me of paternal tenderness led me to turn all the feelings of my heart upon him, and I felt myself his daughter. I accepted his presents, hiding none of my caprices from him, for I saw how he loved to gratify them. I heard one fatal evening that all Paris believed me the mistress of the poor old man. I was told that it was then beyond my power to recover an innocence thus gratuitously denied me. They said that the man who had abused my inexperience could not be lover, and would not be my husband. The week in which I made this horrible discovery the duke left Paris. I was shamefully ejected from the house where he had placed me, and which did not belong to him. Up to this point I have told you the truth as though I stood before God; but now, do not ask a wretched woman to give account of sufferings which are buried in her heart. The time came when I found myself married to Danton. A few days later the storm uprooted the mighty oak around which I had thrown my arms. Again I was plunged into the worst distress, and I resolved to kill myself. I don't know whether love of life, or the hope of wearying ill-fortune and of finding at the bottom of the abyss the happiness which had always escaped me were, unconsciously to myself, my advisers, or whether I was fascinated by the arguments of a young man from Vendome, who, for the last two years, has wound himself about me like a serpent round a tree,—in short, I know not how it is that I accepted, for a payment of three hundred thousand francs, the odious mission of making an unknown man fall in love with me and then betraying him. I met you; I knew you at once by one of those presentiments which never mislead us; yet I tried to doubt my recognition, for the more I came to love you, the more the certainty appalled me. When I saved you from the hands of Hulot, I abjured the part I had taken; I resolved to betray the slaughterers, and not their victim. I did wrong to play with men, with their lives, their principles, with myself, like a thoughtless girl who sees only sentiments in this life. I believed you loved me; I let myself cling to the hope that my life might begin anew; but all things have revealed my past,—even I myself, perhaps, for you must have distrusted a woman so passionate as you have found me. Alas! is there no excuse for my love and my deception? My life was like a troubled sleep; I woke and thought myself a girl; I was in Alencon, where all my memories were pure and chaste. I had the mad simplicity to think that love would baptize me into innocence. For a moment I thought myself pure, for I had never loved. But last night your passion seemed to me true, and a voice cried to me, 'Do not deceive him.' Monsieur le marquis," she said, in a guttural voice which haughtily challenged condemnation, "know this; I am a dishonored creature, unworthy of you. From this hour I accept my fate as a lost woman. I am weary of playing a part,—the part of a woman to whom you had brought back the sanctities of her soul. Virtue is a burden to me. I should despise you if you were weak enough to marry me. The Comte de Bauvan might commit that folly, but you—you must be worthy of your future and leave me without regret. A courtesan is too exacting; I should not love you like the simple, artless girl who felt for a moment the delightful hope of being your companion, of making you happy, of doing you honor, of becoming a noble wife. But I gather from that futile hope the courage to return to a life of vice and infamy, that I may put an eternal barrier between us. I sacrifice both honor and fortune to you. The pride I take in that sacrifice will support me in my wretchedness, —fate may dispose of me as it will. I will never betray you. I shall return to Paris. There your name will be to me a part of myself, and the glory you win will console my grief. As for you, you are a man, and you will forget me. Farewell."

She darted away in the direction of the gorges of Saint-Sulpice, and disappeared before the marquis could rise to detain her. But she came back unseen, hid herself in a cavity of the rocks, and examined the young man with a curiosity mingled with doubt. Presently she saw him walking like a man overwhelmed, without seeming to know where he went.

"Can he be weak?" she thought, when he had disappeared, and she felt she was parted from him. "Will he understand me?" She quivered. Then she turned and went rapidly towards Fougeres, as though she feared the marquis might follow her into the town, where certain death awaited him.

"Francine, what did he say to you?" she asked, when the faithful girl rejoined her.

"Ah! Marie, how I pitied him. You great ladies stab a man with your tongues."

"How did he seem when he came up to you?"

"As if he saw me not at all! Oh, Marie, he loves you!"

"Yes, he loves me, or he does not love me—there is heaven or hell for me in that," she answered. "Between the two extremes there is no spot where I can set my foot."

After thus carrying out her resolution, Marie gave way to grief, and her face, beautified till then by these conflicting sentiments, changed for the worse so rapidly that in a single day, during which she floated incessantly between hope and despair, she lost the glow of beauty, and the freshness which has its source in the absence of passion or the ardor of joy. Anxious to ascertain the result of her mad enterprise, Hulot and Corentin came to see her soon after her return. She received them smiling.

"Well," she said to the commandant, whose care-worn face had a questioning expression, "the fox is coming within range of your guns; you will soon have a glorious triumph over him."

"What happened?" asked Corentin, carelessly, giving Mademoiselle de Verneuil one of those oblique glances with which diplomatists of his class spy on thought.

"Ah!" she said, "the Gars is more in love than ever; I made him come with me to the gates of Fougeres."

"Your power seems to have stopped there," remarked Corentin; "the fears of your *ci-devant* are greater than the love you inspire."

"You judge him by yourself," she replied, with a contemptuous look.

"Well, then," said he, unmoved, "why did you not bring him here to your own house?"

"Commandant," she said to Hulot, with a coaxing smile, "if he really loves me, would you blame me for saving his life and getting him to leave France?"

The old soldier came quickly up to her, took her hand, and kissed it with a sort of enthusiasm. Then he looked at her fixedly and said in a gloomy tone: "You forget my two friends and my sixty-three men."

"Ah, commandant," she cried, with all the naivete of passion, "he was not accountable for that; he was deceived by a bad woman, Charette's mistress, who would, I do believe, drink the blood of the Blues."

"Come, Marie," said Corentin, "don't tease the commandant; he does not understand such jokes."

"Hold your tongue," she answered, "and remember that the day when you displease me too much will have no morrow for you."

"I see, mademoiselle," said Hulot, without bitterness, "that I must prepare for a fight."

"You are not strong enough, my dear colonel. I saw more than six thousand men at Saint-James,—regular troops, artillery, and English officers. But they cannot do much unless *he* leads them? I agree with Fouche, his presence is the head and front of everything."

"Are we to get his head?—that's the point," said Corentin, impatiently.

"I don't know," she answered, carelessly.

"English officers!" cried Hulot, angrily, "that's all that was wanting to make a regular brigand of him. Ha! ha! I'll give him English, I will!"

"It seems to me, citizen-diplomat," said Hulot to Corentin, after the two had taken leave and were at some distance from the house, "that you allow that girl to send you to the right-about when she pleases."

"It is quite natural for you, commandant," replied Corentin, with a thoughtful air, "to see nothing but fighting in what she said to us. You soldiers never seem to know there are various ways of making war. To use the passions of men and women like wires to be pulled for the benefit of the State; to keep the running-gear of the great machine we call government in good order, and fasten to it the desires of human nature, like baited traps which it is fun to watch,—I call *that* creating a world, like God, and putting ourselves at the centre of it!"

"You will please allow me to prefer my calling to yours," said the soldier, curtly. "You can do as you like with your running-gear; I recognize no authority but that of the minister of war. I have my orders; I shall take the field with veterans who don't skulk, and face an enemy you want to catch behind."

"Oh, you can fight if you want to," replied Corentin. "From what that girl has dropped, close-mouthed as you think she is, I can tell you that you'll have to skirmish about, and I myself will give you the pleasure of an interview with the Gars before long."

"How so?" asked Hulot, moving back a step to get a better view of this strange individual.

"Mademoiselle de Verneuil is in love with him," replied Corentin, in a thick voice, "and perhaps he loves her. A marquis, a knight of Saint-Louis, young, brilliant, perhaps rich,—what a list of

The Chouans

temptations! She would be foolish indeed not to look after her own interests and try to marry him rather than betray him. The girl is attempting to fool us. But I saw hesitation in her eyes. They probably have a rendezvous; perhaps they've met already. Well, to-morrow I shall have him by the forelock. Yesterday he was nothing more than the enemy of the Republic, to-day he is mine; and I tell you this, every man who has been so rash as to come between that girl and me has died upon the scaffold."

So saying, Corentin dropped into a reverie which hindered him from observing the disgust on the face of the honest soldier as he discovered the depths of this intrigue, and the mechanism of the means employed by Fouche. Hulot resolved on the spot to thwart Corentin in every way that did not conflict essentially with the success of the government, and to give the Gars a fair chance of dying honorably, sword in hand, before he could fall a prey to the executioner, for whom this agent of the detective police acknowledged himself the purveyor.

"If the First Consul would listen to me," thought Hulot, as he turned his back on Corentin, "he would leave those foxes to fight aristocrats, and send his solders on other business."

Corentin looked coldly after the old soldier, whose face had brightened at the resolve, and his eyes gleamed with a sardonic expression, which showed the mental superiority of this subaltern Machiavelli.

"Give an ell of blue cloth to those fellows, and hang a bit of iron at their waists," he said to himself, "and they'll think there's but one way to kill people." Then, after walking up and down awhile very slowly, he exclaimed suddenly, "Yes, the time has come, that woman shall be mine! For five years I've been drawing the net round her, and I have her now; with her, I can be a greater man in the government than Fouche himself. Yes, if she loses the only man she has ever loved, grief will give her to me, body and soul; but I must be on the watch night and day."

A few moments later the pale face of this man might have been seen through the window of a house, from which he could observe all who entered the cul-de-sac formed by the line of houses running parallel with Saint-Leonard, one of those houses being that now occupied by Mademoiselle de Verneuil. With the patience of a cat watching a mouse Corentin was there in the same place on the following morning, attentive to the slightest noise, and subjecting the passers-by to the closest examination. The day that was now beginning was a market-day. Although in these calamitous times the peasants rarely risked themselves in the towns, Corentin presently noticed a small man with a gloomy face, wrapped in a goatskin, and carrying on his arm a small flat basket; he was making his way in the direction of Mademoiselle de Verneuil's house, casting careless glances about him. Corentin watched him enter the house; then he ran down into the street, meaning to waylay the man as he left; but on second thoughts it occurred to him that if he called unexpectedly on Mademoiselle de Verneuil he might surprise by a single glance the secret that was hidden in the basket of the emissary. Besides, he had already learned that it was impossible to extract anything from the inscrutable answers of Bretons and Normans.

"Galope-Chopine!" cried Mademoiselle de Verneuil, when Francine brought the man to her. "Does he love me?" she murmured to herself, in a low voice.

The instinctive hope sent a brilliant color to her cheeks and joy into her heart. Galope-Chopine looked alternately from the mistress to the maid with evident distrust of the latter; but a sign from Mademoiselle de Verneuil reassured him.

"Madame," he said, "about two o'clock *he* will be at my house waiting for you."

Emotion prevented Mademoiselle de Verneuil from giving any other reply than a movement of her head, but the man understood her meaning. At that moment Corentin's step was heard in the adjoining room, but Galope-Chopine showed no uneasiness, though Mademoiselle de Verneuil's look and shudder warned him of danger, and as soon as the spy had entered the room the Chouan raised his voice to an ear-splitting tone.

"Ha, ha!" he said to Francine, "I tell you there's Breton butter *and* Breton butter. You want the Gibarry kind, and you won't give more than eleven sous a pound; then why did you send me to fetch it? It is good butter that," he added, uncovering the basket to show the pats which Barbette had made. "You ought to be fair, my good lady, and pay one sou more."

His hollow voice betrayed no emotion, and his green eyes, shaded by thick gray eyebrows, bore Corentin's piercing glance without flinching.

"Nonsense, my good man, you are not here to sell butter; you are talking to a lady who never bargained for a thing in her life. The trade you run, old fellow, will shorten you by a head in a very few days"; and Corentin, with a friendly tap on the man's shoulder, added, "you can't keep up being a spy of the Blues and a spy of the Chouans very long."

Galope-Chopine needed all his presence of mind to subdue his rage, and not deny the accusation which his avarice had made a just one. He contented himself with saying:—

"Monsieur is making game of me."

Corentin turned his back on the Chouan, but, while bowing to Mademoiselle de Verneuil, whose heart stood still, he watched him in the mirror behind her. Galope-Chopine, unaware of this, gave a glance to Francine, to which she replied by pointing to the door, and saying, "Come with me, my man, and we will settle the matter between us."

Nothing escaped Corentin, neither the fear which Mademoiselle de Verneuil could not conceal under a smile, nor her color and the contraction of her features, nor the Chouan's sign and Francine's reply; he had seen all. Convinced that Galope-Chopine was sent by the marquis, he caught the man by the long hairs of his goatskin as he was leaving the room, turned him round to face him, and said with a keen look: "Where do you live, my man? I want butter, too."

"My good monsieur," said the Chouan, "all Fougeres knows where I live. I am—"

"Corentin!" exclaimed Mademoiselle de Verneuil, interrupting Galope-Chopine. "Why do you come here at this time of day? I am scarcely dressed. Let that peasant alone; he does not understand your tricks any more than I understand the motive of them. You can go, my man."

Galope-Chopine hesitated a moment. The indecision, real or feigned, of the poor devil, who knew not which to obey, deceived even

Corentin; but the Chouan, finally, after an imperative gesture from the lady, left the room with a dragging step. Mademoiselle de Verneuil and Corentin looked at each other in silence. This time Marie's limpid eyes could not endure the gleam of cruel fire in the man's look. The resolute manner in which the spy had forced his way into her room, an expression on his face which Marie had never seen there before, the deadened tones of his shrill voice, his whole demeanor,—all these things alarmed her; she felt that a secret struggle was about to take place between them, and that he meant to employ against her all the powers of his evil influence. But though she had at this moment a full and distinct view of the gulf into which she was plunging, she gathered strength from her love to shake off the icy chill of these presentiments.

"Corentin," she said, with a sort of gayety, "I hope you are going to let me make my toilet?"

"Marie," he said,—"yes, permit me to call you so,—you don't yet know me. Listen; a much less sagacious man than I would see your love for the Marquis de Montauran. I have several times offered you my heart and hand. You have never thought me worthy of you; and perhaps you are right. But however much you may feel yourself too high, too beautiful, too superior for me, I can compel you to come down to my level. My ambition and my maxims have given you a low opinion of me; frankly, you are mistaken. Men are not worth even what I rate them at, and that is next to nothing. I shall certainly attain a position which will gratify your pride. Who will ever love you better, or make you more absolutely mistress of yourself and of him, than the man who has loved you now for five years? Though I run the risk of exciting your suspicions,—for you cannot conceive that any one should renounce an idolized woman out of excessive love,—I will now prove to you the unselfishness of my passion. If the marquis loves you, marry him; but before you do so, make sure of his sincerity. I could not endure to see you deceived, for I do prefer your happiness to my own. My resolution may surprise you; lay it to the prudence of a man who is not so great a fool as to wish to possess a woman against her will. I blame myself, not you, for the failure of my efforts to win you. I hoped to do so by submission and devotion, for I have long, as you well know, tried to make you happy according to my lights; but you have never in any way rewarded me."

"I have suffered you to be near me," she said, haughtily.

"Add that you regret it."

"After involving me in this infamous enterprise, do you think that I have any thanks to give you?"

"When I proposed to you an enterprise which was not exempt from blame to timid minds," he replied, audaciously, "I had only your own prosperity in view. As for me, whether I succeed or fail, I can make all results further my ends. If you marry Montauran, I shall be delighted to serve the Bourbons in Paris, where I am already a member of the Clichy club. Now, if circumstances were to put me in correspondence with the princes I should abandon the interests of the Republic, which is already on its last legs. General Bonaparte is much too able a man not to know that he can't be in England and in Italy at the same time, and that is how the Republic is about to fall. I have no doubt he made the 18th Brumaire to obtain greater advantages over the Bourbons when it came to treating with them. He is a long-headed fellow, and very keen; but the politicians will get the better of him on their own ground. The betrayal of France is another scruple which men of superiority leave to fools. I won't conceal from you that I have come here with the necessary authority to open negotiations with the Chouans, *or* to further their destruction, as the case may be; for Fouche, my patron, is deep; he has always played a double part; during the Terror he was as much for Robespierre as for Danton—"

"Whom you basely abandoned," she said.

"Nonsense; he is dead,—forget him," replied Corentin. "Come, speak honestly to me; I have set you the example. Old Hulot is deeper than he looks; if you want to escape his vigilance, I can help you. Remember that he holds all the valleys and will instantly detect a rendezvous. If you make one in Fougeres, under his very eyes, you are at the mercy of his patrols. See how quickly he knew that this Chouan had entered your house. His military sagacity will show him that your movements betray those of the Gars—if Montauran loves you."

Mademoiselle de Verneuil had never listened to a more affectionate voice; Corentin certainly seemed sincere, and spoke confidingly. The poor girl's heart was so open to generous impressions that she was on the point of betraying her secret to the serpent who had her in his folds, when it occurred to her that she had no proof beyond his own words of his sincerity, and she felt no scruple in blinding him.

"Yes," she said, "you are right, Corentin. I do love the marquis, but he does not love me—at least, I fear so; I can't help fearing that the appointment he wishes me to make with him is a trap."

"But you said yesterday that he came as far as Fougeres with you," returned Corentin. "If he had meant to do you bodily harm you wouldn't be here now."

"You've a cold heart, Corentin. You can draw shrewd conclusions as to the ordinary events of human life, but not on those of passion. Perhaps that is why you inspire me with such repulsion. As you are so clear-sighted, you may be able to tell me why a man from whom I separated myself violently two days ago now wishes me to meet him in a house at Florigny on the road to Mayenne."

At this avowal, which seemed to escape her with a recklessness that was not unnatural in so passionate a creature, Corentin flushed, for he was still young; but he gave her a sidelong penetrating look, trying to search her soul. The girl's artlessness was so well played, however, that she deceived the spy, and he answered with crafty good-humor, "Shall I accompany you at a distance? I can take a few solders with me, and be ready to help and obey you."

"Very good," she said; "but promise me, on your honor,—no, I don't believe in it; by your salvation,—but you don't believe in God; by your soul,—but I don't suppose you have any! what pledge *can* you give me of your fidelity? and yet you expect me to trust you, and put more than my life—my love, my vengeance—into your hands?"

The slight smile which crossed the pallid lips of the spy showed Mademoiselle de Verneuil the danger she had just escaped. The man, whose nostrils contracted instead of dilating, took the hand of his victim, kissed it with every mark of the deepest respect, and left the room with a bow that was not devoid of grace.

Three hours after this scene Mademoiselle de Verneuil, who feared the man's return, left the town furtively by the Porte Saint-Leonard, and made her way through the labyrinth of paths to the cottage of Galope-Chopine, led by the dream of at last finding happiness, and

also by the purpose of saving her lover from the danger that
threatened him.

During this time Corentin had gone to find the commandant. He had
some difficulty in recognizing Hulot when he found him in a little
square, where he was busy with certain military preparations. The
brave veteran had made a sacrifice, the full merit of which may be
difficult to appreciate. His queue and his moustache were cut off,
and his hair had a sprinkling of powder. He had changed his
uniform for a goatskin, wore hobnailed shoes, a belt full of pistols,
and carried a heavy carbine. In this costume he was reviewing about
two hundred of the natives of Fougeres, all in the same kind of dress,
which was fitted to deceive the eye of the most practised Chouan.
The warlike spirit of the little town and the Breton character were
fully displayed in this scene, which was not at all uncommon. Here
and there a few mothers and sisters were bringing to their sons and
brothers gourds filled with brandy, or forgotten pistols. Several old
men were examining into the number and condition of the cartridges
of these young national guards dressed in the guise of Chouans,
whose gaiety was more in keeping with a hunting expedition than
the dangerous duty they were undertaking. To them, such
encounters with Chouannerie, where the Breton of the town fought
the Breton of the country district, had taken the place of the old
chivalric tournaments. This patriotic enthusiasm may possibly have
been connected with certain purchases of the "national domain."
Still, the benefits of the Revolution which were better understood
and appreciated in the towns, party spirit, and a certain national
delight in war, had a great deal to do with their ardor.

Hulot, much gratified, was going through the ranks and getting
information from Gudin, on whom he was now bestowing the
confidence and good-will he had formerly shown to Merle and
Gerard. A number of the inhabitants stood about watching the
preparations, and comparing the conduct of their tumultuous
contingent with the regulars of Hulot's brigade. Motionless and
silent the Blues were awaiting, under control of their officers, the
orders of the commandant, whose figure they followed with their
eyes as he passed from rank to rank of the contingent. When
Corentin came near the old warrior he could not help smiling at the
change which had taken place in him. He looked like a portrait that
has little or no resemblance to the original.

"What's all this?" asked Corentin.

"Come with us under fire, and you'll find out," replied Hulot.

"Oh! I'm not a Fougeres man," said Corentin.

"Easy to see that, citizen," retorted Gudin.

A few contemptuous laughs came from the nearest ranks.

"Do you think," said Corentin, sharply, "that the only way to serve France is with bayonets?"

Then he turned his back to the laughers, and asked a woman beside him if she knew the object of the expedition.

"Hey! my good man, the Chouans are at Florigny. They say there are more than three thousand, and they are coming to take Fougeres."

"Florigny?" cried Corentin, turning white; "then the rendezvous is not there! Is Florigny on the road to Mayenne?" he asked.

"There are not two Florignys," replied the woman, pointing in the direction of the summit of La Pelerine.

"Are you going in search of the Marquis de Montauran?" said Corentin to Hulot.

"Perhaps I am," answered the commandant, curtly.

"He is not at Florigny," said Corentin. "Send your troops there by all means; but keep a few of those imitation Chouans of yours with you, and wait for me."

"He is too malignant not to know what he's about," thought Hulot as Corentin made off rapidly, "he's the king of spies."

Hulot ordered the battalion to start. The republican soldiers marched without drums and silently through the narrow suburb which led to the Mayenne high-road, forming a blue and red line among the trees and houses. The disguised guard followed them; but Hulot, detaining Gudin and about a score of the smartest young fellows of the town, remained in the little square, awaiting Corentin, whose mysterious manner had piqued his curiosity. Francine herself told the astute spy, whose suspicions she changed into certainty, of her mistress's departure. Inquiring of the post guard at the Porte Saint-Leonard, he learned that Mademoiselle de Verneuil had passed that way. Rushing to the Promenade, he was, unfortunately, in time to see her movements. Though she was wearing a green dress and hood, to be less easily distinguished, the rapidity of her almost distracted step enabled him to follow her with his eye through the leafless hedges, and to guess the point towards which she was hurrying.

"Ha!" he cried, "you said you were going to Florigny, but you are in the valley of Gibarry! I am a fool, she has tricked me! No matter, I can light my lamp by day as well as by night."

Corentin, satisfied that he knew the place of the lovers' rendezvous, returned in all haste to the little square, which Hulot, resolved not to wait any longer, was just quitting to rejoin his troops.

"Halt, general!" he cried to the commandant, who turned round.

He then told Hulot the events relating to the marquis and Mademoiselle de Verneuil, and showed him the scheme of which he held a thread. Hulot, struck by his perspicacity, seized him by the arm.

"God's thunder! citizen, you are right," he cried. "The brigands are making a false attack over there to keep the coast clear; but the two columns I sent to scour the environs between Antrain and Vitre have not yet returned, so we shall have plenty of reinforcements if we need them; and I dare say we shall, for the Gars is not such a fool as to risk his life without a bodyguard of those damned owls. Gudin," he added, "go and tell Captain Lebrun that he must rub those fellows' noses at Florigny without me, and come back yourself in a flash. You know the paths. I'll wait till you return, and *then* — we'll avenge those murders at La Vivetiere. Thunder! how he runs," he added, seeing Gudin disappear as if by magic. "Gerard would have loved him."

On his return Gudin found Hulot's little band increased in numbers by the arrival of several soldiers taken from the various posts in the town. The commandant ordered him to choose a dozen of his compatriots who could best counterfeit the Chouans, and take them out by the Porte Saint-Leonard, so as to creep round the side of the Saint-Sulpice rocks which overlooks the valley of Couesnon and on which was the hovel of Galope-Chopine. Hulot himself went out with the rest of his troop by the Porte Saint-Sulpice, to reach the summit of the same rocks, where, according to his calculations, he ought to meet the men under Beau-Pied, whom he meant to use as a line of sentinels from the suburb of Saint-Sulpice to the Nid-aux-Crocs.

Corentin, satisfied with having delivered over the fate of the Gars to his implacable enemies, went with all speed to the Promenade, so as to follow with his eyes the military arrangements of the commandant. He soon saw Gudin's little squad issuing from the valley of the Nancon and following the line of the rocks to the great valley, while Hulot, creeping round the castle of Fougeres, was mounting the dangerous path which leads to the summit of Saint-Sulpice. The two companies were therefore advancing on parallel lines. The trees and shrubs, draped by the rich arabesques of the hoarfrost, threw whitish reflections which enabled the watcher to see the gray lines of the squads in motion. When Hulot reached the summit of the rocks, he detached all the soldiers in uniform from his main body, and made them into a line of sentinels, each communicating with the other, the first with Gudin, the last with Hulot; so that no shrub could escape the bayonets of the three lines which were now in a position to hunt the Gars across field and mountain.

"The sly old wolf!" thought Corentin, as the shining muzzle of the last gun disappeared in the bushes. "The Gars is done for. If Marie had only betrayed that damned marquis, she and I would have been united in the strongest of all bonds—a vile deed. But she's mine, in any case."

The twelve young men under Gudin soon reached the base of the rocks of Saint-Sulpice. Here Gudin himself left the road with six of them, jumping the stiff hedge into the first field of gorse that he came to, while the other six by his orders did the same on the other side of the road. Gudin advanced to an apple-tree which happened to be in the middle of the field. Hearing the rustle of this movement through the gorse, seven or eight men, at the head of whom was Beau-Pied, hastily hid behind some chestnut-trees which topped the bank of this particular field. Gudin's men did not see them, in spite of the white reflections of the hoar-frost and their own practised sight.

"Hush! here they are," said Beau-Pied, cautiously putting out his head. "The brigands have more men than we, but we have 'em at the muzzles of our guns, and we mustn't miss them, or, by the Lord, we are not fit to be soldiers of the pope."

By this time Gudin's keen eyes had discovered a few muzzles pointing through the branches at his little squad. Just then eight voices cried in derision, "Qui vive?" and eight shots followed. The balls whistled round Gudin and his men. One fell, another was shot in the arm. The five others who were safe and sound replied with a volley and the cry, "Friends!" Then they marched rapidly on their assailants so as to reach them before they had time to reload.

"We did not know how true we spoke," cried Gudin, as he recognized the uniforms and the battered hats of his own brigade. "Well, we behaved like Bretons, and fought before explaining."

The other men were stupefied on recognizing the little company.

"Who the devil would have known them in those goatskins?" cried Beau-Pied, dismally.

"It is a misfortune," said Gudin, "but we are all innocent if you were not informed of the sortie. What are you doing here?" he asked.

"A dozen of those Chouans are amusing themselves by picking us off, and we are getting away as best we can, like poisoned rats; but by dint of scrambling over these hedges and rocks—may the lightning blast 'em!—our compasses have got so rusty we are forced to take a rest. I think those brigands are now somewhere near the old hovel where you see that smoke."

"Good!" cried Gudin. "You," he added to Beau-Pied and his men, "fall back towards the rocks through the fields, and join the line of sentinels you'll find there. You can't go with us, because you are in uniform. We mean to make an end of those curs now; the Gars is with them. I can't stop to tell you more. To the right, march! and don't administer any more shots to our own goatskins; you'll know ours by their cravats, which they twist round their necks and don't tie."

Gudin left his two wounded men under the apple-tree, and marched towards Galope-Chopine's cottage, which Beau-Pied had pointed out to him, the smoke from the chimney serving as a guide.

While the young officer was thus closing in upon the Chouans, the little detachment under Hulot had reached a point still parallel with that at which Gudin had arrived. The old soldier, at the head of his men, was silently gliding along the hedges with the ardor of a young man; he jumped them from time to time actively enough, casting his wary eyes to the heights and listening with the ear of a hunter to every noise. In the third field to which he came he found a woman about thirty years old, with bent back, hoeing the ground vigorously, while a small boy with a sickle in his hand was knocking the hoarfrost from the rushes, which he cut and laid in a heap. At the noise Hulot made in jumping the hedge, the boy and his mother raised their heads. Hulot mistook the young woman for an old one, naturally enough. Wrinkles, coming long before their time, furrowed her face and neck; she was clothed so grotesquely in a worn-out goatskin that if it had not been for a dirty yellow petticoat, a distinctive mark of sex, Hulot would hardly have known the gender she belonged to; for the meshes of her long black hair were twisted up and hidden by a red worsted cap. The tatters of the little boy did not cover him, but left his skin exposed.

"Ho! old woman!" called Hulot, in a low voice, approaching her, "where is the Gars?"

The twenty men who accompanied Hulot now jumped the hedge.

"Hey! if you want the Gars you'll have to go back the way you came," said the woman, with a suspicious glance at the troop.

"Did I ask you the road to Fougeres, old carcass?" said Hulot, roughly. "By Saint-Anne of Auray, have you seen the Gars go by?"

"I don't know what you mean," replied the woman, bending over her hoe.

"You damned garce, do you want to have us eaten up by the Blues who are after us?"

At these words the woman raised her head and gave another look of distrust at the troop as she replied, "How can the Blues be after you?

I have just seen eight or ten of them who were going back to
Fougeres by the lower road."

"One would think she meant to stab us with that nose of hers!" cried
Hulot. "Here, look, you old nanny-goat!"

And he showed her in the distance three or four of his sentinels,
whose hats, guns, and uniforms it was easy to recognize.

"Are you going to let those fellows cut the throats of men who are
sent by Marche-a-Terre to protect the Gars?" he cried, angrily.

"Ah, beg pardon," said the woman; "but it is so easy to be deceived.
What parish do you belong to?"

"Saint-Georges," replied two or three of the men, in the Breton
patois, "and we are dying of hunger."

"Well, there," said the woman; "do you see that smoke down there?
that's my house. Follow the path to the right, and you will come to
the rock above it. Perhaps you'll meet my man on the way. Galope-
Chopine is sure to be on watch to warn the Gars. He is spending the
day in our house," she said, proudly, "as you seem to know."

"Thank you, my good woman," replied Hulot. "Forward, march!
God's thunder! we've got him," he added, speaking to his men.

The detachment followed its leader at a quick step through the path
pointed out to them. The wife of Galope-Chopine turned pale as she
heard the un-Catholic oath of the so-called Chouan. She looked at
the gaiters and goatskins of his men, then she caught her boy in her
arms, and sat down on the ground, saying, "May the holy Virgin of
Auray and the ever blessed Saint-Labre have pity upon us! Those
men are not ours; their shoes have no nails in them. Run down by
the lower road and warn your father; you may save his head," she
said to the boy, who disappeared like a deer among the bushes.

* * * * *

Mademoiselle de Verneuil met no one on her way, neither Blues nor
Chouans. Seeing the column of blue smoke which was rising from
the half-ruined chimney of Galope-Chopine's melancholy dwelling,
her heart was seized with a violent palpitation, the rapid, sonorous

beating of which rose to her throat in waves. She stopped, rested her hand against a tree, and watched the smoke which was serving as a beacon to the foes as well as to the friends of the young chieftain. Never had she felt such overwhelming emotion.

"Ah! I love him too much," she said, with a sort of despair. "To-day, perhaps, I shall no longer be mistress of myself—"

She hurried over the distance which separated her from the cottage, and reached the courtyard, the filth of which was now stiffened by the frost. The big dog sprang up barking, but a word from Galope-Chopine silenced him and he wagged his tail. As she entered the house Marie gave a look which included everything. The marquis was not there. She breathed more freely, and saw with pleasure that the Chouan had taken some pains to clean the dirty and only room in his hovel. He now took his duck-gun, bowed silently to his guest and left the house, followed by his dog. Marie went to the threshold of the door and watched him as he took the path to the right of his hut. From there she could overlook a series of fields, the curious openings to which formed a perspective of gates; for the leafless trees and hedges were no longer a barrier to a full view of the country. When the Chouan's broad hat was out of sight Mademoiselle de Verneuil turned round to look for the church at Fougeres, but the shed concealed it. She cast her eyes over the valley of the Couesnon, which lay before her like a vast sheet of muslin, the whiteness of which still further dulled a gray sky laden with snow. It was one of those days when nature seems dumb and noises are absorbed by the atmosphere. Therefore, though the Blues and their contingent were marching through the country in three lines, forming a triangle which drew together as they neared the cottage, the silence was so profound that Mademoiselle de Verneuil was overcome by a presentiment which added a sort of physical pain to her mental torture. Misfortune was in the air.

At last, in a spot where a little curtain of wood closed the perspective of gates, she saw a young man jumping the barriers like a squirrel and running with astonishing rapidity. "It is he!" she thought.

The Gars was dressed as a Chouan, with a musket slung from his shoulder over his goatskin, and would have been quite disguised were it not for the grace of his movements. Marie withdrew hastily into the cottage, obeying one of those instinctive promptings which are as little explicable as fear itself. The young man was soon beside her before the chimney, where a bright fire was burning. Both were voiceless, fearing to look at each other, or even to make a movement. One and the same hope united them, the same doubt; it was agony, it was joy.

"Monsieur," said Mademoiselle de Verneuil at last, in a trembling voice, "your safety alone has brought me here."

"My safety!" he said, bitterly.

"Yes," she answered; "so long as I stay at Fougeres your life is threatened, and I love you too well not to leave it. I go to-night."

"Leave me! ah, dear love, I shall follow you."

"Follow me!—the Blues?"

"Dear Marie, what have the Blues got to do with our love?"

"But it seems impossible that you can stay with me in France, and still more impossible that you should leave it with me."

"Is there anything impossible to those who love?"

"Ah, true! true! all is possible—have I not the courage to resign you, for your sake."

"What! you could give yourself to a hateful being whom you did not love, and you refuse to make the happiness of a man who adores you, whose life you fill, who swears to be yours, and yours only. Hear me, Marie, do you love me?"

"Yes," she said.

"Then be mine."

"You forget the infamous career of a lost woman; I return to it, I leave you—yes, that I may not bring upon your head the contempt that falls on mine. Without that fear, perhaps—"

"But if I fear nothing?"

"Can I be sure of that? I am distrustful. Who could be otherwise in a position like mine? If the love we inspire cannot last at least it should be complete, and help us to bear with joy the injustice of the world. But you, what have you done for me? You desire me. Do you think that lifts you above other men? Suppose I bade you renounce your ideas, your hopes, your king (who will, perhaps, laugh when he hears you have died for him, while I would die for you with sacred joy!); or suppose I should ask you to send your submission to the First Consul so that you could follow me to Paris, or go with me to America,—away from the world where all is vanity; suppose I thus tested you, to know if you loved me for myself as at this moment I love you? To say all in a word, if I wished, instead of rising to your level, that you should fall to mine, what would you do?"

"Hush, Marie, be silent, do not slander yourself," he cried. "Poor child, I comprehend you. If my first desire was passion, my passion now is love. Dear soul of my soul, you are as noble as your name, I know it,—as great as you are beautiful. I am noble enough, I feel myself great enough to force the world to receive you. Is it because I foresee in you the source of endless, incessant pleasure, or because I find in your soul those precious qualities which make a man forever love the one woman? I do not know the cause, but this I know—that my love for you is boundless. I know I can no longer live without you. Yes, life would be unbearable unless you are ever with me."

"Ever with you!"

"Ah! Marie, will you not understand me?"

"You think to flatter me by the offer of your hand and name," she said, with apparent haughtiness, but looking fixedly at the marquis as if to detect his inmost thought. "How do you know you would love me six months hence? and then what would be my fate? No, a mistress is the only woman who is sure of a man's heart; duty, law, society, the interests of children, are poor auxiliaries. If her power lasts it gives her joys and flatteries which make the trials of life endurable. But to be your wife and become a drag upon you,—rather than that, I prefer a passing love and a true one, though death and misery be its end. Yes, I could be a virtuous mother, a devoted wife; but to keep those instincts firmly in a woman's soul the man must not marry her in a rush of passion. Besides, how do I know that you will please me to-morrow? No, I will not bring evil upon you; I leave

246

Brittany," she said, observing hesitation in his eyes. "I return to Fougeres now, where you cannot come to me—"

"I can! and if to-morrow you see smoke on the rocks of Saint-Sulpice you will know that I shall be with you at night, your lover, your husband,—what you will that I be to you; I brave all!"

"Ah! Alphonse, you love me well," she said, passionately, "to risk your life before you give it to me."

He did not answer; he looked at her and her eyes fell; but he read in her ardent face a passion equal to his own, and he held out his arms to her. A sort of madness overcame her, and she let herself fall softly on his breast, resolved to yield to him, and turn this yielding to great results,—staking upon it her future happiness, which would become more certain if she came victorious from this crucial test. But her head had scarcely touched her lover's shoulder when a slight noise was heard without. She tore herself from his arms as if suddenly awakened, and sprang from the cottage. Her coolness came back to her, and she thought of the situation.

"He might have accepted me and scorned me," she reflected. "Ah! if I could think that, I would kill him. But not yet!" she added, catching sight of Beau-Pied, to whom she made a sign which the soldier was quick to understand. He turned on his heel, pretending to have seen nothing. Mademoiselle de Verneuil re-entered the cottage, putting her finger to her lips to enjoin silence.

"They are there!" she whispered in a frightened voice.

"Who?"

"The Blues."

"Ah! must I die without one kiss!"

"Take it," she said.

He caught her to him, cold and unresisting, and gathered from her lips a kiss of horror and of joy, for while it was the first, it might also be the last. Then they went together to the door and looked cautiously out. The marquis saw Gudin and his men holding the paths leading to the valley. Then he turned to the line of gates where the first rotten trunk was guarded by five men. Without an instant's pause he jumped on the barrel of cider and struck a hole through the thatch of the roof, from which to spring upon the rocks behind the house; but he drew his head hastily back through the gap he had made, for Hulot was on the height; his retreat was cut off in that direction. The marquis turned and looked at his mistress, who uttered a cry of despair; for she heard the tramp of the three detachments near the house.

"Go out first," he said; "you shall save me."

Hearing the words, to her all-glorious, she went out and stood before the door. The marquis loaded his musket. Measuring with his eye the space between the door of the hut and the old rotten trunk where seven men stood, the Gars fired into their midst and sprang forward instantly, forcing a passage through them. The three troops rushed towards the opening through which he had passed, and saw him running across the field with incredible celerity.

"Fire! fire! a thousand devils! You're not Frenchmen! Fire, I say!" called Hulot.

As he shouted these words from the height above, his men and Gudin's fired a volley, which was fortunately ill-aimed. The marquis reached the gate of the next field, but as he did so he was almost caught by Gudin, who was close upon his heels. The Gars redoubled his speed. Nevertheless, he and his pursuer reached the next barrier together; but the marquis dashed his musket at Gudin's head with so good an aim that he stopped his rush. It is impossible to depict the anxiety betrayed by Marie, or the interest of Hulot and his troops as they watched the scene. They all, unconsciously or silently, repeated the gestures which they saw the runners making. The Gars and Gudin reached the little wood together, but as they did so the latter stopped and darted behind a tree. About twenty Chouans, afraid to fire at a distance lest they should kill their leader, rushed from the copse and riddled the tree with balls. Hulot's men advanced at a run to save Gudin, who, being without arms, retreated from tree to tree, seizing his opportunity as the Chouans reloaded. His danger was soon over. Hulot and the Blues met him at the spot where the marquis had thrown his musket. At this instant Gudin perceived his adversary sitting among the trees and out of breath, and he left his comrades firing at the Chouans, who had retreated behind a lateral hedge; slipping round them, he darted towards the marquis with the agility of a wild animal. Observing this manoeuvre the Chouans set up a cry to warn their leader; then, having fired on the Blues and their contingent with the gusto of poachers, they boldly made a rush for them; but Hulot's men sprang through the hedge which served them as a rampart and took a bloody revenge. The Chouans then gained the road which skirted the fields and took to the heights which Hulot had committed the blunder of abandoning. Before the Blues had time to reform, the Chouans were entrenched behind the rocks, where they could fire with impunity on the Republicans if the latter made any attempt to dislodge them.

While Hulot and his soldiers went slowly towards the little wood to meet Gudin, the men from Fougeres busied themselves in rifling the dead Chouans and dispatching those who still lived. In this fearful war neither party took prisoners. The marquis having made good his escape, the Chouans and the Blues mutually recognized their respective positions and the uselessness of continuing the fight; so that both sides prepared to retreat.

"Ha! ha!" cried one of the Fougeres men, busy about the bodies, "here's a bird with yellow wings."

And he showed his companions a purse full of gold which he had just found in the pocket of a stout man dressed in black.

"What's this?" said another, pulling a breviary from the dead man's coat.

"Communion bread—he's a priest!" cried the first man, flinging the breviary on the ground.

"Here's a wretch!" cried a third, finding only two crowns in the pockets of the body he was stripping, "a cheat!"

"But he's got a fine pair of shoes!" said a soldier, beginning to pull them off.

"You can't have them unless they fall to your share," said the Fougeres man, dragging the dead feet away and flinging the boots on a heap of clothing already collected.

Another Chouan took charge of the money, so that lots might be drawn as soon as the troops were all assembled. When Hulot returned with Gudin, whose last attempt to overtake the Gars was useless as well as perilous, he found about a score of his own men and thirty of the contingent standing around eleven of the enemy, whose naked bodies were thrown into a ditch at the foot of the bank.

"Soldiers!" cried Hulot, sternly. "I forbid you to share that clothing. Form in line, quick!"

"Commandant," said a soldier, pointing to his shoes, at the points of which five bare toes could be seen on each foot, "all right about the money, but those boots," motioning to a pair of hobnailed boots with the butt of his gun, "would fit me like a glove."

"Do you want to put English shoes on your feet?" retorted Hulot.

"But," said one of the Fougeres men, respectfully, "we've divided the booty all through the war."

"I don't prevent you civilians from following your own ways," replied Hulot, roughly.

"Here, Gudin, here's a purse with three louis," said the officer who was distributing the money. "You have run hard and the commandant won't prevent your taking it."

Hulot looked askance at Gudin, and saw that he turned pale.

"It's my uncle's purse!" exclaimed the young man.

Exhausted as he was with his run, he sprang to the mound of bodies, and the first that met his eyes was that of his uncle. But he had hardly recognized the rubicund face now furrowed with blue lines, and seen the stiffened arms and the gunshot wound before he gave a stifled cry, exclaiming, "Let us be off, commandant."

The Blues started. Hulot gave his arm to his young friend.

"God's thunder!" he cried. "Never mind, it is no great matter."

"But he is dead," said Gudin, "dead! He was my only relation, and though he cursed me, still he loved me. If the king returns, the neighborhood will want my head, and my poor uncle would have saved it."

"What a fool Gudin is," said one of the men who had stayed behind to share the spoils; "his uncle was rich, and he hasn't had time to make a will and disinherit him."

The division over, the men of Fougeres rejoined the little battalion of the Blues on their way to the town.

* * * * *

Towards midnight the cottage of Galope-Chopine, hitherto the scene of life without a care, was full of dread and horrible anxiety. Barbette and her little boy returned at the supper-hour, one with her heavy burden of rushes, the other carrying fodder for the cattle. Entering the hut, they looked about in vain for Galope-Chopine; the miserable chamber never looked to them as large, so empty was it. The fire was out, and the darkness, the silence, seemed to tell of some disaster. Barbette hastened to make a blaze, and to light two *oribus*, the name given to candles made of pitch in the region between the villages of Amorique and the Upper Loire, and still used beyond Amboise in the Vendomois districts. Barbette did these things with the slowness of a person absorbed in one overpowering feeling. She listened to every sound. Deceived by the whistling of the wind she went often to the door of the hut, returning sadly. She cleaned two beakers, filled them with cider, and placed them on the long table. Now and again she looked at her boy, who watched the baking of the buckwheat cakes, but did not speak to him. The lad's eyes happened to rest on the nails which usually held his father's duck-gun, and Barbette trembled as she noticed that the gun was gone. The silence was broken only by the lowing of a cow or the splash of the cider as it dropped at regular intervals from the bung of the cask. The poor woman sighed while she poured into three brown earthenware porringers a sort of soup made of milk, biscuit broken into bits, and boiled chestnuts.

"They must have fought in the field next to the Berandiere," said the boy.

"Go and see," replied his mother.

The child ran to the place where the fighting had, as he said, taken place. In the moonlight he found the heap of bodies, but his father was not among them, and he came back whistling joyously, having picked up several five-franc pieces trampled in the mud and overlooked by the victors. His mother was sitting on a stool beside the fire, employed in spinning flax. He made a negative sign to her, and then, ten o'clock having struck from the tower of Saint-Leonard, he went to bed, muttering a prayer to the holy Virgin of Auray. At dawn, Barbette, who had not closed her eyes, gave a cry of joy, as she heard in the distance a sound she knew well of hobnailed shoes, and soon after Galope-Chopine's scowling face presented itself.

"Thanks to Saint-Labre," he said, "to whom I owe a candle, the Gars is safe. Don't forget that we now owe three candles to the saint."

He seized a beaker of cider and emptied it at a draught without drawing breath. When his wife had served his soup and taken his gun and he himself was seated on the wooden bench, he said, looking at the fire: "I can't make out how the Blues got here. The fighting was at Florigny. Who the devil could have told them that the Gars was in our house; no one knew it but he and the handsome garce and we—"

Barbette turned white.

"They made me believe they were the gars of Saint-Georges," she said, trembling, "it was I who told them the Gars was here."

Galope-Chopine turned pale himself and dropped his porringer on the table.

"I sent the boy to warn you," said Barbette, frightened, "didn't you meet him?"

The Chouan rose and struck his wife so violently that she dropped, pale as death, upon the bed.

"You cursed woman," he said, "you have killed me!" Then seized with remorse, he took her in his arms. "Barbette!" he cried, "Barbette! —Holy Virgin, my hand was too heavy!"

"Do you think," she said, opening her eyes, "that Marche-a-Terre will hear of it?"

"The Gars will certainly inquire who betrayed him."

"Will he tell it to Marche-a-Terre?"

The Chouans

"Marche-a-Terre and Pille-Miche were both at Florigny."

Barbette breathed a little easier.

"If they touch a hair of your head," she cried, "I'll rinse their glasses with vinegar."

"Ah! I can't eat," said Galope-Chopine, anxiously.

His wife set another pitcher full of cider before him, but he paid no heed to it. Two big tears rolled from the woman's eyes and moistened the deep furrows of her withered face.

"Listen to me, wife; to-morrow morning you must gather fagots on the rocks of Saint-Sulpice, to the right and Saint-Leonard and set fire to them. That is a signal agreed upon between the Gars and the old rector of Saint-Georges who is to come and say mass for him."

"Is the Gars going to Fougeres?"

"Yes, to see his handsome garce. I have been sent here and there all day about it. I think he is going to marry her and carry her off; for he told me to hire horses and have them ready on the road to Saint-Malo."

Thereupon Galope-Chopine, who was tired out, went to bed for an hour or two, at the end of which time he again departed. Later, on the following morning, he returned, having carefully fulfilled all the commissions entrusted to him by the Gars. Finding that Marche-a-Terre and Pille-Miche had not appeared at the cottage, he relieved the apprehensions of his wife, who went off, reassured, to the rocks of Saint-Sulpice, where she had collected the night before several piles of fagots, now covered with hoarfrost. The boy went with her, carrying fire in a broken wooden shoe.

Hardly had his wife and son passed out of sight behind the shed when Galope-Chopine heard the noise of men jumping the successive barriers, and he could dimly see, through the fog which was growing thicker, the forms of two men like moving shadows.

"It is Marche-a-Terre and Pille-Miche," he said, mentally; then he shuddered. The two Chouans entered the courtyard and showed their gloomy faces under the broad-brimmed hats which made them look like the figures which engravers introduce into their landscapes.

"Good-morning, Galope-Chopine," said Marche-a-Terre, gravely.

"Good-morning, Monsieur Marche-a-Terre," replied the other, humbly. "Will you come in and drink a drop? I've some cold buckwheat cake and fresh-made butter."

"That's not to be refused, cousin," said Pille-Miche.

The two Chouans entered the cottage. So far there was nothing alarming for the master of the house, who hastened to fill three beakers from his huge cask of cider, while Marche-a-Terre and Pille-Miche, sitting on the polished benches on each side of the long table, cut the cake and spread it with the rich yellow butter from which the milk spurted as the knife smoothed it. Galope-Chopine placed the beakers full of frothing cider before his guests, and the three Chouans began to eat; but from time to time the master of the house cast side-long glances at Marche-a-Terre as he drank his cider.

"Lend me your snuff-box," said Marche-a-Terre to Pille-Miche.

Having shaken several pinches into the palm of his hand the Breton inhaled the tobacco like a man who is making ready for serious business.

"It is cold," said Pille-Miche, rising to shut the upper half of the door.

The daylight, already dim with fog, now entered only through the little window, and feebly lighted the room and the two seats; the fire, however, gave out a ruddy glow. Galope-Chopine refilled the beakers, but his guests refused to drink again, and throwing aside their large hats looked at him solemnly. Their gestures and the look they gave him terrified Galope-Chopine, who fancied he saw blood in the red woollen caps they wore.

"Fetch your axe," said Marche-a-Terre.

"But, Monsieur Marche-a-Terre, what do you want it for?"

"Come, cousin, you know very well," said Pille-Miche, pocketing his snuff-box which Marche-a-Terre returned to him; "you are condemned."

The two Chouans rose together and took their guns.

"Monsieur Marche-a-Terre, I never said one word about the Gars—"

"I told you to fetch your axe," said Marche-a-Terre.

The hapless man knocked against the wooden bedstead of his son, and several five-franc pieces rolled on the floor. Pille-Miche picked them up.

"Ho! ho! the Blues paid you in new money," cried Marche-a-Terre.

"As true as that's the image of Saint-Labre," said Galope-Chopine, "I have told nothing. Barbette mistook the Fougeres men for the gars of Saint-Georges, and that's the whole of it."

"Why do you tell things to your wife?" said Marche-a-Terre, roughly.

"Besides, cousin, we don't want excuses, we want your axe. You are condemned."

At a sign from his companion, Pille-Miche helped Marche-a-Terre to seize the victim. Finding himself in their grasp Galope-Chopine lost all power and fell on his knees holding up his hands to his slayers in desperation.

"My friends, my good friends, my cousin," he said, "what will become of my little boy?"

"I will take charge of him," said Marche-a-Terre.

"My good comrades," cried the victim, turning livid. "I am not fit to die. Don't make me go without confession. You have the right to take my life, but you've no right to make me lose a blessed eternity."

"That is true," said Marche-a-Terre, addressing Pille-Miche.

The two Chouans waited a moment in much uncertainty, unable to decide this case of conscience. Galope-Chopine listened to the rustling of the wind as though he still had hope. Suddenly Pille-Miche took him by the arm into a corner of the hut.

"Confess your sins to me," he said, "and I will tell them to a priest of the true Church, and if there is any penance to do I will do it for you."

Galope-Chopine obtained some respite by the way in which he confessed his sins; but in spite of their number and the circumstances of each crime, he came finally to the end of them.

"Cousin," he said, imploringly, "since I am speaking to you as I would to my confessor, I do assure you, by the holy name of God, that I have nothing to reproach myself with except for having, now and then, buttered my bread on both sides; and I call on Saint-Labre, who is there over the chimney-piece, to witness that I have never said one word about the Gars. No, my good friends, I have not betrayed him."

"Very good, that will do, cousin; you can explain all that to God in course of time."

"But let me say good-bye to Barbette."

"Come," said Marche-a-Terre, "if you don't want us to think you worse than you are, behave like a Breton and be done with it."

The two Chouans seized him again and threw him on the bench where he gave no other sign of resistance than the instinctive and convulsive motions of an animal, uttering a few smothered groans, which ceased when the axe fell. The head was off at the first blow. Marche-a-Terre took it by the hair, left the room, sought and found a large nail in the rough casing of the door, and wound the hair about it; leaving the bloody head, the eyes of which he did not even close, to hang there.

The two Chouans then washed their hands, without the least haste, in a pot full of water, picked up their hats and guns, and jumped the gate, whistling the "Ballad of the Captain." Pille-Miche began to sing in a hoarse voice as he reached the field the last verses of that rustic song, their melody floating on the breeze:—

"At the first town
Her lover dressed her
All in white satin;

"At the next town
Her lover dressed her
In gold and silver.

"So beautiful was she
They gave her veils
To wear in the regiment."

The tune became gradually indistinguishable as the Chouans got further away; but the silence of the country was so great that several of the notes reached Barbette's ear as she neared home, holding her boy by the hand. A peasant-woman never listens coldly to that song, so popular is it in the West of France, and Barbette began, unconsciously, to sing the first verses:—

"Come, let us go, my girl,
Let us go to the war;
Let us go, it is time.

"Brave captain,
Let it not trouble you,
But my daughter is not for you.

"You shall not have her on earth,
You shall not have her at sea,
Unless by treachery.

"The father took his daughter,
He unclothed her
And flung her out to sea.

"The captain, wiser still,
Into the waves he jumped
And to the shore he brought her.

"Come, let us go, my girl,
Let us go to the war;
Let us go, it is time.

"At the first town
Her lover dressed her,"
Etc., etc.

As Barbette reached this verse of the song, where Pille-Miche had begun it, she was entering the courtyard of her home; her tongue suddenly stiffened, she stood still, and a great cry, quickly repressed, came from her gaping lips.

"What is it, mother?" said the child.

"Walk alone," she cried, pulling her hand away and pushing him roughly; "you have neither father nor mother."

The child, who was rubbing his shoulder and weeping, suddenly caught sight of the thing on the nail; his childlike face kept the nervous convulsion his crying had caused, but he was silent. He opened his eyes wide, and gazed at the head of his father with a stupid look which betrayed no emotion; then his face, brutalized by ignorance, showed savage curiosity. Barbette again took his hand, grasped it violently, and dragged him into the house. When Pille-Miche and Marche-a-Terre threw their victim on the bench one of his shoes, dropping off, fell on the floor beneath his neck and was afterward filled with blood. It was the first thing that met the widow's eye.

"Take off your shoe," said the mother to her son. "Put your foot in that. Good. Remember," she cried, in a solemn voice, "your father's shoe; never put on your own without remembering how the Chouans filled it with his blood, and *kill the Chouans*!"

She swayed her head with so convulsive an action that the meshes of her black hair fell upon her neck and gave a sinister expression to her face.

"I call Saint-Labre to witness," she said, "that I vow you to the Blues. You shall be a soldier to avenge your father. Kill, kill the *Chouans*, and do as I do. Ha! they've taken the head of my man, and I am going to give that of the Gars to the Blues."

She sprang at a bound on the bed, seized a little bag of money from a hiding-place, took the hand of the astonished little boy, and dragged him after her without giving him time to put on his shoe, and was on

258

her way to Fougeres rapidly, without once turning her head to look at the home she abandoned. When they reached the summit of the rocks of Saint-Sulpice Barbette set fire to the pile of fagots, and the boy helped her to pile on the green gorse, damp with hoarfrost, to make the smoke more dense.

"That fire will last longer than your father, longer than I, longer than the Gars," said Barbette, in a savage voice.

While the widow of Galope-Chopine and her son with his bloody foot stood watching, the one, with a gloomy expression of revenge, the other with curiosity, the curling of the smoke, Mademoiselle de Verneuil's eyes were fastened on the same rock, trying, but in vain, to see her lover's signal. The fog, which had thickened, buried the whole region under a veil, its gray tints obscuring even the outlines of the scenery that was nearest the town. She examined with tender anxiety the rocks, the castle, the buildings, which loomed like shadows through the mist. Near her window several trees stood out against this blue-gray background; the sun gave a dull tone as of tarnished silver to the sky; its rays colored the bare branches of the trees, where a few last leaves were fluttering, with a dingy red. But too many dear and delightful sentiments filled Marie's soul to let her notice the ill-omens of a scene so out of harmony with the joys she was tasting in advance. For the last two days her ideas had undergone a change. The fierce, undisciplined vehemence of her passions had yielded under the influence of the equable atmosphere which a true love gives to life. The certainty of being loved, sought through so many perils, had given birth to a desire to re-enter those social conditions which sanction love, and which despair alone had made her leave. To love for a moment only now seemed to her a species of weakness. She saw herself lifted from the dregs of society, where misfortune had driven her, to the high rank in which her father had meant to place her. Her vanity, repressed for a time by the cruel alternations of hope and misconception, was awakened and showed her all the benefits of a great position. Born in a certain way to rank, marriage to a marquis meant, to her mind, living and acting in the sphere that belonged to her. Having known the chances and changes of an adventurous life, she could appreciate, better than other women, the grandeur of the feelings which make the Family. Marriage and motherhood with all their cares seemed to her less a task than a rest. She loved the calm and virtuous life she saw through the clouds of this last storm as a woman weary of virtue may sometimes covet an illicit passion. Virtue was to her a new seduction.

"Perhaps," she thought, leaving the window without seeing the signal on the rocks of Saint-Sulpice, "I have been too coquettish with him —but I knew he loved me! Francine, it is not a dream; to-night I shall be Marquise de Montauran. What have I done to deserve such perfect happiness? Oh! I love him, and love alone is love's reward. And yet, I think God means to recompense me for taking heart through all my misery; he means me to forget my sufferings—for you know, Francine, I have suffered."

"To-night, Marquise de Montauran, you, Marie? Ah! until it is done I cannot believe it! Who has told him your true goodness?"

"Dear child! he has more than his handsome eyes to see me with, he has a soul. If you had seen him, as I have, in danger! Oh! he knows how to love—he is so brave!"

"If you really love him why do you let him come to Fougeres?"

"We had no time to say one word to each other when the Blues surprised us. Besides, his coming is a proof of love. Can I ever have proofs enough? And now, Francine, do my hair."

But she pulled it down a score of times with motions that seemed electric, as though some stormy thoughts were mingling still with the arts of her coquetry. As she rolled a curl or smoothed the shining plaits she asked herself, with a remnant of distrust, whether the marquis were deceiving her; but treachery seemed to her impossible, for did he not expose himself to instant vengeance by entering Fougeres? While studying in her mirror the effects of a sidelong glance, a smile, a gentle frown, an attitude of anger, or of love, or disdain, she was seeking some woman's wile by which to probe to the last instant the heart of the young leader.

"You are right, Francine," she said; "I wish with you that the marriage were over. This is the last of my cloudy days—it is big with death or happiness. Oh! that fog is dreadful," she went on, again looking towards the heights of Saint-Sulpice, which were still veiled in mist.

She began to arrange the silk and muslin curtains which draped the window, making them intercept the light and produce in the room a voluptuous chiaro-scuro.

"Francine," she said, "take away those knick-knacks on the mantelpiece; leave only the clock and the two Dresden vases. I'll fill those vases myself with the flowers Corentin brought me. Take out the chairs, I want only this sofa and a fauteuil. Then sweep the carpet, so as to bring out the colors, and put wax candles in the sconces and on the mantel."

Marie looked long and carefully at the old tapestry on the walls. Guided by her innate taste she found among the brilliant tints of these hangings the shades by which to connect their antique beauty with the furniture and accessories of the boudoir, either by the harmony of color or the charm of contrast. The same thought guided the arrangement of the flowers with which she filled the twisted vases which decorated her chamber. The sofa was placed beside the fire. On either side of the bed, which filled the space parallel to that of the chimney, she placed on gilded tables tall Dresden vases filled with foliage and flowers that were sweetly fragrant. She quivered more than once as she arranged the folds of the green damask above the bed, and studied the fall of the drapery which concealed it. Such preparations have a secret, ineffable happiness about them; they cause so many delightful emotions that a woman as she makes them forgets her doubts; and Mademoiselle de Verneuil forgot hers. There is in truth a religious sentiment in the multiplicity of cares taken for one beloved who is not there to see them and reward them, but who will reward them later with the approving smile these tender preparations (always so fully understood) obtain. Women, as they make them, love in advance; and there are few indeed who would not say to themselves, as Mademoiselle de Verneuil now thought: "To-night I shall be happy!" That soft hope lies in every fold of silk or muslin; insensibly, the harmony the woman makes about her gives an atmosphere of love in which she breathes; to her these things are beings, witnesses; she has made them the sharers of her coming joy. Every movement, every thought brings that joy within her grasp. But presently she expects no longer, she hopes no more, she questions silence; the slightest sound is to her an omen; doubt hooks its claws once more into her heart; she burns, she trembles, she is grasped by a thought which holds her like a physical force; she alternates from triumph to agony, and without the hope of coming happiness she could not endure the torture. A score of times did

Mademoiselle de Verneuil raise the window-curtain, hoping to see the smoke rising above the rocks; but the fog only took a grayer tone, which her excited imagination turned into a warning. At last she let fall the curtain, impatiently resolving not to raise it again. She looked gloomily around the charming room to which she had given a soul and a voice, asking herself if it were done in vain, and this thought brought her back to her preparations.

"Francine," she said, drawing her into a little dressing-room which adjoined her chamber and was lighted through a small round window opening on a dark corner of the fortifications where they joined the rock terrace of the Promenade, "put everything in order. As for the salon, you can leave that as it is," she added, with a smile which women reserve for their nearest friends, the delicate sentiment of which men seldom understand.

"Ah! how sweet you are!" exclaimed the little maid.

"A lover is our beauty—foolish women that we are!" she replied gaily.

Francine left her lying on the ottoman and went away convinced that, whether her mistress were loved or not, she would never betray Montauran.

* * * * *

"Are you sure of what you are telling me, old woman?" Hulot was saying to Barbette, who had sought him out as soon as she had reached Fougeres.

"Have you got eyes? Look at the rocks of Saint-Sulpice, there, my good man, to the right of Saint-Leonard."

Corentin, who was with Hulot, looked towards the summit in the direction pointed out by Barbette, and, as the fog was beginning to lift, he could see with some distinctness the column of white smoke the woman told of.

"But when is he coming, old woman?—to-night, or this evening?"

"My good man," said Barbette, "I don't know."

"Why do you betray your own side?" said Hulot, quickly, having drawn her out of hearing of Corentin.

"Ah! general, see my boy's foot—that's washed in the blood of my man, whom the Chouans have killed like a calf, to punish him for the few words you got out of me the other day when I was working in the fields. Take my boy, for you've deprived him of his father and his mother; make a Blue of him, my good man, teach him to kill Chouans. Here, there's two hundred crowns,—keep them for him; if he is careful, they'll last him long, for it took his father twelve years to lay them by."

Hulot looked with amazement at the pale and withered woman, whose eyes were dry.

"But you, mother," he said, "what will become of you? you had better keep the money."

"I?" she replied, shaking her head sadly. "I don't need anything in this world. You might bolt me into that highest tower over there" (pointing to the battlements of the castle) "and the Chouans would contrive to come and kill me."

She kissed her boy with an awful expression of grief, looked at him, wiped away her tears, looked at him again, and disappeared.

"Commandant," said Corentin, "this is an occasion when two heads are better than one. We know all, and yet we know nothing. If you surrounded Mademoiselle de Verneuil's house now, you will only warn her. Neither you, nor I, nor your Blues and your battalions are strong enough to get the better of that girl if she takes it into her head to save the ci-devant. The fellow is brave, and consequently wily; he is a young man full of daring. We can never get hold of him as he enters Fougères. Perhaps he is here already. Domiciliary visit? Absurdity! that's no good, it will only give them warning."

"Well," said Hulot impatiently, "I shall tell the sentry on the Place Saint-Leonard to keep his eye on the house, and pass word along the other sentinels, if a young man enters it; as soon as the signal reaches me I shall take a corporal and four men and—"

"—and," said Corentin, interrupting the old soldier, "if the young man is not the marquis, or if the marquis doesn't go in by the front door, or if he is already there, if—if—if—what then?"

Corentin looked at the commandant with so insulting an air of superiority that the old soldier shouted out: "God's thousand thunders! get out of here, citizen of hell! What have I got to do with your intrigues? If that cockchafer buzzes into my guard-room I shall shoot him; if I hear he is in a house I shall surround that house and take him when he leaves it and shoot him, but may the devil get me if I soil my uniform with any of your tricks."

"Commandant, the order of the ministers states that you are to obey Mademoiselle de Verneuil."

"Let her come and give them to me herself and I'll see about it."

"Well, citizen," said Corentin, haughtily, "she shall come. She shall tell you herself the hour at which she expects the *ci-devant*. Possibly she won't be easy till you do post the sentinels round the house."

"The devil is made man," thought the old leader as he watched Corentin hurrying up the Queen's Staircase at the foot of which this scene had taken place. "He means to deliver Montauran bound hand and foot, with no chance to fight for his life, and I shall be harrassed to death with a court-martial. However," he added, shrugging his shoulders, "the Gars certainly is an enemy of the Republic, and he killed my poor Gerard, and his death will make a noble the less—the devil take him!"

He turned on the heels of his boots and went off, whistling the Marseillaise, to inspect his guard-rooms.

* * * * *

Mademoiselle de Verneuil was absorbed in one of those meditations the mysteries of which are buried in the soul, and prove by their thousand contradictory emotions, to the woman who undergoes them, that it is possible to have a stormy and passionate existence between four walls without even moving from the ottoman on which her very life is burning itself away. She had reached the final scene of the drama she had come to enact, and her mind was going over and over the phases of love and anger which had so powerfully stirred

The Chouans

her during the ten days which had now elapsed since her first meeting with the marquis. A man's step suddenly sounded in the adjoining room and she trembled; the door opened, she turned quickly and saw Corentin.

"You little cheat!" said the police-agent, "when will you stop deceiving? Ah, Marie, Marie, you are playing a dangerous game by not taking me into your confidence. Why do you play such tricks without consulting me? If the marquis escapes his fate—"

"It won't be your fault, will it?" she replied, sarcastically. "Monsieur," she continued, in a grave voice, "by what right do you come into my house?"

"Your house?" he exclaimed.

"You remind me," she answered, coldly, "that I have no home. Perhaps you chose this house deliberately for the purpose of committing murder. I shall leave it. I would live in a desert to get away from—"

"Spies, say the word," interrupted Corentin. "But this house is neither yours nor mine, it belongs to the government; and as for leaving it you will do nothing of the kind," he added, giving her a diabolical look.

Mademoiselle de Verneuil rose indignantly, made a few steps to leave the room, but stopped short suddenly as Corentin raised the curtain of the window and beckoned her, with a smile, to come to him.

"Do you see that column of smoke?" he asked, with the calmness he always kept on his livid face, however intense his feelings might be.

"What has my departure to do with that burning brush?" she asked.

"Why does your voice tremble?" he said. "You poor thing!" he added, in a gentle voice, "I know all. The marquis is coming to Fougeres this evening; and it is not with any intention of delivering him to us that you have arranged this boudoir and the flowers and candles."

The Chouans

Mademoiselle de Verneuil turned pale, for she saw her lover's death in the eyes of this tiger with a human face, and her love for him rose to frenzy. Each hair on her head caused her an acute pain she could not endure, and she fell on the ottoman. Corentin stood looking at her for a moment with his arms folded, half pleased at inflicting a torture which avenged him for the contempt and the sarcasms this woman had heaped upon his head, half grieved by the sufferings of a creature whose yoke was pleasant to him, heavy as it was.

"She loves him!" he muttered.

"Loves him!" she cried. "Ah! what are words? Corentin! he is my life, my soul, my breath!" She flung herself at the feet of the man, whose silence terrified her. "Soul of vileness!" she cried, "I would rather degrade myself to save his life than degrade myself by betraying him. I will save him at the cost of my own blood. Speak, what price must I pay you?"

Corentin quivered.

"I came to take your orders, Marie," he said, raising her. "Yes, Marie, your insults will not hinder my devotion to your wishes, provided you will promise not to deceive me again; you must know by this time that no one dupes me with impunity."

"If you want me to love you, Corentin, help me to save him."

"At what hour is he coming?" asked the spy, endeavoring to ask the question calmly.

"Alas, I do not know."

They looked at each other in silence.

"I am lost!" thought Mademoiselle de Verneuil.

"She is deceiving me!" thought Corentin. "Marie," he continued, "I have two maxims. One is never to believe a single word a woman says to me—that's the only means of not being duped; the other is to find what interest she has in doing the opposite of what she says, and behaving in contradiction to the facts she pretends to confide to me. I think that you and I understand each other now."

"Perfectly," replied Mademoiselle de Verneuil. "You want proofs of my good faith; but I reserve them for the time when you give me some of yours."

"Adieu, mademoiselle," said Corentin, coolly.

"Nonsense," said the girl, smiling; "sit down, and pray don't sulk; but if you do I shall know how to save the marquis without you. As for the three hundred thousand francs which are always spread before your eyes, I will give them to you in good gold as soon as the marquis is safe."

Corentin rose, stepped back a pace or two, and looked at Marie.

"You have grown rich in a very short time," he said, in a tone of ill-disguised bitterness.

"Montauran," she continued, "will make you a better offer still for his ransom. Now, then, prove to me that you have the means of guaranteeing him from all danger and—"

"Can't you send him away the moment he arrives?" cried Corentin, suddenly. "Hulot does not know he is coming, and—" He stopped as if he had said too much. "But how absurd that you should ask me how to play a trick," he said, with an easy laugh. "Now listen, Marie, I do feel certain of your loyalty. Promise me a compensation for all I lose in furthering your wishes, and I will make that old fool of a commandant so unsuspicious that the marquis will be as safe at Fougeres as at Saint-James."

"Yes, I promise it," said the girl, with a sort of solemnity.

"No, not in that way," he said, "swear it by your mother."

Mademoiselle de Verneuil shuddered; raising a trembling hand she made the oath required by the man whose tone to her had changed so suddenly.

"You can command me," he said; "don't deceive me again, and you shall have reason to bless me to-night."

"I will trust you, Corentin," cried Mademoiselle de Verneuil, much moved. She bowed her head gently towards him and smiled with a kindness not unmixed with surprise, as she saw an expression of melancholy tenderness on his face.

"What an enchanting creature!" thought Corentin, as he left the house. "Shall I ever get her as a means to fortune and a source of delight? To fling herself at my feet! Oh, yes, the marquis shall die! If I can't get that woman in any other way than by dragging her through the mud, I'll sink her in it. At any rate," he thought, as he reached the square unconscious of his steps, "she no longer distrusts me. Three hundred thousand francs down! she thinks me grasping! Either the offer was a trick or she is already married to him."

Corentin, buried in thought, was unable to come to a resolution. The fog which the sun had dispersed at mid-day was now rolling thicker and thicker, so that he could hardly see the trees at a little distance.

"That's another piece of ill-luck," he muttered, as he turned slowly homeward. "It is impossible to see ten feet. The weather protects the lovers. How is one to watch a house in such a fog? Who goes there?" he cried, catching the arm of a boy who seemed to have clambered up the dangerous rocks which made the terrace of the Promenade.

"It is I," said a childish voice.

"Ah! the boy with the bloody foot. Do you want to revenge your father?" said Corentin.

"Yes," said the child.

"Very good. Do you know the Gars?"

"Yes."

"Good again. Now, don't leave me except to do what I bid you, and you will obey your mother and earn some big sous—do you like sous?"

"Yes."

"You like sous, and you want to kill the Gars who killed your father—well, I'll take care of you. Ah! Marie," he muttered, after a pause, "you yourself shall betray him, as you engaged to do! She is too violent to suspect me—passion never reflects. She does not know the marquis's writing. Yes, I can set a trap into which her nature will drive her headlong. But I must first see Hulot."

Mademoiselle de Verneuil and Francine were deliberating on the means of saving the marquis from the more than doubtful generosity of Corentin and Hulot's bayonets.

"I could go and warn him," said the Breton girl.

"But we don't know where he is," replied Marie; "even I, with the instincts of love, could never find him."

After making and rejecting a number of plans Mademoiselle de Verneuil exclaimed, "When I see him his danger will inspire me."

She thought, like other ardent souls, to act on the spur of the moment, trusting to her star, or to that instinct of adroitness which rarely, if ever, fails a woman. Perhaps her heart was never so wrung. At times she seemed stupefied, her eyes were fixed, and then, at the least noise, she shook like a half-uprooted tree which the woodsman drags with a rope to hasten its fall. Suddenly, a loud report from a dozen guns echoed from a distance. Marie turned pale and grasped Francine's hand. "I am dying," she cried; "they have killed him!"

The heavy footfall of a man was heard in the antechamber. Francine went out and returned with a corporal. The man, making a military salute to Mademoiselle de Verneuil, produced some letters, the covers of which were a good deal soiled. Receiving no acknowledgment, the Blue said as he withdrew, "Madame, they are from the commandant."

Mademoiselle de Verneuil, a prey to horrible presentiments, read a letter written apparently in great haste by Hulot:—

"Mademoiselle—a party of my men have just caught a messenger from the Gars and have shot him. Among the intercepted letters is one which may be useful to you and I transmit it—etc."

"Thank God, it was not he they shot," she exclaimed, flinging the letter into the fire.

She breathed more freely and took up the other letter, enclosed by Hulot. It was apparently written to Madame du Gua by the marquis.

"No, my angel," the letter said, "I cannot go to-night to La Vivetiere. You must lose your wager with the count. I triumph over the Republic in the person of their beautiful emissary. You must allow that she is worth the sacrifice of one night. It will be my only victory in this campaign, for I have received the news that La Vendee surrenders. I can do nothing more in France. Let us go back to England—but we will talk of all this to-morrow."

The letter fell from Marie's hands; she closed her eyes, and was silent, leaning backward, with her head on a cushion. After a long pause she looked at the clock, which then marked four in the afternoon.

"My lord keeps me waiting," she said, with savage irony.

"Oh! God grant he may not come!" cried Francine.

"If he does not come," said Marie, in a stifled tone, "I shall go to him. No, no, he will soon be here. Francine, do I look well?"

"You are very pale."

"Ah!" continued Mademoiselle de Verneuil, glancing about her, "this perfumed room, the flowers, the lights, this intoxicating air, it is full of that celestial life of which I dreamed—"

"Marie, what has happened?"

"I am betrayed, deceived, insulted, fooled! I will kill him, I will tear him bit by bit! Yes, there was always in his manner a contempt he could not hide and which I would not see. Oh! I shall die of this! Fool that I am," she went on laughing, "he is coming; I have one night in which to teach him that, married or not, the man who has possessed me cannot abandon me. I will measure my vengeance by his offence; he shall die with despair in his soul. I did believe he had a soul of honor, but no! it is that of a lackey. Ah, he has cleverly deceived me, for even now it seems impossible that the man who abandoned me to Pille-Miche should sink to such back-stair tricks. It is so base to deceive a loving woman, for it is so easy. He might have killed me if he chose, but lie to me! to me, who held him in my thoughts so high! The scaffold! the scaffold! ah! could I only see him guillotined! Am I cruel? He shall go to his death covered with caresses, with kisses which might have blessed him for a lifetime—"

"Marie," said Francine, gently, "be the victim of your lover like other women; not his mistress and his betrayer. Keep his memory in your heart; do not make it an anguish to you. If there were no joys in hopeless love, what would become of us, poor women that we are? God, of whom you never think, Marie, will reward us for obeying our vocation on this earth,—to love, and suffer."

"Dear," replied Mademoiselle de Verneuil, taking Francine's hand and patting it, "your voice is very sweet and persuasive. Reason is attractive from your lips. I should like to obey you, but—"

"You will forgive him, you will not betray him?"

"Hush! never speak of that man again. Compared with him Corentin is a noble being. Do you hear me?"

She rose, hiding beneath a face that was horribly calm the madness of her soul and a thirst for vengeance. The slow and measured step with which she left the room conveyed the sense of an irrevocable resolution. Lost in thought, hugging her insults, too proud to show the slightest suffering, she went to the guard-room at the Porte Saint-Leonard and asked where the commandant lived. She had hardly left her house when Corentin entered it.

"Oh, Monsieur Corentin," cried Francine, "if you are interested in this young man, save him; Mademoiselle has gone to give him up because of this wretched letter."

Corentin took the letter carelessly and asked,—

"Which way did she go?"

"I don't know."

"Yes," he said, "I will save her from her own despair."

He disappeared, taking the letter with him. When he reached the street he said to Galope-Chopine's boy, whom he had stationed to watch the door, "Which way did a lady go who left the house just now?"

The boy went with him a little way and showed him the steep street which led to the Porte Saint-Leonard. "That way," he said.

At this moment four men entered Mademoiselle de Verneuil's house, unseen by either the boy or Corentin.

"Return to your watch," said the latter. "Play with the handles of the blinds and see what you can inside; look about you everywhere, even on the roof."

Corentin darted rapidly in the direction given him, and thought he recognized Mademoiselle de Verneuil through the fog; he did, in fact, overtake her just as she reached the guard-house.

"Where are you going?" he said; "you are pale—what has happened? Is it right for you to be out alone? Take my arm."

"Where is the commandant?" she asked.

Hardly had the words left her lips when she heard the movement of troops beyond the Porte Saint-Leonard and distinguished Hulot's gruff voice in the tumult.

"God's thunder!" he cried, "I never saw such fog as this for a reconnaissance! The Gars must have ordered the weather."

"What are you complaining of?" said Mademoiselle de Verneuil, grasping his arm. "The fog will cover vengeance as well as perfidy. Commandant," she added, in a low voice, "you must take measures at once so that the Gars may not escape us."

"Is he at your house?" he asked, in a tone which showed his amazement.

"Not yet," she replied; "but give me a safe man and I will send him to you when the marquis comes."

"That's a mistake," said Corentin; "a soldier will alarm him, but a boy, and I can find one, will not."

"Commandant," said Mademoiselle de Verneuil, "thanks to this fog which you are cursing, you can surround my house. Put soldiers everywhere. Place a guard in the church to command the esplanade on which the windows of my salon open. Post men on the Promenade; for though the windows of my bedroom are twenty feet above the ground, despair does sometimes give a man the power to

The Chouans

jump even greater distances safely. Listen to what I say. I shall probably send this gentleman out of the door of my house; therefore see that only brave men are there to meet him; for," she added, with a sigh, "no one denies him courage; he will assuredly defend himself."

"Gudin!" called the commandant. "Listen, my lad," he continued in a low voice when the young man joined him, "this devil of a girl is betraying the Gars to us—I am sure I don't know why, but that's no matter. Take ten men and place yourself so as to hold the cul-de-sac in which the house stands; be careful that no one sees either you or your men."

"Yes, commandant, I know the ground."

"Very good," said Hulot. "I'll send Beau-Pied to let you know when to play your sabres. Try to meet the marquis yourself, and if you can manage to kill him, so that I sha'n't have to shoot him judicially, you shall be a lieutenant in a fortnight or my name's not Hulot."

Gudin departed with a dozen soldiers.

"Do you know what you have done?" said Corentin to Mademoiselle de Verneuil, in a low voice.

She made no answer, but looked with a sort of satisfaction at the men who were starting, under command of the sub-lieutenant, for the Promenade, while others, following the next orders given by Hulot, were to post themselves in the shadows of the church of Saint-Leonard.

"There are houses adjoining mine," she said; "you had better surround them all. Don't lay up regrets by neglecting a single precaution."

"She is mad," thought Hulot.

"Was I not a prophet?" asked Corentin in his ear. "As for the boy I shall send with her, he is the little gars with a bloody foot; therefore—"

He did not finish his sentence, for Mademoiselle de Verneuil by a sudden movement darted in the direction of her house, whither he

273

followed her, whistling like a man supremely satisfied. When he overtook her she was already at the door of her house, where Galope-Chopine's little boy was on the watch.

"Mademoiselle," said Corentin, "take the lad with you; you cannot have a more innocent or active emissary. Boy," he added, "when you have seen the Gars enter the house come to me, no matter who stops you; you'll find me at the guard-house and I'll give you something that will make you eat cake for the rest of your days."

At these words, breathed rather than said in the child's ear, Corentin felt his hand squeezed by that of the little Breton, who followed Mademoiselle de Verneuil into the house.

"Now, my good friends, you can come to an explanation as soon as you like," cried Corentin when the door was closed. "If you make love, my little marquis, it will be on your winding-sheet."

But Corentin could not bring himself to let that fatal house completely out of sight, and he went to the Promenade, where he found the commandant giving his last orders. By this time it was night. Two hours went by; but the sentinels posted at intervals noticed nothing that led them to suppose the marquis had evaded the triple line of men who surrounded the three sides by which the tower of Papegaut was accessible. Twenty times had Corentin gone from the Promenade to the guard-room, always to find that his little emissary had not appeared. Sunk in thought, the spy paced the Promenade slowly, enduring the martyrdom to which three passions, terrible in their clashing, subject a man,—love, avarice, and ambition. Eight o'clock struck from all the towers in the town. The moon rose late. Fog and darkness wrapped in impenetrable gloom the places where the drama planned by this man was coming to its climax. He was able to silence the struggle of his passions as he walked up and down, his arms crossed, and his eyes fixed on the windows which rose like the luminous eyes of a phantom above the rampart. The deep silence was broken only by the rippling of the Nancon, by the regular and lugubrious tolling from the belfries, by the heavy steps of the sentinels or the rattle of arms as the guard was hourly relieved.

"The night's as thick as a wolf's jaw," said the voice of Pille-Miche.

"Go on," growled Marche-a-Terre, "and don't talk more than a dead dog."

"I'm hardly breathing," said the Chouan.

"If the man who made that stone roll down wants his heart to serve as the scabbard for my knife he'll do it again," said Marche-a-Terre, in a low voice scarcely heard above the flowing of the river.

"It was I," said Pille-Miche.

"Well, then, old money-bag, down on your stomach," said the other, "and wriggle like a snake through a hedge, or we shall leave our carcasses behind us sooner than we need."

"Hey, Marche-a-Terre," said the incorrigible Pille-Miche, who was using his hands to drag himself along on his stomach, and had reached the level of his comrade's ear. "If the Grande-Garce is to be believed there'll be a fine booty to-day. Will you go shares with me?"

"Look here, Pille-Miche," said Marche-a-Terre stopping short on the flat of his stomach. The other Chouans, who were accompanying the two men, did the same, so wearied were they with the difficulties they had met with in climbing the precipice. "I know you," continued Marche-a-Terre, "for a Jack Grab-All who would rather give blows than receive them when there's nothing else to be done. We have not come here to grab dead men's shoes; we are devils against devils, and sorrow to those whose claws are too short. The Grande-Garce has sent us here to save the Gars. He is up there; lift your dog's nose and see that window above the tower."

Midnight was striking. The moon rose, giving the appearance of white smoke to the fog. Pille-Miche squeezed Marche-a-Terre's arm and silently showed him on the terrace just above them, the triangular iron of several shining bayonets.

"The Blues are there already," said Pille-Miche; "we sha'n't gain anything by force."

"Patience," replied Marche-a-Terre; "if I examined right this morning, we must be at the foot of the Papegaut tower between the ramparts and the Promenade,—that place where they put the manure; it is like a feather-bed to fall on."

"If Saint-Labre," remarked Pille-Miche, "would only change into cider the blood we shall shed to-night the citizens might lay in a good stock to-morrow."

Marche-a-Terre laid his large hand over his friend's mouth; then an order muttered by him went from rank to rank of the Chouans suspended as they were in mid-air among the brambles of the slate rocks. Corentin, walking up and down the esplanade had too practiced an ear not to hear the rustling of the shrubs and the light sound of pebbles rolling down the sides of the precipice. Marche-a-Terre, who seemed to possess the gift of seeing in darkness, and whose senses, continually in action, were acute as those of a savage, saw Corentin; like a trained dog he had scented him. Fouche's diplomatist listened but heard nothing; he looked at the natural wall of rock and saw no signs. If the confusing gleam of the fog enabled him to see, here and there, a crouching Chouan, he took him, no doubt, for a fragment of rock, for these human bodies had all the appearance of inert nature. This danger to the invaders was of short duration. Corentin's attention was diverted by a very distinct noise coming from the other end of the Promenade, where the rock wall ended and a steep descent leading down to the Queen's Staircase began. When Corentin reached the spot he saw a figure gliding past it as if by magic. Putting out his hand to grasp this real or fantastic being, who was there, he supposed, with no good intentions, he encountered the soft and rounded figure of a woman.

"The devil take you!" he exclaimed, "if any one else had met you, you'd have had a ball through your head. What are you doing, and where are you going, at this time of night? Are you dumb? It certainly is a woman," he said to himself.

The silence was suspicious, but the stranger broke it by saying, in a voice which suggested extreme fright, "Ah, my good man, I'm on my way back from a wake."

"It is the pretended mother of the marquis," thought Corentin. "I'll see what she's about. Well, go that way, old woman," he replied, feigning not to recognize her. "Keep to the left if you don't want to be shot."

He stood quite still; then observing that Madame du Gua was making for the Papegaut tower, he followed her at a distance with diabolical caution. During this fatal encounter the Chouans had posted themselves on the manure towards which Marche-a-Terre had guided them.

"There's the Grande-Garce!" thought Marche-a-Terre, as he rose to his feet against the tower wall like a bear.

"We are here," he said to her in a low voice.

"Good," she replied, "there's a ladder in the garden of that house about six feet above the manure; find it, and the Gars is saved. Do you see that small window up there? It is in the dressing-room; you must get to it. This side of the tower is the only one not watched. The horses are ready; if you can hold the passage over the Nancon, a quarter of an hour will put him out of danger—in spite of his folly. But if that woman tries to follow him, stab her."

Corentin now saw several of the forms he had hitherto supposed to be stones moving cautiously but swiftly. He went at once to the guard-room at the Porte Saint-Leonard, where he found the commandant fully dressed and sound asleep on a camp bed.

"Let him alone," said Beau-Pied, roughly, "he has only just lain down."

"The Chouans are here!" cried Corentin, in Hulot's ear.

"Impossible! but so much the better," cried the old soldier, still half asleep; "then he can fight."

When Hulot reached the Promenade Corentin pointed out to him the singular position taken by the Chouans.

"They must have deceived or strangled the sentries I placed between the castle and the Queen's Staircase. Ah! what a devil of a fog! However, patience! I'll send a squad of men under a lieutenant to the foot of the rock. There is no use attacking them where they are, for those animals are so hard they'd let themselves roll down the precipice without breaking a limb."

The cracked clock of the belfry was ringing two when the commandant got back to the Promenade after giving these orders and taking every military precaution to seize the Chouans. The sentries were doubled and Mademoiselle de Verneuil's house

The Chouans

became the centre of a little army. Hulot found Corentin absorbed in contemplation of the window which overlooked the tower.

"Citizen," said the commandant, "I think the *ci-devant* has fooled us; there's nothing stirring."

"He is there," cried Corentin, pointing to the window. "I have seen a man's shadow on the curtain. But I can't think what has become of that boy. They must have killed him or locked him up. There! commandant, don't you see that? there's a man's shadow; come, come on!"

"I sha'n't seize him in bed; thunder of God! He will come out if he went in; Gudin won't miss him," cried Hulot, who had his own reasons for waiting till the Gars could defend himself.

"Commandant, I enjoin you, in the name of the law to proceed at once into that house."

"You're a fine scoundrel to try to make me do that."

Without showing any resentment at the commandant's language, Corentin said coolly: "You will obey me. Here is an order in good form, signed by the minister of war, which will force you to do so." He drew a paper from his pocket and held it out. "Do you suppose we are such fools as to leave that girl to do as she likes? We are endeavoring to suppress a civil war, and the grandeur of the purpose covers the pettiness of the means."

"I take the liberty, citizen, of sending you to—you understand me? Enough. To the right-about, march! Let me alone, or it will be the worse for you."

"But read that," persisted Corentin.

"Don't bother me with your functions," cried Hulot, furious at receiving orders from a man he regarded as contemptible.

At this instant Galope-Chopine's boy suddenly appeared among them like a rat from a hole.

"The Gars has started!" he cried.

278

"Which way?"

"The rue Saint-Leonard."

"Beau-Pied," said Hulot in a whisper to the corporal who was near him, "go and tell your lieutenant to draw in closer round the house, and make ready to fire. Left wheel, forward on the tower, the rest of you!" he shouted.

To understand the conclusion of this fatal drama we must re-enter the house with Mademoiselle de Verneuil when she returned to it after denouncing the marquis to the commandant.

When passions reach their crisis they bring us under the dominion of far greater intoxication than the petty excitements of wine or opium. The lucidity then given to ideas, the delicacy of the high-wrought senses, produce the most singular and unexpected effects. Some persons when they find themselves under the tyranny of a single thought can see with extraordinary distinctness objects scarcely visible to others, while at the same time the most palpable things become to them almost as if they did not exist. When Mademoiselle de Verneuil hurried, after reading the marquis's letter, to prepare the way for vengeance just as she had lately been preparing all for love, she was in that stage of mental intoxication which makes real life like the life of a somnambulist. But when she saw her house surrounded, by her own orders, with a triple line of bayonets a sudden flash of light illuminated her soul. She judged her conduct and saw with horror that she had committed a crime. Under the first shock of this conviction she sprang to the threshold of the door and stood there irresolute, striving to think, yet unable to follow out her reasoning. She knew so vaguely what had happened that she tried in vain to remember why she was in the antechamber, and why she was leading a strange child by the hand. A million of stars were floating in the air before her like tongues of fire. She began to walk about, striving to shake off the horrible torpor which laid hold of her; but, like one asleep, no object appeared to her under its natural form or in its own colors. She grasped the hand of the little boy with a violence not natural to her, dragging him along with such precipitate steps that she seemed to have the motions of a madwoman. She saw neither persons nor things in the salon as she crossed it, and yet she was saluted by three men who made way to let her pass.

"That must be she," said one of them.

"She is very handsome," exclaimed another, who was a priest.

"Yes," replied the first; "but how pale and agitated—"

"And beside herself," said the third; "she did not even see us."

At the door of her own room Mademoiselle de Verneuil saw the smiling face of Francine, who whispered to her: "He is here, Marie."

Mademoiselle de Verneuil awoke, reflected, looked at the child whose hand she held, remembered all, and replied to the girl: "Shut up that boy; if you wish me to live do not let him escape you."

As she slowly said the words her eyes were fixed on the door of her bedroom, and there they continued fastened with so dreadful a fixedness that it seemed as if she saw her victim through the wooden panels. Then she gently opened it, passed through and closed it behind her without turning round, for she saw the marquis standing before the fireplace. His dress, without being too choice, had the look of careful arrangement which adds so much to the admiration which a woman feels for her lover. All her self-possession came back to her at the sight of him. Her lips, rigid, although half-open, showed the enamel of her white teeth and formed a smile that was fixed and terrible rather than voluptuous. She walked with slow steps toward the young man and pointed with her finger to the clock.

"A man who is worthy of love is worth waiting for," she said with deceptive gaiety.

Then, overcome with the violence of her emotions, she dropped upon the sofa which was near the fireplace.

"Dear Marie, you are so charming when you are angry," said the marquis, sitting down beside her and taking her hand, which she let him take, and entreating a look, which she refused him. "I hope," he continued, in a tender, caressing voice, "that my wife will not long refuse a glance to her loving husband."

Hearing the words she turned abruptly and looked into his eyes.

"What is the meaning of that dreadful look?" he said, laughing. "But your hand is burning! oh, my love, what is it?"

"Corentin! ah! I understand it all; he wrote the letter; he has deceived me with diabolical art—as he alone can deceive."

With a piercing cry she flung herself on the sofa, tears rushing from her eyes. Doubt and confidence were equally dreadful now. The marquis knelt beside her and clasped her to his breast, saying, again and again, the only words he was able to utter:—

"Why do you weep, my darling? there is no harm done; your reproaches were all love; do not weep, I love you—I shall always love you."

Suddenly he felt her press him with almost supernatural force. "Do you still love me?" she said, amid her sobs.

"Can you doubt it?" he replied in a tone that was almost melancholy.

She abruptly disengaged herself from his arms, and fled, as if frightened and confused, to a little distance.

"Do I doubt it?" she exclaimed, but a smile of gentle meaning was on her lover's face, and the words died away upon her lips; she let him take her by the hand and lead her to the salon. There an altar had been hastily arranged during her absence. The priest was robed in his officiating vestments. The lighted tapers shed upon the ceiling a glow as soft as hope itself. She now recognized the two men who had bowed to her, the Comte de Bauvan and the Baron du Guenic, the witnesses chosen by Montauran.

"You will not still refuse?" said the marquis.

But at the sight she stopped, stepped backward into her chamber and fell on her knees; raising her hands towards the marquis she cried out: "Pardon! pardon! pardon!"

Her voice died away, her head fell back, her eyes closed, and she lay in the arms of her lover and Francine as if dead. When she opened her eyes they met those of the young man full of loving tenderness.

"Marie! patience! this is your last trial," he said.

"The last!" she exclaimed, bitterly.

Francine and the marquis looked at each other in surprise, but she silenced them by a gesture.

"Call the priest," she said, "and leave me alone with him."

They did so, and withdrew.

"My father," she said to the priest so suddenly called to her, "in my childhood an old man, white-haired like yourself, used to tell me that God would grant all things to those who had faith. Is that true?"

"It is true," replied the priest; "all things are possible to Him who created all."

Mademoiselle de Verneuil threw herself on her knees before him with incredible enthusiasm.

"Oh, my God!" she cried in ecstasy, "my faith in thee is equal to my love for him; inspire me! do here a miracle, or take my life!"

"Your prayer will be granted," said the priest.

Marie returned to the salon leaning on the arm of the venerable old man. A deep and secret emotion brought her to the arms of her lover more brilliant than on any of her past days, for a serenity like that which painters give to the martyrs added to her face an imposing dignity. She held out her hand to the marquis and together they advanced to the altar and knelt down. The marriage was about to be celebrated beside the nuptial bed, the altar hastily raised, the cross, the vessels, the chalice, secretly brought thither by the priest, the fumes of incense rising to the ceiling, the priest himself, who wore a stole above his cassock, the tapers on an altar in a salon,—all these things combined to form a strange and touching scene, which typified those times of saddest memory, when civil discord overthrew all sacred institutions. Religious ceremonies then had the savor of the mysteries. Children were baptized in the chambers where the mothers were still groaning from their labor. As in the olden time, the Saviour went, poor and lowly, to console the dying. Young girls received their first communion in the home where they had played since infancy. The marriage of the marquis and Mademoiselle de Verneuil was now solemnized, like many other unions, by a service contrary to the recent legal enactments. In after years these marriages, mostly celebrated at the foot of oaks, were scrupulously recognized and considered legal. The priest who thus preserved the ancient usages was one of those men who hold to their principles in the height of the storm. His voice, which never made the oath exacted by the Republic, uttered no word throughout the tempest that did not make for peace. He never incited, like the Abbe Gudin, to fire and sword; but like many others, he devoted himself to the still more dangerous mission of performing his priestly functions for the souls of faithful Catholics. To accomplish this perilous ministry he used all the pious deceptions necessitated by persecution, and the marquis, when he sought his services on this occasion, had found him in one of those excavated caverns which are known, even to the present day, by the name of "the priest's hiding-place." The mere sight of that pale and suffering face was enough to give this worldly room a holy aspect.

All was now ready for the act of misery and of joy. Before beginning the ceremony the priest asked, in the dead silence, the names of the bride.

"Marie-Nathalie, daughter of Mademoiselle Blanche de Casteran, abbess, deceased, of Notre-Dame de Seez, and Victor-Amedee, Duc de Verneuil."

"Where born?"

"At La Chasterie, near Alencon."

"I never supposed," said the baron in a low voice to the count, "that Montauran would have the folly to marry her. The natural daughter of a duke!—horrid!"

"If it were of the king, well and good," replied the Comte de Bauvan, smiling. "However, it is not for me to blame him; I like Charette's mistress full as well; and I shall transfer the war to her—though she's not one to bill and coo."

The names of the marquis had been filled in previously, and the two lovers now signed the document with their witnesses. The ceremony then began. At that instant Marie, and she alone, heard the sound of muskets and the heavy tread of soldiers,—no doubt relieving the guard in the church which she had herself demanded. She trembled violently and raised her eyes to the cross on the altar.

"A saint at last," said Francine, in a low voice.

"Give me such saints, and I'll be devilishly devout," added the count, in a whisper.

When the priest made the customary inquiry of Mademoiselle de Verneuil, she answered by a "yes" uttered with a deep sigh. Bending to her husband's ear she said: "You will soon know why I have broken the oath I made never to marry you."

After the ceremony all present passed into the dining-room, where dinner was served, and as they took their places Jeremie, Marie's footman, came into the room terrified. The poor bride rose and went to him; Francine followed her. With one of those pretexts which never fail a woman, she begged the marquis to do the honors for a moment, and went out, taking Jeremie with her before he could utter the fatal words.

"Ah! Francine, to be dying a thousand deaths and not to die!" she cried.

This absence might well be supposed to have its cause in the ceremony that had just taken place. Towards the end of the dinner, as the marquis was beginning to feel uneasy, Marie returned in all the pomp of a bridal robe. Her face was calm and joyful, while that of Francine who followed her had terror imprinted on every feature, so that the guests might well have thought they saw in these two women a fantastic picture by Salvator Rosa, of Life and Death holding each other by the hand.

"Gentlemen," said Marie to the priest, the baron, and the count, "you are my guests for the night. I find you cannot leave Fougeres; it would be dangerous to attempt it. My good maid has instructions to make you comfortable in your apartments. No, you must not rebel," she added to the priest, who was about to speak. "I hope you will not thwart a woman on her wedding-day."

An hour later she was alone with her husband in the room she had so joyously arranged a few hours earlier. They had reached that fatal bed where, like a tomb, so many hopes are wrecked, where the waking to a happy life is all uncertain, where love is born or dies, according to the natures that are tried there. Marie looked at the clock. "Six hours to live," she murmured.

"Can I have slept?" she cried toward morning, wakening with one of those sudden movements which rouse us when we have made ourselves a promise to wake at a certain hour. "Yes, I have slept," she thought, seeing by the light of the candles that the hands of the clock were pointing to two in the morning. She turned and looked at the sleeping marquis, lying like a child with his head on one hand, the other clasping his wife's hand, his lips half smiling as though he had fallen asleep while she kissed him.

"Ah!" she whispered to herself, "he sleeps like an infant; he does not distrust me—me, to whom he has given a happiness without a name."

She touched him softly and he woke, continuing to smile. He kissed the hand he held and looked at the wretched woman with eyes so sparkling that she could not endure their light and slowly lowered her large eyelids. Her husband might justly have accused her of coquetry if she were not concealing the terrors of her soul by thus evading the fire of his looks. Together they raised their charming heads and made each other a sign of gratitude for the pleasures they had tasted; but after a rapid glance at the beautiful picture his wife presented, the marquis was struck with an expression on her face which seemed to him melancholy, and he said in a tender voice, "Why sad, dear love?"

"Poor Alphonse," she answered, "do you know to what I have led you?"

"To happiness."

"To death!"

Shuddering with horror she sprang from the bed; the marquis, astonished, followed her. His wife motioned him to a window and raised the curtain, pointing as she did so to a score of soldiers. The moon had scattered the fog and was now casting her white light on the muskets and the uniforms, on the impassible Corentin pacing up and down like a jackal waiting for his prey, on the commandant, standing still, his arms crossed, his nose in the air, his lips curling, watchful and displeased.

"Come, Marie, leave them and come back to me."

"Why do you smile? I placed them there."

"You are dreaming."

"No."

They looked at each other for a moment. The marquis divined the whole truth, and he took her in his arms. "No matter!" he said, "I love you still."

"All is not lost!" cried Marie, "it cannot be! Alphonse," she said after a pause, "there is hope."

At this moment they distinctly heard the owl's cry, and Francine entered from the dressing-room.

"Pierre has come!" she said with a joy that was like delirium.

The marquise and Francine dressed Montauran in Chouan clothes with that amazing rapidity that belongs only to women. As soon as Marie saw her husband loading the gun Francine had brought in she slipped hastily from the room with a sign to her faithful maid. Francine then took the marquis to the dressing-room adjoining the bed-chamber. The young man seeing a large number of sheets knotted firmly together, perceived the means by which the girl expected him to escape the vigilance of the soldiers.

"I can't get through there," he said, examining the bull's-eye window.

At that instant it was darkened by a thickset figure, and a hoarse voice, known to Francine, said in a whisper, "Make haste, general, those rascally Blues are stirring."

"Oh! one more kiss," said a trembling voice beside him.

The marquis, whose feet were already on the liberating ladder, though he was not wholly through the window, felt his neck clasped with a despairing pressure. Seeing that his wife had put on his clothes, he tried to detain her; but she tore herself roughly from his arms and he was forced to descend. In his hand he held a fragment of some stuff which the moonlight showed him was a piece of the waistcoat he had worn the night before.

"Halt! fire!"

These words uttered by Hulot in the midst of a silence that was almost horrible broke the spell which seemed to hold the men and their surroundings. A volley of balls coming from the valley and reaching to the foot of the tower succeeded the discharges of the Blues posted on the Promenade. Not a cry came from the Chouans. Between each discharge the silence was frightful.

But Corentin had heard a fall from the ladder on the precipice side of the tower, and he suspected some ruse.

"None of those animals are growling," he said to Hulot; "our lovers are capable of fooling us on this side, and escaping themselves on the other."

The spy, to clear up the mystery, sent for torches; Hulot, understanding the force of Corentin's supposition, and hearing the noise of a serious struggle in the direction of the Porte Saint-Leonard, rushed to the guard-house exclaiming: "That's true, they won't separate."

"His head is well-riddled, commandant," said Beau-Pied, who was the first to meet him, "but he killed Gudin, and wounded two men. Ha! the savage; he got through three ranks of our best men and would have reached the fields if it hadn't been for the sentry at the gate who spitted him on his bayonet."

The commandant rushed into the guard-room and saw on a camp bedstead a bloody body which had just been laid there. He went up to the supposed marquis, raised the hat which covered the face, and fell into a chair.

"I suspected it!" he cried, crossing his arms violently; "she kept him, cursed thunder! too long."

The soldiers stood about, motionless. The commandant himself unfastened the long black hair of a woman. Suddenly the silence was broken by the tramp of men and Corentin entered the guardroom, preceding four soldiers who bore on their guns, crossed to make a litter, the body of Montauran, who was shot in the thighs and arms. They laid him on the bedstead beside his wife. He saw her, and found strength to clasp her hand with a convulsive gesture. The dying woman turned her head, recognized her husband, and shuddered with a spasm that was horrible to see, murmuring in a voice almost extinct: "A day without a morrow! God heard me too well!"

"Commandant," said the marquis, collecting all his strength, and still holding Marie's hand, "I count on your honor to send the news of my death to my young brother, who is now in London. Write him that if he wishes to obey my last injunction he will never bear arms against his country—neither must he abandon the king's service."

"It shall be done," said Hulot, pressing the hand of the dying man.

"Take them to the nearest hospital," cried Corentin.

Hulot took the spy by the arm with a grip that left the imprint of his fingers on the flesh.

"Out of this camp!" he cried; "your business is done here. Look well at the face of Commander Hulot, and never find yourself again in his way if you don't want your belly to be the scabbard of his blade—"

And the older soldier flourished his sabre.

"That's another of the honest men who will never make their way," said Corentin to himself when he was some distance from the guard-room.

The marquis was still able to thank his gallant adversary by a look marking the respect which all soldiers feel for loyal enemies.

* * * * *

In 1827 an old man accompanied by his wife was buying cattle in the market-place of Fougeres. Few persons remembered that he had killed a hundred or more men, and that his former name was Marche-a-Terre. A person to whom we owe important information about all the personages of this drama saw him there, leading a cow, and was struck by his simple, ingenuous air, which led her to remark, "That must be a worthy man."

As for Cibot, otherwise called Pille-Miche, we already know his end. It is likely that Marche-a-Terre made some attempt to save his comrade from the scaffold; possibly he was in the square at Alencon on the occasion of the frightful tumult which was one of the events of the famous trial of Rifoel, Briond, and la Chanterie.

ADDENDUM

The following personages appear in other stories of the Human Comedy.

Berthier, Alexandre
  The Gondreville Mystery

Brigaut, Major
  Pierrette

Casteran, De
  The Seamy Side of History
  Jealousies of a Country Town
  Beatrix
  The Peasantry

Cibot, Jean (alias Pille-Miche)
  The Seamy Side of History

Corentin
  The Gondreville Mystery
  Scenes from a Courtesan's Life
  The Middle Classes

Esgrignon, Charles-Marie-Victor-Ange-Carol, Marquis d' (or Des Grignons)
  Jealousies of a Country Town

Falcon, Jean (alias Beaupied or Beau-Pied)
  The Muse of the Department
  Cousin Betty

Ferdinand
  Beatrix

Fontaine, Comte de
  Modeste Mignon
  The Ball at Sceaux
  Cesar Birotteau
  The Government Clerks

Fouche, Joseph
  The Gondreville Mystery
  Scenes from a Courtesan's Life

Guenic, Gaudebert-Calyste-Charles, Baron du
  Beatrix

Hulot (Marshal)
  The Muse of the Department
  Cousin Betty

La Billardiere, Athanase-Jean-Francois-Michel, Baron Flamet de
  Cesar Birotteau
  The Government Clerks

Leroi, Pierre
  The Seamy Side of History
  Jealousies of a Country Town

Loudon, Prince de
  Modeste Mignon

Louis XVIII., Louis-Stanislas-Xavier
  The Seamy Side of History
  The Gondreville Mystery
  Scenes from a Courtesan's Life
  The Ball at Sceaux
  The Lily of the Valley
  Colonel Chabert
  The Government Clerks

Montauran, Marquis Alphonse de
  Cesar Birotteau

Montauran, Marquis de (younger brother of Alphonse de)
  The Seamy Side of History
  Cousin Betty

Stael-Holstein (Anne-Louise-Germaine Necker) Baronne de
  Louis Lambert
  Letters of Two Brides

Talleyrand-Perigord, Charles-Maurice de

The Chouans

The Gondreville Mystery
The Thirteen
Letters of Two Brides
Gaudissart II.

Troisville, Guibelin, Vicomte de
The Seamy Side of History
Jealousies of a Country Town
The Peasantry

Valois, Chevalier de
Jealousies of a Country Town

Verneuil, Duc de
Jealousies of a Country Town

Vissard, Charles-Amedee-Louis-Joseph Rifoel, Chevalier du
The Seamy Side of History

A Passion in the Desert

Translated by Ernest Dowson

A Passion in the Desert

"The whole show is dreadful," she cried coming out of the menagerie of M. Martin. She had just been looking at that daring speculator "working with his hyena,"—to speak in the style of the programme.

"By what means," she continued, "can he have tamed these animals to such a point as to be certain of their affection for—"

"What seems to you a problem," said I, interrupting, "is really quite natural."

"Oh!" she cried, letting an incredulous smile wander over her lips.

"You think that beasts are wholly without passions?" I asked her. "Quite the reverse; we can communicate to them all the vices arising in our own state of civilization."

She looked at me with an air of astonishment.

"But," I continued, "the first time I saw M. Martin, I admit, like you, I did give vent to an exclamation of surprise. I found myself next to an old soldier with the right leg amputated, who had come in with me. His face had struck me. He had one of those heroic heads, stamped with the seal of warfare, and on which the battles of Napoleon are written. Besides, he had that frank, good-humored expression which always impresses me favorably. He was without doubt one of those troopers who are surprised at nothing, who find matter for laughter in the contortions of a dying comrade, who bury or plunder him quite light-heartedly, who stand intrepidly in the way of bullets;—in fact, one of those men who waste no time in deliberation, and would not hesitate to make friends with the devil himself. After looking very attentively at the proprietor of the menagerie getting out of his box, my companion pursed up his lips with an air of mockery and contempt, with that peculiar and expressive twist which superior people assume to show they are not taken in. Then, when I was expatiating on the courage of M. Martin, he smiled, shook his head knowingly, and said, 'Well known.'

"'How "well known"?' I said. 'If you would only explain me the mystery, I should be vastly obliged.'

"After a few minutes, during which we made acquaintance, we went to dine at the first restauranteur's whose shop caught our eye. At dessert a bottle of champagne completely refreshed and brightened up the memories of this odd old soldier. He told me his story, and I saw that he was right when he exclaimed, 'Well known.'"

When she got home, she teased me to that extent, was so charming, and made so many promises, that I consented to communicate to her the confidences of the old soldier. Next day she received the following episode of an epic which one might call "The French in Egypt."

During the expedition in Upper Egypt under General Desaix, a Provencal soldier fell into the hands of the Maugrabins, and was taken by these Arabs into the deserts beyond the falls of the Nile.

In order to place a sufficient distance between themselves and the French army, the Maugrabins made forced marches, and only halted when night was upon them. They camped round a well overshadowed by palm trees under which they had previously concealed a store of provisions. Not surmising that the notion of flight would occur to their prisoner, they contented themselves with binding his hands, and after eating a few dates, and giving provender to their horses, went to sleep.

When the brave Provencal saw that his enemies were no longer watching him, he made use of his teeth to steal a scimiter, fixed the blade between his knees, and cut the cords which prevented him from using his hands; in a moment he was free. He at once seized a rifle and a dagger, then taking the precautions to provide himself with a sack of dried dates, oats, and powder and shot, and to fasten a scimiter to his waist, he leaped on to a horse, and spurred on vigorously in the direction where he thought to find the French army. So impatient was he to see a bivouac again that he pressed on the already tired courser at such speed, that its flanks were lacerated with his spurs, and at last the poor animal died, leaving the Frenchman alone in the desert. After walking some time in the sand with all the courage of an escaped convict, the soldier was obliged to stop, as the day had already ended. In spite of the beauty of an Oriental sky at night, he felt he had not strength enough to go on. Fortunately he had been able to find a small hill, on the summit of which a few palm trees shot up into the air; it was their verdure seen from afar which had brought hope and consolation to his heart. His fatigue was so great that he lay down upon a rock of granite, capriciously cut out like a camp-bed; there he fell asleep without taking any precaution to defend himself while he slept. He had made the sacrifice of his life. His last thought was one of regret. He repented having left the Maugrabins, whose nomadic life seemed to smile upon him now that he was far from them and without help. He was awakened by the sun, whose pitiless rays fell with all their force on the granite and produced an intolerable heat—for he had had the stupidity to place himself adversely to the shadow thrown by the verdant majestic heads of the palm trees. He looked at the solitary trees and shuddered—they reminded him of the graceful shafts crowned with foliage which characterize the Saracen columns in the cathedral of Arles.

But when, after counting the palm trees, he cast his eyes around him, the most horrible despair was infused into his soul. Before him stretched an ocean without limit. The dark sand of the desert spread further than eye could reach in every direction, and glittered like steel struck with bright light. It might have been a sea of looking-glass, or lakes melted together in a mirror. A fiery vapor carried up in surging waves made a perpetual whirlwind over the quivering land. The sky was lit with an Oriental splendor of insupportable purity, leaving naught for the imagination to desire. Heaven and earth were on fire.

The silence was awful in its wild and terrible majesty. Infinity, immensity, closed in upon the soul from every side. Not a cloud in the sky, not a breath in the air, not a flaw on the bosom of the sand, ever moving in diminutive waves; the horizon ended as at sea on a clear day, with one line of light, definite as the cut of a sword.

The Provencal threw his arms round the trunk of one of the palm trees, as though it were the body of a friend, and then, in the shelter of the thin, straight shadow that the palm cast upon the granite, he wept. Then sitting down he remained as he was, contemplating with profound sadness the implacable scene, which was all he had to look upon. He cried aloud, to measure the solitude. His voice, lost in the hollows of the hill, sounded faintly, and aroused no echo—the echo was in his own heart. The Provencal was twenty-two years old:—he loaded his carbine.

"There'll be time enough," he said to himself, laying on the ground the weapon which alone could bring him deliverance.

Viewing alternately the dark expanse of the desert and the blue expanse of the sky, the soldier dreamed of France—he smelled with delight the gutters of Paris—he remembered the towns through which he had passed, the faces of his comrades, the most minute details of his life. His Southern fancy soon showed him the stones of his beloved Provence, in the play of the heat which undulated above the wide expanse of the desert. Realizing the danger of this cruel mirage, he went down the opposite side of the hill to that by which he had come up the day before. The remains of a rug showed that this place of refuge had at one time been inhabited; at a short distance he saw some palm trees full of dates. Then the instinct which binds us to life awoke again in his heart. He hoped to live long enough to await the passing of some Maugrabins, or perhaps he might hear the sound of cannon; for at this time Bonaparte was traversing Egypt.

This thought gave him new life. The palm tree seemed to bend with the weight of the ripe fruit. He shook some of it down. When he tasted this unhoped-for manna, he felt sure that the palms had been cultivated by a former inhabitant—the savory, fresh meat of the dates were proof of the care of his predecessor. He passed suddenly from dark despair to an almost insane joy. He went up again to the top of the hill, and spent the rest of the day in cutting down one of the sterile palm trees, which the night before had served him for shelter. A vague memory made him think of the animals of the desert; and in case they might come to drink at the spring, visible from the base of the rocks but lost further down, he resolved to guard himself from their visits by placing a barrier at the entrance of his hermitage.

In spite of his diligence, and the strength which the fear of being devoured asleep gave him, he was unable to cut the palm in pieces, though he succeeded in cutting it down. At eventide the king of the desert fell; the sound of its fall resounded far and wide, like a sigh in the solitude; the soldier shuddered as though he had heard some voice predicting woe.

But like an heir who does not long bewail a deceased relative, he tore off from this beautiful tree the tall broad green leaves which are its poetic adornment, and used them to mend the mat on which he was to sleep.

Fatigued by the heat and his work, he fell asleep under the red curtains of his wet cave.

In the middle of the night his sleep was troubled by an extraordinary noise; he sat up, and the deep silence around allowed him to distinguish the alternative accents of a respiration whose savage energy could not belong to a human creature.

A profound terror, increased still further by the darkness, the silence, and his waking images, froze his heart within him. He almost felt his hair stand on end, when by straining his eyes to their utmost he perceived through the shadow two faint yellow lights. At first he attributed these lights to the reflections of his own pupils, but soon the vivid brilliance of the night aided him gradually to distinguish the objects around him in the cave, and he beheld a huge animal lying but two steps from him. Was it a lion, a tiger, or a crocodile?

The Provencal was not sufficiently educated to know under what species his enemy ought to be classed; but his fright was all the greater, as his ignorance led him to imagine all terrors at once; he endured a cruel torture, noting every variation of the breathing close to him without daring to make the slightest movement. An odor, pungent like that of a fox, but more penetrating, more profound, —so to speak, —filled the cave, and when the Provencal became sensible of this, his terror reached its height, for he could no longer doubt the proximity of a terrible companion, whose royal dwelling served him for a shelter.

Presently the reflection of the moon descending on the horizon lit up the den, rendering gradually visible and resplendent the spotted skin of a panther.

This lion of Egypt slept, curled up like a big dog, the peaceful possessor of a sumptuous niche at the gate of an hotel; its eyes opened for a moment and closed again; its face was turned towards the man. A thousand confused thoughts passed through the Frenchman's mind; first he thought of killing it with a bullet from his gun, but he saw there was not enough distance between them for him to take proper aim —the shot would miss the mark. And if it were to wake! —the thought made his limbs rigid. He listened to his own heart beating in the midst of the silence, and cursed the too violent pulsations which the flow of blood brought on, fearing to disturb that sleep which allowed him time to think of some means of escape.

Twice he placed his hand on his scimiter, intending to cut off the head of his enemy; but the difficulty of cutting the stiff short hair compelled him to abandon this daring project. To miss would be to die for CERTAIN, he thought; he preferred the chances of fair fight, and made up his mind to wait till morning; the morning did not leave him long to wait.

He could now examine the panther at ease; its muzzle was smeared with blood.

"She's had a good dinner," he thought, without troubling himself as to whether her feast might have been on human flesh. "She won't be hungry when she gets up."

It was a female. The fur on her belly and flanks was glistening white; many small marks like velvet formed beautiful bracelets round her feet; her sinuous tail was also white, ending with black rings; the overpart of her dress, yellow like burnished gold, very lissome and soft, had the characteristic blotches in the form of rosettes, which distinguish the panther from every other feline species.

This tranquil and formidable hostess snored in an attitude as graceful as that of a cat lying on a cushion. Her blood-stained paws, nervous and well armed, were stretched out before her face, which rested upon them, and from which radiated her straight slender whiskers, like threads of silver.

If she had been like that in a cage, the Provencal would doubtless have admired the grace of the animal, and the vigorous contrasts of vivid color which gave her robe an imperial splendor; but just then his sight was troubled by her sinister appearance.

The presence of the panther, even asleep, could not fail to produce the effect which the magnetic eyes of the serpent are said to have on the nightingale.

A Passion in the Desert

For a moment the courage of the soldier began to fail before this danger, though no doubt it would have risen at the mouth of a cannon charged with shell. Nevertheless, a bold thought brought daylight to his soul and sealed up the source of the cold sweat which sprang forth on his brow. Like men driven to bay, who defy death and offer their body to the smiter, so he, seeing in this merely a tragic episode, resolved to play his part with honor to the last.

"The day before yesterday the Arabs would have killed me, perhaps," he said; so considering himself as good as dead already, he waited bravely, with excited curiosity, the awakening of his enemy.

When the sun appeared, the panther suddenly opened her eyes; then she put out her paws with energy, as if to stretch them and get rid of cramp. At last she yawned, showing the formidable apparatus of her teeth and pointed tongue, rough as a file.

"A regular petite maitresse," thought the Frenchman, seeing her roll herself about so softly and coquettishly. She licked off the blood which stained her paws and muzzle, and scratched her head with reiterated gestures full of prettiness. "All right, make a little toilet," the Frenchman said to himself, beginning to recover his gaiety with his courage; "we'll say good morning to each other presently;" and he seized the small, short dagger which he had taken from the Maugrabins.

At this moment the panther turned her head toward the man and looked at him fixedly without moving. The rigidity of her metallic eyes and their insupportable luster made him shudder, especially when the animal walked towards him. But he looked at her caressingly, staring into her eyes in order to magnetize her, and let her come quite close to him; then with a movement both gentle and amorous, as though he were caressing the most beautiful of women, he passed his hand over her whole body, from the head to the tail, scratching the flexible vertebrae which divided the panther's yellow back. The animal waved her tail voluptuously, and her eyes grew gentle; and when for the third time the Frenchman accomplished this interesting flattery, she gave forth one of those purrings by which cats express their pleasure; but this murmur issued from a throat so powerful and so deep that it resounded through the cave like the last vibrations of an organ in a church. The man, understanding the importance of his caresses, redoubled them in such a way as to surprise and stupefy his imperious courtesan. When he felt sure of having extinguished the ferocity of his capricious companion, whose hunger had so fortunately been satisfied the day before, he got up to go out of the cave; the panther let him go out, but when he had reached the summit of the hill she sprang with the lightness of a sparrow hopping from twig to twig, and rubbed herself against his legs, putting up her back after the manner of all the race of cats. Then regarding her guest with eyes whose glare had softened a little, she gave vent to that wild cry which naturalists compare to the grating of a saw.

"She is exacting," said the Frenchman, smilingly.

He was bold enough to play with her ears; he caressed her belly and scratched her head as hard as he could. When he saw that he was successful, he tickled her skull with the point of his dagger, watching for the right moment to kill her, but the hardness of her bones made him tremble for his success.

The sultana of the desert showed herself gracious to her slave; she lifted her head, stretched out her neck and manifested her delight by the tranquility of her attitude. It suddenly occurred to the soldier that to kill this savage princess with one blow he must poniard her in the throat.

He raised the blade, when the panther, satisfied no doubt, laid herself gracefully at his feet, and cast up at him glances in which, in spite of their natural fierceness, was mingled confusedly a kind of good will. The poor Provencal ate his dates, leaning against one of the palm trees, and casting his eyes alternately on the desert in quest of some liberator and on his terrible companion to watch her uncertain clemency.

The panther looked at the place where the date stones fell, and every time that he threw one down her eyes expressed an incredible mistrust.

She examined the man with an almost commercial prudence. However, this examination was favorable to him, for when he had finished his meager meal she licked his boots with her powerful rough tongue, brushing off with marvelous skill the dust gathered in the creases.

"Ah, but when she's really hungry!" thought the Frenchman. In spite of the shudder this thought caused him, the soldier began to measure curiously the proportions of the panther, certainly one of the most splendid specimens of its race. She was three feet high and four feet long without counting her tail; this powerful weapon, rounded like a cudgel, was nearly three feet long. The head, large as that of a lioness, was distinguished by a rare expression of refinement. The cold cruelty of a tiger was dominant, it was true, but there was also a vague resemblance to the face of a sensual woman. Indeed, the face of this solitary queen had something of the gaiety of a drunken Nero: she had satiated herself with blood, and she wanted to play.

The soldier tried if he might walk up and down, and the panther left him free, contenting herself with following him with her eyes, less like a faithful dog than a big Angora cat, observing everything and every movement of her master.

When he looked around, he saw, by the spring, the remains of his horse; the panther had dragged the carcass all that way; about two thirds of it had been devoured already. The sight reassured him.

It was easy to explain the panther's absence, and the respect she had had for him while he slept. The first piece of good luck emboldened him to tempt the future, and he conceived the wild hope of continuing on good terms with the panther during the entire day, neglecting no means of taming her, and remaining in her good graces.

He returned to her, and had the unspeakable joy of seeing her wag her tail with an almost imperceptible movement at his approach. He sat down then, without fear, by her side, and they began to play together; he took her paws and muzzle, pulled her ears, rolled her over on her back, stroked her warm, delicate flanks. She let him do what ever he liked, and when he began to stroke the hair on her feet she drew her claws in carefully.

The man, keeping the dagger in one hand, thought to plunge it into the belly of the too confiding panther, but he was afraid that he would be immediately strangled in her last convulsive struggle; besides, he felt in his heart a sort of remorse which bid him respect a creature that had done him no harm. He seemed to have found a friend, in a boundless desert; half unconsciously he thought of his first sweetheart, whom he had nicknamed "Mignonne" by way of contrast, because she was so atrociously jealous that all the time of their love he was in fear of the knife with which she had always threatened him.

This memory of his early days suggested to him the idea of making the young panther answer to this name, now that he began to admire with less terror her swiftness, suppleness, and softness. Toward the end of the day he had familiarized himself with his perilous position; he now almost liked the painfulness of it. At last his companion had got into the habit of looking up at him whenever he cried in a falsetto voice, "Mignonne."

At the setting of the sun Mignonne gave, several times running, a profound melancholy cry. "She's been well brought up," said the lighthearted soldier; "she says her prayers." But this mental joke only occurred to him when he noticed what a pacific attitude his companion remained in. "Come, ma petite blonde, I'll let you go to bed first," he said to her, counting on the activity of his own legs to run away as quickly as possible, directly she was asleep, and seek another shelter for the night.

The soldier waited with impatience the hour of his flight, and when it had arrived he walked vigorously in the direction of the Nile; but hardly had he made a quarter of a league in the sand when he heard the panther bounding after him, crying with that saw-like cry more dreadful even than the sound of her leaping.

"Ah!" he said, "then she's taken a fancy to me, she has never met anyone before, and it is really quite flattering to have her first love." That instant the man fell into one of those movable quicksands so terrible to travelers and from which it is impossible to save oneself. Feeling himself caught, he gave a shriek of alarm; the panther seized him with her teeth by the collar, and, springing vigorously backwards, drew him as if by magic out of the whirling sand.

"Ah, Mignonne!" cried the soldier, caressing her enthusiastically; "we're bound together for life and death but no jokes, mind!" and he retraced his steps.

From that time the desert seemed inhabited. It contained a being to whom the man could talk, and whose ferocity was rendered gentle by him, though he could not explain to himself the reason for their strange friendship. Great as was the soldier's desire to stay upon guard, he slept.

On awakening he could not find Mignonne; he mounted the hill, and in the distance saw her springing toward him after the habit of these animals, who cannot run on account of the extreme flexibility of the vertebral column. Mignonne arrived, her jaws covered with blood; she received the wonted caress of her companion, showing with much purring how happy it made her. Her eyes, full of languor, turned still more gently than the day before toward the Provencal, who talked to her as one would to a tame animal.

"Ah! mademoiselle, you are a nice girl, aren't you? Just look at that! So we like to be made much of, don't we? Aren't you ashamed of yourself? So you have been eating some Arab or other, have you? That doesn't matter. They're animals just the same as you are; but don't you take to eating Frenchmen, or I shan't like you any longer."

She played like a dog with its master, letting herself be rolled over, knocked about, and stroked, alternately; sometimes she herself would provoke the soldier, putting up her paw with a soliciting gesture.

Some days passed in this manner. This companionship permitted the Provencal to appreciate the sublime beauty of the desert; now that he had a living thing to think about, alternations of fear and quiet, and plenty to eat, his mind became filled with contrast and his life began to be diversified.

Solitude revealed to him all her secrets, and enveloped him in her delights. He discovered in the rising and setting of the sun sights unknown to the world. He knew what it was to tremble when he heard over his head the hiss of a bird's wing, so rarely did they pass, or when he saw the clouds, changing and many colored travelers, melt one into another. He studied in the night time the effect of the moon upon the ocean of sand, where the simoom made waves swift of movement and rapid in their change. He lived the life of the Eastern day, marveling at its wonderful pomp; then, after having reveled in the sight of a hurricane over the plain where the whirling sands made red, dry mists and death-bearing clouds, he would welcome the night with joy, for then fell the healthful freshness of the stars, and he listened to imaginary music in the skies. Then solitude taught him to unroll the treasures of dreams. He passed whole hours in remembering mere nothings, and comparing his present life with his past.

At last he grew passionately fond of the panther; for some sort of affection was a necessity.

Whether it was that his will powerfully projected had modified the character of his companion, or whether, because she found abundant food in her predatory excursions in the desert, she respected the man's life, he began to fear for it no longer, seeing her so well tamed.

He devoted the greater part of his time to sleep, but he was obliged to watch like a spider in its web that the moment of his deliverance might not escape him, if anyone should pass the line marked by the horizon. He had sacrificed his shirt to make a flag with, which he hung at the top of a palm tree, whose foliage he had torn off. Taught by necessity, he found the means of keeping it spread out, by fastening it with little sticks; for the wind might not be blowing at the moment when the passing traveler was looking through the desert.

It was during the long hours, when he had abandoned hope, that he amused himself with the panther. He had come to learn the different inflections of her voice, the expressions of her eyes; he had studied the capricious patterns of all the rosettes which marked the gold of her robe. Mignonne was not even angry when he took hold of the tuft at the end of her tail to count her rings, those graceful ornaments which glittered in the sun like jewelry. It gave him pleasure to contemplate the supple, fine outlines of her form, the whiteness of her belly, the graceful pose of her head. But it was especially when she was playing that he felt most pleasure in looking at her; the agility and youthful lightness of her movements were a continual surprise to him; he wondered at the supple way in which she jumped and climbed, washed herself and arranged her fur, crouched down and prepared to spring. However rapid her spring might be, however slippery the stone she was on, she would always stop short at the word "Mignonne."

One day, in a bright midday sun, an enormous bird coursed through the air. The man left his panther to look at his new guest; but after waiting a moment the deserted sultana growled deeply.

A Passion in the Desert

"My goodness! I do believe she's jealous," he cried, seeing her eyes become hard again; "the soul of Virginie has passed into her body; that's certain."

The eagle disappeared into the air, while the soldier admired the curved contour of the panther.

But there was such youth and grace in her form! she was beautiful as a woman! the blond fur of her robe mingled well with the delicate tints of faint white which marked her flanks.

The profuse light cast down by the sun made this living gold, these russet markings, to burn in a way to give them an indefinable attraction.

The man and the panther looked at one another with a look full of meaning; the coquette quivered when she felt her friend stroke her head; her eyes flashed like lightning—then she shut them tightly.

"She has a soul," he said, looking at the stillness of this queen of the sands, golden like them, white like them, solitary and burning like them.

"Well," she said, "I have read your plea in favor of beasts; but how did two so well adapted to understand each other end?"

"Ah, well! you see, they ended as all great passions do end—by a misunderstanding. For some reason ONE suspects the other of treason; they don't come to an explanation through pride, and quarrel and part from sheer obstinacy."

"Yet sometimes at the best moments a single word or a look is enough —but anyhow go on with your story."

"It's horribly difficult, but you will understand, after what the old villain told me over his champagne. He said—'I don't know if I hurt her, but she turned round, as if enraged, and with her sharp teeth caught hold of my leg—gently, I daresay; but I, thinking she would devour me, plunged my dagger into her throat. She rolled over, giving a cry that froze my heart; and I saw her dying, still looking at me without anger. I would have given all the world—my cross even, which I had not got then—to have brought her to life again. It was as though I had murdered a real person; and the soldiers who had seen my flag, and were come to my assistance, found me in tears.'

"'Well sir,' he said, after a moment of silence, 'since then I have been in war in Germany, in Spain, in Russia, in France; I've certainly carried my carcase about a good deal, but never have I seen anything like the desert. Ah! yes, it is very beautiful!'

"'What did you feel there?' I asked him.

"'Oh! that can't be described, young man! Besides, I am not always regretting my palm trees and my panther. I should have to be very melancholy for that. In the desert, you see, there is everything and nothing.'

"'Yes, but explain—'

"'Well,' he said, with an impatient gesture, 'it is God without mankind.'"

Printed in the United States
62246LVS00004B/130